I0582393

2022 Paperback Edition

Copyright © 2022 by Kate Church

All Rights Reserved

First Edition 2022

ISBN PAPERBACK: 978-1-7358183-2-0
ISBN EBOOK: 978-1-7358183-3-7

Library of Congress Control Number: TXu 2-342-781

Printed in the United States of America

Illustrations by Kate Church

Cover Art by Alexander von Ness

#   Seeking the Wolf

Kate Church

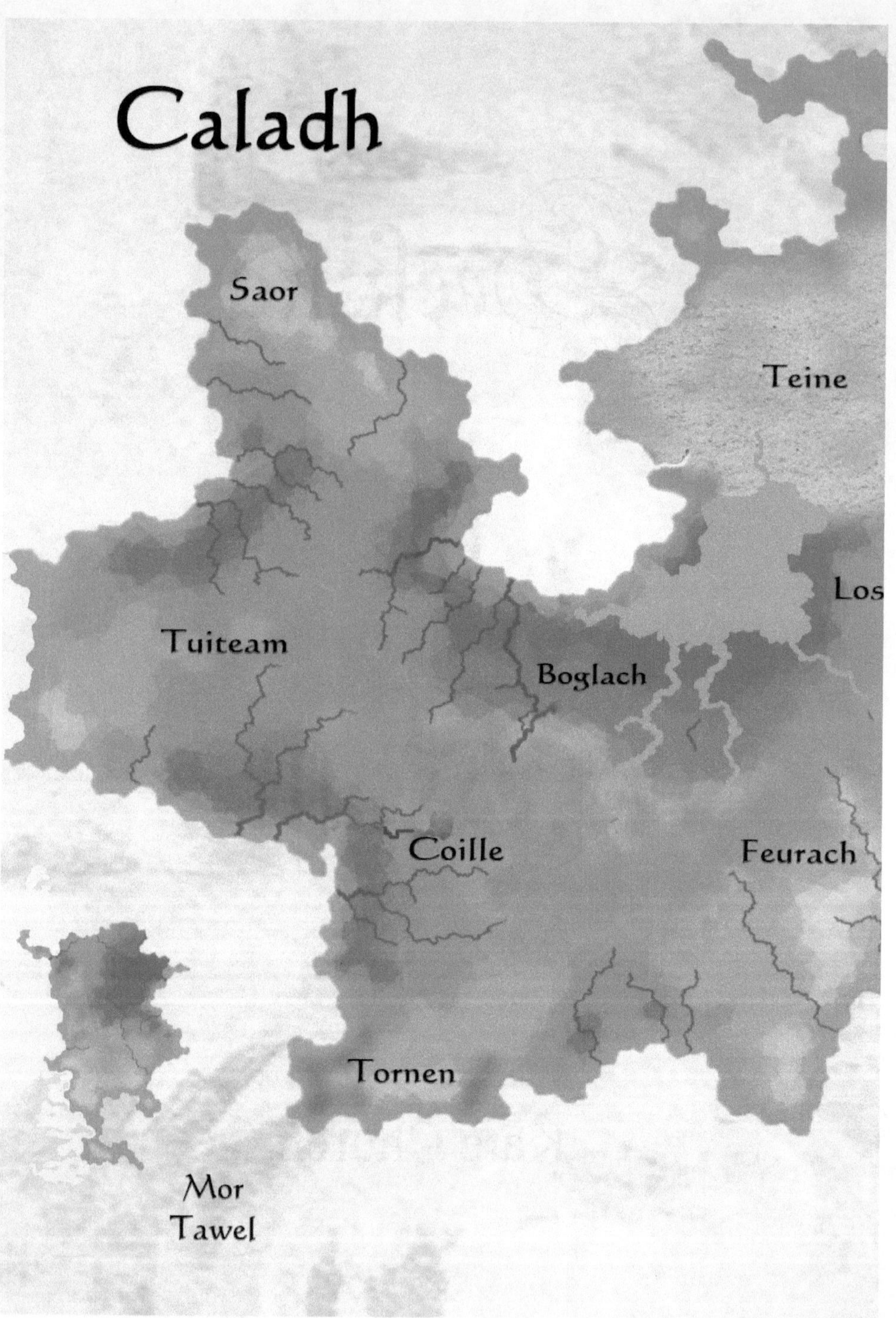

Caladh
Saor
Teine
Los
Tuiteam
Boglach
Coille
Feurach
Tornen
Mor
Tawel

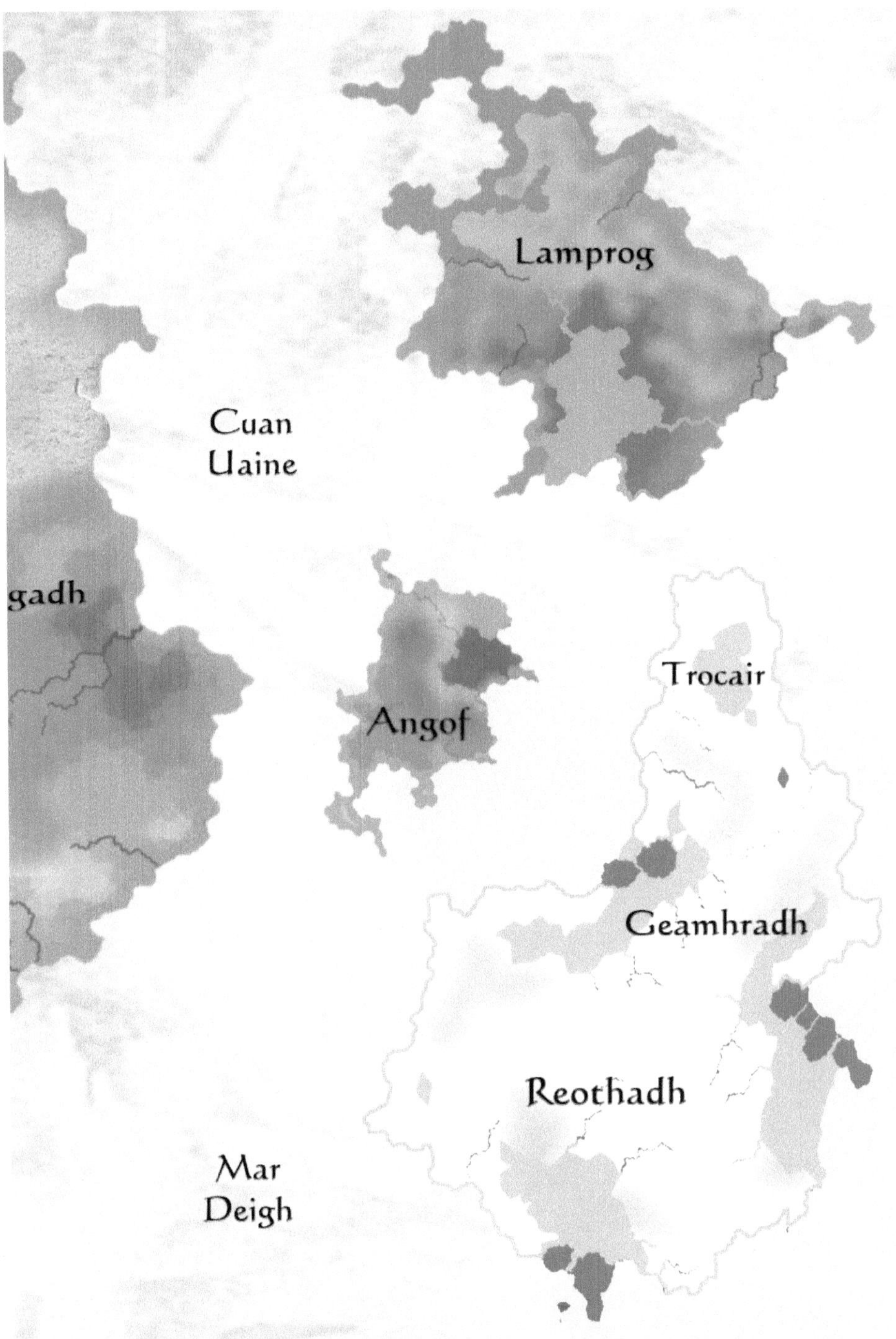

Lamprog
Cuan
Uaine
gadh
Angof
Trocair
Geamhradh
Reothadh
Mar
Deigh

A young lad rushes through the streets, not taking even a brief moment for breath or chatter, to deliver urgent news from the Knight Commander. Nearly breathless and weary legged, he trudged through the snow-covered terrain of his homeland. Given strict instruction to deliver a single phrase to King Edric with all haste, he knew there would be no room for the feeble excuses of a young lad, or he might soon find his head without a pair of shoulders as the last messenger who failed at his task. He must not be delayed.

The streets were bright from the newly fallen snow and with each rushed step he could feel the chill of the snow rush upwards towards his core. The northern part of the island yielded warmer temperatures than in the south but was no less potent. The frozen tundra took notice of his careless steps and raked its cool touch across patches of his exposed flesh. Given the time of year and location, a grown man would succumb to frostbite within minutes of exposure and frozen solid in a matter of hours without the proper attire let alone a young lad as himself.  Thankfully, the young lad paid the wicked tundra no mind and continued on his way leaving the wicked wilds to search for its next victim.

Castle Trocair was in sight now and soon he would be housed within the warmth of its walls.  The walls were vast and made of a black stone that shined in the moonlight giving it a glass-like appearance.  The young lad's stride was brought to a screeching halt as he was knocked back by two burly foot soldiers standing watch over the castle's gate.  Their armor was dark with large plates covering the majority of their bodies.  The plates were made of something similar to the castle's walls as they too shone brightly in the moon's light.  The young lad dropped his head slightly hoping to catch his breath while bringing himself closer to the foot soldier's armor, anxious to obtain a closer look.  The plates while made of a beautiful black stone that was designed to cover the chainmail that was carefully concealed beneath them providing additional defense but not warmth.

"What purpose do ye have at Castle Trocair in this late hour?" one of the men shouted.

Muttering through panted breaths, "I must…speak with...King Edric," the lad insisted.

"No one speaks with the king at this hour," the second man chimed in.

"State your purpose whelp!" the first man demanded.

Still panting the young lad urged, "I have…a message...please...it's of utter...importance."

The foot soldiers glanced at one another before jerking the lad upright.

"Very well, what's the message?" the second soldier urged.

The young lad's panting was beginning to slow, "Only the King may know.  I was given strict instruction not to speak of it to anyone but King Edric."

"Who so ordered it, whelp?" the first soldier demanded.

"The Knight Commander," he paused briefly, "his name is Elgar," the young lad said with confidence.

They turned quickly towards each other and then one of them waved his hand frantically to someone just out of the lad's line of sight.  Soon the once nearly visible black bars fixed to the gate began to slide out of place creating a loud grinding sound, piercings the lad's ears, forcing him to cover them quickly with his cold hands.  The large black gate slowly began to creak open as if it had not been opened in centuries further explaining the grinding sounds heard moments before.  The young lad's task was nearly complete.  As the gap between the door and frame grew wider the young lad could not help but stand there in awe of the castle's grandeur.  A vast darkness surrounded by a world of soft blue moonlight, had the moon stayed in that night and the lad surely would not have been able to see the castle next to the night's sky.  Lifting his gaze higher, he watched the castle's tower shoot up towards the stars and dwarfed all before it.  It was a beacon and as its shadow was cast over the land, it became clear it was built for all to see and fear.

Both foot soldiers stepped behind the young lad urging him forward with a shove, "Move quickly now, King Edric shan't be kept waiting."

The young lad nodded and quickly stepped forward not wanting to agitate the guards further.  Still taking in his surroundings he noted nearly everything inside the castle's walls was made of that same black stone.  Not a cart of wood or splinter in sight.  How could anyone possibly stay warm in such a place he wondered.  While the castle's constructions would prevent fire from wreaking havoc upon it, this would only encourage the cold to take a foothold there.  They continued forward towards a second and slightly smaller gate.  No words were spoken by either party, but the gate only opened enough for the men and young lad to enter.  Just as they entered, two men charged out towards the wall in their absence and the gate closed quickly behind them.  The king clearly left nothing to chance and no border unguarded.

After trudging two full days in the frozen tundra, the warmth from the castle washed over the young lad with such force that it nearly took his breath away.  His limbs ached and burned causing his pace to slow, but due to the nature of his business with the King he did his best to maintain his composure despite the overwhelming discomfort.  The doors to the king's inner circle swung open and into the vast stone court the young lad stepped in.  The walls were curved like the black water that created them had been frozen in time, appearing alive but never free.  Their reflection was brighter than that of the exterior and far more majestic than its exterior would have someone believe.  As the young lad stood there in awe once more, a guard took the opportunity to remind him of where he stood and his supposed purpose by placing a hand in his back, thrusting him forward.

"Your King awaits, whelp," he pushed the young lad forward again, "Do you intend to keep him waiting?"

The young lad shook his head and quickly scurried towards the King who was impatiently waiting on his dark throne.

"My Lord," the young lad bowed, "I have a message for you from the Knight Commander.  He said-"

"What proof do you have that Commander Elgar sent you to me?" he said sharply.

The young lad shook his head and swallowed hard, clearly unprepared for his message to be questioned, "None," he muttered softer than he intended.

"Then before you begin, what can you tell me of Commander Elgar to prove that you indeed carry his message?" the King added with a heavy rasp to his voice.

King Edric was an old king with a face covered in deep grooves embedded within weathered skin.  His hair was pale and coarse with a beard to match.  This was not a king of legend, but he easily commanded a room through a deep and mighty voice.  Even in this late hour, he sat before his subjects and the young lad in full armor with a voice that resonated throughout the hall each time he spoke.  He would be heard.

"Wolf in the South," the young lad muttered almost as if asking a question rather than telling a fact.

"Go on," the King gestured for the lad to be brought forward.

He was now within feet of the King and rather than continue to stare upon his flesh, his gaze fell towards the floor as a sign of submission.  To gaze at the King for an extended period would not have been permitted for any reason and being fond of his head, he opted for submission rather than bravado.

The young lad knelt before the king, "My Lord, the hunt was successful.  A large female wolf was captured and is now detained in the Ice Tower."

King Edric grinned with delight before allowing a menacing laugh to escape, "The line of Tuiteam will soon be broken and their people enslaved!"  He gestured for the young lad to stand.  "Bring the beast to me," he grinned with delight, "it's time to break her spirit and breed her for war."  He stood slowly and cast his hands, willing all who gathered to celebrate their triumph of which they did as he stepped towards the young lad, "What of Commander Elgar?  Why does he not bring me this prodigious news himself?"

"He was injured bringing down the beast but will be well again soon."

King Edric frowned slightly and only for a moment.

"He will be well again I assure you," the young lad blurted out attempting to reassure the King that one of the most valuable pieces of his army could not be conquered so easily.

King Edric nodded and waved the young lad away.  He was not fazed by the young lad's attempt at reassurance for he knew the Commander well.  Edgar was a man of iron and while he may bend, the King believed he could not be broken by one man or beast.  King Edric watched carefully as the young lad scurried out almost as fast as he came in.  He found delight in intimidating the meek and exuding power over the ferocious.  For centuries, the line of Tuiteam had ruled over Caladh, but King Edric was willing to yield no longer.  For a king that cannot command the beings and beasts of all lands, shall not hold power over them.

I awoke from my slumber to the sensation of water dripping on my face, each drop weighted and sharp.  My body felt heavy, weak, drained of nearly all life.  As I pried my eyes open, my surroundings were slowly coming into focus. There was a faint light radiating from nearby candle, but the light's reach was no match for the darkness leaving a vast portion of my surroundings cloaked in darkness.  I attempted to focus my gaze and stand but was met with resistance.  Something was wrong.  I ran my fingers along the stone beneath me.  It was icy and damp prompting me to take another listen rather than glance at my surroundings since my eyes were failing to focus on the darkness.  There were waves mounting an assault on the rock nearby, crashing against them in thunderous repetition.  A clear indication there was a storm brewing and as I wet my lips with the tip of my tongue, I could taste the salt. I was near the coast.

There was an opening on the far wall that may provide valuable insight regarding my location if I could just get a bit closer. I pulled my legs in tight and forced myself upward with what little energy I could muster. Before I was able to fully stand, I was jolted back towards the stone floor causing the chains that restrained me to crack violently against it. These restraints were clearly meant for beasts not man as they were anchored low towards the ground along with being thick and weighted to provide additional restraint. In my altered state, I rebelled against my restraints causing them to crack like lightening in midsummer storm. If I were hidden, I would not be for long.

The chains failed to yield to my will causing me to temporarily collapse onto the stone floor from exhaustion. My mind and body felt in a fog, and I needed to eat and soon before my senses diminish further. The opening once more drew my attention. The waves sounded very near for that not to lead towards the outside. However, there was no light shining through, not even moonlight prompting additional speculation regarding my location. I placed my hands upon the stone floor again and followed the cracks in it towards a corner where ice had formed from water that had slowly seeped through a crack in the wall. Feeling my way up onto the wall I noticed the temperature changing. This was indeed an exterior wall and resting alongside it would certainly bring death.

I quickly pulled together what my eyes were seeing with memories in my mind and concluded, this was not any ordinary prison.  While most of the world is covered in light and warmth, there is only one place on Caladh that could potentially contain such subzero temperatures.  This was the Ice Tower of Reothadh, located in one of the most remote regions in the world.  Most of Reothadh is isolated by chilling temperatures and mountains of ice making it difficult to grown or sustain life.  However, over the centuries these factors have not detoured hunters who venture this far south in hopes of seeking the riches held within the mountains of Geamhradh.

According to legend, an ancient Lord sealed the wealth and knowledge of his kingdom away in those mountains just before the great divide fractured the world, but they were soon discovered and seized by a man.  This man who had been marooned on this island claimed the treasure as his own and dubbed himself the Lord of Trocair.  Now only his heirs possess the knowledge to access the mountain's treasures further validating their claim to the region and over all life on Caladh.  Opposition would be futile as not only is the land hostile and prone to violence, but the people who call this region home are equally hostile and known to be savages.  Neither factor has stopped hunters and royals waging war over it for centuries.  Those who survive here are primarily located on the northern part of the island where the temperature remains brisk but tolerable.  Escaping the tower will be challenging, but the real struggle will be surviving the long trek to Castle Trocair in hopes of bartering passage off this island.

I needed to change.  It was the only way to heighten my senses and regain the strength that was needed to break free.  I am not sure why I was brought here, but I was determined to not linger here only to find out.  I have changed quickly in a number of situations with far more distractions than there are presently but in my weakened state it may take more time than anticipated.  I sat back upon my heels and began to concentrate.  This time the transition started small, a sensation of heat being igniting my fingertips and climbing towards my shoulders followed by my pulse beginning to race.  The sensation would soon engulf my body and in what felt like a blink I would no longer be that of a young elven woman but of a beast.

A sinister laugh echoed across the room's emptiness and broke my concentration.  I was not alone.

"Oh you, my darling girl, are the real treasure," a low voice broke through the darkness, "and they do not even know what you are."

"I know not of what you speak sir," I kept my tone soft to appear docile in hopes the man was bluffing and would take pity on a humble prisoner.

The man stepped into the candle's path giving me only portions of his physique to quickly analyze as a potential threat.  He was extremely tall regardless of my current perspective with long locks of sand that fell onto his shoulders as he lowered a dark hood from atop of his head.  His movement was swift and agile, much like that of a spirit, as opposed to the sluggish and weighted steps of man.  While I heard him take his initial step, all others were lost to me, this one was trained to be unseen.  I merely blinked and he was upon me causing my eyes to flare.

"Oh, but you do know what I speak of," he grinned, "your eyes give you away shapeshifter."

I heard the same sinister laugh within him if only for a moment when he spoke again.

"Bright orbs of honeycomb that turn to fire when the heart…or body are ignited with extreme emotion, truly remarkable."

His gaze determined and focused, unwavering from his target, which at the present moment appeared to be me.  I could feel my skin igniting from the internal fire once more as he brought his face in closer to mine.  The man before me was not human, his instincts were far too keen.  He was heavily cloaked in dark armor but with his face nearly upon mine he could not shield me from his bright eyes.  He was elven.

"Shapeshifters are that of legend good sir," a slight growl escaped as the words exited my body.  "So, tell me, what business does an elf have in the icy wasteland of Reothadh?"

"My business is my own," he snapped, "but I would suggest you forego your quest for my purpose here and start focusing on what I might have to offer you."  He turned briefly towards the opening in the wall before looking back at me and whispering, "Dawn approaches and I'm sure King Edric, in due time, will uncover the mystery of what you truly are."

He did not move a muscle and his gaze was unwavering once more.

"How do I know I will not be your pawn?" I muttered.

"You do not," he grinned, "but better to be in my hands than theirs that I can assure you."

Locked away and weak in this frozen wasteland I was left with few options. Changing into a savage beast might present the option of vanquishing the elf before me, but I would not be able to hold my form for an extended period without further rest and nourishment. My only survivable option would be to accept his offer and hope he leads us both safely out of this tower. I said nothing but nodded to reflect my understanding and approval of his offer.

"This might hurt," he whispered, "but only for a moment," he grinned once more.

My eyes widened in a moment of panic just before watching his eyes turn dark. I could feel the braces around my neck and ankles begin to vibrate just before exploding, causing fragments to ricochet from the walls nearby. He was a man of his word, at least for now.

"Someone will have heard that," he stood quickly, "we need to move." He turned towards the candle while gesturing for me to follow. "Quickly now, we cannot linger here."

Gathering my strength, I rose slowly to follow his lead. Other than the opening on the far wall that I had noticed earlier, I was unaware of any other potential exit and as I drew myself closer to it, I realized the opening was barely large enough for a small child to penetrate. There must be another way. He stepped toward the dark space where he first appeared to me from earlier and moments later, I felt a rush of arctic air blow through.  There was a door leading to another level and based on that breeze it was not likely to be any warmer than this one.  As I began to contemplate what monsters may loom ahead, the elf pressed onward.

I moved through the opening further into darkness where the elf had all but disappeared.  At least that is what I thought until I was greeted by his hand on my shoulder.  Thankfully, I do not startle easy, or I would have shrieked at his sudden touch.  He gestured for me to scan the room.  As I panned the room, I noticed figures off to the one side resting on the floor.  More than likely these figures were in their final stages of life, or they would have been jolted awake by the explosion that occurred upstairs.  These men were not a threat, but I would need to keep up in the future if I had any hope of making it down the remaining floors alive.

We moved swiftly and quietly down the next two floors, barely giving the rooms a second glance.  Each looked remarkably similar to the one before.  They were eerily quiet with a musty odor, probably from the unrelenting moisture that has been seeping through the stone over the decades.  The cells were nearly as inhospitable as the land surrounding the tower with the one exception of the slight temperature change.  Each step across the stone seemed to sting as the feeling in my fingers that was once nearly lost was beginning to return to me.  While the temperature may have only been rising slightly the sun was not and we were still heavily cloaked in darkness, permitting us to move throughout the tower with minimal effort.  If anyone was alerted to our presence, they were not making it known.

As we were making our way towards the next stone stairwell, I noticed a faint scent of blood in the air, and it was growing stronger with each step we took.  My vision may have been lagging due to my weakened state, but my sense of smell never leads me astray.  This was the scent of death and as the stairwell opened into a large partially lit room the origin of the odor became apparent.  The walls and floor were made of stone like the floors above, but these were heavily painted in the lives of this tower's victims.  Filthy instruments and buckets of rotten flesh sporadically placed throughout the room making it apparent this room has been known to contain multiple victims at once.  Based on the scent in the air, there were victims here recently in addition to what would appear to be years of carnage painted throughout the room.  We needed to move and fast, or this may very well be our final resting place.

I nudged the elf to press onward.  This room was making me uneasy and neither one of us could afford to lose focus.  The unfortunate part was just as we started to press onward towards the stairwell when voices were faintly heard down the stairwell ahead.  At most they were two floors to the south, but the longer we listened we could tell those voices were on the move.  I reached for the man's shoulder and pulled him closer.

"Is this the only way out?"  I whispered.

He nodded before adding, "I will go, wait here."

Before I had a chance to respond he vanished in the stairwell.  While I understood I needed to stay hidden, I was determined not to waste the only moments I may have before we are discovered.  I stepped over to grasp one of the few candles still burning in the room before starting my search.  If there was going to be a fight, I was not going into it empty handed or on an empty stomach.  There must be something here, I just needed to find it.  The closer I stepped towards one of the buckets throughout the room, the more pungent the odor became.  This bucket was used recently as the blood found within was still flowing.  It could not have been here more than a few hours at a maximum since this once flowed through someone's veins.  If there was nourishment here, I am not sure I would have any desire to consume it.

A commotion from the floor below drew my attention back towards the stairwell.  There clearly had been a scuffle of sorts and one of the voices we previously heard was rapidly climbing the stairwell.  This being was humanoid but clearly not human as the speech greatly differed.  It was a language I had never heard and while curious that part of me would need to be curbed or I would soon be discovered.  Rather than making a dash towards the dark wall where we entered, I opted to cower beneath the large wooden slab I was standing nearby.  Depending on the creature advancing in my direction, the scent remaining from the previous captive would more than likely cloak my very own or no amount of cowering would conceal my location.  I lowered myself quietly placing the candle into the blood-filled bucket before retreating into the shadow where I began to focus my energy on that stairwell.

The light's rays began entering the large room in just a few breaths, I would have never made it to the wall in time. This humanoid was quite vast in size for without even standing fully erect his head nearly grazed the ceiling. He walked with a slight hunch, whether from injury or long term in this enclosed environment, I cannot say. The light proceeded the creature as he moved into the room and closer to me, permitting me to only see portions of his features at any given moment due to the ever-shifting light. He did not linger on any one portion of the room, but he mumbled perpetually. It was difficult to say whether he was disgruntled about something or just the type to mutter to themselves since his speech was very gruff and difficult to discern.

As the moments dragged on, he didn't appear to be searching for someone but something. He maneuvered throughout the room and began up-heaving nearby crates. The beast was distracted in his search and now had his back to me. From this angle he appeared even larger with scars and hair covering most of his back. There were recovered lash marks across both shoulders, and he donned no covering of his upper body, only a makeshift drapery from the waist down. What could he have possibly been looking for? I tried not to dwindle on the thought when this may be my only chance, however, there was something about his behavior I could not quite comprehend. Given a different situation, I may have been prompted to stay and study the creature but for now, I must keep moving.

I began to glide out from under the slab remaining low to the floor for standing now could potentially cause the light to shift alerting him to my presence. I had barely cleared the slab when I noticed what had drawn his attention, buckets nestled along one of the walls. I could not see what he was doing with them, but he was captivated by them. I continued to glide along the stone floor in slow, steady movements. The sounds of him masticating cloaked my movements more than I had hoped, but even after my quick search earlier I was unaware of any nourishment housed here. What could he possibly be ingesting? I needed to banish this thought and continue my advancement towards the stairwell.

The opening was within my reach, I just needed to concentrate for a few more moments and I would be out of his reach. I pulled myself upright against the dark wall, attempting to blend in its shadows before escaping to the next floor just before I glanced at him once more. His skin was dark and heavily scarred nearly everywhere, not just his back, from what was probably restraints or more likely, torture. In addition, from this angle I could finally see what not only drew but kept the beast's attention. He was devouring the contents of the buckets. What foul manner of beast consumes dead flesh I do not know, but as I felt my stomach turn, I knew I could wait no longer.

The beast continued to gulp down the putrid liquid as I slinked myself along the dark wall. He did not appear to be taking notice of my movement but as I scanned the buckets laid before him, I noticed they were all nearly consumed. I flattened myself against the stone wall as best as I could and pressed onward, never taking my eyes off the beast. My fingers crept along the stone blocks of the wall providing guidance while my focus remained on the beast and soon enough my fingertips grasp a rounded edge. I took my eyes of the beast for a moment to peer around the edge and into the opening. Nothing in sight down the stairwell, but there was a glimmer of something shiny left within the lock, a key had been left behind of which I thought was rather odd.

As I began to turn my head back towards the beast, I noticed something in the air changed causing me to freeze in my current position. The once very loud gulping and sloshing that radiated from the beast's feast had ceased and now, the smell that once seemed so far away was now nearly upon me. I may have stopped moving but my eyes were drawn towards the odor. The beast was no longer feasting upon the decay of the dead and dismembered, he was staring directly at me and breathing heavily. I did not have time to question whether I was on the dinner menu or up for interrogation, just that I needed to move. I watched a bucket crash to the stone floor just before his large over-sized feet began to slide forward. Unarmed and malnourished I knew this was a foe I could not defeat outright but he could be outsmarted.

Remembering the key, I noticed just a moment before, it may be what I need to stop or at the very least slow him down. If it did in fact lock the door it was left in. Without another thought, I knew that had to be my plan.  This beast was not as slow as I hoped, so I would only have one chance to get this right and timing would be everything.  I stood quickly and grasped the door with both hands before throwing myself back towards the stairwell, willing the door to follow my lead and seal off the opening.  It swung towards the latch faster than I expected and I heard the latch swing down with a loud clang that echoed throughout the space.

I released the door from my grasp and reached for the key but not before the beast found the handle on the other side. I could feel his eyes on me, watching me, through the small opening while jostling the handle about.  He was taunting me. With each jerk of the handle, it made me recoil slightly, sending an unwelcome feeling of panic throughout my body. After taking another moment to analyze the movement I noticed he was not trying to unlatch the door just merely keep my focus on it.  I rotated the key quickly until it would not turn anymore then out of spite, I continued to apply pressure to it until I felt it break off.  If he wanted me, he would have to breakdown the door to do so.  I felt the look of satisfaction clearly washing over my face in a large demonic grin.  I had won this round.

Peering at him through the opening, I noticed he did not appear to be infuriated with his predicament but amused as I held up the remains of the broken key for him to see.  Upon waking here, I have always been a step behind and here is where that step was starting to catch up with me.  I tried not to let my grin fade with his amusement, but I felt the sensation of my triumph quickly fading.  I turned sharply and clung to the shadows to continue my descent.  With each step I widened the gap between the beast and I, but that did not stop him from expressing his displeasure with the conundrum he now found himself in.  He continued to jostle the handle about and began slamming himself against the door causing the noise to echo down the stairwell after me.  If my attempt at escaping had gone unnoticed before, this type of racket would certainly bring that hope to a screeching halt.

While at first, I tried to remain quiet and hidden amongst the shadows, I now knew it would be fruitless if I did not start to cover more ground.  The stairwell seems to spiral downward continually with no end in sight and I saw nothing of an exit, forcing my pace to quicken out of sheer panic.  The temperature did not appear to rise as I continued downward either which prompted further curiosity as to how anything is expected to survive here.  Thankfully, the air did not seem as foul as it once did allowing my body to relax slightly and fall into my natural stride.

No sooner did my stride fall into place when I crashed into something causing my body to ricochet off its surface and onto the stone steps.  I reached up to grasp the sides of my head in anguish while trying to gather my wits about me.  As if the whirlwind of stairs had not nearly driven me to delirium, the abrupt stop might be the catalyst my mind needs to finish off the task.  Before I could even bring the space back into focus, I began to stand.  Remaining sprawled out on the stone steps would have surely been a disadvantage and one I could not afford at this stage of my escape.

Using the wall as a guide, I began to stand.  Until I could fully focus my vision, I would need to check my surroundings by scent and touch alone.  Extending one hand out in front of me and the other supporting my aching mind I took a step forward, nothing so far.  Yet, there was a filthy smell lingering in the air here and if it would not have been mixed with several conflicting scents, I could have possibly recognized it.  In this place, it is difficult to discern any one particular smell as there are so many at any one given moment but there was a portion of the scent I recognized.  On the mainland there was a marsh, Boglach, a wasteland known to house vile creatures that lived in the foul murky water.  I know of no one that can recall the original state of that place, but centuries of vegetation rot and decay accompanied by countless victims has not suppressed the odor.  There was a piece of that odor here now, I was sure of it.

Continuing my advancement at this point would not be wise until I determine what broke my stride.  Turning my head slightly to check my blind spots, I noticed my vision was beginning to clear and once again I could take in a portion of my surroundings.  It was still quite dark and there has not been an opening to the outside in ages which could explain some of the odor, though I was not entirely convinced that was the only cause.  I did not notice anything towards either side of me, but as a turned my attention back to the path ahead I could see something moving slightly, just off center.  I narrowed my focus on the object and waited. The odds of finding anything other than foe here was improbable, but I was not ready to cast all hope into the fire just yet.

The movement was rhythmic but non-advancing. Whatever it was, it was breathing. This foe was biding its time and that meant I could not afford to. I slowly began back tracking one step at a time with a steady increase to my speed, never taking my eyes off the shadow. Unfortunately, in my hyper-focused state, I stumbled over a broken step causing me to jerk suddenly. Quickly glancing down to regain my footing I noticed something primordial and sluggish covering large portions of the steps. It appeared amphibian like in consistency and given the chance to run it through my fingers I am sure it would behave in a similar fashion. The steps remained intact despite its present meaning this was not an acid giving me some relief.

Glancing back towards the shadow I noticed it had vanished. I had not felt or heard a presence move past me, but something told me this creature would not have retreated without cause. Fear and curiosity began waging an epic battle for a foothold within me. Behind me still lies the beast locked away and before me something unknown. I could not turn back, so curiosity triumphs this round. With no creature in sight, I bent down to observe the liquid more closely. It was indeed from the marsh, same undeniably foul odor. However, the longer the liquid remained on my skin the number my skin was becoming. I quickly rubbed my fingers on the wall nearby in an attempt to remove as much of it as possible. This is what pleased the beast, he knew what creature was lying in wait for me if I pressed onward.

I was not sure what had stopped my stride previously, but I realized that was no longer important as continuing downward was no longer an option.  I must retreat and search for another potential exit, there must be another way out.  Rather than turn and flee at a rapid rate, I opted for a laggard retreat.  Since the creature vanished when I jerked previously, I assumed it would be more likely to strike or pursue me with similar movements.  I turned slightly to give me better footing as I began my ascent back towards the beast making sure to not take my eyes off the stairwell below.

I had not made more than a few steps when I felt something dripping onto my shoulder.  The liquid was warmer than what had been excreted onto the stairs below, but this was just as sluggish.  I turned my attention towards the ceiling where I was greeted by a raspy, hissing sound.  Hidden carefully in the dark, I was unable to clearly see what creature it was being projected from, but that sound was my cue to flee.  Against my better judgement, I pivoted and fled down the stairwell.  This creature was cunning and continuing my ascent towards the beast would only trap me, further complicating my escape.  Where is that elf when he is truly needed?

It was difficult to get an initial foothold due to the slime, but once I did, my stride quickly returned.  As the hissing sound was growing louder, I knew the creature was not struggling to maneuver through the tight corridor as I was, and it was gaining on me.  Attempting to outrun the creature would be superfluous.  It was agile and more abreast of the tower's layout than I.  Time was running out.  With each stride, my temperature was rising and in one final leap I dropped to all fours and was born again as a wolf.

Within seconds, all of my senses returned to their heightened state, and I felt the beast blood coursing through my veins like fire.  With each stride, I gained ground and rapidly distanced myself from the creature.  The hissing sound that was once so threatening now was nothing more than a whisper in the distance stairwell behind me.  I did not have the strength to maintain this form for long but when faced with a dire situation as this one, once changed the only way to bring me out of it would be to remove the catalyst or welcome my own demise.

In what felt like only a moment later, my stride was brought to a screeching halt once again.  The primordial secretions that once coated several steps beneath my feet, now covered the floor of almost an entire room.  The foul odor was heavily concentrated in the air here and was starting to singe my nasal cavity.  If I had not transformed when I did, I may not have noticed the scent growing stronger with enough time to stop before leaping into it.  The once narrow stairwell had gradually funneled into what felt like a hot spring enclosed in stone.  The room appeared to be steaming but with no apparent heat source in sight, I was not sure how this could have been possible.  The heat of the room forced a dramatic change in temperature and if that was not stifling enough, the foul odor was beginning to suffocate me.

I took a few deep breaths and held my position hoping a solution would present itself before the creature had time to close the gap between us.  Despite the darkness, I was now able to see quite clearly and there was something large coiled in the center of the room.  Rhythmic breathing just as before, whatever the creature in the stairwell was, it had company.  Promptly, I panned the room for an exit, but my efforts were in vain.  If I were going to be taken again, it would not be alive.  I pivoted and rushed back up the stairwell to face the creature, hoping to take the creature by surprise.  Using the outer wall as a guide, I ran just off center in hopes of throwing the creature off target and this time it worked.

As I ascended the staircase, I heard the hissing sound once more growing louder and louder.  I drew in a quick breath and listened again.  I was nearly upon it when all went silent.  I had continued my ascent when I noticed a portion of the creature attempting to cloak itself against the dark walls.  I did not slow my pace but gathered my strength and went in to strike.  My bite does not contain any poison, but when primal, I am able to unleash a ferocity unmatched by anything created by man.  I propelled myself towards the creature ripping into and through one of its appendages with minimal difficulty.  Blood began to pour from the opening like a volcano erupting after decades of being dormant and while it was quite warm, it tasted of river bottom.  The creature expelled a cry from its body that reverberated throughout the staircase certainly waking all within the tower walls and in that moment, I was able to fully see the creature exposed and vulnerable. This was a nathair.

Nathairs are a vile serpent-like creatures found within the marsh with the physique of not only a serpent but of a man as well. Their bodies were that of pure muscle with a venom potent enough to liquefy a victim's insides within minutes of exposure. They are the type to lie in wait for their victims rather than attack outright due to their weakened underbelly, hence, their need to cloak. I have never known them to be found anywhere outside of the marsh as they are highly sensitive to lower temperatures. The sauna I briefly encountered might explain how it was surviving here, but how it arrived here was another matter.

Out of the corner of my eye I noticed the nathair was advancing, stretching to place its fangs within reach of my back. While its fangs would never be given the chance, that did not stop it from brutalizing my back with what was left of its tail and arms. I snapped towards it forcing it to recoil, if only temporarily, giving me the opportunity, I needed to unleash a fury upon it. I snapped rapidly creating several openings into its lower half and with each bite it cried out more in pain but continued to engage me. In the midst of the savagery, a pain seared down one of my hind legs. I do not believe I was bitten for I was still very much alive, but this wound would remove some of the advantage I had.

I could not risk lunging towards its throat, but I was close enough to sink my teeth into its abdomen in time to exact my pound of flesh. I pressed downward onto what was left of its tail to slow the writhing before lashing out once more.  As I bit down into its flesh for what I hoped would be the last time, I felt the blood from within it start to grow cold and its body collapsed beneath me.  If it had not passed on, it would do so shortly.  Rather than release its flesh from my grasp, I thrashed it about until a substantial chunk was torn away and flung against the wall nearby.  I glanced at the nathair once more to confirm its demise before taking a moment to assess my own wound.

As I turned to view my hind leg, my eyes spotted a second nathair slithering into striking distance.  My focus had been heavily on the attacking nathair, permitting me to temporarily forget entirely about its companion.  As I heard the rattle of its tail, I knew this was the male and he would not perish as easily.  This one was larger in size with plum colored skin containing sporadic streaks of violet throughout and out of his skin appeared serrated barbs which were no doubt its primary defense against beasts like myself.  With very little skin free of them, it would be difficult to sink my teeth into his flesh without receiving a few puncture wounds in the process.

He reared back to strike, revealing a soft and unguarded underbelly for my viewing.  I pushed past the pain and lunged towards him; fangs boldly displayed.  With the element of surprise on his side, this quite possibly was the only chance I would have to sink my fangs into his belly, crippling his defenses.  Our bodies collided in such a way that if it were not for the barbs lodged into my flesh and my teeth into his, we would have rebounded off on another with enough force to knock us both unconscious.  I thrashed about attempting to pull myself free but the more I struggled the further the barbs penetrated and hooked into my skin.  The pain seemed nearly unbearable and as the moments ticked on, my body began to go numb from the toxins, permitting the pain to fade away.

Refusing to be become the nathair's latest meal, I lashed out once more catching a rib within my bite and with a jerk, I heard it crack within my grasp.  He cried out with a blood curdling scream that nearly deafened me, this time I hurt him.  While temporarily pain free, I thrashed about in such a way that I was thrown from his grasp and down the stairwell where the elusive elf appeared once more.  Standing there cloaked in shadow, he drew a weapon from his back and cast it towards the nathair abruptly freeing his head from his body.  I watched him fall lifeless towards the ground just a few feet from his mate.  It would have been tragic had they not been trying to devour me.

I stood slowly as I knew this escape was far from over, but I collapsed quickly as my muscles were rapidly disintegrating.  The elf bent down to bring himself within my field of vision.

"So, shapeshifters are that of legend did you say," he whispered with a fair amount of sarcasm.

In my current state I was unable to speak, but that did not stop me from letting out a groan reflecting my disgust.

"What a magnificent creature you are," he glanced into my eyes for only a moment before turning to assess our surroundings, "no wonder tales of your kind have fallen into legend."

His reaction did not surprise or flatter me, as a shapeshifter I knew I was unlike anything else in nature.  When changed, I am nearly three times the weight and height of any of nature's woodland or ice wolves with a ferocity unmatched by any beast of that same caliber.  While my fur may change with my environment, my eyes never will, giving me away on more than one occasion.  They glow like the brightest of honeycombs when my emotions run high and have been known to glow as embers when provoked.  They are unmistakable.

Rising gracefully, he stepped towards the dead nathairs. I do not believe he wished to get a better look, but it only took a moment before I noticed him shifting the bodies around.  He was looking for something and he found it moments later with minimal effort.  I watched him pull his blade from amongst the carnage before wiping it clean on an exterior portion of his cloak, a wise decision.  I watched him with growing anxiety.  I understood the need to retrieve his weapon, but it was too quiet here.  We cannot linger.

I pulled my legs underneath me and stood slowly before turning to make my way down the stairs.  While the assault only concluded moments ago, I could already feel its poison coursing through me, devouring the walls and tissues that kept my body pulled together.  A faint cracking sound from behind prompted me to hunker down for cover, preparing for what may be another attack when I heard a sinister laugh echoing down that stairwell towards me.  I rose once more and snorted reflecting the lack of amusement I presently felt towards him. He appeared to be stalling needlessly and that was beginning to infuriate me.  A low growl escaped me, and he turned in my direction just before another cracking sound broke through the silence.  Upon taking a closer look, I noticed he was removing something from the nathair's bodies, their fangs to be more specific but why?

He placed them in a small pouch at his side and rose to his feet, "If protected, these are still lethal long after the serpent has passed on."

He must have felt me watching him with growing curiosity.

"We must go," he sauntered by speaking in a soft but stern tone, "you will need time to rest as the journey will be lengthy and quite disagreeable in your current condition."

His behavior was perplexing and often irritating, but I could not deny that I would not have made it this far without him.  As he continued his descent, I followed him without question.  Arriving back at the enclosed hot springs, I stopped just shy of the last step and watched over the elf carefully. Sauntering about throughout the room, he seemed to be carefully taking mental notes along with randomly picking up items as he went taking no notice of the secretions that had heavily coated the floor.  Perhaps the armor he wore provided a significant barrier against it and that is why he did not seem the slightest bit concerned about it.  However, I was interested as to what he was taking notes for and what he could have possibly been fetching throughout the room.

I turned away hoping to prevent the stench from seeking further refuge in my nasal cavity.  When I did, I noticed several crimson patches pushing through my already reddened coat.  Reluctantly, I began to whimper softly.  I was afraid to lick my own wounds for fear of the toxin creeping into my system, but they needed tending to.  Turning back in search of the elf, I found he had once again disappeared.  Just as before, he vanished without a trace or sound, it was astonishing really.  Standing at the ready, I prepared for an attack by an unseen foe, but nothing came.  Treading carefully, I began to walk the perimeter of the room as the secretions appeared to be isolated towards the center.

With much of my body and limbs now numb it was difficult for me to even stand let alone stroll around the perimeter, but I was not going to give up just yet.  Shuffling my paws across the lukewarm stone was better than stumbling, just not as stealthy as I would prefer to be.  Scanning the room repeatedly I noticed vary little variances between the floors and based on what I could see there was not a way out of this room.  Just as I was about to give up the search, I faintly heard something moving beneath the stone just off center in the room.  It was not a voice but movement.  There was some shuffling followed by the occasional sound of metal being tapped against the stone.

Stepping carefully through the secretions, I drew myself closer to the sound.  This creature was being careless and that gave me the advantage.  As I reached the center, I found a trapdoor cleverly hidden in plain sight as a drain.  This what the male nathair was concealing when I stumbled upon this room earlier and now, the door was beginning to open.  The door snapped back revealing the elf who previously disappeared.  I shook my head in confusion as he casually hopped up and out of the opening.

"Well," he uttered impatiently, "get in."

I snorted at his demand knowing that I could barely walk at this point, let alone leap into a hole in the floor.

He scoffed, "Shapeshifter, should you decide to return to your more desirable and trim state it would be my pleasure to carry you about."  He grinned, "However, in your current state I'm afraid I cannot."

I see this elf has a sense of humor today and I am not the least bit amused.  I stepped towards the opening and dropped into the drain with a thud.  Not the least bit graceful but with exhaustion and the toxins settling in nicely that was now impossible.  The elf followed along in near perfect grace and silence of which I was considerably jealous of at this point.  Much to my surprise, he did not stop to gloat.  I struggled to get back on what I assumed was my feet only to find out it was my chest, and I was now sliding across the floor nearly on my face with my rear in the air.  Unfortunately, it was only after I heard a significant amount of snickering coming from behind me that prompted my curiosity as to what could have possibly amused the elf in such a way when I soon understood.

The trapdoor shut moments later, and I felt the elf place his hand on my back.

"Let me help you," he said softly, "it will take only a moment."

Out of my peripheral vision I saw his eyes turn dark once more and I felt warmth radiating from his touch. It wasn't quick like lightening striking, but I felt something within me change. The pain that once felt so terribly far away was racing back causing my stomach to tousle about. Pain continued to spread throughout my body but soon began to fade again. His hand lifted from my back just before I heard him speak again.

"That should help," he sighed, "I'm not as strong as an elder, which I'm confident would have done better, but it is a start."

I nuzzled against him gently as a form of appreciation. He seemed to understand the gesture as he stroked my back a few times as confirmation before pressing onward. Before his touch, my life force was nearly spent and now, I was temporarily revived enough to press onward. The tunnel we were now in was dark and vile, clearly not a designed for safe passage of anything other than waste. It began tapering just shy of the entrance making it difficult for both of us to remain standing. The elf crouched and maneuvered down the tunnel with surprising comfort, clearly, he had been here before and I followed in a low crawl. This was significantly more difficult for me, but I had little choice in the matter.

I kept low and skulked a few paces behind the elf's posterior, close enough to draw in his scent even through the foul odor of the nathairs that was still wafting through the air.

He smelt of ash and soot despite an overall clean appearance. This would explain how he was able to maneuver throughout the tower with very little disturbance until I was free of my restraints. They could not smell or hear him. Nevertheless, I appeared to be the treasure and the temptation in a high stakes game of cat and mouse, but who was the cat?

Continuing through the tunnel we crossed several junctions but passed them with barely a second glance. When, finally, I caught the scent of salty sea water rushing towards me through one of the tunnels. There must be an opening nearby. I broke away from the elf to pursue the scent, quickening my pace as the scent grew stronger. My tracking instincts were locked on and I was closing in on my target. A few quick turns later, I felt the blistering cold firing through the tunnel at me and I reminded where I was. While the Ice Tower held many perils within its walls, the land it called home was just as cruel and unforgiving.

I reached the end of the tunnel and found myself facing a large, heavily barred grate exiting towards the coastline. The wind and ice I heard previously was now issuing an assault through the grate and onto my forelimbs. In that moment, I was grateful to be a wolf as it provided additional warmth and stability I may not have had in elven form. Peering through the grate, I scanned the perimeter for any sign of life, but there was nothing. The moon was shining just above the horizon casting radiate light to dance across the undisturbed ice, but the sun was beginning to rise. The land was dead and the only life to be found here would be hidden in the cruel waves of the Mar

Deigh or remained inside the tower.  My absence must have alerted the elf and he soon rushed in behind me.

"There is another way," he whispered, "follow me."

A growl began to reverberate in my throat just before flowing outward towards the elf.  I had no intention of continuing to explore the tower in my current state or otherwise.  Even the slightest opportunity we could escape through this hatch and into the night was worth the risk.

"We need to leave quietly," he sighed, "if we do this anyone in or out of the tower will be alerted to our presence."

There was a chance he was correct in that assumption, but I still wanted to chance it.  The significant drop was a bit concerning but not something that should hinder either one of us.  It may take a moment to recover from the impact but not enough to delay our escape.  I slammed my paws against the grate attempting to press the matter and I felt the grate begin to give way.  I shifted my body against the elf trying to give myself a wider birth and I slammed myself against the grate once more.  While the grate was beginning to cave from the sudden pressure that was being forced on it, the sound echoing through the tunnel would be difficult to ignore.  Thankfully, there are several junctions that may permit the sound to lose its way before being found by an unwanted guard.

Just as I was about to slam myself against the grate for the third time, I felt the elf's arm reach around me just before a crackling sound began to flood my eardrums.  The elf fractured the hinges causing the grate to shift and now with each gust from the coast it rattled against the metal of the tunnel.

Glancing through the grate once more, I quickly evaluated our potential landing zone and noted that once we were down there, we would find no coverage nearby. With us facing the coastline, we would have to maneuver around the tower before advancing north which would make us vulnerable for a longer period than desired.

I glanced back towards the elf but could not see more than my own fluff as the narrow tunnel barely permitted me to squeeze through let alone him alongside me. It was time. I slammed my paws into the metal grate once more launching it outward with such a force it disappeared into the frozen tundra of the coastline. I crept towards the opening and scanned the perimeter once more, all clear. I extended myself out of the tunnel ever so slightly and leapt towards the surface, hoping my reach would grasp snow rather than ice. Unfortunately, the impact was greater than anticipated causing the ice to rupture beneath me and if it were not for my claws latching onto the surface my limbs would have buckled under the pressure.

Pausing briefly, I felt the wind shift and what once was assaulting the tower now drew its attention towards my flesh. This was no ordinary breeze, more like an assault from the Gods. Infuriated with the poison that has infected these lands, they are seeking their vengeance by cursing all who venture here. I refused to give them the satisfaction. Hunkering down I crept towards the tower wall to wait for the elf. As I approached the wall, I noticed there were not any openings on this side of the tower except for one or two near its peak. Perhaps the King found leaving prisoners exposed to the elements was not the wisest practice when located this far south.  An act of cruelty rather than generosity I have no doubt.

Gradually following the curve of the tower wall, I watched as the edge of the coast disappeared and gave way to a vast open landscape of white leading up to the mountains of Geamhradh.  Colossal mountains of stone and ice punctured their way through the clouds casting an illusion of peaks floating high above.  The snow that rested on their peaks appeared soft and angelic but in my present location it was firm and unwelcoming to my touch.  Centuries of salt and ice compacted on the coastal edge has insured that tower's base will not falter but navigating it would be difficult for the elf as he has no means to provide traction.  As I was scanning the surrounding area, I found the elf had followed my lead and was just a few paces shy of reaching my hind limbs.  Glancing towards him briefly before returning my attention towards the mountains for there our real journey will begin.

"Wait," he whispered, "you changed, how?"

I glanced back towards him briefly and snorted as if I could have possibly answered him even if I wanted to.  What once was the color of autumn leaves and chestnuts was now snow white with flecks of ash.  A cloaking mechanism to help ensure our survival in the event our environment should change, but there is no way he could have possibly known that.  The elf slid into my peripheral vision and began pointing towards to different points near the base of the mountains that lie ahead that were likely to be concealed points of entry, but somehow, he knew they were there.  This elf knows more than what his lips are uttering and in time, I will draw it out of him.

With my sheer size and speed, I could easily make it to those mountains with the elf astride, but in the vast openness surrounding the tower it would limit my mobility should any disruptions in our path be encountered.  A clanging sound was finding its way to us, movement was stirring within the tower walls, based on that sound we would not have long to decide.  Seeing how there was no means for me to communicate my thoughts to him in the present moment, it was up to me to weigh our odds quickly and advance or retreat accordingly.  I listened carefully once more, the clanging amplifying and becoming sharper in tone with each passing moment.  Whatever foul beast had discovered our absence, they were nearing the end of our escape tunnel and soon would be able to decipher our location.  There could be no debate or second thoughts, we needed to move.

Pivoting sharply, I took the elf by surprise and dropped my snout under his bottom just enough to launch him into the air providing me the time I needed to fully drop underneath him for the catch.  Not a single sound escaped him in the toss, but his body grew tense at the sudden upheaval as one would have expected.  However, true to form he landed onto my back with grace and poise, hardly a hair out of place, just before clinging cautiously to my fur.  Our thoughts lined up in near synchronization and he was primed for the jaunt ahead.

Before I had even risen fully on all fours, we were moving.  He stayed low and tight against my upper back and neck causing less drag as I attempted to accelerate.  The pain near my hind quarters was more evident now, but I could not let it distract me from seeking the base of the mountain pass that lay ahead.  Keep moving, stay focused I told myself.  I have been captured once before by some hunters on the mainland and I assured myself I would never let that happen again.  While there are few shapeshifters found scattered amongst the lands, these hunters were not educated in such matters and merely wanted to skin me for the potential reward or favor brought if donned by a certain nobleman's shoulders.  The mere thought fueled my cause to advance further and dismiss the pain until it was safe to attend to it properly.

I did not need to turnaround to know the Ice Tower would soon be shrinking behind us in the distance.  However, while my initial thought was to seek Glacial Pass carefully hidden inside of the Geamhradh Mountains, I now realize that would be a folly for that pass places me closer to King Edric's castle.  He commands these lands, and it would only have been under his explicit instruction that I be obtained and detained in the Ice Tower.  Proceeding further north would place me directly within his reach and my present company's appearance would hardly permit us to simply blend into our surroundings.

We must turn back and advance towards the coast.  The waters here are treacherous, and we could by no means wade in them or swim across them, but there may be a chance we could seek refuge from one of the cargo ships I have known to be found nearby.  This could potentially buy us some time as wolfs are often too large and dangerous to be found concealed in enclosed spaces without an ample food supply being provided to them.  The beasts of the tower would know this causing them to focus their search efforts elsewhere provided we were able reach the coast unseen.

I promptly changed direction with this new thought in mind and while up until now the elf had been silent, I could now hear his voice struggling to project its way through the wind and ice that was swirling around us.  It was heavily muffled, and he was wasting precious breath for I had no intention of stopping to take in his thoughts as the sun was now rising.  While my second thought cost us time, I refused to relent or heed to the wishes of the elf I carry in tow.  When I did not yield to his demands, he began tugging at the fur just behind my ear.  A snarl escaped me, and I felt the tugging lessen, but it did not cease altogether.  He did not approve of the change in direction and was not shy about sharing his disapproval with me.

Bounds were made in mere seconds and soon I was racing along the coastline seeking a path to make our descent.  There was nothing to be found.  Meters passed along in seconds, and we were rapidly running out of coastline to search when a pier was sighted just shy of the southernmost point of the island.  A ship was not spotted but I could hear voices slicing their way through the quickly churning waves.  It took a moment to discern but they were clearly facing towards us rather than departing, which was pleasing news.  I slowed my pace and continued the search along the rim.

The elf slid off my back, I felt the weight of the journey already waning on me and my energy nearly depleted.  I knew I would not have long before collapsing was my only option.  We needed to get out of sight and quickly before anyone else could potentially witness my transformation.  No one else must learn of my secret as both of our lives now depend on it.  I ventured closer to the edge and spotted a narrow path to the pier; however, it was several stories below us and heavily coated in ice.  There was no way I could make the leap without potentially shattering my body or my companion's.  My head dropped in disappointment as we were certain to be found in the morning light if we lingered here any longer.  In that moment, fatigue and disappointment overcame me and I collapsed onto the ice before me.

The shapeshifter once so large and ferocious, now lies lifeless and bleeding on the ice before me.  I have worked too hard to get her out just to watch her pass on just steps from the tower.  I turned quickly to scout the cliff's edge for any type of rock or protrusion I could anchor a rope to before making our descent.  It was the only option we had to get us both out of sight quick enough without leaving a trace and thankfully, with her in humanoid form she would be light enough for me to shoulder.  With minimal difficulty I found a thick ice spike protruding from the cliffside that I was able to encircle with a rope I had on hand and fasten down upon it, all I needed now was her.  I stepped towards her and noticed the blood was pooling underneath her.  While slow in movement, she was still bleeding, and I could not fully mend her here.  I draped my cloak over her and slung her over my shoulder just before sloughing away the reddened ice and snow.  They must not know we were here, or it would all be for naught.

She was incredibly light and soft to my touch, nothing like I would have expected from the wolf that slayed a nathair in the tower.  This will make the descent easier than anticipated.  I grasped the rope firmly in one hand and held onto her tightly with the other.  There was not any magic I could use to teleport us downward, but while a one-handed descent poses a challenge I am rarely, if ever, not up for the challenge.  I stepped off the cliff's edge and began abseiling us towards the icy floor below.  Each step downward felt more daunting than the one before, but there was no room for fault or self-pity.

We reached the floor faster than expected and I could now hear the voices of human men barking orders over the sounds of crashing waves.  I released the rope promptly and took a moment reposition the shapeshifter in my grasp.  I needed the men to take pity on her and allow us on board.  Having a woman slung over my shoulder screams captive, not kin and while magic can buy you some grace, it has been known to not work on everyone.  I need them to believe I came here to rescue my kin, not a shapeshifter, for if her secret were revealed too soon, we would both become targets of King Edric's wrath.

I was nearly upon them before they were alerted to my presence.  Human men lack keen senses and are easily surprised when distracted.  I altered my course, staying clear of the men in power as they would be least likely to accept my offer and permit us aboard.  However, a small cluster of men unloading crates were within a few paces of us and I decided there is where I would make our case.  As I approached them, I could see some of the dock men focusing heavily on the mass I now carry and attempting to assess the situation. While I was carrying someone, they more than likely would not be able to tell that from their location, let alone my intentions.  The men were heavily battered and filthy from the grunt work they probably had been completing since shortly after being taken from their mother's womb.

"Greetings," I paused giving me time to gauge their reaction which remained that of surprise, "my kin and I seek passage on your vessel.  Would you permit us aboard?"

One of the men cleared their throat before speaking, "Passage may only be granted by our lord, King Edric, good sir."

The nearby crates were temporarily concealing us, permitting a few moments that would have otherwise been impossible to obtain and I could see these men needed some persuasion which was something I would happily give to them. I carefully focused on each of their faces just before widening my eyes, letting the magic channel through them.  The magic I possess does not require that of a wand or staff as warlocks and clerics wield. I am elven and as such the only humanoid found on Caladh that is born with such an innate gift.

"I request you reconsider as we are short on time and *we* need shelter," I insisted.

Within moments, I watched their expression transition from apprehension to concern which is exactly what I wanted them to feel. Suggesting that my kin and I needed to seek refuge was not enough before as the shapeshifter could not be seen, the word "we" struck a chord with them. In that moment they knew the mass was a someone, not a something. It was written all over their faces.

"What do you need?" a younger man spoke.

I turned towards him and bowed my head slightly to reflect my appreciation. As I scanned the man before me, I noticed his appearance did not differ much from the others, only slightly younger in years. Their clothes were heavily tattered and void of all color the fabric once contained. There were multiple repairs throughout, and they relied on layers rather than robust fabrics to control the temperature.

"Keep her hidden and take her aboard," I insisted, "it will appear less conspicuous should one of you handle this task than I."

"Who is she?" another one asked.

I focused my attention heavily on him, "In time, all will be revealed, now move."

The man quickly began searching for what I can only assume was to be a vessel for her passage aboard as I laid her down gently on the ground. Human men tend to fall prey to elven magic more so than any other species and this time I was relieved to not be met with a difficult challenge. While the men attended to the task at hand, an older man's voice was drawing near the crates. While I have ability to maneuver about unseen at times and persuade others, coercion over a large group is not in my power.  I would need to silence this man in order to give the others time to conceal her.

There was a slight gap between the crates, and it was there I focused on the man walking towards us.  He was older than the ones nearby suggesting he was of higher rank but no more than half life at best.  He continued to bark at them, permitting me to move in behind him unnoticed.  It was in that moment I pulled a bantam blade from beneath one of my bracers and struck him quickly and deeply in the nape of his neck.  He fell limp into my arms, and I quickly scurried towards the icy waters edge with the man in tow where he would meet his final resting place.  His death would be one of many should we be found and the hunger of the Mar Deigh was all too eager to consume.

I returned to the men to find them heavily focused on her.  At first, I could not conceive of what could have possibly captivated their attention so intently, but as I stepped closer, I became equally as drawn to her.  The wind had peeled my cloak back from her face and shoulders exposing her beauty and majesty for all to see.  In the morning light, her once white fur had given way to a sun-kissed beauty with long locks of paprika and fiery embers.  Never before had I seen such rich colors in beast nor man.  I forced myself to look away and refocus on the task at hand.  I rushed over to cover her before picking her up and placing her in an open crate nearby.

"Cover her quickly and get her aboard," I insisted, "I will clear the way."

I did not wait for a reply or rebuttal before turning my attention towards the vessel. It was not old as I would have predicted but heavily weathered and battered from its many journeys. Its haul was vast and seated deep in the icy water that was temporarily its home. I scanned it carefully, taking note of all points of entry. Much of the crew were now ashore and moving the cargo into a large opening at the base of the cliff just shy of the pier. This was one of two entrances to the Ice Tower and by far the most watched. The fastest and most secluded path would be to dive into the icy waters and swim to the haul. However, this would, also, be the most dangerous path for the water temperature found here would cast out all life within a matter of breaths. Then I realized my path was with her. I abandoned her once before to scout the path ahead and she nearly became the tower's newest victim. I could not be so careless again.

I returned to the men who were now working diligently at their assigned duties and the shapeshifter was nowhere to be found.

"Where is she?" I demanded.

One of the men pointed to a crate not a few paces away, "We shut the crate up to keep her warm, but she's barely breathing."

"Open it," I demanded.

"But sir, there's not time," the same man uttered, "any moment now someone will be by to inquire as to the delay."

I stepped forward and grabbed the man by his tunic, "I said open it."

I could feel the man tremble within my grasp as I stared deep into his eyes.  The words came out as a growl and while this man may not have feared me before, he certainly does now.  He nodded anxiously in hopes that would be sufficient for me to let him go and it was.  I released my grasp and found the other men were already opening the crate without so much as a second glance.  They did not remove it entirely but enough that I could see her and feel her once more.  I laid my hand upon her back and felt little to no movement.  This land had no need to exact a pound of flesh from her as her life was already being siphoned with each breath she took.

My eyes refused to look away from her, "Do what you must to get us on board," I paused, "I need to be with her now or she will pass all too soon."

"Aye," replied the men, "there is place in the haul, near that rudder, where you should be safe."

I nodded.  Without giving it another thought, I slipped into the crate and carefully pulled her into my arms just as they began nailing the crate closed above me.  Once inside the crate I felt my body temperature begin to rise again but hers did not falter.  I just did not understand it.  When I touched her for the first time, she was abnormally warm despite the frigid temperatures that surrounded her and now she appears almost mortal.  The thought perplexed me and the more I thought of it, the more concerned I became.

There was some mumbling from the men just before I felt the crate begin to shift.  I listened carefully for any sign of disobedience and soon put the matter to rest as we began moving south at a rather quick pace.  The closer we drew to the cargo entrance the noisier it became.  There were several voices of human men barking orders along with a distinct sound of whips cracking and tools at work.  Human men were weak and easily controlled, yet they continued to insist they should be the rulers of all life on Caladh.  The populace does not need to be dominated to flourish but nurtured.  Something that they have yet to learn despite centuries of being among us.  They were the ones who began the strife that has infected these lands and they will be the ones who shall perish first if they continue to choose poorly.

It was not long before I felt the wind shift as our path was changing direction.  The crate was being moved aboard and soon I would have the time to tend to her properly.  I lifted my cloak slightly from her side and watched as the crimson liquid continued to seep from her wounds accompanied by a foul bile that was attempting to gain a foothold nearby.  Placing my hand over it, I applied a slight pressure and watched her recoil slightly, she was still amongst the living, at least for now.  As I felt the men drop the crate onto the deck, several voices were heard in the distance, bellowing in our direction.  The guards of the tower knew she was missing.  However, from what I could discern, they were still seeking a wolf, not an elven woman.  She had chosen wisely, and we were safe, for now.

Once aboard there was several other voices casually passing by the men.  The commentary was friendly and filled with light humor which surprised me.  Serfs such as these generally do not bond to comrades as they were expendable, but perhaps those aboard this vessel were unique in that capacity.  I continued to listen carefully to the voices surrounding us along with mapping out the layout of the ship by counting steps and direction changes.  Then we stopped. The crate was temporarily secure but once opened those clues would be the only way for me to know exactly how to get us out if we needed to leave in a hurry.

I could hear and feel the crate being tugged at, but this time was not with a tool as they had used previously.  They were attempting to keep the noise from radiating throughout what I can only assume was a vacant portion of the haul.  There was a faint light beginning to shine through an opening near the seam between the lid and the base.  They were opening it and as the opening grew larger, the faint amber light grazed my cheekbones.  Not a word was uttered but shortly after the tugging began the men stopped before turning to scurry down a nearby corridor.

Waiting patiently, I listened for any sign of movement or life nearby and when I was sure there was nothing, I began to shift in the crate.  The haul was temporarily vacant, and I would need this time to get what was needed for her. However, there was a peculiar draw I felt towards her that tore at my insides with the thought of leaving her, but I had no choice.  I laid her aside and began forcing the top of the crate upwards.  It was surprisingly effortless considering the difficulty the men appeared to have with it, but then again, I am not built like most men.

Once the top was removed, I scanned the room taking in the full layout for any potential hiding places or resources we would need while aboard the ship.  The room while dimly lit by candlelight still permitting me to view a small nook between the vessel's keel and the rudder.  The nook was only partially in view from where I stood but it could easily be concealed by sliding a crate or two closer to it.  I stepped out of the crate to examine it further and was relieved to observe the space was larger than anticipated.  Moving quickly, I gathered any spare shreds of cloth and nourishment nearby, I was unsure of the vessel's next destination or where it may lay berth which means I would need to prepare for the worst.  Then again, I am traveling in the company a shapeshifter, the worst thing that could happen would be she turns to devour all the life onboard, but I digress.  I made quick use of the time spent gathering supplies and padding the space before returning to the crate where she remained still.  I lifted her gently out of the crate and placed her just in front of the nook where I would be able to examine her more closely.

The candlelight was too distant to see clearly, so I summoned an orb of light to aid in my task, with a mere snap of my fingers it appeared in the air, following me like a moth to a flame.  As I pulled my cloak back from her body once more, taking notice she was minimally covered in soft leathers, quite similar in color to her sun-kissed skin and she was barefoot.  My cloak was saturated at several points from her partially open wounds, and it was time I addressed those before they tore fully open once more.  I pulled some supplies from beneath a patch in my armor and began removing portions of her leather clothing.

The wounds were barely seeping at this point, and while I was relieved to find that she did not recoil from my touch, it pained me at the same time, for it meant she was fading further from our world. Placing my hand upon her, I pulled my energy towards that point and attempted to seal the opening, to which I failed miserably. Assisting her the mortal way, was now my only option. I grasped her cool flesh tightly in my fingers and began stitching. While precision was important, I was more concerned with how little time we had before we would have company once more. Once finished, I used a portion of the cloth I was able to find to wipe off any excess blood that had pooled on her body. While I was anxious to see her awake, I am sure she would not be comforted by finding her body heavily coated in her own blood. Thankfully, it was still relatively damp allowing it to wipe off with minimal difficulty, but she was terribly cold.

With this portion of the ship below sea level warming her up would be challenging but not impossible. I placed her inside the nook just before pulling the crate towards us concealing our location from anyone who was not within eyesight of the nook. I crouched down and removed the upper portion of my armor exposing my torso to the cool air that was drifting throughout the cabin. While I am resistant to the elements, I am not immune to them and soon enough I would need warmth just as much as she did, but for now, I would offer mine to her. Carefully crawling into the nook beside her,

I pulled her towards my chest just before encircling us in the warmth of my cloak's embrace.

While my body temperature dropped slightly from grasping a shapeshifting icicle, her temperature was beginning to stabilize which relaxed my mind if but temporarily.  With my arms wrapped around her I was able to take her in fully and appreciate more of what captivated me earlier.  Her locks, while vibrant, were long and curly while restrained at multiple points by beautifully woven leather bands.  They and the locks they held were lovely.  The shorter locks just towards the peak of her forehead fell nonchalantly down across her large almond eyes and onto her speckled cheeks.  She radiated a scent of freshly fallen rain and honeysuckle.  It reminded me of my homeland, which I rarely thought of these days.

While I could not see much of her flesh any longer, I could feel it beneath my fingertips, remarkably smooth and supple for someone living in the wilds.  However, a large scar near one of her shoulders drew my attention.  I lifted the cloak slightly to get a better view and there I saw an equally large scar on her chest, she had been run threw at one point and survived.  Based on the healing patterns of the scar it was not mended by a skilled healer nor an amateur healer such as myself.  The wound was reopened on multiple occasions for one reason or another, further prolonging the healing process.  I am astonished the scar tissue has not inhibited her from using her arm naturally, but then again in the limited time I have been in her presence I cannot say I was entirely focused on how she moved.

I laid there, with her wrapped in my arms, listening to the waves crashing against the hull.  Peaceful moments such as these were rarely found in the world we live in and when presented with such an opportunity I refused to deny its appeal. While elves do not sleep, at times we are able to fall into a trance like state as a way of reinvigorating our senses, but even now I am reluctant to take my eyes from her.  Repairing the exterior damage from the nathair's poisonous barbs was only one step of many in her recovery and I had no way of knowing whether her eyes would ever open to me again.  This thought haunted me and when I was certain we would not be disturbed for some time I permitted my eyes to close.

# Tuiteam

The three Princes of Tuiteam strutted with pride as they entered their father's bedchamber for what would more than likely be the last time.  King Baylon had fallen ill several days ago and last evening his condition took a turn for the worst. While it was understood Prince Ferand, the eldest, would succeed him on the throne, there were stirrings of sibling rivalry and secret campaigns by a nameless being to usurp the throne.  While there was no denying Prince Ferand's birthright, the populace was questioning his intentions as their ruler. Despite being highly trained and educated in the politics of ruling a kingdom, he never actively participated in such matters giving him a false perspective on how to apply those teachings. In addition, he was found to have a wandering eye that relished in lustful encounters of the flesh which would surely not please the Lady Rosalyn, his betrothed.

Their betrothal was agreed upon shortly after her birth but had been delayed on multiple occasions due to Ferand's preoccupation with other potential suitors. With the lands now being infected with turmoil from the southwest, it was vital the kingdoms of Tuiteam and Losgadh unite under one ruler. Seeing how Tuiteam and Losgadh were the only two prospering kingdoms of men on the mainland this alliance was the obvious choice to keep the surviving kingdoms of men alive and thriving. King Itheal of Losgadh appeared remarkably young considering his time on the throne but was by no means as inexperienced as Prince Ferand in the art of ruling a kingdom. However, his docile nature opened him up to becoming overrun when the slightest amount of pressure was applied. Thankfully, with only the elven kingdom of Lamprog on an isle to their east and Castle Tuiteam to the west their borders were secure from all but the creatures of Boglach and those found north in Tiene.

The princes stood at their father's bedside taking in what would be their father's last lucid moments when they were discourteously interrupted by a knight bounding through the bedchamber door.

"King Baylon! I need to speak with you!" he shouted.

"Are you a fool?!" Prince Berenger shouted firmly at the knight, "Our father, your KING, lay dying and you have the audacity to bound into his bedchamber in such a fashion!" He stepped towards the knight slamming his hands into the man's breastplate pushing him back towards the door before insisting, "Leave us now or face my wrath," he growled.

Prince Berenger was much larger and more muscular than his brothers due to his excessive training and time spent on the battlefield. While his tone was generally very calm and collected, when provoked, he of all the princes would be the one to fear. He had a commanding presence that radiated from his body and through his voice when he spoke. While he had no interest in the duties of a young noble, attempting to ignore his orders or silence him would surely be met with imprisonment. This day was no exception.

"Commander Berenger, I must speak with him," the knight insisted.

Prince Berenger did not take kindly to the knight's disobedience, "Guards! Seize this man!"

"I cry for mercy, King Baylon!" the knight shouted once more as the guards approached him, "She has been found!"

Prince Berenger waved the guards to remove the knight when a faint voice was heard crackling nearby.

"Wait," King Baylon whispered, "are you certain?"

The attention of the room was drawn back towards the King, unsure whether to press him about the matter or wait for further explanation to come in time.

Prince Ferand refused to wait and interjected himself into the conversation, "Speak quickly and freely good sir for your King has little time."

"We received word a female wolf was captured by King Edric and detained in the Ice Tower," the knight paused waiting for any sign of recognition from the princes but there was nothing.

The princes were confounded with the knight's behavior over a wolf. While these were rarely found in the wilds, one found should not permit such disrespectful behavior nor would it alter their course in any manner.

Prince Berenger turned towards the knight and spoke firmly once more, "It will take decades for King Edric to breed an army of wolves large enough to overrun our lands. Why do you bring us this news?"

The knight knelt before Prince Berenger but only addressed the King, "This is the beast your prisoner spoke of."

The princes exchanged glances before turning their disarray back towards the knight. Prince Berenger drew his sword and placed it carefully on the underside of the knight's jaw. The knight's body constricted from the sudden threat, but he did not attempt to flee or flinch away from it.

"Speak plainly knight or you will find your shoulders without a head," Prince Berenger urged.

King Baylon spoke once more, "Berenger, stand down and let the man speak without scourge," his voice was weak but firm.

"The Jagare were dispatched when news of the wolf reached our borders," he spoke quickly, "then a message was returned to us this eve confirming our suspicions."

The princes looked blankly at the knight, unsure what it all meant.

"You dispatched some of our finest assassins and hunters without the King's consent?" Prince Berenger pressed the knight.

The king's wispy voice was heard once more, "Come hither, my sons, I shall tell ye of a secret that my body has been tirelessly carrying for far too long."

He placed his hands beside him on the bed tapping gently hoping they would heed his call without any additional prompting, and they flocked to him without question.

"Take the passage through the lower halls and into the tomb of our ancestors.  Hidden there will be a very unusual prisoner," the king stopped to catch his breath before continuing, "because I have offered my unceasing protection he remains there willingly.  You, too, will give him your solemn vow and in doing so he will not harm you."

"Who is this man and why does he need our protection?" Prince Ferand interjected.

"For legends are true my son," the King paused, "this prisoner is no ordinary being," he smiled faintly and then appeared to cough out the remaining words, "Conall is a shapeshifter."

The princes pulled away in surprise at the revelation of a fairy tale come to life before leaning in further in hopes that the tale was not over.

"But how did this come to pass?" muttered Prince Ferand, "Shapeshifters faded from Caladh long ago, if they ever truly existed to begin with."

The King turned his attention towards Prince Berenger and the two remaining princes exchanged glances between themselves and then between their father and Berenger at a frantic rate.

"Berenger," they spoke in unison, "you know of what he speaks?"

Prince Berenger leaned against one of the bed's posts before speaking softly, "Myself and a scouting party were venturing through Boglach near its western border months ago when we stumbled upon a wolf," he sighed, "I was under the impression that the wolf was destroyed during an escape attempt but now I feel foolish for not inquiring about it sooner."

"You knew of this prisoner!?!" Prince Ferand spat.

Prince Berenger shook his head, "No, I assumed it to be a wolf, just as it appeared to be and never gave it another thought."

Prince Ferand rolled his eyes and scoffed, "So, what happens now?"

The princes' attention was now drawn back to their father.

"Shapeshifters are mythological beings that have power unlike any man can create or possess," King Baylon whispered, "You must recover her. She alone will give you what you need to rule over all Caladh unopposed."

"No one would dare oppose us while in the company of shapeshifters," Prince Ferand grinned with delight.

"Don't be daft Ferand," Prince Berenger swatted his brother's shoulder, temporarily knocking him off balance, "while these beasts have supernatural abilities, they are not exactly dragons nor are they friendly to our kind. Two would never be enough to overthrow the legions of men and beasts King Edric intends to send our way."

"But these we can control," Ferand snapped back, "No one can control a dragon, that is unless you would like to give it a go?" he snickered knowing all too well his brother despised backing down from a challenge.

The King's frail body began to gasp for air, fighting to remain with them. They both stopped bantering and turned back towards their father, silently praying that this would not be the end.

King Baylon whispered, "Seek her and find a way to convince her to come willingly," he coughed, "once here, take her to him and give her an incentive to want to stay with him."

"Father," Prince Urie finally spoke in a soft, child-like tone, "what would he want with her?"

Prince Urie was by far the unruliest of the princes and constantly getting into mischief. He had little desire to be trained or educated in the inner working of ruling a kingdom as there was little chance, he would ever sit upon the throne. Everyone knew this and therefore did not press the matter. He spoke little and behaved more as a fly on the wall than as a son of the King and this pleased his brothers greatly.

King Baylon mumbled, "If given time, she will learn to trust him and then they will do what nature demands of them," he gasped for air, "thus giving you an unstoppable might in their growing numbers."

"I do not understand," Prince Urie uttered unsure what his father could have possibly meant.

Prince Ferand scoffed at Prince Urie's childlike inquiry before returning his attention to the matter at hand, "How could that possibly aid our cause as they cannot be controlled?"

King Baylon replied, "You protect and defend them, and they become yours," he cleared his throat before continuing, "you do not need to control them directly, but should you possess or control something they care for and then they will owe you their allegiance," he paused, "which would transcend time itself, further protecting our bloodline."

Prince Urie spoke up again, trying to be heard, "I still don't understand, what would nature demand of them once inside our walls?"

His brothers snickered at the young prince's lack of experience and understanding. Due to their mother's untimely passing and the result of their father's second union, Prince Urie was born nearly a decade after Prince Berenger. They often forget the gap in age they have with him and in that, a vast difference of experiences.

Prince Ferand uttered through his snickering, "He means to bed her and sire bairns."

"Beshrew thee Ferand!" Prince Urie shouted, "Just because I have not bedded half of the kingdom does not mean I am a fool!"

Ferand stood quickly knocking over his seat causing a loud thud to echo throughout the King's bedchamber, "I would hold your tongue if I were you," he leaned towards him, "or if you would prefer, I could gladly cut it out for you."

His gaze was unwavering and while Prince Ferand had not been crowned ruler of Tuiteam as of this eve, he would be in due time leaving no room for sibling rivalry or insolence. By the time the princes returned their attention to their father, he had already passed on leaving them in silence pondering over their foolishness.

"Knight, can this shapeshifter be safely extracted from the tower?" Prince Ferand's gaze did not leave his father's face when he spoke.

"Aye," the knight remained knelt, "Prince Ferand if it be your will."

"What source do you have that brings you this confidence?"

"The Jagare are both cunning and resourceful, they will breach the tower," he took a deep breath before adding, "or they will die trying."

"Then let it be done, I have a coronation to plan," Prince Ferand insisted, "and I wish to meet this Conall.  I want to know more about his kind and what our father had promised him."

The knight nodded before standing and quickly exiting the room clearly rattled by the overwhelming confusion that he encountered.  He knew it was not of his rank to speak of such matters but leaving this crucial part of his strategy to the last moments of life would certainly leave more questions than answers.  The doors closed quickly behind the knight, and it was time to prepare for all that had been set in motion.  Prince Ferand took a moment, a very short moment, of solace with his brothers before turning away.  His silent departure was short lived as before he reached the bedchamber doors, he began uttering his wishes for the day and days to come.

"My Queen must be brought here with haste as I will need an heir to secure my throne and our father's legacy.  I will, also, need preparations for my coronation to take place on the morrow or a day passed at the latest.  Tuiteam will not be seen without a ruler on the throne," he continued to strut down the long corridor growing further and further from the bedchamber until his voice became nothing more than a faint echo upon the stone walls.

The remaining princes stayed behind, pondering over all that they had just heard and the loss of their father, unsure of exactly what should be the next move.  While Tuiteam would need a ruler, their minds returned to the brief tale they had just been told.  Both princes had heard of the legends of shapeshifters and understood the capabilities of the Jagare, but neither could fully comprehend the door their father had opened by wittingly restraining such a beast.  Prince Berenger was one to believe talk meant little over those who acted, and he had no intention of waiting for an escort to meet the shapeshifter, Conall.  He kissed his father's brow briefly before exiting the chamber without uttering a word, while Prince Urie remained, face buried in his hands, weeping softly.

It was the heat that woke me just before I permitted my eyes to peel open, revealing the darkness that surrounded me once more.  I was in an enclosed space, and I was not alone.  There was a man lying very close to me, breathing slowly and his skin cool to the touch.  I could feel the warmth from my skin radiate onto his, briefly warming where I touched.  Exhaustion no longer overcame me and while I was famished, my body was mending, permitting my temperature to return to normal.  I lifted my head upwards slightly to draw in a better view of my location and when I did, his breathing changed.

"Calm yourself," he whispered, "you're safe here."

It was the elf from the tower, "Where are we and who are you?" I whispered.

"We are on a cog, passage was bartered while you were...recovering," he whispered without even opening his eyes, "and who I am still doesn't concern you."

"Shall I have your name then?" I quickly added, "I'd like to know that in the least."

"My kin call me Drayk," he uttered, "and you are?"

"Eira," I whispered, "I am called Eira."

He made a sound as if he were pleased, but the reason eluded me.

"You saved me, why?" I asked softly.

"In my travels I have encountered males of your kind but never a female," his eyes began to open allowing their brightness to draw my attention to them in the dark space. "Consider it my honor if you will," he added.

I watched his face carefully in the dark, trying not to stare into his eyes for longer than necessary.  Before when I saw him, he seemed different, but I could not place what was different just yet.

"Care for some light?" he interjected breaking my focus, "I would hate to strain your eyes further if only for a more intimate look upon my flesh."

I felt my skin flush in frustration and refused to speak of the matter further.  I knew he could see my eyes upon him but to have it pointed out so boldly infuriated me.  Elves are generally very poise and polite, however, Drayk is audacious and very brash.  He clearly was accustomed to rattling cages.

"How long have we been aboard?" I mumbled trying to change the subject.

"Two or three days now, it's difficult to discern," he whispered just before light appeared to engulf the small nook, I found us in, "is that more to your liking?"

An awkward smile rushed across my face before I nodded.

My eyes were quickly drawn back towards his lily-white skin and bright eyes. They reminded me of the elven king's jewels when met with the sun's light, diverging and iridescent. His long sandy hair fell playfully onto his strong jaw and as I brushed it back from his face I was greeted with color once more. There was a bluish grey trail that began near his right eye and flowed down his neck onto his chest and back growing more vibrant as it descended. I ran my fingers along it pondering the purpose or outlay of such an enduring mark. I must have lingered there longer than he anticipated as he cleared his throat to break my focus.

"It was a gift," he said.

"What does it mean?" I asked.

"That I cannot tell you," he uttered, "for each it is different."

"There is so much about you I don't understand," I muttered.

"That's where your curiosity is misplaced," his arms tightened around me bringing my lips within inches of his once more, "you want to know too much and with that you miss what is right in front of you."

I held my breath in anticipation but nothing further was said.

With growing curiosity, I asked, "Which is?"

His one eyebrow arched ever so slightly reflecting his amusement with my curiosity, "You've been on the run for too long Eira," he smirked just before placing his lips ever so slightly on my forehead.

The kiss caused a shutter to run through my body. There was a part of me that wanted to admit how right he was and another part that knew it did not matter if he was.

"Are you alright?" he uttered with his lips barely parted from my skin.

"Of course," I stated attempting to sound aloof at the situation.

Unfortunately, all we both detected was apprehension in my voice.

"Do I frighten you?"

I thought over the question, realizing in my own way I did fear him, not because of his strength but of his knowledge. He held within his body a secret that I have concealed for centuries, and that knowledge was power if given to the right person. I thought about uttering something to that effect, but ultimately decided to say nothing as we both knew the answer.

"I'm not the one you should fear Eira," he whispered.

I tilted my head back just enough to bring his eyes back into focus and when I did, they were there waiting to meet my gaze.

"If I wanted you dead, I would have left you in the tower," he grinned, "and if I wanted to bed you, I could have already done so or would do so now if I so desired."

He applied slight pressure with his fingertips before dragging his hands down my back slowly just before resting them casually on my hips, reminding me how physically close we had become.  His point was proven and while the events of my escape was not without flaws, he has been protecting me ever since my eyes opened in the tower.  The why I was so desperately concerned with, need not be as important as what comes next.

"Thank you," I whispered as there was nothing further, I could think to say in this moment.

"Think nothing of it," he smiled briefly before turning and slinking out of the nook where the light followed him instinctively, "Would you care for a bite?  You must be famished."

His sudden departure left me wanting but with the thought of something to eat dancing along the tip of my tongue I could hardly think of anything else.  I crept out of the nook behind him, just in time to witness him donning a tunic followed by a portion of his armor that remained on the floor beyond the boundaries of the nook.  He dressed slower than foreseen while I watched with growing curiosity.  Perhaps that is what he desired, my eyes upon him or perhaps he, too, was recovering from an injury or aliment that was unseen to me.

The armor he wore was much darker in color and contained far too many layers to be entirely elven made, but it appeared to have been started by one of his kin.  Over the years and through his travels, it would appear the other layers were added or altered by other races which would explain its unusual style.  The marking that was so difficult to see before was now quite apparent and while it, too, was elven in origin, it was not at the same time.  The marking that was hidden from me previously was pleasantly in view now.  The color ran over his shoulder and down his back, poetically flowing into slender curls that cleverly hugged the muscles of his back, moving as he moved.  Against his lily-white skin, the brightness of the markings blue and grey tones shown more muted than I am sure was intended, but no less noticeable.  Before I had long to ponder its meaning once more, he spoke breaking my focus.

"You watch me, why?" he asked.

"Forgive me, I-" I stumbled over my words.

"You didn't realize I knew you were watching me," he interjected.

To say I was dumbfounded would have been an understatement.  While I consider myself to be perceptive and cunning, Drayk misses nothing.  There could not have been more than ten or fifteen seconds that passed at most while I was watching, and he still knew I was watching.

"Forgive me," I uttered.

He turned sharply and tossed a partial loaf of bread in my direction, "There is nothing to forgive.  Besides, I am not offended that your body lusts for me," I felt my breathing change at what he was suggesting, "perhaps, I too, would entertain such a notion had the woman in question dazzle me with her body rather than her questions."

"My body does not lust for you," I said sharply before I began devouring the bread, not taking a moment to breathe for fear of adding fuel to his fire.

"Then perhaps you should inform your eyes of your lack of interest, for they now appear to be controlled by your burning loins rather than your mind as it should be."

A playful grin was painted across his face as he returned to my side with a flagon of what appeared to be water, but its bitter aftertaste suggested this was a watered-down version of ale. More than likely thinned to sustain the serfs on unpredictably long journeys at sea, but it was better than nothing. I wanted to protest his accusation further, but I quickly reminded myself that had I not been so apparent with my observations he may not have felt the need to point them out so confidently.

"Who commands this vessel?" I asked softly, desperately trying to divert the conversation.

"They are neither friend nor foe," he turned towards me, "that I am sure of."

"Do you know where it berths?" I pressed.

He looked down at me with his left eyebrow raised and I was starting to gain the impression that my curiosity amuses him, if but a little. I was about to press the matter further when I heard something in the distance. It was large, breaking through the water at a remarkable speed. I dropped down to lean into the nook for a better listen when I heard it again.

"What do you hear?" he whispered.

"Quiet," I insisted, "now's not the time to give ourselves away."

I listened again. Carefully hidden among the crashing waves I could hear the wail of something large, very large, moving in our direction.  I jerked back and in doing so startled Drayk, who had drawn himself towards me in an attempt to have a better listen to what I was hearing.

"We have to get off this vessel," I insisted trying not to raise my voice above a whisper, "now!"

"We cannot," he insisted, "we are miles from shore."

I grabbed a corner of his armor and jerked him down towards the nook, "Listen," I paused, "it is coming."

"I am unfamiliar with the sound of this foe," he paused, "what is it?"

"Havsdrake," I said frankly not wanting to draw out the discussion further.

There was a brief glimpse of vexation that rushed across his face, "Grab what you can, we need to depart before it strikes, or risk being lost to the depths below."

I dropped to the nook searching for anything that would be invaluable to surviving our sudden departure and found little.  I glanced over my shoulder to inquire as to our potential location when I noticed Drayk had vanished again.  I hoped he had plans to return but one can never be too certain in situations like this.  I grasped his cloak along with a few scraps of unused dressings before continuing my search throughout the remainder the room.

The light that once so cleverly followed Drayk's every will and movement had now dissipated and I was standing in near complete darkness.  My eyes adjusted quicker this time and I was able to float towards potential areas of interest but quickly abandoned my search as the havsdrake's wail was growing deafening to my ears.  If the serfs aboard were not abreast of the situation, they would be shortly.  Havsdrakes are one of several highly unpredictable sea creatures that roam the oceans of Caladh.  The smaller, meek havsdrakes can be found flourishing near the coastline as they prefer the tepid water and camouflage the coral provides, but the larger ones are rarely found near the coastline due to their tremendous size which only the deepest depths of the ocean's floor can shelter them.  When I was a youngling, I was told that one of the largest havsdrake ever encountered would have taken two moons to cross, but I have never seen such a creature.

The water surrounding the ship was beginning to clash violently with the vessel's wooden haul signaling that my time to depart was rapidly dwindling.  I wrapped Drayk's cloak around me, covering most of my body and face, just before advancing towards the door.  If the havsdrake intends to wreak havoc on this vessel, I need to find Drayk and get out of here.  I grasped the door and pulled it open slowly.  The cargo hold opened into sleeping quarters for the serfs and the while the wails from the havsdrake were quickly becoming deafening to my ears it remained a lullaby to theirs.

Moonlight radiated throughout the space from a partially open hatch directly above a jury-rigged staircase that has been heavily overused.  I would need to navigate through a maze of sleeping men, both suspended in the air by hammocks and sprawled out on the floor, in order to reach the staircase.  I took my first step towards the light relying on my nimbleness to carry me through each step in a poetic dance across the wooden floor.  My final step placed me just shy of the staircase where I was once again greeted by Drayk's bright eyes.

"I have bought us some time," he whispered, "let us go now."

I nodded just before we began our ascent up the rickety staircase which seemed to creak in unison with the haul each time the ship rocked in the unrelenting waves.  Stepping through the opening I noticed on-deck was nearly as quiet as the crew quarters below.  The few serfs that were roaming the deck did not appear to be deterred by our presence and that permitted me to rush onto the stern castle unhindered in hopes I would find the havsdrake had altered its course.  We were not so fortunate this night.

In the distance, I watched the water break against the curves of its scales just before its body projected itself upward towards the moon in this beautiful display of light.  Its body was paler than I expected, similar to that of the sky just after a spring rain, with what appeared to be coral or seaweed projecting from several points on its back and head.  It quickly arched itself back into the water with swiftness and grace.  I stood there in admiration of this beautiful creature and pondered if it, too, was misunderstood.  With such cunning abilities and cognition, it would indeed make a powerful ally if ever captured.  I continued to stand there unable to pull myself from its sight when I felt someone from behind pull me back onto my heels.

"And just who might you be fair maiden?" a low gruff voice mumbled into my ear, "I do not recall you being let aboard, but I'm sure you'd be a welcome sight for the men below."

As the man spoke, I could smell and feel the bitter and foul odor of his breath penetrating through the fabric of Drayk's cloak. It was nauseating and while, normally, I would just find a way to break his concentration long enough to flee, given our situation that was not an option. He reached for me, wrapping his arms tightly around mine temporarily restraining me, I would need to free myself before I could incapacitate him. I jerked my upper body forward and then back again with such an unexpected force the blow broke his nose. He released his grip from me to aid his wounded face just before crying out in pain. Without allowing another moment to pass, I extended my leg to execute a semi-circular kick that fractured the man's neck on impact, thereby relieving him of his previous discomfort. As the man fell to the deck with a thud, I realized it would not be long before someone had heard that or potentially already did. I scanned the deck in search of Drayk and found the once so passive deckhands were now rapidly approaching. Retreating towards the most wayward point of the stern castle's edge, I scanned its length for any potential step down and during that time I noticed the height of the waves had dramatically increased, crashing against the stern and splashing the water on deck. The havsdrake that was once a mere glimmer in the moonlight was now circling the ship.

The serfs to my posterior were now chaotically scurrying about the deck exclaiming obscenities as they were now very aware of the havsdrake presence and its proximity to their vessel.  They moved about with no particular direction or purpose in a strange madness that seemed to consume them.  Thankfully, I appeared to be immune to the ailment that now consumed their minds.  Through the sound of crashing waves and screams, I heard a flood of voices rushing from the chambers below.  Serfs were being commanded towards their stations in a frivolous attempt to conquer or at the very least, detour the havsdrake from its intended course.  This mission would be a folly as these men were already doomed.  Leaping from this vessel would be their only chance.

I abandoned the stern castle and ventured forth towards the forecastle.  As I rushed past the serfs on deck, several took notice of me but that did not slow my progression.  The most northern edge of the forecastle was within my sight, and I knew that is where I would need to take my leap.  The water would be cold but bearable and while the shore may be far, enduring it was just another cost of my freedom.  Within seconds, I leapt from the vessel's edge and felt a mist of salty sea water cling to my face and body.  Its cool touch brought forth a wave of goosebumps that started at my toes and ended at the tips of my fingers.

For a brief moment, I felt what flight must have felt like for some, effortless and exhilarating.  However, my free fall was broken, and my body jolted to a sudden stop.  The cloak must have snagged itself upon a loose board or protruding weaponry that I could not have foreseen before I leapt so suddenly.  I jostled myself about for a moment attempting to loosen the hold it had when I noticed that the ship was not holding it but Drayk.  His face was painstakingly strained from the sudden jolt and his nostrils were flared with agitation.  I stared into his eyes hoping he would have the strength to just set me free, but after a few moments I realized that hope was in vain.

I closed my eyes as I pulled my arms upwards towards the moonlit sky, drawing in one final breath.  I felt my body relax just enough to slip free of the cloak and I fell smoothly into the water below.  The cool water rushed over my warm skin and clung to me tighter than one's true love.  The upheaval the havsdrake was causing beneath the surface was greater than what could be seen from above.  I felt the pull of its might towards a central point and at the point is where it would bring its crushing blow to the cog.  Upon opening my eyes, I was able to fully appreciate the physical phenomenon of a havsdrake.  As its size could never fully be appreciated from the surface.

Its movement was incredibly alacritous and precise, nothing it appeared to do was without purpose.  When I realized it was not detoured by my presence, I took to the surface to begin the lengthy swim ashore.  Water was something I needed to survive as most do, however, every part of it surrounding my body felt unnatural to me.  The current wrapped itself around me with a constant and unrelenting draw back towards the cog.  My mind and body were now locked into an intense battle with the sea and while the havsdrake may not have been directly pursuing me, the sea was.  The waves were picking me up and carrying me back making each body length I swam only inches in gain.  Buckets and buckets of water were cast against my face and body with each breath, forcing me to choke through the water to draw in more air as the sea relentlessly exuded its dominance over me.  The struggle compelled me to acknowledge yet another error in judgment that may yet cost me my life.  I could feel myself tiring already, but I needed to remember to use my mind rather than fight the sea's salty waves with brute strength.  Taking in one final deep breath, I plunged below the surface in hopes of escaping the violent waves on the surface.

Even under the surface there was a current still present, but the ever rising and crashing waves no longer distressed me as they once did.  Movement under the surface was smoother and less resistant, allowing me to place more distance between the cog and I.  Glancing downward revealed a deeply blackened void providing further understanding how the havsdrake could carefully conceal itself in the sea.  I tried not to focus on the darkened depths below, but the thought of other creatures hidden there ever watchful of my movements was becoming a growing concern in my mind.

Rising to the surface once more to regain the breath lost, I worked quickly to observe my location and the distance I had traveled.  This would be vital in determining how I proceeded forth as to not expend all my strength.  The air rushed in my lungs quicker than I expected and I took several moments to inhale as much as I could before reorienting myself.  The sound of men shrieking at their impending doom was thunderous in conjunction with the sounds of the havsdrake's destruction and while I felt a brief moment of sorrow, I felt nothing more as I knew there was nothing I could do for them.  In the distance, I watched as several of them throw themselves from the cog in hopes of meeting a better end but as the ship began to collapse under the sea's demands and the havsdrake's might, nothing they did would have saved them.

I slowly began to backpedal my way towards the shore, fearful of taking my eyes off the ship.  My concern grew as to the Havsdrake's next action, but in truth, I believe my concern was with the untimely end of the elf I met in the tower.  There was no sign of him, and I felt that tug at my insides more so than expected.  The havsdrake's actions seemed like such a waste of life, but when threatened, we are all capable of such violence.  As I continued backwards the waves soon began to calm and the sinking ship was fading in the distance along with the cries of its crew.  When all had disappeared, I turned back towards where I presumed land to be and struggled onward.

I was deep within the struggle of treading water when I noticed doldrums had settled in.  In the distance, I watched as the sun slowly began to rise, causing light and warmth to flood the surface of the sea, bringing my attention back to the stillness of it.  Aside from the ripples radiating from my body, the surface was disconcertingly still.  While my experience in and on the sea have been limited, I have lived near its beauty and violence all my life.  To my knowledge, I cannot recall a witnessing a sea as calm as this one in the wee hours of the morning ever before.  Perhaps I was further out to sea than expected or was this the calm before another storm?  Dropping below the surface, I quickly scanned the darkness for any signs of an impending misfortune when I noticed a glimmer of stardust faintly flickering beneath me.  The glimmer was wispy and fleeting, but I was certain there was something there.  If this were to be a beast of malicious intentions, there would be no outmaneuvering it.  I could only trust that my animalistic nature would not misguide me.  I tipped my head back towards the surface and drew in a few deep breaths before once again dropping below the surface.

However, when I glanced towards the glimmer again, it had vanished, further provoking my fear and curiosity over what it may have been.  I began to spin about in the water only further increasing the height and length of the ripples that extended from me.  I needed to calm myself or every creature within a mile would be alerted to my presence if they were not already.  I slowly brought my limbs to a halt and floated back towards the surface, still nothing.  Perhaps the glimmer was only seen by chance, or it was a ruse to draw my attention elsewhere.  Either thought became unsettling in my belly and I was still no closer to land further adding to my apprehension.

Slowly drawing in breath after breath, smooth and effortless, I felt myself relax if but briefly.  My arms lay lifeless in the water beside me and as I drifted to a standstill, I allowed the water to wrap itself around me, clinging to each hair and pore it could grasp.  While the water was crisp, it felt silky, not grainy as I expected.  I lay for several moments longer than I should when I stopped pondering the mystery of the depths below and just started slowly dragging my legs against the water's stillness, propelling me forward once more.

After what felt like a hundred strokes, I turned over and permitted my arms to join in on the task.  Unfortunately, I turned over a bit less gracefully than I had hoped and in doing so caused something beneath me to jolt.  Jerking myself to a sudden stop, I drew in a few quick breaths and plunged myself downward.  Shapeshifters are not known to be strong swimmers, so it was not without difficulty, but I suppose we all can do remarkable things when they are demanded of us.  Each stroke pulled me further away from the light and closer to something much larger than myself.  Continuing my descent, I felt the water shift and a current pulling me towards something. I allowed the current to pull me, giving my muscles a much-needed break.

The current was quick and twisting, nearly the opposite of a water current generally found near a northern coastline. So, either I was further out to sea than I foresaw or something else was creating the current.  Just as I began to comprehend that concept, the current ceased and the water was still once more.  When nothing lay before me, I turned sharply only to be greeted by a pair of large, round eyes the shade of a long-lost blue.  My gut reaction was to flee, but with those eyes only a few body lengths from mine I could do nothing more than gaze upon them with fear and trembling as those eyes were part of something much larger.  The eyes held my focus, but mine were soon drawn away to take in the large scales that were tightly woven onto the body of large marine monster.  We both may have been beasts but before me was a dragon of the sea. Legions of men could not best this beast while in the sea and therefore, my ferocity would make me appear no more than a timid, lost hare in its eyes.

I watched it, watching me for several moments when I noticed a familiar glimmer reflecting from its crest. It has followed me from the shipwreck with just as much, if not more, curiosity than I presented previously. The sunlight from above broke through the surface and onto the seaweed-like appendages that branched from several points of its body. As it hovered in the depths, those appendages shifted in waves of colorful light make it glimmer and sparkle like stars in the night sky. I blinked quickly to refocus my vision when I noticed it appeared closer to me than before. Was it advancing, or was I? As the space between us was closing, its beautifully vibrant pearl scales were clear to see as each one reflected the light just slightly different than the one before. This would explain how it appeared bluer to me in the moonlight. Each appeared to be cleverly crafted with edges that resembled those of snowflakes, delicate and flowing, although I am certain they would not be as soft.

I slowly pushed my hands forward towards the Havsdrake in a sign of submission and to stress that I was bearing no ill will, only wishing to part in peace. It did not appear amused, and its eyes did not falter from its target, me. I could feel my flesh igniting once more as it did in the tower from the emotions that were rapidly overcoming me, I needed to calm myself. While the havsdrake is a monstrous beast, it was not threatening me, merely observing as I was doing to it. I knew that my time below the surface was limited as my lungs beginning to ache, but I was concerned about the reaction it would have if I bolted away from it so unexpectedly. I decided to stay and tempt fate into choosing another path for me.

Slowly, I began shifting my legs in the water to move me closer to the havsdrake as I may never get another chance and had it wished to take me, the distance would make little difference. The havsdrake snorted at my feeble attempt to be coy. It knew I wanted a closer look while it probably already knew what I was, allowing me that up close and personal glimpse was not something it intended to encourage. It quickly projected itself forward and around me, into the darkness. The sudden burst of speed sent me into a spiral, distorting my vision and my perception of where the surface was. I felt my lungs giving way, I needed to get to the surface. I thrashed about to regain my balance before ascending when another wave struck me from behind further toppling me into the deep. I closed my eyes and wound myself tightly into a ball hoping to control some of the agitation I was experiencing from being jostled. I listened carefully for at a young age I learned to trust my ears over my eyes since our eyes can easily be deceived. I could hear the havsdrake's call echoing in the distance as before the vessel went down, clearly signally it was no longer nearby. Hanging there suspended and rotating in the current, I felt my lungs collapsing from the pressure.

I extended a handout hoping to latch onto something nearby when I was greeted with a needle-like and fervent sensation that started at the palm of my hand and painfully gnawed its way up towards my back. It was fire coral. The searing pain engulfed my arm and was starting into my shoulder. When I extended my hand, it changed my course, and I was now tumbling into a bed of coral. Unknowingly so, I opened my mouth as a foolish response to the pain and quickly took in water. I felt myself choking on it. My eyes opened wide and when they did, I noted the change in terrain and colors surrounding me. The havsdrake's momentum propelled me a great distance from the wreckage and based on what I could see, it brought me closer to land. Whether an act of kindness or in error, that did not matter now as I was given another chance at life.

Extending my body, I planted my feet temporarily onto a smaller patch of coral, gritting my teeth as my feet were now engulfed in the searing pain as well, before projecting myself towards the surface. Powering through the pain was my only option as I could hold my breath no longer. My body and lungs were crying out in anguish and my heart was beating in such a thunderous rhythm I felt its demanding present throughout my body only amplifying the pain. I pressed onward. With each stroke I felt the water warming from the morning sun's light and with its rays, the water all around me was illuminated from its presence. Just a little further.

I burst through the surface just as my lungs gave out and I began flailing and gasping for air. I worked quickly to regain my composure as I would not want to draw an undue attention in my direction more so than I probably already had.

Each breath was agony and delight encapsulated into one moment.  The fire coral had made its point as I was not from there and clearly not welcome to return.  I continued to whip myself around until at last land was in sight.  It was not as near as I had hoped but there was land to be found.  Taking in several deeper breaths, I began to rush towards the shore.  If the havsdrake wanted to come and claim me, this was its chance.

The surface felt warmer than I expected after my brief time spent below, but still significantly cooler than waters found to the north towards Tiene and Saor.  Either the vessel took a wrong turn, or its destination was not towards Castle Trocair as originally suspected.  I was clearly further north, but not venturing towards Lamprog either.  As I swam through the pain, I took what moments I could to orient myself with my surroundings.  Where was the sun? What can I hear? What can I smell?  Anything that would provide me with valuable insight as to my location and potentially give me an edge if and when I was able to greet the shore.

There was a soft breeze waltzing across the water's surface now, filling my nostrils once again with salt.  The scent and texture of the breeze became so strong I had to stop and violently expel it before it consumed my nasal cavity.  The salt burned my insides further aggravating my already battered body.  I desperately needed a few days of rest, but rest rarely comes for the hunted.  There was a price that must be paid to exist in this world and unfortunately for myself and other shapeshifters, the price is non-negotiable, and nothing is off limits.  While some want us just for the satisfaction of the hunt, others seek something far greater and it is in the cruel hearts of men, that the majority of my kind have perished, and the remaining seek darkness.

I tried to relax my body once more in hopes that floating would alleviate some of the discomfort I was feeling now and while it may not have alleviated my pain, it did not antagonize it as swimming did.  I drifted further and further towards the shore with each sway of my legs and the growing waves.  While this was a brief moment of peace found amongst the water's embrace, I longed to be released of its hold and return to the forests of Lamprog where I could be carefully hidden amongst King Aldon's magic.  At least there, I may walk among them unsuspected and without fear.  Elves have been known to be spotted amongst other races, however due to their nature, they do not seek strife commonly found on the mainland or remaining islands.  The elves have proven to be valuable allies in the past and given the opportunity I see no reason they would stray from that path.

Spinning myself like a barrel, I rotated over onto my front allowing my eyes to focus on the shore versus the red that had nearly consumed all of the pale blue that once was there.  With this in sight, I felt my body and mind rejuvenate slightly causing a flood of energy to flow throughout me.  I burst towards the shore with such speed that, if witnessed, one would have thought I was on the hunt.  I missed the sensation of dirt breaking beneath my feet as I sprang into action and pollen powdering my hair as I rushed through the meadows.  Out of everything that has been taken from me in my life, those sensations, that feeling of sweet freedom, is what propelled me forward and permitted my mind to embrace the hurt instead of collapsing from it.

I reached the rocky shore and dropped to knees before crawling the remainder of the way to the forest's edge.  Out of exhaustion and overcome with emotion, I cowered on the forest floor, just shy of a cluster of tall trees, where the foliage was dense, and my scent obscured.  There I found comfort in the crashing waves and softness of the moss beneath me.  It was there I closed my eyes and implored there is where I would be when they opened again.

# Trocair

King Edric awoke late in the morning to a thunderous charge of men rushing though the castle gates. They were heavily armored and shouting orders that ricocheted amongst the men. The king rose out of bed and signaled for his chamberlain to enter and assist him. The chamberlain entered without question or further instruction.

"Good morning, King Edric, I trust you slept well," the chamberlain bowed whilst presenting the king with his wardrobe for the morning.

"Stop being a fool," the king scoffed, "how could anyone sleep with all that nonsense about the gate?"

"My apologies King Edric," the chamberlain bowed lower, "there's news from the tower."

King Edric stood quickly and tore the garments from the chamberlain's arms, "What news?!?!" he growled.

"I cannot say your majesty," the chamberlain stood erect with his head hanging low and quickly began dressing the king.

"Hurry you fool!" King Edric shouted.

"Yes, your majesty," the chamberlain muttered while rushing through the final steps of dressing his highness.

Once the final piece of the royal jewels slid onto his shoulders, the king tore himself from the chamberlain's presence bursting through the bedchamber doors, stampeding through the long hall towards the great hall.  His jaunt was interrupted when he heard voices radiating into the hall from the war room.  Only a select few of the king's inner circle were permitted there without his presence and should they be there now, surely meaning a grave error had occurred and death would soon follow for some.  King Edric altered his course just in time to burst through the war room doors, startling all within.

"King Edric," several knights knelt before him in shock, "your majesty, we were unaware you'd be joining us."

"Have you forgotten whose castle you have stumbled into?!" the King sneered, "Is this not my war room?!" the King continued to shout before he was forced to stop to cough up what would certainly have been this morning's phlegm, nearly choking on it in the process.

"Of course, King Edric," a deep voice flowed into the room behind his highness, "none of these men would be so foolish to have done so."  The man stepped forward and placed his hand upon the King's shoulder, "Forgive my delay King Edric, it is I who summoned these men here."

The King recognized this man and with the exuberance of a child he turned sharply bringing the man into view. The Knight Commander, Elgar, was not a man in the prime of his life any longer, but he was not a childhood companion of the King either. He was a burly man with shoulder length dark locks heavily streaked in grey and white, badly broken from years of abuse and neglect. The face they shadowed was heavily scarred from battle ailments including slashes above his eyes and two ample grooves into his one cheek and gnawing their way down onto his neck. These grooves were surrounded by several pock marks reflecting a poor man's mending more than likely completed on a battlefield long lost to us now. The eyes found just to the north were dark and shaded by his perpetual scowl which caused him to have a very unwelcoming appearance, much like King Edric.

"Commander Elgar!" the King burst with excitement while grasping the man's shoulders firmly just before hugging him, "I did not expect to see you so soon my friend. I was told you were injured during the attack."

"Aye," Commander Elgar shook his head, "just a scratch," he uttered being modest as they both understood a scratch would have never kept him from reporting favorable news to the King, but to elaborate on an ailment would have just been considered whining, which was never acceptable.

The King smiled at the Commander which was extremely rare especially in the presence of others, "Good," he turned just before stepping towards the war table, "what news do you bring me?" the King growled with anticipation.

Commander Elgar stepped towards the far side of the table, placing a fair amount of distance between the King and himself, "The wolf has fled the tower."

"Impudent fools!" King Edric slammed his fists onto the war table with such force the pieces atop bounced about before several cascaded towards the floor, "No one escapes my tower!"

"The beast is clearly more cunning and powerful than we anticipated, your majesty," Commander Elgar responded.

"Then you should have tried harder!" King Edric shouted at Commander Elgar, "You have failed me!"

Commander Elgar rushed towards his King and placed his hand gently upon the King's shoulder, "I have not failed you nor will I."

The King threw his hands up, knocking the Commander back onto his heels, just before beginning to pace about the room.

"The beast was given aid," Commander Elgar spoke softly in an effort to calm the king's wrath, "your tower is impenetrable, it could not have escaped otherwise."

"Then we have a traitor amongst us," the King sneered, "find him!"

The Commander nodded in agreement before signaling the other men in the room to flee towards the grounds.

"What of my wolf?" the King's tone softened slightly, "Is there any reason to believe that she was injured during the escape?"

"Since she was not found, if injured," he paused, "I believe they are repairable."

The King nodded before adding, "Who else knows of her escape?"

"A handful of men in the tower, maybe more.  The men were brought here under false pretenses to help insure the wolf's presence and escape remain isolated to as few men as possible," the Commander attempted to sound reassuring, but it only came across as hollow.

"Then keep it as such.  Too many lives have already been lost in pursuit of such a beast and I will not have the men fleeing over secret whispers and scuttlebutt."

The Commander nodded in agreement before fleeing from the King's sight, leaving them both to ponder what really happened the tower.

Prince Berenger watched carefully over his brothers in the hours following their father's death.  Ferand, the future king, took little time to grieve and attacked the tasks of his coronation and nuptials with all haste.  He was becoming greedier and more power hungry with each passing hour, an unwelcome sight for all in his wake.  Ferand's undeniable beauty and charisma were what drew the people to him.  He was silver-tongued and flirtatious, giving him a mannerism quite pleasing towards the opposite sex, but deadly towards his own for one could never know what side he was truly on.  His locks were trimmed short on the sides but left longer at the top so they might fall to one side or another, giving him a rebellious appearance while still permitting the ladies to indulge in its softness.  The eyes that were found beneath were an equal shade of brown surrounded by his pale but smooth white skin and not a wrinkle or scar in sight.  The two brothers were remarkable similar in body type, but with Ferand choosing the life of luxury over responsibility, he significantly lacked the muscle and power of his brother, Berenger. However, as Berenger was now witnessing, the overbearing side of Ferand would quickly need to be controlled or he would soon fall out of favor with the populace as they would never side with a wicked king.

Berenger waited patiently for Ferand's demands to cease, but when they failed to do so in a timely fashion, Berenger took the anointed king harshly by the nape of his neck and ushered him into a secluded hall behind the throne room.  Ferand did not appreciate being handled in such a manner in front of his subjects, however, he knew that resisting the one person who could and would defend him until his dying breath would not be the wisest course of action for him to take.  Therefore, he uttered nothing nor displayed any sign of disapproval of his behavior until he was sure they were alone and away from prying eyes.  There is where he took out his vengeance upon him.  In a low voice he began issuing a vicious tongue lashing as attempting a physical altercation would have only been met with defeat.

"Never choose to lay a hand on me in the presence of my subjects or I shall wreck thee and all you hold dear," Ferand hissed keeping his voice low.

"Then you would destroy yourself my brother," Berenger hissed back, "now, stop acting like a youngling.  I will wait no longer for your *precious* time."

Berenger turned about giving Ferand no time for a rebuttal and it quickly became clear he was to follow his brother without question or instruction.  They walked together in near perfect synchronization not uttering a sound but understanding completely the destination in mind.  The beautiful light grey stone halls, bright and full of warm light, soon gave way to more primitive walls that were shadowed from all but candlelight.  They continued to journey through several corridors and even backtracking through others to insure they were not being followed just before reaching what appeared to be two dead end pathways.

They looked at each other with an inkling of disarray about them as if the pathway had changed in some way and it caught them off their guard.  Berenger rarely hesitated, as in most cases the hesitation would end in defeat, but caution when in the presence of magic has its benefits.  He closed his eyes and stepped into the pathway towards his left and in doing so the wall vanished and a stairwell appeared.  Once both princes' feet were firmly placed across the threshold, the wall reappeared sealing them inside.  Berenger may not have been able to see Ferand in the dark but that did not stop him from overhearing the grumbling and groaning he was uttering under his breath.  Berenger placed a hand upon the encrusted stone wall for guidance until his eyes brought things into focus and they began their descent.  Each step descended them further into the earth and darkness until one final step brought them onto a dusty stone floor where Berenger was able to locate and ignite a torch to aid their journey further into the tomb of their ancestors.

"The path is longer than I remember," Ferand spoke softly.

"Aye brother," Berenger uttered, "it is, but you would know the path better if ye ventured here more often."

Berenger glanced over his shoulder with a disapproving look towards Ferand and a mere scoff was all that was given in return. While the brothers had a close relationship, both knew when it was best not to goad the other and this was one of those moments. They were soon greeted by a large, heavily bolted iron door. The door was wider than it was tall and covered in several sheets of additional plating, all of which appeared to be added after the door's original construction. In addition to the plating, there were several sliding bolts and locking mechanisms for which great strength and keys would be required for entry.

Berenger placed a hand upon one of the plates just before running his fingers along the edge. He examined the door for a few moments and then quickly began flipping the slide bolts up then jerking them back with loud clangs that echoed wildly throughout the chamber. He then pulled a pouch from beneath his armor that contained the keys needed for entry. One by one he placed the keys in their corresponding locks and when the last key was turned the door appeared to have exhaled and was now slightly ajar. Berenger took a deep breath and pulled the door open wide revealing a large cavern filled with light rising from basins of oil and fire scattered throughout the perimeter of the space. They stepped into the hall of their ancestors and without prompting, the door inhaled and shut quickly behind them. Berenger placed a hand on the hilt of his sword, tempting to draw it, but in his memory of the wolf, one sword could not possibly best him regardless of who wielded it.

"Kindly remove your hand from your sword," a low male voice penetrated through the cavern, "I bear no ill will towards the Princes of Tuiteam."

"How did you-" Berenger began to say but was rudely interrupted.

"I am no prince," Ferand barked, "I am your anointed king," his voice began to quiver, "show yourself."

"I have no king," the voice replied.

"You insolent fool!" Ferand spat.

Berenger placed a hand on Ferand and stepped forward trying to determine the location of the voice.

"Forgive my brother," Berenger spoke softly as to not upset the shapeshifter, "he is still grieving over the loss of our father, King Baylon."

"And you are not?" the voice changed pitch, sounding concerned if but briefly.

"I have not felt the pain of this loss thus far, but I'm certain I soon will," Berenger responded quickly as to not appear deceitful.

"You grieve another," the voice fell soft.

"Aye, that I do."

A deafening silence filled the room and, in that moment, Berenger realized there was more to this shapeshifter than he initially predicted.  Everything we say and do was picked up on and remembered by him.  He sensed things, deeply personal things, that would otherwise be incomprehensible by ordinary man.

"I do not wish to speak my grief," Berenger added, "would you not come into the light?"

A man stepped forward from behind a large angelic statue and rested his shoulder on one of the lower arches in the angel's wings.  The man wore little to cover his body, only a pair of heavily worn leather breeches, leaving little to the imagination.  He was quite tall and muscular but not bulky allowing him to appear more like that common folk when clothed.  His hair was the color of walnuts when dried over an open fire and filled with wind braids making it appear shorter than it clearly was if it would have fallen naturally.  Thick, masculine eyebrows cloaked the dark eyes hidden beneath them, but they were very misshapen over his right eye from multiple scars in different stages of healing.

The princes stepped towards him hoping to get a better look even though they would have never admitted such.  As they grew closer the man's eyes grew wide and allowed them to see how large and round, they were with bright honeycomb centers.  The scarring that once appeared isolated to his brow was now, also, found through both the upper and lower lip on his right-hand side.  This scar was deeper more jagged than the others causing a peculiar indent in his already swollen lips.

"Are you Conall?" Ferand spoke sounding surprised.

Conall grinned, "Where you expecting something more majestic?"

"Our apologies," Berenger spoke up, "our expectations were deluded by childhood tales and our father's sudden passing gave us little time to discuss details of your physical appearance."

"Come now Commander," Conall stepped towards them with the grace of a cat but the threat of a dragon, "deceit doesn't become you."  Conall sighed clearly appearing irritated at this mindless banter, "There are no such tales of our appearance, or we would not have stayed hidden for as long as we have.  Suchlike numerous others, you are just appalled at how natural my humanoid form appears."

"Aye," Berenger sighed, "that I am."

Ferand stepped towards Conall and began circling him, initiating an unspoken predatory dance. Conall did not appear amused at this typical exertion of masculinity and left his gaze resting upon Berenger as in his eyes he was the alpha male regardless of Ferand's new title.

"Why have you come?" Conall demanded.

"To inquire as to the details of your arrangement with the late King Baylon," Berenger spoke.

Conall folded his arms across his chest with displeasure at their continued presence, "Surely, you must know of our arrangement, or you would not have graced me with your presence." Conall scoffed, "Stop being coy, either tell me what you truly desire of me or grant me my freedom."

"Your freedom was never a term mentioned in the agreement," Ferand blurted out in frustration, "do you take us for fools?"

"Unless you execute me, I will outlive you and your grandchildren," Conall grinned, "provided you are able to sire a wee bairn."

"How dare you!" Ferand spat, "I should have you executed for such insolence!"

"But you will not," Conall jabbed, "you need me, or all this would be for naught."

Ferand drew his fists up in anger as a low growl escaped his throat. He may have wanted to strike Conall, but he knew he spoke the truth. Ferand may not have been able to execute the man, but he would not be spoken to in such a tone and definitely not by some prisoner. Ferand drew his fist back and swung to strike Conall's taunt jaw. Fortunately, Conall sensed the impending attack and dodged Ferand's attempt causing Ferand to stumble forward, losing his balance. Conall countered his attempt by lunging forward and down, catching Ferand by the throat before tossing him backwards and hard onto his back. The thud echoed throughout the cavern and Berenger leapt towards them.

"Conall! No!" Berenger shouted while attempting to pull Conall's hand off his brother's throat.

Conall turned towards Berenger releasing a menacing growl from deep within which ignited a fire that was felt across his skin and brightened his eyes. The sudden change startled Berenger and he soon fell back onto his behind before quickly scurrying away from the two of them, eyes wide and mouth agape in reverence.  Conall turned his attention back to Ferand who was writhing beneath his grasp and gasping for air.

"Your feeble attempts at proving your worth have left you vulnerable," Conall growled, "and I will not submit to your will."

Berenger watched in repugnance as the events of Ferand's ego unfolded before him and it quickly reminded him of the day Conall was captured in Coille.  The forest steamed from the tropical morning heat and there lay the remains of hundreds of his men fallen during the night.  The wolf, he now knows to be Conall, was relentless and malevolent showing no mercy towards the souls of all who attempted to stand before him.  The gods have made a mistake to permit such power to be held within one being and no amount of luck or faith would be enough to survive his wrath when provoked.

"Stop!" Berenger cried out, "Forgive King Ferand for he knows not to whom he speaks!"

Conall released his grip from Ferand's neck and grew tall before stepping towards Berenger who was now scrambling to regain his footing.  As a soldier, he knew there was no honor in cowering on the floor as an enemy drew near.  Conall stopped just short of arm's length and tilted his head slightly with amusement.  Berenger drew his shoulders back and with that he grasped the hilt of his sword bringing it out, aimed in Conall's direction.

"Stand down Conall, you will not harm the King of Tuiteam," Berenger said sternly, "upon my life and my honor, I will protect him."

"Then take this pitiful excuse for a king and begone with you.  There is no need for pleasantries, and I care not to toil over this one's ego," Conall glanced towards Ferand who was now returning to his feet.

"Unfortunately, we cannot let this time come to pass without the information we are seeking," Berenger responded.

"Can he be controlled, or does he need to be threatened in order to behave in a civilized manner?" Conall gestured towards a clearly shaken Ferand.

"Can you?" Ferand spat.

"This is me being controlled," Conall insisted, "had we stumbled upon each other in the wild, you both would already be dead."

Berenger knew this to be true and with that sheathed his sword.  Tuiteam needed Conall as an ally, not a prisoner or this arrangement would never hold.  Conall turned and began walking toward the far side of the cavern and the brothers soon followed.

"This arrangement," Berenger spoke with a soft but firm tone, "may we discuss it?"

Conall nodded, "Aye, we may.  I assume you know something of it already or you would not have come."

Ferand spoke up, "Aye, that we do, and it is our understanding that we will protect you for as long as we are able."  He paused appearing to think carefully over the words he was planning to release into the world, "Nevertheless, our father may have been a patient man but never foolish.  He would have never given such a gift without the scale heavily weighted in his favor.  What did he ask of you in return?"

"Power," he mumbled, "my power."

"You mean your allegiance?" Ferand sounded perplexed.

"Power was all he could force me to relinquish, if temporarily at best.  After all, I am an immortal or rather I am incapable of dying in a sense that you know of, and my allegiance would transcend time.  That would be a gift I cannot give, so he had to accept my offer of power instead."

"You speak as if our protection holds no value for you," Ferand added.

"Protection means something different to you," Conall sighed and traced one of the scars just above his brow to emphasize his point, "a point I need not forget to clarify in the future."

The room stood silent as all parties present were painfully aware that this was a fact they could not change.

"There must be more to it than that," Berenger added quizzically, "our protection in exchange for you aligning yourself with us at an undisclosed time in the future would not be enough.  What else are you not telling us?"

Conall stood there, eyeing Berenger disapprovingly but did not utter a word.

Berenger sighed just before speaking again, "This arrangement was never weighted in your favor, and should you desire the scale to be tipped in your favor, I suggest you tell us what we wish to know."

Conall's eyes narrowed as he watched Berenger carefully. He did not appear to wish him ill will, but he pondered why a father that appeared to sacrifice so much for his sons would have hidden so much from them. However, that information may never be known to him, but the thought gave him something knew to chew on.

"King Baylon demanded another as payment," Conall spoke firmly but with a heavy amount of regret in his voice.

"Why would you give up one of your own?" Berenger spoke.

"I am not even sure she exists, but at the time both of our lives were hanging in the balance and now, there's a chance we both could find some peace, if but temporarily."

"I was there when you were taken," Berenger sounded perplexed, "you were injured but not gravely."

"Your king did what he believed was required of him in order to break my spirit and bend my will. However, I heal much faster than any mortal man and I have been on the run for centuries." Conall took in a few deep breaths before adding, "He was not the first to attempt such a task and he will not be the last for that I am certain."

Berenger's eyes wandered throughout the cavern, reliving Conall's capture and the months that followed when he remembered this was not the first time, he and Conall had crossed paths. At the time, he was just another traitor on a slab while several men were working on exacting their pound of flesh in exchange for information.  Hours soon turned into days and although, gravely battered and broken, he did not utter a sound.  That alone was a testament to his character and strength.

"You and I have met before now," Berenger spoke softly.

"Aye, we have."

"You were in so-"

Conall cut him off, "I do not wish to speak of those matters," he glanced towards a stone marker just down the way, "unless you wish to speak of your pain as well."

Berenger shook his head not uttering a sound.

Ferand could sense and unspoken bond before him and refused to let either of them dwindle on something that was no longer relevant, "And you were willingly bring this...pain upon another?"

"You know not of what you seek," Conall insisted.

"You tasked us to seek-" Ferand began to say.

"King Baylon demanded I give him another!" Conall bellowed, "My soul has already made peace with the solitude I have found myself in.  You may have learned of us as legends, but in truth we are fading into legend."  Conall began to walk towards the far end of the cavern, "We are done here."

"The woman you spoke of," Ferand paused hoping to draw Conall back in, "she does exist."

Conall promptly turned back towards Ferand, "Are you certain?"

"Aye, according to our guards she was captured by King Edric and now resides in the Ice Tower of Reothadh."

The appearance of hope on Conall's face was diminishing, "Then she will soon perish," he paused, "no one leaves that tower alive."

"She will," Ferand added sounding confident, "some of our finest have been dispatched to extract her from the tower and as it be my will, it will be done."

"What happens then?"

"She will be brought here, provided she survives the extraction and journey."

"To what end?" Conall sounded unsure for the first time since their encounter began.

"She would be kept safe here, much like yourself," Berenger spoke up.

"Then she would be yet another one of your prisoners," Conall sighed.

"Aye, she will be.  I will not risk losing my kingdom over a few rogue shapeshifters," Ferand said sternly.

"We are not rogues," Conall growled, "we are just the only two that have survived the years of persecution by *your* people."

Ferand was fuming, "Regardless of how you came to be here, you are our prisoner now and you will do as I command!"

He stepped towards Conall puffing out his chest in a pitiful display of superiority that failed to win him any favor with Conall.  Conall merely released a faint growl through his lips as if giving a warning to keep his distance.  Berenger stepped in between the two with his arms outstretched attempting to distance the fiery men before him. Ferand's fiery temper would soon drive a wedge between all of them that shall not be undone.

He thought for a moment on his father's words and understood there was a strong possibility that what was mentioned could not have been the entire story. Shapeshifters are elusive and mythological to nearly every race upon Caladh, what could anyone possibly know of them? While King Baylon indicated a desire to have nature take its course, part of him knew there was nothing natural about any of this. In order to avoid arousing further suspicion or apprehension he would have to choose carefully when and how he inquired. However, he was not willing to risk the kingdom just yet on whether the entirety of the terms mentioned were known to Conall. In the event selected terms were withheld from Conall, then mentioning them to him offhandedly could be catastrophic. They needed him to trust them as the fate of Tuiteam hinged on their agreement.

"Ferand," Berenger bellowed, "I think it is time we left Conall to his solace. He has much to think about."

Ferand scoffed, "As do we brother."

Ferand turned and headed towards the door. He may be king, but he was no match for Conall, and this burdened him greatly. Berenger remained near Conall if but briefly before turning to follow his brother. The room remained silent and by the time he reached the door it had already been opened and Ferand had disappeared into the darkness that lay beyond. He placed his hand upon the door preparing to close it when he heard Conall's voice once more.

"This *King* you brought to me is just like his father," Conall's voice echoed, "his heart dark and filled with greed."

"Your King," Berenger sighed, "it would do you a great service if you remember that."

Without another word, the door swung closed behind Berenger and promptly closed its locks. Berenger quietly removed the keys from their chambers before turning away and rushing towards the stairwell where he was promptly greeted by Ferand's flushed face. He was livid and no amount of flattery was going to soften the savage beast within him.

"I want him tortured Berenger," Ferand puffed, "and I want you to be the man to do it. He cannot be permitted to address me in such a manner without consequences." Ferand stepped down off the bottom step to begin pacing on level ground, "Break him if you must."

Berenger grabbed Ferand by the shoulder and shoved him away from him as fast as he could and bellowed, "I will not torture an innocent man!"

"That is no innocent man I assure you!" Ferand shouted, "He's killed hundreds, if not thousands over the centuries!"

Berenger lowered his voice and continued, "You break him, and all our father's planning will be for naught."

"He is our prisoner; my prisoner and I alone shall decide his fate."

"In a matter of hours, you have become just as deluded as our father was," Berenger spat and turned away from Ferand's sight. "If by some happening the female arrives safely, do you really believe he will bond with her under these conditions? It may not even be possible."

"They will not be given any choice in the matter," Ferand added.

"We cannot demand this of them," Berenger growled back.

"Then you are a fool brother," Ferand growled back.

"Aye, perhaps, but you know not of what you are demanding of them."

"And you do?" Ferand added confidently.

Berenger closed his eyes and let the memory of a long-lost maiden drift into his mind. Long locks carefully braided back away from her rosy cheeks as she giggled in the sunlight. In that brief moment, he felt as if he was transported back to the valley where they so playfully fell in love and just as quickly, she was gone again. A tear fell from his eye, and he quickly brushed it away. Ferand said nothing but stepped towards his brother. Just as he reached to place a hand on his shoulder Berenger turned sharply startling Ferand and causing him to gasp just before grasping his chest in surprise. In that moment, something in Berenger changed.

"My apologies, this should not have been about my wishes. I have sworn an oath to protect, and I will uphold that oath until death wishes to rid me of it." Berenger spoke firmly and confidently, "What does my King wish of me?"

"Seek what information you can of these shapeshifters but do so without arousing suspicion," Ferand paused appearing deep in thought, "send Urie to scour the library as he has been known to frequent there for his studies and see if you can get a status update regarding the extraction.  The plan father put in motion for us hinges around her survival," he lowered his voice before added, "see that she does."

"May I add something brother," Berenger spoke softly trying to appear docile rather than resistant, "I do not believe our father's hope of Conall siring bairns with this woman was part of the terms understood by Conall."

"What makes you believe so?" Ferand sounded perplexed.

"He appeared genuinely astonished at the mere suggestion she exists," he paused and thought for a moment before continuing, "Although, it does seem peculiar that two mythological beings such as themselves would not have found each other by now, would you not say?"

"Aye brother, it does," Ferand began to pace once more, "you would think they would know where to find one another or sense each other in some way."  Ferand brought his hands to his temples and began massaging in concentric circles, "We need answers."

As the door closed behind Berenger and the locks turned over, I listened carefully at the words that were being exchanged between the two.  Unfortunately, due to large amounts of stone and iron found in the door and the wall it was held within, I was unable to decipher much of the conversation other than a few words here and there, but the tone was clear.  It appeared a struggle for power was gaining a foothold as the two were bantering and even though Berenger conceded at the end of their conversation, he had already shown his hand.  His outward appearance projected that of a knight, but there was something in Berenger's voice that gave him away.  Grief and pain radiated from his pores as he thought of it, without uttering a word, I could sense all he felt.  This pain made him vulnerable.  Of the brothers I had met and the father who sired them, this is the one that should be king.  He is tactile and intentional with each action, nothing he does is without purpose and his loss, however, unintentional grants him compassion, an emotion that would be greatly received by his subjects.

I carefully thought over each movement the two made during their impromptu visit.  For all Ferand's posturing, he appeared to know and understand very little.  While he may be in power, he is not accustomed to it, nor does he understand the finesse needed to handle such a delicate situation, forcing him to behave as a varlet or small child would.  Berenger carried himself very differently from his brother and once he understood we had met before his behavior changed.  The memory caught him off guard and while I was sure he did his best to project an appearance of superiority, all I could sense was shame.  He may not have been the one holding the instruments of torture or bending my bones until they fractured but he watched, nonetheless.  His loyalty to the late King Baylon was unfailing, but I was interested to see and hear that his loyalty towards the newly appointed king and brother was not as such.

With nothing other than my thoughts and memories to comfort me, I turned my attention away from their movements and back towards our conversation.  They spoke of the arrangement in his presence and again after their departure.  It was my understanding that the terms set forth by King Baylon were non-negotiable, defend him and his heirs and in turn, they would ensure I was hunted no longer, or vengeance they would permit me to take.  Up until now, King Baylon has held up his end of the agreement, not as I would have hoped, but in truth, I have not been hunted and I am able to reside here in solace. Yet, what I could not foresee is when I was going to be required to hold up my end of the agreement.  The war to end all wars was growing near but still many seasons if not years away.  The thought of being alone and locked in a tomb to an uncertain end was nearly more than I could bare, then I thought of her.

I first learned of a stunning elven beauty with locks of fire rumored to be trouncing her way through the wilds in search of someone lost.  Whether this someone was a child, a lover, or a friend, I do not know, but it was my understanding he was seeking temporary refuge in the Kingdom of Losgadh and that is what brought her near to me.  The populace knew very little of her when inquiries were made, just that she appeared one afternoon.  She was rumored to be an apparition by some, then a rogue assassin, and then a creature from the marsh.  All had the potential to be accurate, but I knew different.  Elven women are rarely left to wander the mainland alone and when found doing so, exile is the cause.  When this is done, the elven king orders the person to become forever marked, so the world might know their shame and be left to the mercy of others.  However, this woman was not marked to my knowledge as it would have been mentioned if this was part of her story. This woman was no lorvisad or one of the banished nor did her appearance suggest she was an elf of Lamprog, as her vibrant locks and sun-kissed skin would have never occurred naturally on the island.  She was a shapeshifter like myself and hiding in plain sight.

In my travels, I have found others like myself, but found it difficult to remain in their company as beasts, such as myself, tend to quickly draw attention when in groups.  The Kingdom of Losgadh, however, held particular fascination for me as that is where not only one was hiding in plain sight but held a position of power.   A young male was frequently seen near King Itheal posing as an ambassador, of sorts, for King Aldon, the elven king.  While shapeshifters may appear elven when in humanoid form, we do not possess the inherent gifts they receive when they come of age.  This one was disciplined and highly dedicated to his cover story which piqued my curiosity.  I desired to learn more.

After observing him for several days and nights, I noticed he did not make attempts to escape nor reach out to anyone else of our kind.  A behavior I found interesting as he did not appear in distress in any way nor was he seeking.  Had this been the one she lost, I would have thought he would be trying harder to find her unless, his sudden disappearance was not so sudden or unplanned.  Either thought did not warrant me remaining in the city.  I needed to find out for myself if the myths were true, so I set out in search of a ghost.  Searching the plains of Feurach for weeks to no avail and left with understanding that either she found who she was searching for or fled for her own protection.  Both could have been true, but if she were truly searching for someone like them, they probably perished soon after their disappearance or they are held captive somewhere, like I was here.

However, something about searching Feurach for her brought life back to me and just as quickly as it was given it was taken away.  I was captured weeks later while battling a creature of the marsh.  A young commander, now known to be Prince Berenger, had brought his soldiers forth to test their might against the ever-expanding marsh.  Once I was discovered, they appeared content to leave the marsh in peace if it meant taking me with them.  I may have been distracted when they stumbled upon me but much to their dismay, I had no intention of being taken so easily.  Many men fell to my wrath that morning depleting my strength leading to my capture, but there is not a day that goes by when I have not wondered what became of her.

# Lira

Hunger drew me from my slumber, and I was greeted with the warmth of the late afternoon sun. The sun was falling once more in the sky and its piercing gaze had drifted through the gaps in the tree's branches. I listened carefully for anything unusual near my resting place before prying my eyes open to find the temporary den as undisturbed as it was when I fell asleep there hours ago. Stretching myself out fully, I groaned at the comfort it brought, before rising and heading towards the shore to forage for anything useful or suspicious. The shore was littered with debris from the wreckage and unfortunately, most of what was scattered across the shore was wooden boards from broken crates and the ropes that once were used to bind them. There would be very little of use or value to be found here, but my eyes remained peeled, holding onto a hope.

Just when I had nearly given up the search, my eyes caught a glimpse of something moving near a bend in the beach.  It was partially covered in sand, but crimson pooled cleverly just out of the tide's reach.  Stepping towards it, I realized it was human.  As its chest rose and fell with each labored breath it took, I knew it was alive and struggling to survive.  Quickly rushing towards it, I stopped myself just outside of his line of sight and watched him for a few moments.  It was one of the men from aboard the cog that went down the morning before.  The tunic and trousers he wore were parchment thin from years of wear and further battery by the elements along with a distinct odor that one would think the sea would have washed away but it had failed to do so.

I did not need to bring myself any closer to know that this man was not gravely injured but was in dire need of healing or he would soon spark an infection that would surely take him.  There were some large gashes across his one arm and torso but nothing that could not be mended by a cleric.  He was fortunate to have survived such an attack.  I slid across the sand and knelt by his side just before rolling him onto his back. He groaned with discomfort from the unexpected movement and his eyes began to peel open despite being heavily coated in sand.  Brushing the sand from his eyes and he looked towards me before mumbling something inaudible.  I shook my head trying to convey to him that I did not understand and hoping he would repeat himself to which he did.

"It is you," he whispered.

Tilting my head slightly towards one of my shoulders in confusion as I pondered what he could have meant.

"You brought the beast upon us" he mumbled, "you should have never been aboard," his voice was now reflecting a fear and agitation not previously heard.

"What of the man who brought me aboard?" I paused, "Does he live?"

"What man?" he muttered sounding confused as there must have been many men aboard the cog before it went down.

"The man in black," I added.

"No, no man in black," he mumbled.

"He is elven," I pulled back my hair and touched the tips of my ears, "like myself," I insisted.

He shook his head back and forth while clearing his throat before fading out of consciousness.

Pulling away from him I felt consumed by thoughts of Drayk and my own well-being.  Scanning the shore once more for any other signs of life of which none were found. Was it possible he was the only survivor or would rumor of a nameless face spread throughout the land as more came to light?  If I were to be alone once more then I would need to silence all who knew of my presence on the cog starting with this man.  I positioned myself behind the man's head, brushing his face and neck with my hands, before closing my eyes and offering this man to the Gods.  May the journey for him be a safer passage than the one I must take and with a flick of my wrists I felt his body slough off its mortal coil.

I stood quickly and fled back towards the foliage that once so carefully camouflaged me, leaving the man where he lay to be consumed by the sea or the scavengers that undoubtably prowl the shorelines at night as nothing further could be gained from me remaining on the shore at least not until nightfall.  After the sun fully sets and the moon begins to rise, that is when I will hunt, but until then I must seek nourishment elsewhere.  While in seclusion and under the magical protection of Lamprog, there was not a need for substantial meals full of beast or sea life.  However, after days of depletion and little to no nutrition, I was left with no choice, but to feast on the flesh of my fellow beast.

The further I stepped from shore the calmer and more bountiful the forest appeared, but this was a great source of confusion for me as I originally believed the ship was traveling northbound on the eastern side of the mainland.  However, if that were the case, then once ashore I would have been greeted by dark sandy dunes quickly followed by lush grass plains but alas, none were to be found here.  It was not home but I was relieved to feel the plush moss beneath my feet accompanied by ferns brushing against my naked legs again.  This was clearly a part of the forests of Coille on the western coastline of Caladh.  A particularly sweet smell was found in the air and soon I found myself actively seeking it over all others.  It was rich and sugary as one would expect fruit to be but pungent like one on the verge of becoming sour.  Its essence captivated my senses, and I anxiously sought the source.

My search brought me to a densely wooded area, heavily cloaked in hanging vines and moss.  While it could be broken through, it was not without difficulty.  At times, I wondered why my curiosity would not cease, but as I broke through the veil of draped foliage the forest opened to an ample grove cloaked by a dense ceiling of tree limbs as tall as cathedrals, my curiosity was rewarded.  Watching the evening light now crawl through the limbs above reminded me of the stained-glass windows enclosing the walls and ceilings to the Towers of Light located in the Kingdom of Losgadh.  Their beauty, while man-made, was unmatched by any other.  Many years ago, a poor soul granted me access if only to look upon my flesh a little longer, while I remember little of him, the memory of those towers I am not likely to forget.  Returning my thoughts to my surroundings I noticed the forest appeared dark and disheartening but once inside, it radiated light, just as the walls of those cathedrals did.  The light bounced off any nearby stone or flower willing to receive its warmth just before the chill of the night would begin to rush in.  The air was filled with a sweetness and warmth only nature could provide and while the scent drew me here, its peace is what beckoned me to stay.

As I walked around the grove I could sense all eyes upon me, which is something I was very accustomed to.  They may not know why they were drawn to me but deep down they could sense something was different and there was something very different about this grove.  The foliage and trees found within were unlike any found in the surrounding area which should have prompted more apprehension from me prior to this moment.  While the world evolves as we do, to see such a random change in an isolated place surely meant magic was involved.  This was a trap and with that thought I could feel my muscles tighten, ready with anticipation.

I rushed back towards the border of the grove, just shy of where I broke through and felt a strong barrier trapping me within.  Running my fingers along its surface, it appeared to spring back towards me with each touch, further proving a magical presence.  While the surface was translucent, its texture was silky and felt of damp flower petals.  Nothing about this was natural and no ordinary elf or warlock could have conjured such a unique barrier.  Turning myself about once more, I stepped back towards the grove's center and attempted to rapidly ascend one of the large trees in hopes that the barrier was isolated to the forest's floor.  The top was nearly within reach when in a quick glance back down, I saw a figure planted at the base of the tall tree.  At first, it just appeared to be watching me but with my hesitation and its growing impatience the figure called to me.

"Eira, my beskyddare," the male voice paused, "we have not much time."

That voice rang painfully familiar in my ears causing my heart to sink into my stomach, sending knots twisting throughout.  There was only one who had ever called me by that name, and I had not heard it uttered in quite some time.  How could this be?  I descended the tree at record speed and once within feet of the forest's floor I leapt down towards him, landing within inches of his feet.  As I glanced up from the forest's floor, I knew this was not a man but an apparition.  I stood slowly taking notice of the man before me and breathing slowly.  His appearance was that of a noble, dressed in the finest of clothes with a bold blue brocade fabric adorned with silver rivets in the shape of tiny pyramids covering most of his arms and shoulders.  His long caramel hair was elegantly drawn back to present some newly adorned jewelry in his left ear.  If I would have encountered him in any other moment, I would not have believed it was him.

"Bryn, my pendang," I uttered breathlessly before staring into his golden eyes, "How can this be?  I believed you were lost to me."

"An accord was struck with King Aldon, and it is by his will that I am here.  Please do not dwell on how this came to be as it took a great deal of magic to locate you and open this portal for me to bring you this message."

"What does he wish of me?" I responded as if I was a pet responding to my master.

"There is a man that seeks you and once found-"

"He will not find me," I insisted.

"He will and when he does, you must not believe his lies."

"Who is this man? How will I know him when I see him?"

"He will offer you your freedom, but this offer is not without consequence," he insisted.

"What must I do?"

"Flee towards the Boglach's eastern border.  It is a difficult path but may slow this man's pursuit."

"And what of you?"

"I am well as you can see."

He smiled ineptly which suggested he may not have been alone and while I longed to see my pendang, my friend, my thoughts quickly turned to concern.

"Once into Feurach," I paused for a moment thinking carefully over my next words when he spoke again.

"Seek the light and there you shall find me," he sighed, "until we meet again my beskyddare."

The fingertips belonging to his right hand gently touched his forehead before they were turned outward and extended towards me. I mimicked the gesture with my left hand. It was distinctly elven but without fully understanding his present location, it was better to appear elven than the shapeshifters we are. I watched his apparition fade from sight, and I was left with the warning he risked so much to provide. There were few who could have channeled such power to not only locate me but project him to me and of the ones that could, I am not certain why they would have.

Bryn and I were not born of the same womb, but he had been the closest thing to a companion in nearly my entire existence. He was younger than I and far more passive. When challenged he quickly folds to the path of least resistance. Do not confuse this with a sign of weakness but as a means for enduring this era. Many years ago, we pledged our undying loyalty to the elves as they were the only true immortals left on Caladh other than ourselves and above all, they believed we were worth protecting. While man would appear to possess great power and wealth, their quickly expanding populace and destructive ways would soon lead to them into their tombs.  If shapeshifters were to endure their destruction, we could not remain in the open unprotected.

His sudden appearance and departure reminded me of how quickly he had faded from my life not so long ago.  It was at a bizarre a few years back when I last saw his face.  We were meandering our way through the crowd when an unusual scent caught my attention, by the time I turned around, he had vanished from my sight.  I spent hours sifting through the crowd and searching for him, his scent, anything that would lead me back to him.  While in the presence of another shapeshifter, we can sense it, but when separated by distance or magic, there is nothing.

My search for him never ceased and that is how I found myself to be in the Ice Tower just days ago.  There were rumors of a shapeshifter wandering the plains of Feurach, but no such creature was ever found there.  My last memory was there and then nothing until the bone chilling cold of the Ice Tower.  More than likely the rumor that led me there was false and, in my desperation, my judgment was clouded.  This world rarely gives second chances, so I could not afford to be so foolish again.

As my attention returned to the grove, I noticed the once beautiful and glowing light radiating from within had faded and darkness washed over the hidden gem.  Dropping into a crouch position, I fully scanned my surroundings once more.  In all my travels throughout the mainland, I could not recall stumbling upon this grove before.  Could it be that the land was beginning to evolve quicker than in previous years or had this been part of the magical illusion used to bring Bryn to me?  The answer perhaps was not important, but while comforted by this place, out of fear of being discovered, I shall not remain.

As I watched my beskyddare fade from my sight, I relived the pain of her loss once more.  I missed her terribly. We were birthed nearly a century apart, both following the fracture, but young enough that we were essentially childhood playmates to one another.  One fateful afternoon we were driven together by chance as I was trapped by a pack of Jagare near the point of Saor, a day's journey or so north of the Kingdom of Tuiteam.  The Jagare are fierce warriors trained by the King himself and later trained by Tuiteam's warrior prince, Berenger.  Their sole duty is to purge the land of any foul creature that poises a potential threat to their kingdom and while they have been known to assassinate certain individuals when given the task, they prefer to weigh the odds in their favor by executing brute force attacks in large numbers rather than one on one combat.

Seeking the Wolf

In my case, I believe they intended to make a sizable floor covering out of my father and I, but I was to never know for sure of what their intentions would have been for me as they were rudely interrupted by my escape.  Eira initially appeared to me as if by magic just near several grouping of tail grass, her fiery locks billowing from the coastal breeze. Despite my best efforts, I found it difficult not to be drawn to her with childlike curiosity as she was like nothing I had encountered before.  However, much to my regret, she had come too late, my father was no longer among the living, and I lay chained there, weeping like a wee bairn.  The Jagare had just finished decapitating him before me and working to rid his body of his hide.

She changed quickly, rushing to my aid, freeing me of my bindings and there is where our story began.  From that day forth, our fates have been ever entwined with one another and I felt oddly protective of her and she of me.  Even now our fates are linked, as the reason for her capture was my untimely departure or she never would have been searching the plains of Feurach.  However, despite our sacrificial and unconditional love for one another, we never felt the call to bond with one another or for me to sire her offspring.  The mere suggestion of it felt unsettling and with that mutual feeling, our friendship endured.

Many moons had passed since we last saw one another and even though my current circumstance prevented me from seeking her out, I knew it would not stop her.  In the few moments we spoke, I knew I had given her enough to get her started and while she was making her way through Coille towards the marsh I could work towards executing our next move. Unfortunately, just as I was contemplating that thought there was a knock at my bedchamber door.

"My Lord," a male voice spoke softly through the door, "the King requests your presence."

"Aye, please let him know I will be right there."

"As you wish my Lord," the voice responded just before turning and walking down the narrow hall, heels clicking loudly against the marble floor.

I quickly jotted down a message on some parchment located on a desk nearby before stepping towards the only window found in my bedchamber. Once there, I held out my arm prompting my korp, a raven-like bird known for their intelligence and excellent navigation senses. The bird recognized my command and heeded my call. I stroked his wings softly just before folding the message and attaching it to his underbelly.

"Take this message to King Aldon," I whispered, "he will be expecting you."

"Gronk-gronk, gronk-gronk," the korp replied.

"You must not be seen, is that understood?"

The korp bobbed its head several times just before taking flight high into the sky. I preferred to send him out once night had fallen but time was of the essence. King Aldon has sworn to protect me at all costs, but it was pertinent that no one in the Kingdom of Losgadh know of what I truly am. While King Itheal appears to have no desire to seek wolves or shapeshifters out, it does not mean that he would willingly let us roam about for fear of another kingdom seizing control of us.  It was a dangerous path I was treading on but vital I remain here until Eira and I could be reunited.

I left my bedchamber a few moments later, trying not to appear suspicious by keeping King Itheal waiting, even though he is a patient man.  Here in Castle Losgadh, the halls and chambers are continuously filled with light as the sun radiates from the gold accents found on nearly everything held within, nearly blinding all who are unaccustomed to its…charm.  While legend has the riches of this world are held in the mountains of Reothadh, I would argue this kingdom would hold their equivalent if not surpass them.  I thought this frequently during my stay and was just appalled at one king's desire to flaunt such wealth without a purpose.  Regardless of my feelings, I had a duty to perform and a persona to project.

Upon reaching the King's main chamber I was redirected to his study, where I found him devouring what appeared to be a type of pigeon for an early lunch while reviewing several bits of parchment that were scattered before him.  I greeted him with a slight bow and stepped towards him, waiting for further instruction.  While normally I would just take a seat as we have grown quite comfortable with one another, I dare not do this with others present.

King Itheal was abnormally young to have taken the throne and even younger in appearance.  It has been rumored he was born half-elven and therefore his allegiance belongs to King Aldon, but in all my time here I have never witnessed anything other than his youthful appearance that was suggestive of him being elven.  In addition, betrothing his only daughter, Lady Rosalyn, to the promiscuous Prince Ferand would have never sat well with members of the elven court. Elves despise promiscuity and never betroth their children as they view them as jewels being birthed out of stone, not pawns they possess.  There are no two that are alike, and they can take as much time as needed to become someone worth bonding to for all eternity.

"Bryn, it is my understanding you made contact," the King mumbled through his chewing which was quite distracting.

"Aye, your majesty, I have," I responded.

"Well, don't be coy," he gestured for me to elaborate.

"Forgive me your majesty," I quietly cleared my throat before continuing, "I was able to locate her near the southern coast of Caladh and have instructed her to venture towards the northwestern portion of Boglach."

"Have you gone mad?!" the King spat out his food before continuing, "That will place her directly in the path of King Baylon!"

"The journey will not be without difficulty, but this is to our advantage since King Baylon will not be looking for her so close to his home," I argued.

"I disapprove of what you have done here," his brow was furled, and he exhaled heavily, "the path you have chosen for her forces her to walk the edge of a very sharp blade."

Unfortunately, what the king did not know was this plan was a distraction for his men.  I needed the vast majority of his men to be elsewhere searching for her where I knew she would not be, giving us a chance to flee east and back to Lamprog.  My message will reach King Aldon long before they have any hope of reaching the far side of the marsh and while they are busy combating the beasts of marsh, King Aldon will have sent over a vessel for our safe passage home.  It was almost too easy.

"I wouldn't have requested it of her if I believed she could not handle the task," I responded assuredly.

"And you are certain she is the key we seek?" he added.

"Aye, that I am," I replied.

King Itheal was led to believe that Eira was the key to unlocking Tiene, a region directly to the north of Losgadh and one heavily guarded by sprites and fire elves.  While there are other beasts and creatures found in the region, these two present the greatest danger next to the region's terrain.  Tiene is riddled with volcanoes, lava fields and deserts making it difficult for anyone other than a native to travel here.  I may have insinuated that she is the long-lost descendant of the tribe, one whom they would be eternally grateful for her safe return, after all, King Aldon requested she be found and returned to Lamprog by any means necessary.  Seeing how this is where Eira was born only further validated my claim and helped push matters along.

Each shapeshifter is presented with similar gifts: the power to change upon a whim, abnormal strength, immortality, heightened senses and so on.  However, the one thing that has continued to fascinate me over the years is our ability to pull our birthplace into our beast and humanoid forms.  I happened to be born in what was now the plains of Feurach on a late autumn day, giving me my caramel locks and lighter complexion.  In Eira's case, this is where her fiery locks and sun-kissed skin originate from since these are far from typical elven traits, the fire elves to the north being the exception. While we can attempt to blend in nearly anywhere, when she arrives in Tiene, she is no longer an outsider and although, she would deny it, I believe that is where she wishes to call home. King Itheal is hopeful returning her to her home may grant him an alliance with the natives as their borders are beginning to suffocate him and his people.  I do not believe such an agreement will occur.

I knew that giving her to the Kingdom of Losgadh was not my only option, but it was the only way I could safely pursue her without further endangering myself.  Elves rarely abandon one of their own, unless they are forced to do so and neither do we.  However, the elves are the only race that merely desires to protect and shield us from this dying world. To bring her home, Eira and I would need to dance on the edge of a blade, but while I am hidden, she is fully exposed. Unfortunately, this was only a portion of what was required to ensure a safe return and the next task would be a bit more challenging as it involved matters of the heart, which I knew little of.

Seeking the Wolf

Shapeshifters are not foreign to the concept of having a mate or indulging in the flesh, however, we do become bonded to the one we select and cannot sire with any race other than our own.  More importantly if one of us should ever lay with a human or elven partner, we would become barren as a mark of dishonor.  Let us call it an act of the gods, if you will, a way of keeping us in balance as there was a time when our options were limitless, and the mainland was filled with our people.  This is no longer our story and while there are other males that roam this world alone, Eira is the only known female amongst us, her bonding to one of our own is imperative to our survival.

The King dismissed me disapprovingly for now and I turned to venture towards the castle gardens as I knew this is where the Lady Rosalyn would be found at this hour.  With her hair and skin, the color of cream, she did not fare well in the sunlight of midday.  She was suited for moonlight and under starlight is where we first met.  I was greeted by a maiden late one evening just after crossing the Cuan Uaine, a bright greenish sea that divided Lamprog from the mainland.  There was a cloak draped over her head, heavily shading her face from my sight.  When I stepped from the vessel towards her, she removed the hood of her cloak, and I was greeted with the most crystal-clear eyes I have ever seen.  They were like two large water droplets that had fallen during an early morning rain.  They instantly captivated me.

Her eyes presented only a fraction of her beauty that I later came to notice, but they were the first features that drew me in.  Her quiet tone and passive nature I grew to love as we shared many mornings conversing over the differences in our two worlds.  As a form of protection, she was confined to Castle Losgadh since her birth nearly twenty years ago and she has never ventured outside of its walls.  As the only living heir of the young king, he could not afford to lose her over childish folly and opted kept her in seclusion.  This made her hungry for adventure and prompted her to read nearly every book housed within the castle's library.  A feat few have accomplished and as a stranger from the east, I further provoked and indulged her curiosity.

I stepped through the garden gates and there she was sitting quietly, starring longingly out across the sea.  The sun's warm light kissed her skin and radiated off her as if she were a beacon heeding to its call.  I stood there quietly for a moment and watched her long wavy locks swirl in the soft morning breeze.  While I knew I was not meant for her world, in this moment, I permitted myself to temporarily get lost in the thought only to be pulled away from it a moment later as I heard her voice call out to me.

"Bryn," she said softly, "will you come and join me?"

I cleared my throat slightly, which I did often in her presence for a reason unknown to me and stepped towards her.

"Forgive me Lady Rosalyn," I paused, "I did not mean to disturb you."

As she turned towards me, I could see her eyes were pooled with droplets of rain that has recently began flowing down onto her cheeks in smooth continuous streaks.  Something was troubling her this beautiful morning and while I knew it was impolite of me to ask it tugged at my heart strings to see her this way.

"What troubles you, my Lady?" I asked softly.

"We are alone, are we not?"

I nodded, "Aye, that we are."

"Then please call me Rose," she smiled and when she did it warmed my heart more than the sun ever could.

"Of course, my lady…I mean, Rose" I smiled back at her and I could feel my cheeks began to flush.

She turned her attention back towards the east where Lamprog could be seen faintly off in the distance.

"In all your years you have never belonged to another?"

"No," I struggled to swallow, nearly choking on the words, "I have not."

"Do you not long for a lover's embrace?" she said sounding hopeful.

"Of course," I said trying to sound assuredly, "however, in my experience, it was not meant to be."

I knelt on one knee just before her and reached up placing my right hand on her cheek, drawing her attention towards me.

"Is this what troubles you?"

She nodded and let out a soft sigh, "It has been so many years, I would sooner pass of old age," she sighed again, "Am I not worthy of being his queen?  Could he possibly love another?" she was beginning to sound frantic.

"No," I answered quickly and sternly.  Upon viewing the shock that washed over her I quickly added, "It is he that is not worthy of you, my Lady."

She watched me carefully over the next few moments before she tore herself away from me and rushed towards balcony's edge.  I watched the light bounce from her beautiful golden dress with each step she took giving her the appearance of a star further wishing it were in the moonlight that I had found her just now rather than in the sun's light.  She did not just radiate the light, she was the light and for a moment, a part of me wished I were the one she held so closely to her heart.

"Wed another!" I blurted out surprising even myself, "Someone worthy of your affection, I beseech thee to not toil over a such a foolish man."

I brought one of my hands up and clasped it over my mouth in shock at the audacity of my rebuttal.  I could hear the faint cries carried across the breeze towards me, she was beginning to weep, and I knew then my own desire had overstepped its bounds.  I quickly stood before rushing towards her, only stopping inches from her.  She did not turn to face me.  I gazed upon her standing there, weak, and vulnerable, thinking how exquisite she appeared in that very moment and how this may be the moment the future could be changed.

"But we are betrothed, Prince Ferand and I," she sniffled, "he is all I ever wanted."

"Betrothals can be broken my Lady," I added as I reached up and placed a hand on her bare shoulder.

While I knew a reciprocating gesture of affection could not be expected as she is promised to another, I was hopeful she would consider it and my words.  I was about to take another step forward when I felt something soft touch the end of my fingers.  The touch felt shocking and warm, the way lightning warms the sand after its brief encounter.  The feeling startled me, but I did what I could not to pull away.  When I looked towards my hand, I noticed the tips of her slender fingers were lightly resting upon mine and I felt a glimmer of hope.  While I knew coveting the Lady Rosalyn was not forbidden, to act upon this desire would certainly mean death to anyone but her betrothed.  Regardless of the risk, I could not pull myself away from her.

# Commander Elgar

Storming through the castle I began barking orders to the few men unfortunately standing nearby, "Assemble the troops for we shall scour Glacial Pass and all that lies to the north. Secure the castle and if the beast seeks its vengeance, it shall be here where it makes its claim."

The men nodded with understanding and began rushing back towards the remaining troops, preparing for the journey ahead. When a few other subordinates stepped towards me.

"Commander Elgar, the dromons remain at the ready, is it your wish to depart from the capital and venture towards the mainland?" one of the men spoke firmly.

"No, that is not my intention," I gestured towards the northwest and the north, "I want each of you to search coastlines in these directions, but only the coastline."

"Commander, do you have reason to believe the beast could potentially swim that great of a distance?"

"No, I do not," I paused, "but this beast had help and until I have the traitor within my grasp, I shall not leave these options untested.  Is that understood?"

"Aye Commander," the men bowed their heads slightly before turning to make their way through the main hall towards the castle gates.

I began pacing throughout the great hall deep in thought.  King Edric was not a reasonable man and errors of this magnitude would not be easily forgotten.  I thought carefully over the layout of the tower and potential traitors amongst the ranks.  When an ideal match did not abruptly present itself, I reevaluated the information provided by the messenger from the tower, and he knew there was more to it then what was shared.

"Fetch my things," I commanded, "I wish to depart for the Ice Tower at once."

I stormed towards the entrance where a young squire was waiting for me with thick heavy dark cloak outstretched for me to receive.

I shook my head disapprovingly and corrected the young squire, "A change dress will be needed," I paused, "fetch my fur cloak at once!"

The young squire appeared nerve-racked but bowed quickly before scurrying off to seek what was requested of him.  Pressing onward through one of the side entrances which opened into the courtyard where I stopped to whistle briefly into my vacant surroundings and waited for a reply.  The snow had begun to fall once more, and it was one of the few welcomed sights in all of Reothadh.  The snow was soft and angelic providing a unique and breathtaking sight when viewed from any angle.  The courtyard was one of the few peaceful places found once inside the castle walls and during the warmer months it is the home to some of the most colorful and fragrant berries found in the region.  When the sun brings them to their ripened state, they radiate the smell of pine that is soon trailed by a hint of bitterness and citrus.  They are irresistible and only grown in this part of the world.

Just as I was appreciating one of the few beauties unique to this native land, a high-pitched call broke through the clouds alerting the world and myself to its presence.  Lavin, an Isfagel, had arrived sooner than expected and rushed towards his master's call.  Isfagels are the largest of frost raptors found in the south dwarfing their native cousins, phoenixes, and are fiercely loyal to their masters.  Having their sheer size and ability to be reborn out of ashes makes their loyalty nearly as unbreakable as an elf to their magic.  It would have been difficult to see at such a distance, but when it broke through the clouds the sun's rays shown through its icy feathers making it challenging to track against the pale grey sky.

I watched its wings slice through the clouds with ease and marveled at its grace as if watching its movement for the first time.  Unfortunately, my observations were interrupted when the young squire returned holding a mass of pale fur and leather.  I jerked the items from the young squire's arms with more frustration that was intended and donned the new garments just as Lavin swooped in and landed softly on the snow-dusted stone before me.  I noticed the young squire watching me with utter fascination as I did not speak to the creature but simply called to it in the playful whistling sounds that I made.  Lavin responded to this musical banter with an equally amusing sound before I pulled myself onto the creature, straddling its back just shy of its wings.

While gesturing for the young squire to come forth I spoke firmly, "Come forth, we must leave at once."

The young squire hesitated to result in an unfavorable stare being placed upon him and my patience was wearing thin. After a few moments, when he still had not budged a muscle, my patience had expired.  Lavin stepped towards the young squire causing him and his shadow to appear as nothing more than a mouse in the snow.  Just as the young squire assumed he was about to be eaten, I grasped one of his arms firmly in my hand before jerking him up and onto the creature just before me.

"I have no time for games," I insisted, "make notes of everything you see as no detail is useless to me."

The boy nodded frantically as he clung to Lavin with every fiber of his being.

"Is that understood?" I pressed him.

"Aye commander!" the boy blurted out as if it was a knee jerk reaction.

"Good," I made a loud high-pitched sound with my voice and although no words were uttered Lavin's wings spread wide, "hold on."

I all but uttered the last words when Lavin leapt into the air. Its immense wings began to flap forcing cyclones of wind and snow to form beneath us aiding our ascent higher and higher into the sky. The young squire was clearly a stranger to flight and his terrified expression left little to the imagination of what he may have been thinking at the time. While I could not have possibly viewed his full expression for myself, I could feel his body stiffen up as a corpse would days after life left it. This made me grin with delight. The creature continued to rise until we were just shy of the clouds, when it capsized and began to glide through the air. There was not another feeling like it known to man and while I had countless flights in my youth alone, it was understood this was not commonplace. This may be the young squire's first and only flight, that is if he did not learn to relax. Despite my will to torment the world's youth, even I did not want him to miss out on all its wonders.

I outstretched my hand before the young squire gesturing for him to view all before him, "Open your eyes boy, you may even catch a cloud."

The young squire said nothing in reply but began to turn his head about just in time to swallow his first cloud. Watching him attempt to cough out a cloud humored me and threw my head back with laughter just as I wrapped one of my arms firmly around the young squire's chest. The young squire shrugged off my laughter and continued to clear his throat not realizing how dry it was becoming since they had taken flight. The air appeared thinner at this altitude and the young squire was having trouble catching his breath.  I called to the creature again and moments later Lavin dropped down slightly in the sky, temporarily shocking the young squire but providing him with the relief he needed.

"Catch your breath," I whispered to him, "then tell me what you see."

The young squire was panting but did his best to heed to my demand.

"Ice," he paused, "I see ice."

"Now beyond that," I nudged.

As the young squire shifted his focus past the shards of icy feathers, snowy mountain peaks came into view.

"We are somewhere above the mountains of Geamhradh," he paused before lowering his voice to a mere whisper, "but how?" he quietly questioned to himself.

"Once in the air," I reached down and stroked Lavin's feathers slowly, "Lavin has the ability to make man's journey disappear in mere blinks of the eye."

If the young squire had not already been witnessing this feat, he may not have believed my claim.  The journey would have been long if left on foot, but with the speed of an Isfagel, the days melt away to only a matter of hours.  The young squire became mesmerized by all he could see and as Lavin lowered himself further to soar between the mountain peaks, he quickly learned how minute he truly was when in the vast wilderness.  While contemplating this thought further, his curiosity was met with my sudden interest in visiting the Ice Tower as no one truly wants to venture there.

"Commander Elgar," the young squire cleared his throat once more, "we are looking for those men, are we not?"

"Who might that be?" I asked attempting to be coy.

"The traitors who let the wolf escape," he said boldly.

I nodded, "And how might you know of such things?"

"I am little, so I can easily slip in and out of rooms unnoticed and in this case, right behind the troops."

"Clever boy," I leaned in and whispered to him, "I may have use for you after all."

# Prince Berenger

While my brothers and I were working tirelessly to locate any information regarding shapeshifters, it was decided that we may need to implore some additional souls to assistant in the task or be forced to venture outside of our walls for answers.  Ferand's coronation was to take place this afternoon but once the celebration had concluded, he has tasked me with the fetching of his betrothed with all haste.  While we sent word that we would be coming for her by messenger shortly after our father's departure from this world, Ferand seems insistent waiting for a reply is frivolous and has ordered me to fetch her.  The task set before me would not be an easy one and the journey would take more than a mere few days, Ferand was deceiving himself by thinking anything different.  However, it is my understanding that he has sent word to the port inside the sound for a vessel to be waiting for us there.  Uncertain as to the condition or operation of the port near the Tiene and

Losgadh border, this was the only logical option with the constrained timeframe we were given.

As the final preparations for the coronation were nearing completion, I received a summons from Ferand beckoning me to his side. I felt the good in him starting to slip away and he was becoming a slave to the power he has been given and the guilty pleasures found within his heart. My hope is that his betrothed would soothe his hungry heart and calm the beast that was growing within. Before I jumped to his command, as if I were a dog being pulled back by its master, I spoke my final orders to the Jagare and sent them forth to scout the path ahead. They were our best chance of making it to Castle Losgadh without interruption and with enough men to make the journey home again. While I knew several would need to remain to protect my brothers and the people of Tuiteam, not all would return as both the land and sea were becoming growing threats.

I did not delay further as I did not want to upset him on such an important day. Rushing towards his chambers I did not even wait for the guards to announce my presence before stepping inside. He did not move from where he stood, nor did he appear pleased with my arrival. I bowed slightly in hopes this would alleviate some of his agitation and I was pleased to see it did by the slight smirk that appeared on his face. He enjoyed having his ego stroked by having so many cater and bow to him, it would serve him well to not relish in it more than necessary as the fragile king needs men like myself to keep him raised high in the sky.

"Have the arrangements been made?" he asked promptly and the smirk I was once so glad to see was gone.

"Aye, they have, and I have left explicit instructions for the guards and remaining Jagare to handle your safety as well as Urie's whilst I am away."

"And what of my betrothed?"

"She should have received our message shortly, if she has not already and be preparing for the journey to her new home."

"No, I meant," he paused, "is she truly as exquisite as they say?"

"For that I'm certain," I responded attempting to sound confident even though I had no means of knowing what beauty she truly possessed.

He nodded but an appearance of apprehension was heavily painted upon his face.

"You knew this day would come brother," I waited for any sign of a reply but when there was nothing I continued, "is there another maiden you desire?"

He scoffed and cast a hand into the air, "Leave us." The room cleared quickly and once the room had been free of all others he continued, "There will always be another, but to be forced to marry one I have not seen or felt beneath me is agony.  Honestly Beri, I do not understand how you can shoulder the day without a woman *relieving* you.  I do not believe I would make it until brunch each day without one…or perhaps two."

He grinned with delight as I raised an eyebrow in disapproval. While I, too, have indulged in the flesh, I have not in some time, nor did I plan too again in the near future for the death of my beloved was still too near to my heart. Of this I have made myself quite clear, but that did not stop him from prodding at me as brothers do.

"Would you rather marry some peasant girl from the market?" I asked hoping to change the focus of the conversation.

"Perhaps," he paused, "our father chose a maiden of a lower class to wed."

"Aye that he did, but she was not a maiden and he had already wed a maiden of noble birth…she just left this world all too soon."

"Mother," he whispered softly.

I nodded, "It was she who wished for you to marry the Lady Rosalyn, would you dishonor her by choosing another?"

"No, I suppose not," he said with a fair amount of disappointment in his voice.

I stepped towards him and pulled at his cloak forcing him to straighten up, "You will soon be crowned a KING of Tuiteam and soon all of Caladh. Banish these thoughts from your mind for you have a duty to perform."

He took a deep breath and placed a hand upon my shoulder, "Aye, of that you are right. Thank you, brother."

It was rare for him to show such appreciation for anyone, but I knew if I made something of that it would quickly turn to anger as he always viewed being kind as a form

of weakness rather than an act of goodwill.  We stood there for
a moment acknowledging that in a matter of moments Ferand
would step through the castle gates into the abbey and would
no longer be my brother but my king.  There were no words
left to say but it was understood that our childhood had passed,
and we were no longer equals.  From this day forward, my life
could and would be sacrificed at any given moment for his.  It
is an oath I took and have every intention of upholding.

  We parted shortly thereafter, and I ventured towards the
abbey to prepare for the procession that was scheduled to
happen at the conclusion of the coronation.  The streets were
heavily lined with people full of excitement and shouting
praises for their new king, ever hopeful of a new and bright
beginning.  I never had the pleasure of witnessing my father's
coronation, but I was alive and well for that of his second
wife's, Urie's mother.  I still remember the sight and smell of
lavender and honeysuckle flowers falling from the balconies
above.  They rained down from above, twirling and twisting as
they glided through the air until they reached the ground we
walked on.  The sound of the crowd calling out to her, and my
father has been blurred into a humming sound in my mind.
Had I closed my eyes, I was confident that today would mirror
that memory and take me back to when life was a little less of a
burden and more about being a boy.

  As a Prince of Tuiteam, I was obligated to attend the
ceremony but as Commander of the royal guard, I would not
have the time to grow complacent during the ceremony.  I
entered the abbey and stepped towards my rightful place near

the throne and waited for Ferand to be welcomed into the abbey. There was music playing softly against the humming sound of the crowd patiently waiting for the rightful moment to welcome Ferand in. We stood there for some time, I watched the gentry growing restless, for unlike the crowd, these men and women have watched the young prince grow into a man, a man of whose intentions were unclear. However, all changed when the doors opened again. The humming transformed itself into a blaring roar of excitement and there before us he stood. The light poured in from behind him surrounding his frame with a bold golden aura.

As he took his first steps forward, the doors to the abbey slowly closed behind him and the crowd's cheerfulness quieted to a whisper. It had begun. His shoulders were no longer draped in sunlight but in a bronze-colored cape trimmed in dark marbled fur that nearly scraped the ground. The cape while long and beautifully crafted, did not distract from the exquisitely embroidered tunic with dark brown leather overlay that resided beneath it. There were gold clasps holding the cape in place with a chain of delicate rings falling onto his chest that were shifting together as he walked creating a soft ring similar to that of bells as they chimed in a soft breeze.

The gentry and my fellow royals bowed slightly as he passed but Urie and I did not waver from our positions. Urie was standing just to my right dressed in nearly identical attire to Ferand, only in fawn colors to match. Standing next to him reminded me of how youthful he really was. With soft supple skin and a scrawny body that had not had the chance to be whipped into shape or abused by elements, very childlike and for a moment, I envied that innocence.  He stood there with his head down and his hands clasped tightly together.  I was not sure if he was praying or plotting his next deviant act, neither suggestion of which I found comforting.

When my attention was returned towards the ceremony, Ferand had stopped a few feet from the throne and was being blessed by our most holy.  Each movement was not without meaning and as the ancient ritual neared its conclusion, my brother knelt with arms extended, palms facing upward.  With his head bowed, he recited the words of our ancestors as the sword of Tuiteam was placed upon his hands.  It was forged of the finest metals with a hilt intricately carved of bone and metal.  Outside of our bloodline, it was to be our most treasured possession.  Ferand raised his gaze and stood slowly, never faltering his hold on the sword or his view upon it, before turning towards his people allowing the chosen crown to be laid upon his head.  Prior to that moment, all may have known he was our anointed king, but this ceremony declared it to all of Caladh.  As the crown found its place and our most holy stepped away, King Ferand sat for the first time on this throne as King of Tuiteam.  Applause filled the room in a series of waves and just when I thought the waves would never cease, King Ferand stood and sheathed his sword just before venturing towards the doors to the abbey.

I signaled for the guards to hold the doors until I could close the gap between myself and King Ferand.  Once I was within reach of him, I signaled for the doors to be opened and with another roar from the crowd our new king was welcomed by his people.  He cast a hand into the air and waved to his people while strutting towards a pack of krigshastar that were waiting for our arrival.  Krigshastar have a large, muscular build similar to wild horses but would dwarf most horses.  They appear to only exist in tree tones, more than likely to help them blend into the forests they are native to, along with multi-pointed antlers protruding from their heads.  The few we have brought to live inside the castle walls of Tuiteam, also, have large spikes that project from the joints on each of their fore limbs, aiding them as an additional form of protection, as if a snap of their tail could not already break bones when whipped into a fury.  These few unique features more than likely formed as a mutation due to growing threats near their homeland.  I have found them only to be gentle beasts and ones we frequently use in our travels.

King Ferand was assisted with mounting one of our largest males and once upon him, he appeared to tower high in the sky over the masses.  I tossed Urie upon one of the smaller beasts before mounting one of my own.  I called her Vide for the trees she was birthed nearby.  She was a younger female, and her spirit was raw, like a peasant child before the world suppresses their hunger to one more befitting of their social station.  I had the pleasure of being present during her birth and since that moment, she has never tolerated another.  Though I have never sired bairns, she is the closest I have come to feeling that emotional bond and I protect her like no other.

Seeking the Wolf


        As Ferand's krigshast stepped off and down the main
path, I followed closely, keeping a careful watch for anyone
suspicious that may have been lurking in the crowd.  At times
it was difficult to focus with all the racket and movement, but I
kept to my duties as we continued to march through the streets.
All seemed to be well until we rounded the final turn that
would lead us to the castle's main entrance.  Something rushed
by me and disappeared just behind Ferand.  I only caught a
glimpse of it, but it was light and had a smoke-like appearance
that left no room for doubt, it was a wisp.  Wisps are a
dangerous omen of our world and usually spotted when a
heavily concentrated amount of magic was being conjured
nearby, but of all the ones capable of such power, only one
resided within our fair city.  Halting Vide, I began scanning the
crowd, there must be something here that we were missing.
When I found nothing, I turned the beast around and saw a tall
dark figure slip into one of the alleys seemingly unnoticed by
all others present.  I pressed my heels into the beast's sides, and
she lunged forward in hasty pursuit.  We dodged in and out of
the populace until reaching the alley, faintly shadowed by the
sun shifting overhead, we decreased our speed and waited for
the figure to reappear.
        Upon reaching the opposite end of the alley, we were
greeted by the once adoring people of our great city.  However,
their expressions turned grim when they saw us closing in on
them.  As I brought my steed to a halt and began whipping her
around in a fury continuing my search for the dark figure, my
attention was drawn towards an extended hand, pointing

upward in my direction.  At first, I thought the person was pointing towards me, then when more hands appeared in the air, I realized it was something behind me.  Slowly I turned and drew my head back, hoping to catch a glimpse of what had captivated the crowd's attention.  When I did, I witnessed what was the dark figure standing atop a nearby building and it was not alone.  They were the Skogar or natives to the woodlands of Coille, south of Tuiteam.  Previously I believed the figure was cloaked or slinking in the shadows, but the shadow was their skin as it was dark caramel with olive undertones.  This aided them in their ability to disappear within the trees and thorns of their homeland.  I have seen their kind seldom in my travels, as they move quickly and tend to disappear high into the trees with minimal effort.  Until this afternoon, however, they have never been so bold as to breach our walls and I was left to assume their appearance here today was no accident.

As I watched a third member join the others on the roof top, I knew something was wrong, my brothers were in danger, and I shouted for Vide to make way towards the king.  She pressed her hooves hard against the stone alley, launching us forward forcing the crowd to flee in panic.  I did my best to maneuver through the panicked souls whilst doing my best to not lose sight of the Skogar above.  Two out of the three continued off the backside of the building while the remaining one leapt in my direction and onto a neighboring rooftop bringing him into focus.  The man was an incredibly tall and thin, much like a tree, and his long dark locks were pulled back into a braid of sorts that fell past the rim of his trousers.  As I attempted to focus my gaze further on the man a streak of bright light began racing towards me from the sky.  I squinted to bring the streak into focus when I realized the bright light was the sun reflecting itself from the bright tip of an arrow.  I swerved in hopes of dodging out of the arrows path when I felt a sharp pain pierce through my lower back and bury itself into Vide.  She reared back from the sudden impact when I felt another one drive into the back of my one leg, further pinning me to her.  I curled myself down towards her back and commanded she press onward to which she heeded despite her own injuries.

As I lay upon her, I watched the blood from our bodies run together and dot the stone causeway below.  I could hear the crowd screaming in terror and with each breath I felt her breathing change with mine.  Each breath labored and I worried for her.  Out of the corner of my eyes, I could see several of my men rush over towards her to halt my anxious steed.

"Lock down the city and protect the King," I urged through a strained voice, "Skogar have invaded the city."

Several soldiers rushed back in Ferand's direction where all I could see was the sight of his cloak billowing behind him.  He was fleeing into the castle, behind its walls, the safest place for him to be if there was to be an assault upon the kingdom.  I extended my arm pointing towards the building I last saw one atop of while pulling myself back into an upright position.  I quickly placed a hand on my side, clasping it tightly in my grasp to slow the quickly pooling liquid that was flooding the fabric of my tunic as two of my men were attempting to withdraw the shaft of the arrow from my leg.

"Take me to the castle," I insisted, "and fetch the cleric," I swallowed deeply as my throat was growing dry. "I must reach the King. Go now and search for the Skogar in my absence."

I did not wait for a reply before touching my krigshast lightly, urging her to advance. She was significantly slower than before, and I cannot recall seeing an exit wound from the first arrow. The thought pulled at my insides and made me feel desperate at the thought of losing her. Just before reaching the castle's entrance, one of the doors swung wide and with a touch of my hand upon her neck, she bolted inside like a child who has just been whipped. Once inside, her pace rapidly diminished to a crawl where she soon collapsed on the stone floor, fracturing the shaft of the arrow. Her collapse tossed me onto the floor just feet away from her where I found myself clinging to the coolness of the stone floor, anxiously hoping it would ease the upheaval my stomach was now feeling.

I watched as several guards and chambermaids swarmed around me, but what I did not see was either of my brothers causing an emptiness to grow in the pit of my stomach. I jostled about to find them when I felt one of maidens begin to disrobe me. I grasped her arm as a strong suggestion to cease in her task and while she did not continue, she looked upon me with concern and then pity. Pity from a woman who more than likely washes our linens and cleans our floors. The thought disturbed me, but when I realized, she was merely trying to help the cleric do her work, I released her arm and permitted her to continue.  They worked quickly to prep the areas and while I was feeling quite tired, barely able to keep my eyes open.  However, even in my groggy state I could hear them chattering amongst themselves, but then I heard something I did not expect.

"Forgive me, my lady, what did you just say?"

The cleric glanced at me briefly then smiled, "My lord, while these wounds are severe," she paused, "the wounds are precise not as I would normally see in the event someone was off their mark."

"Then I was not the target," I whispered under my breath before adding, "Where is the King?"

The woman shook her head and shrugged, "My Lord, we have not seen him."

"And what of Prince Urie? Where is he?"

They shook their heads clearly unsure of what to say.

"Find your King and Prince Urie!" I called out to the room as I attempted to stand, "Go now!" I insisted.

"My Lord," she sighed, "I have only just begun my work to repair the damage, you must rest now."

I glared back at her, "Madam, please do not presume to tell me what I must do," I paused just before I winced my way to a standing position.

"Rest, please," she insisted as she held out her hand for me to grab, "you are not yourself and while my power can accelerate your recovery it will not fully mend you."

I brushed her hand away, "Thank you for what you have done here.  I am grateful."

She nodded back at me and recoiled her hand from my reach just before I turned towards the stable master who was working quickly to save Vide.  Her once beautiful fawn coat was now very tainted with splotches of crimson and while I felt a duty to search for my brothers, I felt motivated to remain here.  I slid myself over to her and as I attempted to crouch down towards her my leg gave way slamming me onto the stone floor.  I winced as I pulled my arm out from under me and reached for her and I began stroking the long bridge of her snout.  She was a tough girl but as I watched the light fading from her eyes I could not help wondering if this is what a father feels for their child when they are hurt or ill in some way, then again, perhaps not I suppose.

I pulled myself towards her and placed my head against hers when we were both jolted back to reality by a clanging sound.  Quickly scanning the room, I searched for the source when I realized it was coming from the stable master.  He had tossed something onto the floor near him that was blood soaked but something dark was shining through.

"What is that?" I asked softly not wanting to startle either of them.

"That is the blade of the first arrow.  Took some doing but she is rid of it now."

I extended my hand towards him, reaching for it.  When he witnessed my struggle, he picked up the piece and dropped it in my hand.  It was heavier and much larger than I anticipated.  Running my fingers across its surface, I felt the coolness of it and took note of its dark coloring, more like glass in clarity, but had the weight of stone.

"Man made?" I inquired.

Without turning towards me he shook his head, "No, I do not believe so."

I slid the blade across what was left of my trousers and watched as it split the linen and into the flesh beneath them with minimal effort.  I examined it again, it did not appear to be metal by its translucent quality, but glass would not be easy to come by in Coille and never this durable.  Picking up my tattered tunic, I tore one of the sleeves off and wrapped it around the blade before putting it into a leather pouch of mine that was lying nearby on the floor.  I was not sure what we had just found, but I was not willing to let it slip through my fingers.

Grazing my fingers across Vide's snout once more I asked, "Will she live?"

"Aye, that she will," he paused, "no need to trouble yourself Commander Berenger."

I nodded and nuzzled her cheek with mine before offering my praises to her and all the staff present for without them, neither of us would remain amongst the living for long.  With a groan, I stood once more and returned to my duties.  Rest would have to wait; my brothers must be found.

Whilst prisoners cannot partake in the festivities of a coronation, I cannot deny the wonder they present to a kingdom's populace.  The thrill of change and the celebration of youth: one of them is constant, the other is fleeting.  At first it appeared as any other, voices cheering wildly accompanied by hoofbeats as the march began, but then something about the commotion from above changed.  There was a desperation to its tone now and while specific voices were inaudible, the general overtone was fear but from what?  Just as I began to contemplate the potential cause, there was a faint crackling sound coming from the door to the chamber.  I diverted away for coverage behind one of the many statues found within the cavern as I was unsure of the intruder.  I listened carefully and waited for the sound to either escalate or dissipate, I did not have to wait long.  The door slowly walked open and slender tree branches began growing and clinging to the wall and door.

I felt my skin tighten and flush with heat.  The branches did not move like any other and as they slowly crept into the cavern, I watched them unfold and grow tall.

They moved about slowly, stretching, and clinging to each surface they touched.  I watched them as they appear to scan the room before extending themselves forward in pursuit of something or someone.  They did not appear to be threatening and with that the heat ceased and my body relaxed.  While I was interested in the trees, my focus shifted towards the open door that was previously unrelenting.  Now would be my chance to make my escape as there may not be another opportunity.  When I was confident the trees had moved past the statue, I was concealing myself behind, I crouched down low and began shuffling my way towards the door, never taking my eyes from them.  There was something peculiar about the way they moved, like they were not really trees or perhaps they were an illusion meant to distract me and were not there at all.  I was only steps from crossing the threshold when I glanced away from the trees to ensure the opening was clear.  As I did so and then turn back to them a moment later, the trees had vanished and three Skogar stood close by watching me carefully when a fourth figure, I had not noticed previously, stepped across the threshold, and spoke to me.

"Calm yourself Conall," he spoke softly, "we are friend not foe."

I recognized this one and stretched myself upward quickly.  He was unlike myself but our paths had crossed before.  He was a youngling the last time we spoke and though his body may have changed, his peaceful soul was still in there and it exuded itself with every movement he made.  From his graceful steps to the gentle stroke of his fingers upon the iron door as he stepped through.

My eyes grew wide with surprise, "Ewan, why have you come?"

He appeared appalled at my inquiry and just as he was about to speak another voice chimed in echoing across the space.

"You have earned my favor, Conall," a women's voice spoke, "you would do well to use this to your advantage."

A woman with locks of silver stepped into the light several paces towards my right taking me by surprise.  Her skin was darker than expected but sinuous and soft in appearance.  She wore little to cover her body, only bands of pale colored delicate fabrics that would draw anyone's attention.  I stepped towards her slowly drawing in her scent and attempting to commit it to memory.  Her scent was difficult to trace as it appeared to change along with her movements and thoughts.  She was using magic to evade me and when I was only a pace or two from her, I was able to appreciate more of her and the wardrobe was not the only thing delicate about her.  She was significantly dwarfed by all those in the room including myself but clearly commanded it.  How could a human female have manifested such power?

Her expression did not shift or show any emotion when she spoke again, "In time all of your questions shall be answered but for now, we must go."

While I knew nothing of her or why the Skogar had come, I refused to squander this opportunity.

"Forgive me but where do you plan to go?  The city is swarming from the coronation."

"Would you prefer to remain here?" she looked displeased with me, and her tone reflected that displeasure.

"No, I suppose not," I uttered.

"Then I suggest you hold your tongue and gather your things," she paused, "oh and do your best to stay as you are." Her gaze fell lower on my body and then back up, "No good will come from showing the people of Tuiteam what you truly are."

"And you think you know?" I said with a sharpness in my voice.

"Conall," she stepped towards me, lightly dragging the fingers her left hand down my abdomen and onto one of my thighs, grinning with delight as she did so, "you do not think I would have created a barrier for King Baylon without knowing what he was hiding, do you?"

It was not unusual for a woman to be drawn to me, in fact, that is part of what keeps a shapeshifter alive.  Our ability to draw someone in and make them feel something more *primal* is one of our greatest unintentional gifts.  Nonetheless, I do not believe this woman would be so weak as to fall for such folly.  This woman was older than she appeared and there was something in her eyes that gave her away. I believe her youthful exterior is an illusion, a powerful one but still an illusion.

"You are a warlock," I muttered softly.

"This surprises you," she replied.

"Aye," I responded.

She turned away and spoke in a disapproving tone, "I was not asking," just before stepping towards the back wall of the cavern, "Now gather your things," she glanced over her shoulder, "I will not mention it again."

"Milady, I have nothing to gather," I responded strong at first but then barely audible as I realized I had nothing left from my life before here.

The thought hurt me more than I had expected and when I looked at her again, her face mirrored my heartache. This was the first time she appeared human to me. Which I am certain was an oversight on her part.

"I am called Haxa," she grinned, "now, bring forth the young prince."

I looked towards Ewan in hopes of finding comfort in the sheer confusion Haxa's last statement caused, but found none, when I felt one of the Skogar step past me carrying something small and lifeless over one of his shoulders. The body appeared to be that of a young man with dark locks. Could this have possibly been the youngest prince of Tuiteam? He seemed so childlike and what purpose would taking him serve. I watched the Skogar carefully as he dropped the prince hard onto the cavern's sandy, stone floor near one of the nearby tombs. What was to become of this young prince? Staring at the young prince, I watched his chest rise and fall faintly with the few shallow breaths he took. He was alive, but I could not be sure for how long as under my ever-watchful eyes a stone coffin near the back of the cavern was now open, and the prince was being lowered inside.

"What will become of this boy?" I inquired.

"If we fail to exit the city then Prince Urie will be yours to do with as you wish," Haxa grinned again.

"And if we do?" I added.

"Then locating him will serve as a distraction for the others," she sighed impatiently.

I turned towards Ewan, who was now standing beside me, and placed a hand on his shoulder, "This is not the way of your people."

"This is what was required," he whispered, "while we questioned the purpose behind her request, her terms were minimal."

"This boy is innocent, Ewan," I pleaded unsure as to my newfound loyalty.

"Prince Urie has been sedated and shall not wake for days," she paused, "should he wake at all," she grinned, "do not fret over such matters.  We should go while there is still fear and panic in their hearts."

Ewan nodded, "Haxa, is it done?"

"Aye," she replied, "Conall please come with me."

"What of the Skogar?" I requested.

"Conall, do not trouble yourself with their escape as their *roots* go deep underground," Haxa spoke softly as if telling me a secret just before gesturing for me to follow her.

We both stepped across the threshold, and I watched her pace quicken as the door closed behind us, locking in place. I followed her with minimal effort as even her quicken steps were still only a fraction of the strides I took. I turned to glance at Ewan, but then I realized there was nothing for me to see. I knew before turning back that there was nothing I could do for them nor anything I could see but I glanced back anyway. I continued watching her carefully as we walked across a large stone platform littered with the bodies of fallen soldiers. My attention was quickly drawn towards them, they were all dead. I rushed towards the stairwell when I felt her hand grasp my arm drawing my attention back towards her.

"Put these on," she thrust a heap of items towards me, "and do so quickly," she insisted.

I set the items onto a nearby step and began removing my trousers when I felt her eyes upon me once more. I never understood mortals and their fascination with the flesh, and it appeared warlocks were no different. They, too, have a lifeline that transcends time; however, they do not bond eternally with a mate as we do, giving them every opportunity to indulge themselves. Waiting for this bond, unfortunately, has been the bane of my existence and I longed to be released from its painful grasp. Alas, I digress. Haxa stood patiently waiting until I donned the final article of this exquisite, yet quite uncomfortable armor. I loathed wearing heavy armor as it limits the finesse of my movements and complicates it when I attempt to change suddenly. A grievance that no doubt would not be appreciated if voiced at this crucial moment, so I remained silent.

"You are now Demetri, a member of the royal guard," she stopped briefly to draw my hair back and place a helmet upon my head, "do not address me or anyone else unless spoken to, is that understood?"

I nodded and she mirrored my understanding with a nod of her own before turning and ascending the stairwell. I watched her carefully once more, searching her body language and movements for any sign of anxiety or apprehension. There was nothing until I saw a faint light creeping its way along the upper portion of the stone stairwell. We must be nearing an opening, but where this opening would lead us to, I did not know. However, as we drew closer to the source of the light, I felt my skin warming with anticipation and the once faint humming, I heard from below was now audible and rushing towards us.

We reached the opening and to my surprise there was not a door present preventing passage in or out of the cavern, only a faint barrier that could be seen when standing from inside, similar to how drapery falls over a glass window. Depending on the fabric, it does not always prevent someone from seeing out but from seeing in and that was my hope with the barrier as well. Drawing her sceptre up from her side, she touched the barrier with its prongs, and we were greeted by a wave of sound and warmth as the barrier had fallen. Her pace quickened once more, and I soon found myself rushing to keep up as I had become distracted by the ever-evolving passageway.  At first, we were in a poorly tended to narrow passage, but it transformed into large halls with vast walls blanketed with exquisite carvings of wood and stone.  It was a different kind of beauty, timeless really, not garish as I would have expected from the line of Tuiteam.

We continued our way through the labyrinth of passages and small rooms, nodding to those we passed along the way, when we reached a larger room filled with members of the royal guard, I felt my insides tugging at me to flee.  I suppressed the urge and followed Haxa as instructed despite my misgivings.  As we walked among them, I listened to their bickering and bantering in an attempt to piece together the events of the day without needing to ask any further questions.  The guards believed the city was under attack and they were still searching for the young prince, of which I already knew he would not be found.

We were on our way out of the room when a voice called out to the men, "There is no sign of Prince Urie.  Search every aspect of the city," he paused before muttering under his breath, "please let him be found."

Without even setting my eyes upon him, I knew the man was Prince Berenger.  While his voice sounded slightly strained and weary, it was him for that I had no doubt.  I glanced back slightly to insure we were not being followed when I noticed his body was heavily wrapped to conceal injuries unknown to me.  While I understood the objective was to retrieve me, I had not realized that the Skogar were willing to harm the royal family in the process.  What could Haxa gain from disabling or eliminating the line of Tuiteam?

As I turned my attention back towards Haxa, Prince Berenger's voice called out to us, "Haxa, come hither," I heard him turn towards us, his tone changed, "I require your assistance."

"As you wish Commander Berenger," she turned and pushed herself past me, "how can I be of assistance?"

"I need to you to place a ward over King Ferand as I believe the Skogar are using the coronation as a means of distraction to place an attack on the King."

"It will be done," she bowed slightly before turning back towards me.

"Oh, and Haxa," he paused, "Demetri is a member of the royal guard, not your puppet.  You will relinquish your hold over him and return him to me now," he insisted.

She chuckled at the suggestion, "Interestingly enough, there was a time when I remember you greatly desired to become one of my *puppets*," a diabolical grin flooded her cheeks.

"For that I am certain you are mistaken as we both know my heart and body have always belonged to another," he scoffed before turning back towards members of the guard.

She pursed her lips, and I could tell she did not approve of Berenger's blatant disregard for her.  Perhaps she just a woman that longed to be every man's fantasy or maybe her own fantasy had extended past its reach.

"Demetri is at your disposal once more," her voice was curt, "I shall take my leave now."

I merely blinked and she vanished from my sight.  I turned quickly to follow her as I am certain attempting to portray a member of the royal guard would not bode well.  I had hoped my sudden departure behind Haxa would go unnoticed but as I heard him speak again my heart sank.

"Demetri," he paused, "you will accompany me along with a few members of the Jagare to scout the borders of Coille."

I turned towards him and nodded quickly to affirm my understanding.  He started to nod in return when I noticed he tilted his head to the side slightly starting to work something over in his mind. I dare not assume what he was thinking, and I opted to take my leave.  Returning to my pursuit of Haxa, I fled the room and rushed towards the next. Taking time to glance in all directions in hopes of spotting her, but again there was nothing when I heard his voice call out to me once more.

"Demetri!" his voice sounded strained.

I kept moving, searching for somewhere that would conceal me, if but temporarily.  Unfortunately, without knowing the layout of the castle, at any one moment a simple hall could turn into a dead end.

He shouted once more, "Demetri, you will stop, or I shall have your head!"

His tone appeared louder now, more robust than before and I knew he was gaining on me.  I rounded another corner only to be met with more guards walking towards me forcing me to backpedal towards the previous hall where the Commander and I collided causing us both to stumble backwards.

"Demetri, I should have you flogged!" he shouted just before hunching over gasping for breath, "I demand to know the meaning of this!"

"I beseech thee, I know not of what came over me," I spoke quickly before bowing down removing my face from sight.

"Haxa, happened to you," he shook his head, "she has a way of…" he hesitated, "changing people."

He returned to an upright position, and I remained as such ever hopeful this conversation would end soon.

"Stand Demetri," he commanded.

I stood as he demanded not wanting to pull anymore focus towards myself than I already had.

"Since when do you wear a helmet," he scoffed before grabbing the helmet by its edge and tossing it backward, "you have not worn one of those since we were children," he sounded playful.

I felt the helmet slide off and watched in slow motion as it fell towards the stone floor, clanging about as it tumbled across the metal of the armor.  When it fell lifeless onto the floor my eyes were drawn back to Prince Berenger, who was now scanning my face with his eyes narrowed then our eyes met.

"You," he uttered breathlessly, "but how?"

My skin began to flush, but I maintained a look of composure as I was hoping to persuade the prince into believing he was mistaken.

"Commander Berenger, how did I do what?" I tilted my head slightly in hopes of conveying a sense of concern and confusion for the prince, he did not buy into the ruse.

"I have known Demetri for years and you are not him," he growled, "Guards!" he shouted, "Seize this man!"

A clanging began to ring in my ears as I watched guards enter my peripheral vision. If they were to take me again, it would not be here and it would not be now. I drew my arm up swiftly while clenching my fist and brought it down like a hammer onto Prince Berenger's shoulder causing him to collapse under the force of it. This he had not anticipated giving me the upper hand. While I did not favor this prince, there was no honor in killing him as his body already lay broken and beaten at my feet. I may not understand him or his way but to protect his own, he has and will do unspeakable things, for that, he has my respect.

In that moment, part of me forgave him just before I opted to turn towards the only opening that did not appear to have guards rushing out of it and pressed onward. Unfortunately, once through the opening I noticed it was a dead end. I quickly grasped the door in my hands before slamming it shut, throwing my body against it in hopes of buying myself some time. This was a trap and while the grandness of the castle was a welcomed sight from the dark cavern that lay beneath, it was no less than a gilded cage. The room was small enough that if I were to pick them off as they crossed the threshold, I could wreak havoc on a large portion of the guard, but that would not stop them from coming.  I braced myself against the door just as guards began slamming objects or themselves against it, trying to break the hold I had on it.  It would not be long before they would be able to break through.  Unfortunately, the room I entered appeared to be no more than a filler space as there was little of use here apart from two very large windows that engulfed nearly the entire one wall.  They could be my best option for an escape.

My time was running out and I could hear the voices through the door growing louder with threats of retaliation and justice.  Unsheathing the sword from my side, I jabbed it into the door frame, wedging it in place and bending it against the door.  This will have to hold them for now.  While within the walls of the city a sword may have been useful, but anything held or worn resembling the royal guard would now appear as a target on me in the crowd.  I reached for the nearest piece of furniture, a small side table probably not meant to hold more than a candle and some tea and thrust it towards one of the windows.  It crashed into the pane, shattering it, causing a cascade of broken glass to rain down onto the surface below.  The screaming grew louder from the mix of frightened shrieks outside of the castle walls and guards who had now created a small opening between the door and the sword that held it.  Before the last shard fell, I leapt out through the opening and felt my lungs expand fully for the first time in months.  I, like many shapeshifters, not meant to be confined indoors as it has the tendency to rot our minds and break us more than any physical pain ever could.  While I believe my mind and body were still strong, I was not as strong as I could have been given my living situation over the past several months.  I cannot go back.

I fell towards the ground with such force that my body became coiled up and continued rotating forward in a series of unpredictable summer salts of which were brought to an abrupt stop when my body slammed into a few wooden barrels that resided just outside a nearby building.  Had they been full at the time of our collision, and it would have been as hitting a stone wall, abrupt and unyielding.  While attempting to shake off my disorientation from the landing, I watched in confusion as people rushed by me, faces elongated and eyes wide, screaming in horror.  I quickly brought my hands into view, wondering if it was even possible for me to change so suddenly without any warning, but when I looked upon my hands, they were still humanoid.  I could not understand their fear.

Standing quickly, I was brought back down by a weakness felt in my left leg, if it were broken, I could not see it.  The pain in it, however, radiated throughout and made it difficult to fully apply my weight on it.  I knew it would heal but not before I could liberate myself from the hold.  For now, I would just have to endure the pain while I searched for cover. Fleeing towards and down a nearby alley my search began for a secluded place where I could remove and dispose of Demetri's armor as they would be looking for me to be wearing that.  After attempting to enter several different buildings without success, I noticed a woman staring at me through a small opening in her doorway just across the way. I held my hands up and then pointed to my one leg hoping she would take pity on me and permit me inside. She opened the door wider, glancing outwards and turning towards both sides. I was unsure if she was looking to alert someone to my presence or if she was looking to ensure my safe passage to her. Either possibility set me on edge and the anticipation was nearly more than I could manage.

I backed myself against a nearby wall and listened for anything harmful nearby which was extremely difficult with the populace still unhinged by the sudden attack on the crown. When my attention returned to her, she was gone, but her door remained ajar. I did not wait to see if anyone was coming towards me when I rushed out into the street towards her open door and upon reaching it, sliding myself inside. I closed it quietly behind myself and turned slowly as I was unsure what or who would be present to greet me. She stepped towards me with her hands outstretched, quivering. I could see a shadowed face behind her looking fearful of me and it tore at my insides to think what a monster I must have become for people to look at me in such a way. I did not know what to say and neither did she, so we stood in silence until a voice behind her spoke softly.

"Are you hurt young man?" an old woman appeared just behind the other, "Or is this blood from another?"

I swallowed deeply unsure how to answer her, so I nodded.

"Come now," she touched my arm lightly and led me towards an old wooden stool not far from the hearth, "sit here and let us help you."

I sat willingly and began scouting the room for any information that might be useful. Despite being the sun being high in the sky, it was fairly dark inside with the only light to be seen was stemming from the hearth. Most of the items and furniture seen were heavily aged and worn from more than likely generations of use. I listened carefully to the two women speaking along with searching the room for any other faces that I might find, but there were none there. However, listening to the two women banter over me was stimulating. Their act of goodwill may have been prompted by entirely different and untrue reasons, but I opted not to correct them on the matter.

The woman returned a short time later lowering herself down in front of me. She held a basin of water with several strips of cloth draped over her arm. Placing the basin adjacent to her, I watched, and she brought herself towards me. I leaned away unsure of her intentions, when I felt her hands slide under one of the pauldrons that had been attached to the armor I was wearing. Her touch startled me, and I grasped her forearm tightly in my hand causing her to gasp and attempt to pull away.

"Please sir," she blurted out, "I mean you no ill will."

I released her arm from my grasp and felt myself release a breath of air that I had clearly been holding. I nodded in response. Should I apologize for being afraid of her touch? Should I ask questions or search for information? None of them seemed appropriate and I was conflicted and afraid of saying the wrong thing, so again, I opted to say nothing. She nodded and continued to remove the pauldrons followed by the cuirass before laying them onto the floor nearby leaving me in a bloody padded jack. As I looked upon the armor, I noted it was considerably damaged in the fall with multiple patches torn away or spattered with blood giving it a gruesome appearance rather than the brilliance they generally were found in. She knelt back down and placed some cloth in the basin long enough to allow the warm liquid to fully saturate it before drawing it back out, squeezing them tightly, forcing the excess water to flee from the fabric's grasp. Her fingers touched my face lightly, pushing my hair back away from my eyes and gliding the cloth across the surface, freeing it from the filth that currently had set up camp there. I closed my eyes, afraid to look at her, as I would be ashamed to admit that I enjoyed her touch a great deal.

She stopped suddenly and I heard droplets of water fall back into the basin once more prompting my eyes to open slightly. She was hunched over the basin of crimson liquid, breathing slowly, and mumbling something to herself. While I was unfamiliar with the words, it sounded as if she was praying or perhaps whispering the words to a lullaby long lost to me. The old woman walked towards her and placed a hand on her shoulder, bringing the woman and her thoughts back to us. When I looked upon her face this time, she appeared saddened by something as opposed to the fear I once saw.

"Forgive me good sir," she spoke softly, "I was lost in thought."

Her eyes returned to mine with the assumption they were still closed and when they were not, I noticed she flinched slightly in surprise but did not take her eyes from mine. I turned away from her not wanting her to dwell on what she saw and felt her hands cup the sides of my face. I felt the burn of her touch as her fingertips began mapping out new and old grooves upon my cheeks and neck. They were painful reminders of all that I have endured in the name of freedom. I placed my hands gently upon her wrists and pulled them down from my face. While she was not harming me in any way, just there was something about the way she looked at me that I could not handle.

"Have I hurt you?" she said softly.

I shook my head.

The older woman stood ever watchful of this and spoke again, "Please forgive my daughter as she lost her husband many months ago in the marsh." She took up the wet cloth the woman was using and began working it through my long locks, "Every soldier she sees now reminds her of him," she sighed, "she will never stop praying for his return."

"Was he not found?" I spoke deeply and softly hoping not to startle them.

The old woman smiled and waved her daughter away, "Go now, my child, I will tend to this man."

The woman looked disappointed but ultimately left without uttering another word, but with tears now streaming down her cheeks.

"We were told little of what happened in the marsh," she paused to dampen the cloth before continuing, "just that the men encountered a formidable beast that took hundreds of good men from our fair city.  The remains were never returned to us, so my daughter will never stop believing that he still lives."

"When was this?" I blurted out faster and louder than I expected causing her eyes to widen.

"A several months ago," she responded sounding concerned, "why do you ask?"

I felt my chest tighten and breath leave me as I knew all too well of the day she spoke of.

"I was there that awful day," my heart sank along with my voice, "the men," I stopped myself, "I mean, we were forced to attack a beast that was just defending itself."

"Can you recall seeing or hearing of a young soldier by the name of William?" the woman asked hastily and hopeful.

I shook my head.

"I suppose not with all those lost that day," she sighed before turning and heading towards the kitchen, "I suppose you think it foolish of us to hope when few survive the marsh."

"Not in the least," I muttered and then I thought of her once more, if but briefly before my thoughts returned to that day.

I knew not of the soldier she spoke of, nor could I have recognized him if he was seen as the men that I slaughtered that day were many. If he would have survived my wrath, the marsh would have consumed him long before now, and I would in part be responsible for this family's unrest. I turned to stand when the older woman's hand pressed lightly on my shoulder, urging me to remain where I was. I did not resist her and as I sat back down, she handed me a plate of something. It did not appear to be much, but fresh bread and a stew of sorts was more than enough to ignite a fire in my empty stomach. I ate everything hastily and without a word when I remembered that I was in the presence of others.

I swallowed the last few bites and wiped my mouth on my sleeve, "Thank you for your kindness, I did not mean to swallow my manners."

She smiled and relieved my hands of the empty plate they now held. I had not realized how long it had been since I had eaten until I felt the hunger pain in my stomach when food was placed before me. She returned quickly with her daughter in tow.

"If you are ready now, my daughter shall finish tending to your," she stopped suddenly and touched my face lightly when I heard her mumble, "your misfortune."

I brought my hand towards my face and searched my face and neck for what she was referring to. Just in front of my one ear was a gash that walked its way downwards from my cheekbone and onto my neck. I felt the slick coolness of blood as it was beginning to set and followed that coolness as the gash branched itself further on my cheek, connecting several smaller cuts along the way.  As I slid my fingertips back and forth across it feeling its length and depth, it comforted me to know that the populace was not running from me in fear, they were running from me because I was splattered with blood and blood frightens many.

"Do not worry, I'm an excellent seamstress and I will do my best to not displease any suitors you may have," she smiled briefly before pulling a needle and thread from her apron.

"I appreciate your thoughtfulness," I paused giving a brief smile, "as I am sure they will as well," I heard myself lie to the woman as I knew otherwise but could not bring myself to witness the pity that would soon consume her had she have known.

She tilted my head slightly towards the one side as she wiped the blood from my jawline once more causing the warm water to burn through the openings in my flesh.  The pain was quickly surpassed by the sensation of the needle piercing the surface at multiple points.  While the pain was irritating, it did not distress me much and as it appeared to distress her.  Her face was pulled tight as if she were clenching her teeth or something to focus her efforts completely on her stitch work which I could appreciate.

"Please relax, you are not hurting me," I said softly, and I could feel her breath wash over me as she exhaled.

"I apologize sir, it has been quite some time since I mended a soldier's wounds."

"Please do not apologize to me," I ran one of my fingers across the thick scar found on my upper lip, "as you can see, I'm no stranger to," I paused and thought carefully over my next few words, "misfortune as your mother so eloquently put it."

"I am sorry that Commander Berenger was so willing to place you in harm's way," her voice was soft but saddened, "and then not tend to your injuries properly."

I wanted to ask her what happened to the woman Prince Berenger longs for, but had I been a member of the guard I am certain that should have already been known to me and asking would only make me appear suspicious. She was nearly finished when I felt her brush my hair back, fully exposing my neck, just before she let out a gasp and fell back on her heels. The older woman rushed over to find her daughter recoiling from me with her hands over her mouth to stop herself from screaming. Both of their eyes widened further when I chose to stand quickly and reach towards them. I was not trying to hurt them, only help them up when I heard something uttered under their breath in concurrence.

"Elf."

I lowered myself and spoke softly, "Aye, that I am."

"You are an impostor," the woman spat, "only humans can be members of the royal guard for elves are not welcome here."

I withdrew my hands and spoke softly once more, "Please help me, I only wish for my freedom."

"You do not deserve freedom," the woman spat again just before standing up and rushing towards the door.

The handle was fully grasped in her hands, and she had just begun to turn it when I spoke suddenly.

"While that is probably true," I mumbled, "but there is a woman out there that does."

I felt the old woman's hands touch my arm causing me to pull away suddenly.

"Go now and we will say nothing," she whispered.

The woman released the door from her grasp suddenly and turned towards us, "Mama," she pointed towards me, "this man is a traitor to the crown," her tone sharpened, "if you let him leave, we shall share the same fate as he."

"Perhaps," she paused, "but I will not be the one who leads him to his death."

The old woman stepped away and I slowly stepped towards the door, the woman did not budge from her position, only stared at me with partially drowned eyes and a scowl.

"Please let me pass," I paused and reached out to touch her when she jerked herself away. I exhaled slowly before reaching around her, grasping the door's handle firmly, "I watched your husband fall to the beast in the marsh," I spoke softly but did not look at her, "you can stop hoping for his return for there will not be one."

To some this may have been cruel, but I believed this was the only kindness left for me to give this family who tried to help me. As I began to open the door, I heard her voice speak to me once more.

"How do you know this?"

"I was there that day.  He was not returned to you because there was nothing left of him to return," I glanced towards her briefly and then opened the door to step out into the street, "Please forgive me."

# Lira

Despite an attack on some poor creature in the night, it held no bearing on the welcoming and fruitful sight I woke to in the light of the wee morning hours.  While I knew remaining in the grove was not an option, I could not help but find peace within its wake.  The light was once more projecting its way through gaps in the treetops and warming the ground beneath me.  The birds were singing, young krigshastar were grazing and the ground was a variable playground for young ekorre.  Ekorre are mischievous furry creatures that are similar in appearance to mice but much larger.  The average ekorre is about the size of a melon with large, pointed ears, keen to pick up on almost any noise, and a long skinny tail with only tufts of fur being projected from the end.  However, do not let their soft fuzzy exterior fool you, they love to play tricks on sleeping travelers and can be fierce in numbers when challenged.  I just thought they were fun.

I lay there listening to them scurrying about in the quiet grove when one opted to burrow in my free-flowing locks of which I did not pay him any mind.  While animals can sense my predatory nature, they are often deceived by my humanoid appearance and scent, but given my unique situation, I am able to communicate with them in a way few others can.  Druids are by far the closest to us in our ability to understand or communicate with animals, but what they lack in blood-borne ability, they make up for in their magic.  I have never found comfort in their presence and when shifted, it is my understanding that they are able to communicate with us freely through non-verbal means of which I find very unsettling as I am unsure where this ability ends.

As I continued to rest there, I replayed the events since my capture once more in my mind.  Focusing carefully on the events of the Ice Tower, I was still unable to comprehend the majority of what happened there that night.  Drayk, while foreign to those lands, moved about with ease and precision.  Perhaps he was once a prisoner in that very tower or perhaps I had been unconscious longer than my mind would permit me to comprehend giving him additional time to explore the tower.  Either seemed plausible, but I could not get that night nor his face out of my mind.  I watched him in my mind, focusing on those eyes and the marking that appeared so foreign to me, yet so familiar.  Then I saw a flash of his face just before I fell into the crashing waves below.  The look snapped my attention back to the bounding ekorre nearby and I felt a pain grow in the pit of my stomach.

Attempting to shake off the brief but emotional attachment I was feeling for him, I reached for the ekorre, now coiled in my hair, and pulled him towards me. At first, he rushed to escape my grasp, but his fear quickly dissipated as I began nuzzling his fluffy cheeks. The simple act of reciprocating my affection was enough to warm my saddened heart. With another nuzzle of our cheeks, I said my goodbyes just before watching him frolic back towards his kin. This felt dangerously like home, but I knew the illusion would not last. I sat upright with legs crossed and pulled back the flap that was barely covering the nathair's puncture wounds. It was still painful to the touch and very charred in appearance. It was not healing as it should. I lowered the flap to begin scanning the grove while I began braiding my long locks.

The grove was overflowing with life, both plant and wildlife. Unless the shipwreck placed me within reach of a remote unknown island, this was Coille not Feurach as I had hoped, and I was significantly further from the Towers of Light than was desirable. This created a nagging question in my mind, what was a cargo vessel from Tuiteam doing delivering goods to the Ice Tower of Reothadh? If there was any validity to this suggestion, I could already sense the answer would not comfort me, but the question tugged at my mind. There must be information being exchanged for wandering ears to capture, I just needed to make sure those wandering ears were mine. In the event an alliance has been created between Tuiteam and Trocair, the remaining regions of Caladh would all be at risk. However, venturing towards Tuiteam would certainly only bring unyielding torment if found, it may not be worth the risk. I did what I could to confine these thoughts to the back of my mind before stepping towards the barrier of the grove.

Stopping just shy of the barrier, I paused briefly hoping it had vanished as Bryn did the day before but other than attempting to step through, there was no other way of testing it as I was unsure of the type of barrier that was conjured. Stepping forward slowly, ever hopeful I would be granted passage, or I would be met with resistance and most likely fall back upon my backside in humiliation for all to see. Either way, someone was going to be amused and as I felt my feet continue to glide upon the plush moss below, I knew it had faded. I was confined to the grove no longer and my journey towards the marsh must now begin.

Once outside of the grove the forest appeared very different from before and when I turned around to view the grove once more, it was gone. It was a portal and whatever or whoever conjured it, I cannot say, but I would find sanctuary here no longer. The sun was bright and high in the sky, giving me time to explore the coast once more and better orient myself to my exact location. Unfortunately, with the overlapping landscapes of the mainland there are not exact borders as would be found on an island, further adding to the conundrum of which I found myself in. At least with following the coastline in either direction would provide a guideline rather than relying on surroundings or pure instinct although it would leave me exposed. Ultimately opting for the forest's protection over the coastline's guidance, I turned away from the light and took my first steps towards the forest's core.

The forest was as I remembered it, lush greenery coating nearly every surface with enormous boulders projecting themselves through the soot below.  The forest was an inevitable playground of life by day all while a dangerous turf war raged in the moonlight.  This region may not have been home to man but between the native Skogar and the druids that now call this region home, this region (much like many others), was in a constant state of unrest.  I have only encountered one of the Skogar at a great distance but understand that they are remarkably similar to shapeshifters and tend to be reclusive.  When closing in on their borders, I generally strive to keep my distance and never infringe upon that at least in the last century or more as they merely tolerate others in their forest rather than attempt to befriend them.  I shall be no exception.

The forest was growing darker now as if a great canopy were being pulled over the forest with each passing step I took.  While I was still able to see some of the light piercing through the treetops, little of it was warming the ground beneath me.  Could I really have been walking that long or had something within the forest changed?  As it is with Lamprog, this forest contains magical beings and properties that have the potential to alter my perception of time and my surroundings making it a variable labyrinth for unknowing souls that enter.  I did not wish to be its next victim.  I scanned the surrounding area for the tallest tree that I could use to lift myself out of the darkness and back into the light.

There was a change in the air as I ascended it with minimal effort, up here the air seemed fresher somehow while the air beneath me was stale and musty.  That could easily explain a portion of my confusion as breathing stale air for too long has a way of polluting the mind.  I reached the tree top and pulled myself up and out into the evening sky.  It was a darker shade of lavender followed by stroke of midnight closing in, accompanied by a warm breeze dancing along the treetops pushing loose leaves and pollen throughout.  I was relieved to feel the breeze drawing my attention towards the east, I was on the right track.  I was not as far as I had hoped, but if changed once the sun sets, it would not be difficult for me to extend my reach further.

Night was the ideal time to travel as it was not uncommon for other predators to be roaming about the forest, providing interested parties with a much-needed distraction. My descent was nothing short of typical until I reached about midway down the tree's trunk.  The air felt and smelt as it did before, but something had changed, and I could sense it.  I lowered myself down fully onto one of the larger branches, wrapping myself around it to appear as part of it should there be any wandering eyes nearby.  If necessary, I would wait the night out until morning hoping whatever may have come here would vacate the area by that time.  Closing my eyes, I could hear a faint rustling sound just due north of me which drew my eyes open again.  I turned my head slowly to face that direction when the noise ceased.  I scanned the area repeatedly for the source to no avail when I opted to give up the search and continue my descent.  I reached the forest floor once more and continued to venture east when I heard the rustling begin again.  I was being followed.  My pace remained unchanged when I noticed a clearing but a few hundred paces ahead.

As I neared the clearing, I realized it was not a clearing at all but a large gorge of rock and debris that fell between two large cliffs.  The foliage of the forest floor attempted to make a home upon the rock in several places but ultimately was denied and coiled back onto itself.  The few trees that were found high upon the rock walls and nooks within were now dead and lifeless, only hanging by the roots that once so diligently provided them life.  The ascent to the rim was steep and could not easily be scaled but treading through the heart of the gorge may prove more treacherous as once inside there would only be one way out.  Bringing my motions to a halt, I listened for any sign of the mysterious follower when I heard a whistling sound behind me.  I did not turnaround or utter a word, just set off at a quick pace with the intent of reaching the rim of the gorge.  Depending on who or what was following me, this should detour them.  Trees that once seemed so far in the distance were now blurred in my peripheral vision and the cliff's rocky slope was becoming dangerously close when I heard the whistling sound again, this time much closer.  I denied my ever-growing curiosity to turnaround and view my attacker in favor of a swift ascent.

Rushing up onto the rocky slope, I felt my bare feet slipping on the stone pieces that were randomly cast across the surface.  As I stretched myself towards the next set of stones, the jagged particles from the last clung to my feet, tearing into my flesh.  Dropping down, I implored my hands to aid in the burden as I continued scurrying towards the peak, they did so without opposition and soon they matched my feet in their tattered appearance.  Through the crashing of rock against rock and my labored breathing, I no longer heard the whistling sound.

With my body only a few paces from the peak, I glanced over my shoulders in hopes of getting a glimpse of those who were seeking me, but there appeared to be no one there.  Nothing other than the forest staring back at me.  I slowed my pace to a crawl to help secure my footing and quiet my frantic ascent.  While creeping towards the peak, I scanned the forest floor for any sign of movement which was difficult as a breeze was beginning to rush in.  Even though I was significantly higher than the forest floor, the breeze that rushed towards me was still filled with soot.  I felt the ground begin to level out beneath me and just as I laid my hand down one final time before standing, I felt something other than rock beneath my fingers.  The surface was overly dry and leathery but significantly softer than anything I would have expected to find here.  I turned my head slowly forward, walking my eyes upward from the rock to my fingers to the object beneath them.  To my surprise, I found my bloody fingers lingering on the foot of a man.

My attention was immediately drawn upwards towards the man it belonged to when I was greeted with a sharp spike pointed directly at me.  I tilted my head slightly to bring him into view when the light radiating off of the side of the spike caused me to squint. I lowered my head and raised my eyes upward and focused on the spike, which was not a spike at all, it was the tip of an arrow. This would have explained the whistling sound I heard earlier. I brought my legs up and under me, preparing to stand when the man spoke.

"Why have you come here?" his voice deep and gruff.

I attempted to stand when the tip of his arrow was brought forward and placed just before my right eye forcing me to back down.

"The vessel I was aboard, sank in the night," I paused trying to gauge his reaction.

"You are not welcome here," he growled.

"And I shall not remain if you permit me to pass," I spoke firmly.

Out of my peripheral vision I found there were now others nearby and they were quickly surrounding me. While I had hoped my presence here to go unnoticed, I should have known that the forest sees all and the Skogar's overwhelming presence was causing my flesh to ignite. The male in charge looked down upon me disapprovingly.

"Bind her," he commanded, "the Elders will want to know what she knows."

I quieted my inner beast and permitted them to bind me as nothing good would come from antagonizing them. The bindings were soft initially, but as my focus remained on observing their behavior, I failed to notice the bindings were hardening. I began flexing against them, testing their strength and my own while bound.  My efforts did not go unnoticed as without warning I felt my entire body slam down against the rock.

"Do not test me," I felt the pressure increase as the man bent down to enter my field of vision before he spoke again, "there's something different about this one."

His brow tightened causing his eyes to narrow.  His eyes, extremely dark and obsidian throughout, not as man or elf possess.  Anger was not the source of his interest any longer, but curiosity was.  While I can control my transformations, the flash fire that rushes across my eyes when I feel threatened has been a struggle for me to manage, giving me away on more than one occasion.  While most read the flash as something magical, something elven, others see and feel something else as this one did.  They do not understand that it is a primal response and takes intense focus and time to master.  I have been struggling to master it since my birth centuries ago.  When well rested and properly nourished it becomes easier to control, but in recent years, as the hunt for us grows stronger, those things have become increasing problematic to obtain.

"We go now," he commanded just before removing himself from my view.

I felt the pressure upon my body give way as the man removed himself from my side.  My body was pulled away from the rock and cast onto the back of one of the Skogar while still bound.  He wrapped an arm around my legs, but there was really no need.  The bindings were not of rope but of long thick vines with thorns scattered about the housing.  However, they did not feel like vines when they were being wrapped around me.  Something about them was different, magical, and with each movement their grasp on me tightened prompting the thought, where these inherently magical or were they spellbound?

I thought over this carefully as we ventured deeper into the mouth of the forest.  As we moved fuller inland, the forest was no less dark, but there was life here.  As we neared what appeared to be a prominent village, the Skogar moved about taking care to not disturb the new growth found there. They did not speak but were clearly communicating with each other and the life around them.  Their heads were turn towards one another, then darting glances towards far off things that were unseen to me.  I watched foliage stretch itself towards the Skogar, thinning itself and growing brighter when it was met with their touch.  With each touch, the foliage would give birth to new seedlings that would almost immediately sprout roots that grappled their way into the soil below in a twisted and magical way of expediting the life cycle of the forest.

With each step, we began encountering other Skogar, one or two in passing at first and now, flocks of them were pouring in around us.  They were ever watchful and keen to know more of the fiery haired maiden that had stumbled across their borders.  Their inquiries at first appeared in quickened glances and widened eyes, but soon grew vocal to become cast upon us from every direction in growing volume.  No sooner were those inquires cast, they were dismissed.  The Skogar that was shouldering me stopped just before lowering me to the ground below where the bindings slowly unwound themselves and drew themselves back into the soil.

A Skogar, not much older than myself, stepped towards me and the crowd fell silent, bowing their heads before him. Could this really be one of the Elders the man spoke of? He appeared barely out of his youth but as I glanced around, they all appeared as such. It was not until he stepped towards me and hunkered down before me that I could see different. I brought myself up and onto my knees keeping my head low, but my eyes unyielding from his. His eyes were black as shadow giving him an emptiness, I had not anticipated but when I thought about it, their eyes were all darkened to hide their humanity. Our eyes often give us away and when no pupil to dilate and no tears to produce beads of laughter or sorrow, they could maintain their illusive response to nearly any situation. Being as such, I was unable to follow their movements and even though I did not feel a surge within me, I knew this man could sense I was not what I appeared to be.

"Framling," he proceeded to stand just before gesturing for me to stand as well, "I am called Yew. How is it you have come to find yourself past the wall of thorns?"

Standing gracefully, I lifted my head upwards, slightly projecting my chin, "A vessel I was aboard sunk in the night," I paused, "I only wish passage through your land."

"And how is it that an *elf* came to be on such a vessel?" he spoke disapprovingly.

"My kin and I were," I paused watching him carefully for any changes in his body language but there was nothing, "I was gravely injured, and it was there we sought refuge."

"But you are elven," he paused, "are you not?"

I nodded before adding, "My kin and I are not skilled healers and therefore, no match for a nathair's poisonous barbs."

He raised an eyebrow disapprovingly, "Nathairs are only found in Boglach, should you have been injured by one, you would not have survived the journey to the coast to board a vessel." He stepped towards me, "Tuiteam is no friend to elves-"

"My kin bartered passage," I snapped, cutting him off and igniting my flesh.

"And what did your *kin* offer these men?" his voice mistrustful.

"I know naught of their arrangement," I spat.

"Hmmmm," he groaned just before falling silent.

His eyes closed and I watched as his brow tightened along with his eyelids. He was concentrating. We remained in silence for several moments before his eyes opened again.

"Tell me," he leaned in, smelling me, studying me, "where did you encounter this nathair?"

"The Ice Tower of Reothadh," I spoke confidently but not forceful as controlling my emotions was critical.

He closed his eyes again and inhaled deeply, searching for any changes in my sense as an animal would when threatened.

"It is rare for King Edric to seek out an elf, let alone a fire elf.  How did you come to be imprisoned there?"

"That is unclear to me," I paused briefly debating on what to divulge to him, "I was taken from the mainland and awoke in the Ice Tower.  I have no memory of my attackers nor of how long I may have been imprisoned there."

His eyes opened again and narrowed, "Surely, you would not have been taken without cause."  He touched my chin softly with two of his long slender fingers, pulling them back slightly, forcing my chin upward and my curly locks to fall back away from my forehead, revealing the wonder of my honeycomb eyes.  "You have something he wants, surely you must know this."

I pulled my chin away from his touch, "I know not of what that man seeks other than his own greed," I growled.

"Take her to the cage," he did not turn away from me, but his body appeared to harden slightly, "perhaps there her memory will return to her."

He turned abruptly and no sooner than his back was towards me, two Skogar scooped me up by my arms and began dragging me away.  I knew then that I had traded one prison for another and this time I would need to find my own escape.

We stood together, myself and the Lady Rosalyn, for several moments when she turned towards me.  The tears from her eyes had dried and she was smiling at me.  The morning breeze has shifted directions causing a fair amount of her long locks to sweep across her face, shading her eyes from my sight. I raised a hand up and clasped several groupings of strands within my fingers and began sliding them back.  They felt weightless in my grasp and smoother than the finest of silks, forcing me to take a second glance.  I heard a faint giggle escape through her lips and the gesture caused a smile to climb up and onto my cheeks.  Then I felt her hand upon my hand.  I wondered if the flutters I felt within my belly and the coolness that rushed over my skin was what all men feel when in the presence of a lady made of such pure starlight the Gods should have been ashamed of themselves for creating her to be a mere mortal.  I cradled her face within my hands and closed my eyes, afraid to look into them for another moment as my heart may burst. I leaned in and placed my cheek against hers, holding mine next to hers for several moments before shifting to the other cheek. While I knew she would not understand the complexity of the gesture, this was the closest thing I could muster to showing her what she has meant...or rather what she means to me.

There was a knock at the door that shook me from my dream. I could have sat there for hours reliving that moment in my mind. The feeling and hope I drew from it far exceeded the regret that had been built in my mind. I should have kissed her. I wanted to kiss her. The thought broke off again when there was another knock at the door.

"My Lord," the man paused, "your presence has been requested by the King."

"Please let him know I will be a moment," I responded hoping to continue thinking of her, if but only for a few moments more.

"My Lord," the door swung open, "please forgive the intrusion, but I was instructed to bring you at once."

The man bowed before me which was something I had never quite grown accustomed to. While I am no Lord, as an emissary of the King Aldon, I was to be treated as such. If they understood what I truly was they would have me shackled and enslaved for the remainder of my unnaturally long life. I nodded quickly just before standing from my seat and fastening my doublet closed. I gestured for the man to step off before me allowing me a moment to glance around the room for anything unbecoming.  When nothing noteworthy came into view, I stepped off and joined in him the hall, just after closing my door behind me.

"To what do I owe the pleasure of his majesty's company at this hour?"

"Word was received from the Kingdom of Tuiteam," he hurried through the corridors.

"What sort of news?" I pried.

"For that, I cannot say for certain, my Lord," he muttered, and he pressed onward, "but based on his majesty's mixed reaction, I would deduce it is disheartening news."

Thoughts began to swirl in my head of who or what was to meet an untimely end when we arrived in the King's study.  I stepped across the threshold and bowed slightly just as the King's backside came into view.  He was pacing hastily while sliding a piece of parchment back and forth between his fingertips, flipping it about as if it were a wee bairn's toy rather than something distressing.

"King Itheal," I paused, "how may I be of service?"

"Pack your belongings," he turned towards me just in time to catch my eyes widen with surprise, "you depart upon the morrow."

I felt my insides tighten and I had to fight the urge to expel my feast from last eve, "To what end?"

"Tuiteam," he stated candidly before placing the parchment down onto a nearby table.

"I do not understand your majesty," I felt the words catch.

"Your presence has been requested."

I felt my heart sink and my mind began to swirl the way it does when one has too much ale.  Who there would even know of me, let alone request my presence?"

"Bryn," he paused, "are you alright?" he spoke softly and placed his hands on my shoulders, forcing my attention to return to him.

I nodded, "My apologies King Itheal.  If it be your wish, I will go."

A grin drew itself onto his cheeks shortly before the sounds of laughter begin to resonate within him.  My response amused him, although, I uncertain as to why.  I turned my head slightly at the gesture, the way an animal would when they hear an unfamiliar sound.  I watched his eyes close as he tossed his head back slightly allowing his tousled creamy locks to drift away from his brow and cheeks as the laughter escaped him.  While his amusement may have befuddled me, it was pleasant to see him so pleased with anything as he seldom permits himself to be seen so informal.

He calmed his laughter just before he spoke once more, "It is not I who wishes it."

"Then whom?" I asked curiously.

"It would be at the Lady Roselyn's request."

I felt the wind knocked out of me and rather than draw breath, I held what little I had in a pitiful attempt to stop this moment from happening.  I saw her face in the foreground of my mind, her beauty of pure starlight and a tender heart that had chosen me over all others to befriend.  The thought of leaving her tore at my insides and sent fire racing through my veins.  Why chose to send me away now?  The question jerked me back into the moment.

"Have I displeased her?" I said sternly.

He smiled again, "Quite the opposite I am afraid," he turned away and stepped back towards a table heavily littered with parchment and texts where he picked up the parchment he had been previously holding.  "King Baylon has died, and Prince Ferand has sent word for the Lady Rosalyn.  His men should arrive upon the morrow with the intention of departing shortly thereafter."

I clenched my teeth, fighting the urge to scream.

"She has requested you accompany her on the journey," I felt my jaw start to relax, "and remain there with her until after her coronation."

King Itheal spun about on his heels, forcing me to compose myself quickly before his eyes were to catch my displeasure.

"You are to act as my emissary and when the moment arrives," his eyes darted towards mine, "present Losgadh's only princess to Tuiteam's anointed king."

I tried to clear the mass of discomfort lodged in my throat as he stepped towards me.

"Is that understood?" he said sternly.

"Aye," I croaked, "it will be done."

He nodded and gestured towards the door to which I bowed my head slightly reflecting my understanding it was my time to remove myself from his presence before turning to exit the study.  No sooner than the door closed behind, I felt my legs grow weak and I began to fall towards the stone floor. Thankfully, I was able to take hold of a pillar nearby, permitting me a moment to compose myself.  My pulse was beating against the wall of my chest in a terrible rhythm that grew louder as my mind attempted to wrap itself around the events that would unfold in the days to come.  While I knew the Lady Rosalyn was betrothed to Prince Ferand, part of me hoped her heart could be swayed to desire another, this was part of King Aldon's hope as well, although I am unsure why the betrothal of two human royals would concern him at all.

I extended my arms, forcing myself to stand fully upright, when I remembered Eira.  Depending on the path she would choose to follow, she could close the gap between us in a matter of days, forcing her into King Itheal's hands without me here to mediate the meet and greet.  There is a chance I could reach King Aldon prior to my departure but once outside of the kingdom the connection Losgadh provided would not be strong enough to locate Eira and portal me to her.  I am unsure as to the power King Aldon draws from here, but it is unlike anywhere else outside of Lamprog.

I rushed my way back towards my bedchamber and quickly began tossing my belongings into a small wooden chest located just shy of my bedside.  Part of me wanted to resign and sleep away my last hours in Castle Losgadh, but the fear I had for these two women could not be ignored and had the potential to consume me.  While my heart rate was beginning to slow, each pulse of it continued to slam against my chest like a hammer on an anvil, forcing the pressure from the point of contact to reverberate throughout my torso. While the pressure was powerful, the tightness it caused took my breath away once more, forcing me to gasp for air. I dropped the doublets I held within my hands and rushed towards the window, slamming my hands against it, thrusting it open. The crisp night air filled my lungs with each gasp I took, quickly bringing my heart rate back to a more natural rhythm. I clung to the stone with such force, that my knuckles turned white, and the stone was beginning to crumble beneath my fingertips. I was growing stronger with each passing day, but my strength could not save me from the choice I was being forced to make. If I were to choose Eira, I would surely lose the Lady Rosalyn and favor of King Itheal and if I should choose Rosalyn, Eira would be lost to me and the fate of our kind along with her. No matter the path I should choose, the outcome will haunt me for the remainder of my existence.

My eyes were drawn up towards the magnificence of the moon reminding me of the night I arrived and there I stood in its graceful light, contemplating the path I would choose, what they would choose if they knew one had to be made. I felt my heart and my legs give way before collapsing onto the stone beneath me. Where I lay prematurely weeping over the woman I would have to sacrifice. Then I saw it, like a beacon skipping across the early morning sky and stopping just shy of the Lady Rosalyn's balcony, a falling star. It was there I saw her, too, staring upon the moon and its light covered her in a shimmering blanket of silver. This was the brightest I had ever seen her appear and even at a distance, there was no denying her beauty.  It was then that I knew I could wait no longer to speak the truth of my feelings towards her for forever leave them to be buried deep within my belly.

I brought myself to my feet while sloughing off the dust from the crumbling stone.  My heart propelled me forward and my once so weary legs, now seemed to be gliding across the stone floor as I sped towards the Lady Rosalyn's bedchamber.  There were few about the castle at this time, seeing the wee morning hour we had found ourselves awake in, making it much easier to arrive at her door unseen.  I was compelled to knock but my heart would not let me for fear of being unheard or being turned away.  Pushing the door open ever so gently, I crept my way inside and closed it behind me with barely a sound.  Never having been in her bedchamber before I was relieved to find it was not unlike my own, quite simple actually.  She may have been a princess in dress and title but her living quarters reflected nothing of the sort.  I was tempted to look about the room when I heard her speaking to someone.  The sound quickly drew my attention and I clung to a nearby wall as I moved out towards the balcony.  It was a large semi-circle that jetted itself out away from the castle walls and was kept very much like her bedchamber.  She clearly spent as much time in her bedchamber as she did out here, comforting me as I knew she belonged in the moonlight.  My eyes quickly found her, feeling my heart skip at the sheer sight of her and she was alone.  She had not moved from when I last saw her and as I let her beauty take my breath away once more, I stepped towards her.

"My lady," I spoke softly hoping not to startle her.

She drew a quick breath at the sound of my voice.

"Lady Rosalyn," I spoke softly again.

I watched her inhale deeply and then exhale just as deeply permitting her shoulders to return to the relaxed state I found her in.

"Bryn," she turned her head toward me slightly, looking at me from over her shoulder, "you should not be here." She turned back towards the moon, "My father will have you flogged for entering my bedchamber at such an hour," she uttered with a hint of amusement in her voice.

"And you," I asked softly and continued walking towards her, "will you have me flogged?"

"Of course not," she paused and turned towards me, forcing her chemise to twist around her, pulling it tighter to her body. "Though, you should not be here, if anyone knew-"

"They will not," I blurted it out, cutting her off, "Rose, no one will know I was here."

"Bryn, you called me Rose," she smiled.

I nodded, unsure of what to say, but I felt my heart skip again at the sound of her voice saying my name.

"You know I enjoy your company, but I must ask," she paused, "why are you here?"

"King Itheal, I mean, your father told me that we are to depart for Tuiteam soon and…" I froze, afraid to tell her what I was really thinking and feeling. My eyes shifted to the moon in hopes of distracting myself long enough to regain my confidence, "It is beautiful, is it not?"

I saw her head turn slightly and glance towards it, "Yes, it is, but Bryn-"

I hastily stepped towards her, stopping just within arm's reach of her and reached out my hand for hers, "You trust me, do you not?"

"Of course, I do," she placed her hand in my mine and once again I was greeted by the warmth of her touch, "Bryn, you are frightening me."

"Please do not wed Prince Ferand."

"Bryn," she sighed, "you know this is what I want."

My grip tightened on her hand, and I pulled myself slowly towards her, "Because your father gave you no other choice.  He has held you prisoner here, forcing you to only see what he wishes."

Her eyes were wide now, filled with concern and confusion.  While I did not want to hurt her, I knew I was running out of time.  After several moments of silence, I felt her other hand find mine and she was rubbing my fingers in between hers.  She was attempting to soothe my troubled heart without compromising a promise verbally made by her father many years before and now being questioned by her heart.

"Rose," I leaned in and placed my lips softly on her cheek just before whispering to her, "if you feel nothing for me, I beseech thee to tell me now."

I could hear her pulse begin to race and her cheeks were beginning to flush.  I pulled away just enough, so when I turned to kiss her other cheek, she could feel my lips graze across her very own.  The sensation of such a brief, but intimate touch caused fire to break through and flood my veins with heat of which I certain she could feel as I was dangerously close to pressing my body to hers.  Her breathing was slow with a slight quiver in it as she exhaled, but she did not appear to be afraid.  Without looking at her, I released her hand from my grasp just before placing it gently upon her lower back, pulling her towards me.  The movement was graceful and as our bodies came together, clinging to one another.  I knew now what had been missing all the many years of my life…it was her.

I leaned in to kiss her cheek again when I felt her lips press themselves against my cheek.  The touch was tender, and I felt my heart begin to ache, longing for her, pleading with her not to stop as the rhythm of my heart grew more frantic.  I placed my other hand softly on the base of her neck, where her pulse felt the strongest and lightly brushed my fingers across her skin.  Her breathing deepened and the sudden change prompted me to pull away to be met with her large crystal blue eyes.  They were brighter in the moonlight, and I found myself weakened at the sight of them watching me.  Her eyes sought their way across my face and down onto my chest where they met her hands, resting peacefully.  I reached for them with my own and covered them, pressing them tightly to my chest, allowing her to feel my heart beating.  Our eyes met once more, and I felt the moment slipping from my grasp.  I closed my eyes willing it to linger just a little longer and to give me strength to say what I came to say.

"Rose, my darling," I whispered, "I beseech thee-"

My words were soon cut off by Rose pressing her lips tightly to mine and her arms were drawing themselves upward around my neck, further pressing her body against mine. At first the kisses were tender and subtle, but with each kiss I felt further drawn to her. I parted my lips and pressed my tongue gently between hers, providing a playful suggestion that she open her mouth to me, further deepening the kiss. I was unsure what had come over me, but the sudden turn caused my flesh to sear beneath the moonlight and I felt the need to pant in between our kisses. Never have I been so taken with a maiden, and I was certain there would never be another that set my soul and flesh ablaze as she.

I was completely consumed by this feeling and by her. I pulled my lips away from hers leaving her panting at the sudden change, when I noticed a faint moan escaped her lips as I began kissing her neck. Her fingers were frantically twirling themselves through my long locks, further pulling me towards her, when I felt my doublet break open. My attention was drawn downwards, curious as to the cause, when I felt her hands sliding underneath it, forcing it back and off my shoulders. It fell towards the stone floor with barely a sound, but the gesture echoed wildly in my mind.

My attention was drawn away from the doublet as the coolness of her fingers continued to press themselves against my exposed chest. I reached for them, pulling them towards my face where I kissed them softly just before leaning in to kiss her again.  Through panted breaths and swollen lips, we had lost none of our desire for one another and with a slight tug from my fingers, I felt her cape fall towards the stone floor. She shivered slightly from the sudden temperature change before I wrapped my arms around her, pulling her tightly against my body before picking her up gently and carrying her to her bed.  I felt her body stiffen at the suggestion the gesture made and in turn, mine did as well.

"Bryn, I am afraid," her attention was drawn towards the bedding beneath us and began biting her lower lip.

For a moment, I was unsure as to what her fear was regarding, but as I looked upon her wide eyes and quivering lips, I knew this fear was about choosing whether or not to give herself to me.  I felt the same fear, only this appeared to be unknown to her in this moment.

"Rose," I kissed her forehead and without pulling away I whispered, "so am I."

This was uncharted territory for both of us and while we may have been taken in by the moment before, it was now all too real.  I looked into her eyes and the once so captivating orbs that stared into mine were now growing cold.

"I care for you, and this," I placed my hand on hers and pulled it onto the bedding, "this can wait."

"Can it?  We shall soon depart, and the opportunity may never present itself again." she muttered.

I felt gutted, "You still intend to wed Prince Ferand," I paused, "do you not?"

She frowned and my mind began to swirl with confusion.  Did I misread her somehow?  Or was there a part of her story she had yet to tell?  I sent pleading thoughts out into the world for anyone, anything to banish these thoughts from my mind when I felt her lips once again pressed against mine, pulling me back into the moment, back to her.  I frantically pulled my tunic from my body and tossed it onto the stone floor, her eyes grew wide and bright once more.  If she wishes to lay with me here on this day, there could never be another and even though the thought of the eternal torment I would suffer being bonded to a woman who loved another, I still wanted her.

I felt her soft hands once again on my chest and then on my face and then onto my back as if she were etching my body into her memory.  Her lips found mine and I quickly found myself lost in their sweet nectar and enticed by the spark they gave that made my lips tingle.  I would have given my soul for more.

"My darling," I spoke softly between our kisses, "oh my darling Rose."

I deepened our kisses once more and pulled her onto my lap.  There she could feel my skin upon hers as our bodies clung to each other once more.  I turned away from her lips to begin kissing her neck when I knew I had to tell her now or risk losing the moment to something more primal.

I whispered, "If you wish it, I will bind myself to you for the remainder of my existence.  A connection I shall not take lightly," I pulled her chin towards me, forcing her to look into my eyes, "but I shall not bind myself to you should you truly love and desire another."

"I do not love another," she spoke quickly before carefully thinking over her next words, "for I do not believe I know what love is," closing her eyes as if what she said or was about to say pained her in some way.

If it pained her to think of it, then I dare not wish to hear it.  I kissed her once more and held the kiss as long as I was able when I felt her break it off, her hands and mind captivated by a large scar found near the base of my rib cage that I had nearly forgotten was there.  One of the only markings that remained from all my years of running.

"Bryn, who did this to you?" she whispered sounding concerned.

"The Jagare," she looked confused, so I continued, "King Baylon's men or rather-"

"Prince Ferand's…" she spoke with words with an increasing airiness to voice making the last word nearly inaudible even for my keen hearing, "I do not understand," her brow tightened.

"I am not sure I want you to," I frowned, "If you still desire to venture to your betrothed, I will willingly go with you, but I fear the journey will change you, for the desires of men are not what you have been led to believe."

Her body shuttered as she exhaled, attempting to expel a portion of the heavy burden that was laid upon her, but should she survive the journey to Tuiteam and agree to wed Prince Ferand, her suffering would be far from over.

"This is a decision I cannot make now as I fear more than my life will be at stake should I choose poorly," she said wearily.

I felt the need to press her as to what she meant by that, but I restrained myself as she already appeared overtaxed by our encounter.  With heart and mind now locked in an intense battle, I was unsure of which would triumph, but looking upon her now, there was no denying I would never not choose her.

"Do not toil over such matters now," I brought my lips to her cheeks and kissed them softly, "you should rest now."

She smiled at me playfully, "What if I have not tired of your company just yet?"

I grinned like a child at her playful response.  She was perfect to me.

"Please kiss me," she whispered, "if I am to be greeted by the early morning's light then let it be in your loving embrace."

Never had someone made such a request of me and should I perish from this world, may I be left with the comfort that on this night her heart chose me.

# Commander Elgar

Our journey to the Ice Tower was temporarily delayed by a looming ice storm that had opted to rush in, but nevertheless myself and the young squire arrived.  The boy opted to stay with Lavin for as long as his flesh would permit, but he was soon forced to renege in favor of warmer accommodations.  He fled into the tower while I remained, scanning everything within my sight before entering the tower.  Most of what would have remained of an escape had vanished due to the constant assault by the elements, further complicating my investigation.  I retreated to the tower to find my men squabbling and punting blame amongst themselves.  A childish tactic of which I would not tolerate.

"Silence!" I commanded, "I will have order!"

The men quickly dissipated and those that remained brought themselves to attention.  I stepped towards each of them, carefully, scanning them for any sign of uneasiness or bewilderment.  The men who showed no signs of these were temporarily requested to escort me to the wolf's chamber, so I may follow in her escape while the remaining men were detained for further questioning.  We began the long ascent towards the upper chambers of the tower in near silence, only the chinks of our armor and landings of boots upon stone would be heard as I continued my investigation.  While I did not linger on any one particular item for more than a mere fraction of a second, it was clear the beast did not escape through the main door, but the few remaining potential points of departure should have been unreachable for a beast of her size.  With or without assistance, it was unclear to me how she could have escaped.

"Kraciun," I broke the silence, "Do we know the point of exit?"

Kraciun was essentially my second in command.  He was a young, powerful soldier that when met without his armor appeared to be carved out of wood, much like I would have been at his age.  His hair was lighter and shorter than most for our part of the world, making me think his father may not have been from Reothadh as he resembled his mother little.  While he was forced to endure a rotation at the tower as all soldiers must, he was seldom found idle, making him the ideal candidate to place in control during one of my frequent absences.  Had word of the wolf's disappearance been conveyed to me by any other and I would have assumed the claim to be false.

"Aye Commander, she fled through a drainage tunnel beneath the nathairs."

I grabbed Kraciun and jerked his body towards me causing his eyes to narrow with frustration when they became met with mine.

"The beast was able to sneak past the nathairs?" I questioned.

He shook his head and pushed himself against me, "She did not sneak past anything, they are dead!" he shouted.

I released him from my grasp and attempted to fathom the true strength of the beast we had detained. I assisted with her capture and against mere men, she was menacing, but even on the brink of starving she was still lethal. She must be recovered.

I gestured for Kraciun to continue forward, "What of the beasts in the chambers above?"

"The ogre still lives, but the remaining guards were slain and hidden in one of the wall passages."

Something about what he said struck me as odd. Beasts do not hide their kills, nor do they flaunt them for that is the way of men. Why let the ogre live but hide the men?

"Have you seen these men?" I demanded.

"Aye Commander, I have."

"What did you see?" I inquired hastily.

"They were slain with a blade primarily inserted at the base of the neck," he paused attempting to search for something in his pocket before continuing, "this incapacitated them quickly, leaving them to bleed out slowly."

"Are you certain it was a blade?"

"Aye, it was but not one of ours," he turned slightly towards me attempting to show me the shape he was creating with his hands, "much smaller and quite sharp.  It pierced through bone and armor in one strike."

"Were any left alive?" I inquired.

He shook his head, "If they were, they were dead before we found them, but the ogre tells a tale that has led the men to believe this tower is cursed."

"Of course, it is cursed," I responded, candidly.

I heard a chuckle escape Kraciun, and I knew he understood what I had meant.  This tower has been a prison to hundreds of men and beasts all of whom have or will perish under its ever-watchful eyes.  If it was not cursed, then those sorts of things do not exist.  However, I pondered what an ogre could have conjured to pollute the minds of men so easily and to what was his purpose in doing so.  It is the answer I intended to draw out of him momentarily.  Kraciun and I spoke little as we ventured the remaining corridors and stairs until we reached a large stone wall that appeared as a dead end. Kraciun stopped near the wall and inserted the key he must have been previously fetching from his pocket.  As the door was pried open new light was brought onto the stone floor beneath me revealing the large pools of dried blood and other bodily fluids. While we often hear of those who have died in battle or of ailments, we are rarely told of what foul stench escapes their bodies in their final hours.  Given the enclosed space we have found ourselves in, it shall be nothing short of months before this chamber can be visited without causing the upheaval in a man's stomach.

"And the men were found here?" I pointed to the floor with surprise as the door he had opened was not without difficulty.

"Aye," he nodded and stepped into the stairwell, "but not just anyone knows of this chamber."

I nodded and followed him out into the stairwell just before shutting the door behind us, leaving the remaining men to wait for our return. I looked upon the door in astonishment as I am unsure how someone or something not of this tower would have known it to have been there. I slammed my hands against it, looking for any signs of weakness or movement, to which I found nothing remarkable.

"If it was after nightfall and you were venturing down this stairwell, how would you know this was here?"

"You would not," he responded confidently, "even I could easily pass it in the dark."

"Hmmm, yet someone not only had the insight to locate it but open it before beast or man could dispose of them."

I directed him to proceed further up into the tower as I needed to grasp how the wolf was freed from its restraints. With no visible passageways in sight, running the stairwell in a panicked state at night could easily become disorienting, especially for a large beast unaccustomed to being indoors. I continued to search the stairwell as we ascended and there was nothing. The stairwell soon plateaued into a large chamber that we have been known to use for the purposes of extracting information from some of our less fortunate guests.  The room appeared as I remembered it to be aside from the large wooden door, heavily battered, that had miraculously floated off its hinges, requiring further explanation.

"What happened to the door?" I continued searching the room while I waited for an explanation.

"It was damaged in the escape," he replied promptly.

"How did no one hear it breaking through?"

"It was heard, but by the time we arrived in the stairwell we were greeted by an ogre, not a wolf."

"Why not just open it?" I stated as I brought my hand to my forehead and began massaging it attempting to soothe the headache that was rapidly growing from irritation.

"It was locked," my eyes darted towards him, "from the outside, but the key was not found."

"Must I be surrounded by fools!" I exclaimed forcing Kraciun to flinch away from me in surprise at the sudden disruption in my tone.

I threw my hands up in frustration before stepping over towards where the door once stood and began searching.  This door could not have locked on its own nor could a wolf have developed the skill necessary to turn a key.  I inspected the frame and stone nearby for any imperfection, any change that would have explained how this could have occurred when I saw it.  Several steps down into the stairwell lay something that just did not belong, it was darker in color but with a glimmer of something at one end.  I stepped back into the stairwell with a torch in hand, when I saw the object reveal itself to me, it was a key or at least part of one at one time.  The teeth were broken off, but there was no denying what the handle was to.  I brought it back and handed it to Kraciun.

His eyes widened, "The ogre was telling the truth."

"Of what truth did he speak of?  What are you not telling me?" I hissed.

"He claimed a woman was fleeing the tower and locked him inside," he blurted out.

"A woman?" I said perplexed, "Do you believe him to be bewitched?"

Kraciun shook his head violently, "But there is something strange about the chamber where the wolf was kept," he rushed towards the ascending stairwell, "I have never seen anything like it."

I quickly fell in behind him as we ran up the stairwell past another chamber or two when his gait was brought to a stop.  The room was dark and cold, colder than the ones below and there was a breeze whipping itself through a small opening nearby.  More than likely a stone was destroyed during a failed escape attempt and never repaired, but while it chilled the room significantly, the air was fresher here.  The room was not unlike any other at first glance, maybe slightly smaller, but upon further inspection I could see large black burns on the stone floor accompanied by broken shackles.  To be clear, they were not just broken, they had nearly been disintegrated.  Something or someone heated them to the point of rupture.

"Warlock perhaps?" Kraciun suggested.

"Perhaps," I mumbled, "but how would they know she was here?"

"Of that I cannot say," Kraciun said quietly as he, too, was clearly deep in thought.

I turned to descend back down the stairwell in search of anything that would lead to more answers than questions. It was not long before Kraciun followed suit and joined in my descent. We walked in silence until the stairwell turned into something else, something dark and foul. Kraciun did not utter a word, but I soon felt his hand upon my shoulder with a drape of cloth outstretched towards me.

"Commander, you should put this on, it will help with the vapors as they grow stronger."

I took the cloth from his hand and held it over my mouth, lessening the foul odor that was beginning to creep into my nasal cavity. We continued onward when I noticed a significant amount of mucus or something that was beginning to coat the stairs and walls. I reached out to touch the wall when I felt Kraciun's hand once more upon my shoulder.

"Commander, you should not touch the secretions," his eyes drifted down the stairwell, "even in death they are still potent."

We continued to find several large scrapes on the walls and what looked to be black ink scattered across different points on the walls and stairs. The fluid was too smooth to be anything other than blood, this must have been where the wolf attacked, taking first blood. It was not until several steps later when I found crimson dappled onto the stairs and smudged into a portion of the stone wall.

"One of them was injured," I muttered.

"Aye, the trail continues into the drain below and then stops suddenly."

I followed the trail to find two nathairs withered and rotting in the stairwell.  There was a steam of sorts being excreted from their decaying bodies, not unlike the vapors that had been wafted up the stairwell at us, but these seemed to sting in a way the others had not.  Looking over the bodies carefully, I was able to see that the one was clearly killed by a beast and the other a blade.  This is something that did not add up to me.  Clearly, someone released it from its bindings and was with it when the ogre was locked away.  However, had it been a warlock, they would not have opted to slay the beast with a blade when their magic would have been much quicker, but both would have benefited from taking a trophy, which they did.  The fangs of the nathairs had been broken off and taken, possibly to study or increase the lethality of a weapon, there was really no way to know.

We continued towards their den paying careful attention to the secretions that were now found slathered on nearly every surface along with holding our breath as the vapors were becoming quite potent.  Their lair was as expected, foul and humid.  King Edric must have installed fire pits beneath this chamber, or they would have never been able to survive here.  Regardless, my attention was drawn towards the blood trail that led directly into a hatch, located in the center of the room.  The door to the hatch had been left open and there was a large blood stain just at the base of the opening, but as I leaned down to get a better look it appeared to dissipate the further away it traveled from the hatch.  The wounds had either been bound or healed by some form of magic prior to continuing or we would have found one of them dead inside the drain.  I dropped myself into the drain and began to creep along the pipeline in search of their next steps.  While the pipeline soon broke off into several other smaller pipelines, I had no means of knowing which one they took or why.

I gestured for Kraciun to search down the tunnels towards the right and I would search the tunnels to the left.  We know they came this way but now there was no sign of them.  We parted ways, leaving us to venture the long dark tunnels alone on nearly our hands and knees.  The tunnels appeared much larger at first but now there was barely room for one to fit through let alone a large beast.  What would have made them choose this path over all others?  They could have easily slipped into the hidden passageway where the bodies were disposed of and taken on the men a few at a time, why venture further into the nathair's lair?  The questions tugged at my mind, further straining my already frustrated mind, when I heard it.  A faint whistling sound echoing though the tunnels, it was Kraciun.  I turned about and began winding my way back through the long road of twists and turns when I smelt and tasted a change in the air.  There was salt in it, and I knew we must have been closing in on an opening.  I scurried towards the sound and found Kraciun hunched over in front of a large opening, temporarily shielding me from the storm that was brewing outside.

At one time there must have been a covering and I wondered if it was removed as a diversion or if this was truly their exiting point.  Either could have been plausible but as we both squeezed ourselves next to the opening, we knew someone or something quite strong did not just remove the covering but tore it from its hinges leaving only jagged metal behind.  I gauged the distance to the surface below and knew that I could not safely make the jump without risking injury to myself or Kraciun, we would need to double back.  While there was a need to double back, I had no intention of going back through the nathair's lair if there was even a remote chance another route was taken.  I ordered Kraciun to return to the barracks and wait for me there as I continued to search the pipelines.  He did so without question.  As I continued crawling through the darkness, with a torch barely lit, I combed through the facts in mind and what I remember from the day the wolf was detained.  There was something about all of it that did not make sense to me.  How did the warlock enter and leave the tower virtually unseen?

After what felt like hours in dampened tunnels and cold stairwells, I arrived back at the barracks.  The men were a bit more on edge with my presence than usual, but that is often the case when the cat comes home after the mice have been out to play.  I selected a few to question and left the remainder to their own devices.  Kraciun greeted me just shy of exiting the chambers and reminded me that the ogre was still being detained in the event I wished to speak with him.  I nodded and gestured for him to lead the way.

"Were you able to locate anything further?" he inquired as we continued walking.

"No, the journey was all for naught," I said before we stopped just shy of a large wooden door.  "Open it," I commanded.

He swung the large door open to reveal a large ogre hunched over and facing the corner.  Despite their large size, when questioned they often behave like dogs of whom have been scolded by their masters and had it not been for their fearsome demeanor outside of those instances, we would have little use for them here.

"Turn around and face me beast!" I demanded before stepping towards him with my arms held firmly at my sides.

Kraciun had not left the doorway, nor did he move after the ogre turned towards me.

"Tell me what you saw, and I will permit you to return to your post," I spoke firmly.

"Grubble, grumble, kronk-konk," the ogre responded with what appeared to be sounds rather than actual words.

"In my tongue you insolent fool!" I shouted.

The ogre's head dipped down slightly at the sound of my voice echoing in the small chamber as if the sound hurt him or frightened him in some way.

"She elf," he mumbled, "alone."

I heard what he had uttered, but I could not help in hoping I misheard him, "Are you certain she was alone?"

He nodded his head vigorously.

"Did she come from above or below?"

He pointed up, "Me go up.  Hungry.  Found elf."

"And you saw no one before her or after her in the stairwell?"

He shook his head, "Elf lock door."

"Why did you not follow?" I insisted.

"Serpent hungry too," he stated this in such a tone I felt as if I was being mocked which displeased me greatly.

"Where were you before you entered the stairwell?" I inquired, curious as to how an elf could have slain so many men without being noticed.

"Hole by serpent.  Me cold."

"There is a pocket in that chamber," Kraciun interjected, "perhaps the commotion woke him, and the elf retreated at the sight of him."

"What did this elf look like?" I pressed the ogre.

"Fire," he tapped his head, "naked," he tapped his chest.

"Are you certain she was naked?" Kraciun injected once more sounding appalled.

I turned towards him with astonishment, "I suggest you step outside to cool your loins as this elf was not here to indulge in the company of men," I uttered with a fair amount of sarcasm.

He scoffed before continuing, "Beast, are you *certain* she wore nothing?"

"She like me," he pulled at a tattered draping only covering a small portion of his lower half.

"If she wore nothing, then those men were killed by someone or something else as she would not have been able to conceal weapons dressed as such," I muttered under my breath.

I placed my hand on the ogre's arm, he recoiled from my touch, and I soon abandoned the gesture.

"He is free to go," I paused, "be sure he is fed."

"Understood," he gestured for the ogre to step out as I remained there, struggling to find the answer that was no closer in my mind.

After several moments, I fled the chamber and the tower in hopes there was some detail outside that was missed. Kraciun along with a few others joined me. We walked towards where the drain exited the tower and only found its cover, lodged forcefully into the ice. There were only so many ways off this island and if not by sea, then she would have already been heading straight for us at Castle Trocair. I refused to believe a fire elf from the north could have survived in such terrain, so I had the men scour the coastline for anything of use. It was not long before I heard one of them calling to me.

"Commander Elgar!" the man shouted through the wind, "Over here!"

The remaining men and I rushed towards the man. As we approached him, I saw he was pointing to something over the edge, "That rope should not be there! The port is only to be accessed from within the tower!"

"Good work," I patted the man on his back, "Now, who is first?"

The men looked startled at my request forcing me to burst out with laughter, "I am only joking men!  Kraciun and I will go, the rest of you meet us down there!"

The men significantly relaxed once they knew their necks were freed of the path that potentially involved a long drop that would be met with a sudden stop.  I grasped the edge firmly before swinging myself out and onto the rope.  The rope was slick from ice clinging to its fibers and cracked at the sudden tension my body provided, but it did not break.  I descended quicker than expected as my grasp struggled to maintain control over the slick surface.  Kraciun appeared to fair better than I as he was lighter with better dexterity.  We reached the bottom and there was only a slender path between the cliff and the icy water's edge.  The port may have been empty now but was it so on the night of?

"Kraciun, when was the last shipment?"

He was silent for several moments, "The ship arrived the eve before the wolf's disappearance."

"And you did not find that suspicious?"

"No," he said firmly, "I controlled the port that night and there were no disruptions."

"Are you certain?" I pressed him further.

"Yes, the cargo was unloaded, and the empty crates returned to the cargo hold prior to its departure the following morning.  Should there have been a stowaway, someone would have seen them."

"Do we know where the vessel was headed?"

"No, we do not."

"How is that possible?"

I began walking down the slender path at the water's edge, unsure of what I was even looking for when I heard him speak again.

"Mercenary vessel," he shrugged, "We've been seeing them more frequently in recent months."

"And that does not strike you as questionable?"

"Aye it does, but Commander, we need supplies to survive."

I nodded knowing all too well the price of survival in this region. I paced near the water's edge in an unaccompanied waltz with the Mar Deigh as my mind was troubled. While I would never know if the elf escaped aboard the vessel or was snuffed out by the inhospitable land, she found herself in, I was confident the wolf remained on the island and in doing so she would have headed directly into the mountains. A dangerous path but one that could be scouted and searched by my men. She will be found.

# Prince Berenger

The castle grounds and city were searched for two full days after Prince Urie's disappearance to no avail. With each passing hour, I grew more and more weary over his well-being, a feeling that was not mutually shared by our eldest brother, Ferand. Since our father's departure from this world to today, Ferand has grown more and more formidable with each passing hour. His hunger for power and control will soon extend past his grasp causing Tuiteam to become a kingdom of ill repute, shaming our bloodline. Just as Urie has disappeared, so had the shapeshifter, Conall. Despite a rigorous search, he has continued to elude us, a fact that disturbs Ferand greatly for a reason unknown to me. While our action with him was limited, he possesses something that Ferand, like our father, believes would be a great asset to us. I am still not convinced. I believe coveting the few that may or may not still exist is a distraction and a costly one. I have no intention of disregarding a direct order to obtain and contain them, but there is little preventing me from continuing the research at one time we were so keen to complete.

Troubled and still not properly rested, I found myself summoned to King Ferand's chambers once more, where upon entering I found him relieving a young maiden of her dress.

I scoffed at the audacity of his summons during such a moment, "Your grace," I growled.

The maiden gasped in surprise, clearly, she was not aware they would have an audience.  As I stepped towards them, I bent down to scoop up her dress before grabbing her arm pulling her away from him.

"You are free to go," I told her and watched her eyes begin to dart between the two of us, "I said go!" I shouted.

She fled the room whimpering like a scolded child as I had just deprived her of potentially her one and only chance to bed a king.  I was not amused at either of their behaviors and just when I heard Ferand about to cast demands upon me, I turned sharply and shoved him violently against one of his bedposts.  My physical strength may have been weakened by my injuries, but I have lost none of my potency.

"If your majesty opts to summon me again only to witness yet another depraved attempt of him freeing another maiden of her virtue," I brought my hand up towards his throat and squeezed just enough that I could hear him gasp for air, "be warned, it will be his last," I growled before releasing him from my grasp and turning away.

"You will address me as befitting of *your* station," he commanded, "and should I wish to have you watch me bed a maiden for whatever need suits me," he stepped towards me clearly flustered, "you shall do so without question."

Without hesitation I rushed towards him, stopping inches from his face and I felt him exhale vigorously. I needed to stop myself from provoking him further. I do not need to like him, but I must follow him, for he is my king now and insolence shall not be tolerated even amongst brothers.

"Very well, *your grace*," I growled, "what is it you wish of me?" I spat.

"You are to arm the troops and make for the Kingdom of Losgadh."

"Your grace, the men are depleted from defending and searching the city," I shook my head, "should we depart now, the hold will be vulnerable to further attack and Conall will potentially escape."

"That's what I'm hoping for," he muttered as he began pulling at the ties of his tunic.

I felt my brow tighten trying to deduce a potential upside to what he is proposing when it came to me.

"You mean to follow him."

He nodded his head, "I have thought over everything carefully and he must know more than he is saying. The attack upon our city appears to have been a ruse for his escape and I believe if found he will lead us to Urie."

"And you believe sending myself and the men to obtain your betrothed will be enough to draw him out?" I questioned.

"Precisely," he stepped towards a large table located on the opposite side of the chamber and placed his hands upon it, "Haxa and a portion of the Jagare will depart with you only to split off here and here," he pointed to two potential locations on a map.  "Haxa has agreed to lower the barrier once they are in range."

"To give the illusion she has left the kingdom," I nodded with understanding.

While my brother has never been a born leader, he was a master at deceit, a fact that has rarely comforted me.

"And what of my men?" I uttered with concern pulling at my vocal cords.

"You will continue onward and bring Princess Rosalyn home," he said confidently, "I dare not trust her well-being to anyone else and Tuiteam needs their Queen now more than ever."

"Understood, I will make the necessary preparations-"

"There is no need," he said abruptly, "the men were given their orders at first light," he looked up at me briefly and smiled, "they are just waiting for their Commander to join them and Berenger, make way towards the sound.  It shall be the safest and quickest route.  A ship will be waiting for you there."

"I will bring her home," I bowed slightly and turned towards the door when a thought was brought forward in my mind, "Haxa," I paused, "are we certain she can be trusted? She was after all walking with the shapeshifter just moments before he was discovered."

He sighed, "We have no choice but to trust her."

"But she was seen with him, and she is one of the only ones who could have unlocked the barrier to the tomb," I argued.

"Should her wish have been to release Conall, she would not have left him in your presence or have cast the barrier that was keeping him here," he blurted out.

I could not help but feel that there was more to Haxa's tale than what was told.  While she had resided in Tuiteam for nearly as long as I could remember, we knew little about her.  She had a way of toying with men, distracting them by pulling a veil over their eyes.  The illusion of her was part of her charm and while the majority of my life we've lived in peace, the times were changing and not just beasts were drawn to our borders.

"Perhaps you are right," I stepped towards the door and pulled it open, "forgive me."

He said nothing, only continued staring at the map that lay before him and we parted in silence.

I quickly returned to my quarters and did what I could to pack little.  For me and my men, this would be no casual stroll through the forest and while the journey would undoubtedly last longer than expected, we could not afford the weight of anything unnecessary.  When I was nearing completion, I called to a passing guard to assist in the donning of my armor.  While at first it felt awkward as I have rarely needed someone's assistance before, but we soon found humor in it.  The laughter felt so freeing that it was not long before our laughter reverberated down the long halls and others joined in.

Most of the men under my command had grown up with me and even though we were not born of the same blood, that did not stop us from behaving like brothers.  The relationship that I had developed with my own brothers was quite different than anything I had with them.  These men would stand shoulder to shoulder with me and charge towards any foe despite the danger.  Even knowing this, I watched them all a bit more closely than I had in the past.  They were heavily taxed by the past few days and while I knew the importance of Princess Rosalyn, I could not help in thinking this would end in disaster.

When we arrived at the castle gate, I noticed most of the men were already saddled and heavily armed, an unsettling sight as I was trying to banish the negative thoughts from my mind.  I made one final round to address the men of the guard towers and the main gate.  King Ferand and I needed this to go as planned, if we had any hope of finding our brother and who was truly behind the attack.  After all, who enters a city only to slink amongst the shadows to obtain nothing more than a view?  The questions were draining life from me and had the coronation concluded as planned, the alliance with Losgadh would be nearly within our reach.  Now, we were several days journey away and the bodies and spirits of the men drained.

I returned to the main gate to find Haxa waiting patiently amongst several members of the Jagare.  They appeared equally as armed as my men, but Haxa appeared quite different.  She was draped in a heavy cloak which concealed much of her body and face, but her hands remained exposed grasping a staff in her long dark fingers.  They were darker than I remembered, nearly blackened now and not as if shadowed, but as if coated in oil.  I found it rather peculiar but forced myself to regain my focus.  Out of all of us, she was the only one who could easily disappear amongst the shadows, a feat in due time she would be forced to employ.

I stepped in their direction, "Haxa, I trust you are well."

"Commander," she appeared to glide next to me and reached an open hand out towards me, "the road is long and there is no room for injured men."

I pulled myself onto a krigshast saddled and waiting for me nearby, pulling me away from her reach, "I have endured worse without your assistance."  I grimaced, "With magic there is always a price and one I am not willing to pay."  I turned to face the gate as her mere presence felt bewitching, "Open the gate!" I commanded.

The large wooden gates opened to a lengthy cobblestone walkway leading towards another gate that remained closed as another security provision.  As the others and I cleared the first gate the second began to open, revealing a wealth of lush greenery found outside the castle's walls.  The intoxicating fragrance pushed away the staleness that had recently consumed our fair city and was now flooding our senses.  When I learned of Ferand's instruction to seek the sound, my initial thought was to lead the troops in a charge until we arrived but something about stepping out towards such beauty made me want to slow down.  This world can be a vile place, but I did not let it have to turn me sour.

We stepped out onto the long stone road that would be the first steps of thousands we would make before we were home again and as we did; I saw and felt the men relax ever so slightly.  Their shoulders fell to a more natural position and the grasps they held upon their weapons no longer appeared to be white knuckled from anxiety and strain.  They were glad to be free of the city, if only for a matter of days.  I, unfortunately, did not share in their delight.  My mind and thoughts were troubled, and my judgment felt clouded over my missing brother.  The city had been searched only to find no sign of the young prince, leaving us to believe he simply vanished.  He knew little of the crown's affairs nor was he in a position to be a threat to anyone, so why take him?

"You appear troubled Commander," Haxa spoke suddenly causing me to jerk at the sound of her voice, "Did I startle you?"

"Only for a moment," I noticed she had not mounted a steed for the journey, "I see you prefer to tire quickly over mounting a beast of burden."

"I never tire," she smirked, "besides, it is easier to slip away when not mounted on a pedestal for all others to see."

"Perhaps," I uttered not willing the conversation to be extended.

She did not respond but continued walking beside me. I got the feeling there was something lingering on the tip of her tongue, waiting for the right time, but it never came.  I took the silence as my chance to toil further over everything that occurred in the last week.  There had not been a moment's peace to be found since our father's passing and I felt my heart sink as I thought of Urie once more.  Whether he had been taken or already dead, his soul may never know peace again.  In the event of his death, I pray that his mother finds him and if not she, then perhaps my love could be a pleasant alternative.  We walked in silence for much of the afternoon before I heard Haxa's voice once more.  Her voice was very near to me but somehow far away, like an echo fading towards the end of a long hall.

*I could give it back to you.*

"Give what back?" I asked.

"Beggin' your pardon Commander," one of the men responded sounding confused, "did you say something?"

I gestured towards him to ignore my previous question and turned slightly towards Haxa over my right shoulder, "Haxa, what do you mean?"

"Forgive me Commander, as I did not utter a word," she replied with a smirk only provoking me.

I rushed my krigshast out and in front of her, stopping her from stepping forward, "I know what I heard," I insisted.

"Perhaps you are mistaken," her smirk grew into a large grin.

"I know what it is I heard!"

Her smile remained just as I began to hear it again, only this time I noticed her lips did not move.

*I could give it back to you.*

Give what back I thought.

*What you had...with her.*

How dare she bring her into this.  She is doing this to toy with me, draw my focus away from something she did not want me to see.  I stared at Haxa trying to understand what was happening.  She was speaking to me, but she was not at the same time.  Somehow, I must have been bewitched by the land or by her and I deeply desired to know how.

*How is not important.*

I felt my eyes grow wide in astonishment.  I am certain I did not utter a word, but she knew exactly what I was thinking.

"Best to carry on, Commander," she pointed the staff towards the road ahead, "for the journey is long and you will soon need your rest."

I returned to walk amongst the troops attempting to keep a fair distance from her when I heard her voice again in my head.

*You loved her.*

I love her still I thought.

*Then let me pluck out the pain and give her back to you.*

This is not real.  No one has the power to bring back the dead.

*I do.  I have been ever watchful of you since she fell lifeless in your arms.  Let me give her back to you.*

She cannot, she is lying to you.  You must shut her out and keep moving.

*If you love her still, why not let me give her back to you?*

Why do you offer me this?  I thought.

*To restore balance.*

But she has been gone too long.

*Does your heart not still yearn for her?  Do you not dream of her loving embrace and her warm body beneath yours?*

Stop this.  You cannot give me what you offer.

*But I can.*

How do I know you are telling me the truth?

*You do not.*

Magic always has a price.

*Aye, that it does.  However, to be with her again, would you not be willing to pay any price?*

What is your price?

*A life for a life.*

Whose life would you take?

*Does it matter?*

Of course, it matters I thought, but then I wondered why it did.  For years I have been grief stricken by her death and nearly driven to take my own life.  For me, there will never be another that could take her place, so what was holding me back?

*Do we have a deal?*

I will need proof you can do what you claim.

*Then name your victim.*

Victim?  What did she mean victim?  I felt struck at the sheer thought that to obtain the proof I desired; I would have to choose someone to die.  The voice came to me again only this time it was preceded by her laughter.

*Yes, your victim shall die but only to rise again.  So, I will say it again, name your victim.*

Demetri.

*Hmmm, how pragmatic of you.*

I turned slightly to glance over my shoulder when I saw a large grin sweep across her face once more, but her eyes were now hidden from me.  She appeared quite relaxed, gliding smoothly along the beaten path, which prompted my curiosity.  In all my years of seeing the wonder of her magic, she always appeared heavily focused when casting.  Seeing her now, suggests that may have all been a ruse and she could have been listening in to our thoughts all along.  A thought that left me most uneasy and to what of her *deal*?  Would she really hold up her end and bring Demetri back and if she did would he be the same as before?  Would she?

We continued onward even as the ever-falling sun was giving way to the night's warm cloak of darkness, and it was time for Haxa and the Jagare to breakaway.  I ordered the remaining men to continue onward before turning and dismounting my krigshast.  When I turned to face them, they were already gone, only leaving faint, rapidly diminishing shadows to be found in their absence.  As I watched their shadows vanish from the land, I felt an uneasiness growing in my belly.  While there was no question, they were the most capable of tracking Conall and detaining him if found, but there was something pulling at my mind and tearing at my thoughts.  Things were about to change, but I did not have the means to know or understand how.

I returned to join my men who, also, were beginning to fade off into the distance.  They were a bit more lighthearted than before as they felt the weight of Haxa and the Jagare's presence lift from their shoulders.  I, too, was soon comforted by their absence and took an active stance at banishing thoughts of them from my mind.  I decided here is where we would make camp.  While the men were appearing more relaxed, they were still drained from the week's endeavors and who could blame them.  I just hope Ferand's plan is executed half as well as he hopes it will.

# Lira

The cage, as they called it, was a large woven sphere made of vines and thorns.  Initially, I did not find this threatening, but once inside, the sphere tightened around me, sealing off the point of entry.  It moved as they moved, prompting further speculation as to their origin and capabilities.  I reached over and snapped one of thorns off, hoping, if magical, the sphere would dissipate once the magic was damaged.  It did not and therefore, was more than likely not magical at all further provoking my curiosity.  However, at the point of breakage, the stem was beginning to bleed.  It was not sending out a stream of crimson as I would be, but a slightly thicker and more translucent substance was now seeping out.  I reached over and broke off another thorn and then another when I felt the cage begin to quake.  The cage projected itself upward towards the treetops as though it were an arrow being released from an unseen bow.  As the sphere rotated slightly and began to free fall back towards the ground, I relaxed my limbs in anticipation of the tumble that would surely follow the impact that never came. Instead, I found myself hovering over a bed of significantly larger thorns and spikes. Had the sphere continued to the point of impact, I would have surely been impaled by them. I studied them carefully for a moment before reaching to clasp another thorn between my fingers, bending it slowly, when I heard Yew speak.

"Why do you wish to hurt my people?" he said sternly.

I could not see him, but his voice carried itself to me with minimal effort suggesting he was nearby.

"That has never been my wish," I paused listening carefully to my surroundings, "but it was you who sentenced me to life in a cage."

"Not life, just time," he paused, "and if that not be your wish, then release him from your grasp."

I felt his voice whisper in my ear but as I turned around, there was nothing. I withdrew my hand from the thorn and felt the cage's rigid grasp soften slightly as if it was a body exhaling a long-held breath. When the thought struck me, they did not just appear treelike in appearance, they were the trees. That is how they were able to close in on me without being seen and how Coille continued to grow over the years without being noticed.

"But how?" I asked soon realizing I may need to provide more context behind such a vague question. "I thought druids and shapeshifters were the only ones to have the power of transfiguration."

"How peculiar," I heard him whisper, "I am curious what you know of shapeshifters to mention them so freely."

"My studies were extensive," I paused, "of course, I am not as youthful as my outward appearance leads people to believe."

When I turned back towards the front of the cage, I found him now within arm's reach, scanning me thoroughly. I did not flinch, but his hard, unrelenting eyes were beginning to make me sweat.

"Of course not," he said smugly, "only man ages nearly as quick as a blade of grass, as I am sure you must know."

"Then you do not age?" I said softly.

"We are not immortals, but our aging process is much different than theirs."

"How so?"

"Well, is not someone curious?" he sneered.

I felt scowl beginning to take over my face which made me appear weak, to which I believe I am not.

"Hmmm," his lips tightened, "you are used to being in control. I can assure you, that will not be the case here."

"What is your fascination with me?" I muttered more as a thought spoken out loud rather than a legitimate question.

The intention made little difference as he responded quickly and sharply, "You treat me as if I am a man after your flesh," he hissed, "I want nothing of it...you give yourself far too much credit," he began circling the cage just shy of the large spikes.

He held out an open hand, palm facing upward, giving the illusion that the unspoken question he was asking was open to my rejection.  Both of us understood, without debate, that this was never the case.

"If I tell you what you wish to know," I glanced up and around at the cage surrounding me, "will you release me from this prison?"

"Perhaps," his expression did not change, and his hand remained open to me.

I extended an open hand towards his, hovering slightly above his, with our palms facing each other.  I was hesitant to grasp his, something in my gut said he already knew too much. In my hesitation, his long slender fingers enclosed around my hand quickly and held it tightly within his.  The sudden touch startled me, but I soon regained my composure.

We remained there in silence for some time when I opted to press him, "I am not the first elf you have seen here recently am I?"

"No," he sighed, "although the others were not so easily detained."

I scoffed just before replaying his words in my mind. He said others.  The odds of finding one elf, banished or otherwise, in Coille would be unusual, but more than one would be nearly impossible.

"Where are they now?" I blurted out just as my other hand was reaching to grasp his arm.

"Some were not what they appeared to be," he released my hand, "one felt remarkably like you."

"What do you mean, *felt*?"

"Ahh, there is that curiosity again," he had a faint grin growing on his face, but it soon disappeared.

"King Edric is seeking wolfs to launch an assault upon Tuiteam."

"And what would make King Edric believe you possessed this knowledge.  Surely, a lorvisad would not keep such valuable information to themselves."

"I was not banished," I spat, "nor could I have been," I added in a much softer tone.

His face turned cold, and the patches around his eyes darkened, "Of course not, for that you would have been marked."

"That would require me to be an elf of Lamprog and as you can clearly see I was birthed in Tiene," I said with a touch more sarcasm than intended, but it did not appear to alter his course in any way.  I continued hoping that my twisted version of the truth would be enough for him to give me the information I now desired, "My kin was taken," I lowered my head slightly, taking my eyes out of his view, "I left willingly to find him."

"And did you?"

"Aye, I believe I have.  That is why I must be going, before he is lost to me for the second time."  I paused thinking carefully over what would be my next request as each came with a price, "Tell me of the one like me."

"Are you not familiar with those like yourself?" he uttered in such a tone, clearly appearing appalled by my request.

"You said one *felt* remarkably like me, what did you mean?" I added.

"Not elven," he said blatantly.

Resisting the urge to snap at him, I muttered, "I take it you have not encountered many elves in your time."

"While that may be true," he lurched forward grasping my neck and was beginning to squeeze, "they all possess magic or rather the magic possesses them.  A gift that you have clearly been denied."

I felt my blood beginning to boil and my heart racing.

"Either release me or execute me, but if you continue to toy with me," I gasped, "I assure you that you that today will be your last," I spat.

His grip relaxed and he pulled his hand away, "Such ferocity from a creature locked away in a cage," he paused, "but I suppose had I been locked away twice in the last fortnight I, too, may be difficult to control."

I inhaled and exhaled heavily, attempting to regain what breath I had lost when I opted to press him again, "What is it you believe you know?"

"This is a ruse, a clever one, but a ruse no less," his voice remained steady, and his body did not shift from its place, "Let us not confuse ourselves as we both know you are not elven, but merely humanoid."

I found myself irritated with his accusation no matter how founded it may have been, "What be your plan for me?"

He smiled and clasped his hands together just out in front of his chest, "Eira, I am one of the forest kind, and have no desire to keep you here," he sighed, "In fact, I would like nothing more than for you to leave this place."

"Then why detain me?"

"For what you know of course," he sounded surprised.

"What makes you certain that any knowledge I may possess is worth the risk?"

"Nothing is by coincidence," he whispered, "and the risk you believe you pose does not frighten us."

"And what of information I wish to know?"

"Should you choose to be civilized, you may walk among us but know your time here is running out."

I accepted his offer and nodded quickly just before watching the cage withdraw itself into the ground, where it disappeared without a trace.

"But how?" I muttered.

"You are much more inquisitive than the last one," he turned and lowered himself towards the ground, "but he never gave up looking for you."

Bryn.

I rushed towards him and knelt before him, "He was here? You physically saw him here? When? Was he alright?" I blurted the inquisitions at him like a volley of arrows not realizing I have not given him a chance to reply before releasing the next one from my lips.

"Calm yourself," he placed his hands in a triangular shape, palms outward, just before me and began tracing an unseen pattern.

I watched him carefully, unsure as to the purpose behind the gesture, then he stopped.

"The kin you spoke of that assisted you in bartering passage, is he, too, like you?" he spoke softly in a monotone voice.

"Not in the least," I said, frankly.

"And yet you trusted him?"

"Aye, I did, he presented the only option that gave me a chance of leaving the tower alive, so I took it."

"Where is he now?"

"He was aboard the vessel when it sank in the night."

"But yet, you survived?" he sounded confused.

"Call it an act of the gods, I care not," I dismissed rehashing over the questions that had been nagging me since I arrived on shore.  "What of the man you spoke of?"

"He was captured in the marsh many moons ago," he paused, "Did this elf say why he was helping you?"

"No, I pressed him for the information, but there was not time for storytelling.  Do you know where he is now?"

"Aye, he was being detained within Tuiteam's walls, presumably to be studied, but the minds of men are easily manipulated."

I felt my heart sink, so the message he sent was a trap. A ploy to lure me elsewhere while he was locked away in a prison.

"How do you know of such things?" I said softly.

"He stayed with us for some time, we learned from each other, cared for each other," he paused and held out a hand once more for me to take, "here you, too, could live peacefully should you desire it."

I heard Bryn's words echo in my mind; you must not believe his lies. Could this have been the man he spoke of?

"What makes you believe you could offer such a gift?"

"Our borders are well protected, at least for now, and with any good fortune your kin shall return to us."

"How can you be certain of this?"

"I know things that you do not," he said abruptly, "now, please calm yourself or that wound will never fully heal."

"How did you-"

"That, too, is not important," he paused, "Tell me more of the elf from the tower."

I was confused by the sudden turn in conversation back to Drayk. What was it about this one elf that fascinated him so?

"He was an elf from Lamprog with long creamy locks and bright eyes, cloaked heavily in black. He was nimble, nearly unseen by all including myself, yet had little magical skill. I know naught else."

"Yet somehow, he knew you were there and had the skill to assist you in escaping the tower, how peculiar?" he paused and began rubbing his temples, "Is there naught else you can remember?"

I shook my head as I was afraid he would catch the lie in my voice had he heard it and I was oddly protective of Drayk.  Something about him, a feeling I got when I was around him that he did not wish others to know of him as if he was something ill-fated or forbidden.  He continued rubbing his temples for several moments in silence as if concentrating heavily on something I could not see or hear, then he spoke again.

"Tell me of the tower," he demanded.

"It was bone-chilling and smelled of death-"

"No," he stopped me, "tell me of what you found within."

"There were foul creatures and dying men inside," I paused, "at least from what I could see.  I was terribly weak at the time."

"No men?" he glanced up in surprise.

"None that I can recall in the tower, but we fled in the wee morning hours while all was silent."  I stopped, "Is this really what you wish to know?"

"There is a great deal more I would wish to learn from you," he placed a hand on my shoulder, "but I fear you will not linger here willingly."

My eyes widened, "You shall not keep me here," I stood quickly and began backing away from him, "I need to find him."

He rose to his knees but did not budge further, "If you would only stay, I assure you that you will see him again," he held his hands up in that same triangular shape.

"Your promises mean naught," I spat, "you abandoned my kin to die in King Baylon's prison and yet, you promise me a life of peace."

"He was not abandoned by me or anyone here," his voice rose, "but we had to wait for an opportunity to enter the city."

He stood and stepped towards me, arms extended, and I felt my heart rate slow.  I suddenly felt myself relax, if but slightly, but how?

"An accord was struck to enter the city while the barrier was down and provided the warlock and *my* kin are as skilled as I believe them to be, he should already be free of his prison."

"How does a warlock know of his presence in Tuiteam?" I asked puzzled at the mere suggestion that our existence was no longer that of legend.

His arms dropped suddenly and while I still felt relief it was not as strong as it once was, "For without her, they would not have been able to keep him confined for as long as they have."

The Bryn I knew was strong, but Yew made it sound like he could break down walls with his bare hands.  That was not the Bryn I knew, and it told me there was more than just a few years of life that I had missed.

"Forgive me, I must go to him," I said just before turning to be greeted by two Skogar I did not even know were there.  I turned my head slightly, but I had no intention of looking back at him, "Have you never loved someone?  Felt the need to be near someone even though it may be dangerous for you?"

"Should you choose to leave now," he sighed, "I assure you there will be more suffering before the end."

"That is a chance I must take, for my life is nothing without him."

I turned my attention back towards the Skogar standing in front of me and shoved them violently back, taking them both by surprise.  Yew did not utter a sound, but I felt his eyes watching me as my pace began to quicken.  When I was nearly out of sight, I changed, adding a sudden burst to my speed and my coat quickly darkened to mask myself against the dark forest floor.  If nothing else, I hope my transition gave him the satisfaction that he appeared to crave.

As I fled their inner sanctum, the darker the forest had become, reminding how late the hour had become.  While my time with the Skogar had been brief, it flowed together in a series of riddles and contradictions that devoured time itself.  None of which I had time to decipher the meaning behind, Bryn was near.  I do not know if it be my imagination or something else, but I could feel him somehow.  With each step towards Tuiteam, I felt something within me growing stronger.  A hunger that turned into an ache, tearing at my insides, and beseeching me to give in to it.  This sensation drove me to rush towards the castle with no regard for the danger that may lay nearby or the exhaustion that I would soon feel.

Many hours had passed, and my legs were beginning to burn from all the miles I had traveled.  I could not stop to rest now.  The path ahead would be riddled with thorns and sacrifices, all of which would be worth it for us to be together again.  If there was even a chance, he had made it out alive, I had to try.  After laying a great distance between myself and them, I witnessed the phenomenon that was the wall of thorns.  It was not unlike the cage but much larger.  I, now, understood what Yew meant when he said they are well protected.  It would have taken several men, one stacked upon another to reach the top and only small openings were found throughout, presumably to permit small plants and animals to enter or flee if necessary.  There was nothing large enough for me to slip in my present form or otherwise.  However, the moonlight crept its way through, giving me the understanding that if I continued to flee carelessly, I would surely be seen as what lay beyond this barrier was not nearly as secluded as what was housed within.

Quickly changing back to my elven form, I was consumed by the exhaustion and fell towards the forest floor, panting.  You must get up.  You must keep moving.  I brought myself back from the brink and stood, searching the forest floor for any sign of water.  I soon found water trickling down a nearby tree trunk and carefully cupped my hands beneath it to catch it.  Lapping up all I could, for the journey was far from over, I instantly felt better.  I returned my attention towards the wall of thorns.  I believe it could be scaled but not without permitting the thorns to have a taste first.  I could not see a way around and time was slipping away.  I dare not rush towards

Tuiteam in the light, for I would surely be seen, so I must continue onward.

Feeling my way through the thorns and vines I began to make my way towards the top, in hopes there would be a clearer view of the path ahead from there.  Each step further strained my already weakened body, and my arms and legs were quickly becoming riddled with puncture wounds from the thorns.  Just another scratch I had to tell myself to keep moving.  Well, it may have started that way at first, but as I neared the top, the moonlight shone in upon me to reveal dark crimson streaks now streaming down my arms and parts of my legs.  I did not toil over them long, in less than a day they would be gone again and no more than a memory of what was necessary to bring us together again.

Laying down along the wall permitted me to blend in slightly more so than being perched up for all to see as I needed to scan everything near the wall and out into a clearing that lay ahead.  The forest was still alarmingly quiet, but I could see a pack of krigshastar grazing ahead.  Several of them were alerted to my presence and were carefully watching me from afar.  All appeared as it should and I slowly lowered myself over the other side, opting to jump the remaining distance rather than be raked over the thorns any longer.  I landed with cat-like precision and remained crouched scanning for any change.  There was nothing.  Using the tree line as a guide, I ventured out into the clearing.  The krigshastar were skittish at first, but after realizing they were not going to be my next meal, they went on with their very early morning graze.

The clearing was lush with greenery and filled with a freshness that was not found inside Coille forest.  The moss and soil found previously beneath my feet had been replaced by grass and I was reminded of the time I found Bryn.  This may have been his birthplace, but his home would always be with me.  I took in as much as my lungs could hold and pressed onward knowing I would not find peace until he was found.

With the thought of the Jagare potentially nearby I could not risk changing again, but there was a great distance I needed to cover.  I began sprinting to the north, stopping periodically to further scan the unfamiliar surroundings before pressing onward.  The light was beginning to grow in the distance, and I knew daybreak was near.  I had clearly been running longer than I anticipated when I heard it.  A man's voice, soft and barely audible at first, but quickly growing louder.  He was breathing heavily between words, but I could clearly hear him speaking to himself or someone else.

*It is not safe here.  Must keep moving.*

I thought briefly of conversation with Yew and instinctively I thought to myself, perhaps this could be him, it must be him, please keep going.  I will follow your voice and I will find you.  Just keep going.

*It is you.  Is it really you?*

The man's voice changed, almost sounding surprised.  He heard me, but how?  I was certain I did not utter a sound.

*Of course, I heard you.*

I have been searching for you for so long.  I thought.

*And I you.  I sense that you are near.*

I stopped for a moment, to listen for his footsteps, when I heard them in the east. He was treading through a waterway and the rocks were cracking beneath his thunderous steps. I quickly pivoted and raced in that direction. I am almost to you. Please stay there.

*Find the stream and follow it, for there you shall find me.*

My pace quickened, tearing what little breath I kept within my lungs out in a painful display. I reached the stream and turned sharply towards the direction I last heard him. His breathing has settled to a more natural rhythm and all I could hear now was the breaking of water against his skin.

*I can feel you now and smell you. You are bleeding.*

None of that matters now.

I rushed down the stream to a slight opening where the water pooled. There was a man wading in the water. His hair was long and twirled into wind braids that I desperately wanted to run my fingers through. His shoulders were broader than I remembered, and he smelled different to me, but a welcome different. I stood there panting for several moments, watching him, when I noticed he was starting to turn towards me.

Please do not. I am afraid if you do it will all be a dream and this pool shall become my grave.

*I assure you I am no dream.*

I stepped towards him and slid myself into the water behind him and watched his body quiver as the ripples collided with his lower back. I felt my breathing change, as did his, assured that at any moment he would be taken from me again.

His heart was pounding loudly like a drum and quickening in tempo.  My heart quickly met his rhythm and while something inside me said I should wait, I could not any longer.  I reached up to pull his damp hair away from his shoulders when I felt him flinch.  It hurt me to see and feel him recoil at my touch and my heart broke a little over what I knew I may never understand.  I closed my eyes before placing my cheek against his shoulder and he began to relax underneath my touch.  Nearly everything about him felt different and I wondered if I, too, felt different to him.

*For months, I searched for you but found nothing.*

His thought broke off, but I refused to open my eyes, afraid he would vanish if I did, when I felt him turn towards me.

*I will not vanish unless you send me away.*

The thought of me ever sending him away broke the hold the moment had on me, and my eyes opened to him.  This was not Bryn.

# Conall

After fleeing the woman's home, I sought refuge in an
abandoned hovel near the outskirts of the city.  While
remaining there unseen was not without difficulty, I needed
somewhere to rest during the waking hours to prepare me for
the countless hours I would need to spend scouring the city for
an exit after nightfall.  True to his word, there was no stone in
the city that was left unturned as the search continued for the
lost prince.  Watching the royal guard scurry about throughout
the city made the thought of being rid of this place seem
terribly far out of reach.  While I took no pleasure in ridding
Tuiteam of a few more of its guards, the ever-changing
wardrobe they provided was invaluable to remaining
concealed.  In my first night there I took down no less than five
and by the second night more than twenty, all while remaining
as I was.  The livestock and milk found at a small farm nearby

provided me with the strength I needed to take on such a force. I would not have been able to survive without it.

By the morning of the third day, I noticed a significant portion of the royal guard and the Jagare had fled the city, along with Commander Berenger. While their destination was unclear to me, they were heavily armed, and I could feel the warlock's magic fading from the castle. Either she had perished, which was highly unlikely, or she was fleeing the city. Best be her wish that the Skogar locate her first, for if I do, there will be nothing left of her to find. Having had time to dwindle over her actions in the castle, I, now, know that she had no intention of helping me escape, but as to the ruse or her agreement with the Skogar, I know naught as to the why. Coille borders Tuiteam to the south but has never posed a threat to them or anyone else for that matter. They are forest kind and to willfully align themselves with a warlock, the reward or threat must have been great. While this interested me greatly, I was reminded that one shapeshifter could not change the fate of man, nor should he. My intent should only be to inform Yew of Haxa's betrayal and then to seek out the maiden shapeshifter with hair of fire, for she was the key all would soon be seeking.

As the sun was setting, I donned the royal guard's armor and made my way towards a cluster of men that were gathering for the night's patrol. As per their way, one of the men continually barked orders at the remaining and those orders were to be followed without question. I casually fell in line but stayed near the outside in hopes it would be less conspicuous when I broke away from the pack. I listened carefully to his orders, not because I had intention of following them, but as a gauge for where the men would be and when. Thus, giving me the opportunity to disappear into the night. Once far enough outside of the walls, I could change to put more ground between us without them even realizing they were looking for me. The men know naught of what I am, nor my appearance and this omission would be my advantage.

The men began filing through a secondary and more secluded opening in the wall near the south side. It was almost too perfect. I mimicked their behavior and marched through the gate, out into the world for the first time in months. While it was intoxicating and had it not been for the armed soldiers around me, I had stopped just to breathe it all in, instead I kept moving. We were soon divided into three separate groupings, each of which were instructed towards a different location that they were to scout. I rushed to be included with the men bound for the coastline as this would have been the easiest to disappear in. I meshed with them better than I had anticipated and even though the other men were squabbling and bickering amongst themselves, I found myself lost in the last moments of the setting sun. It is easy to forget the light when you never see it, but when it is there, it is almost impossible to ignore. The beauty of the sun wrapped in rings of rust and amber, made me think of her once more. Perhaps it was all a ruse to keep me bound to them or bound to the hope of something more...or perhaps all of it means nothing. For so long I have searched and killed in the name of survival, but I never thought to ask myself what am I fighting for?

A man placed a hand on my shoulder, "Peaceful looking, is it not?"

"Aye, that it is," I brushed away the remnants of tears I did not even know were there and kept moving.

I sensed he wanted to say something more as he remained walking at my side, but I could not bring myself to entertain the quiet yearnings of this man. We walked together for some time when a fork appeared to us in the road, one path lead towards the coast and the other down a long dense patch of forest. While our feet had carried us nearly a thousand paces from the castle walls, it still appeared too near for the throngs of Skogar to lie in wait. This is where I would make my escape. Slowing my pace, I watched as most of the other guards pressed onward, relatively unconcerned by my lack of enthusiasm for the hunt that was at hand. Seemed rather odd that so many people would be swayed by a few to hunt another humanoid over minute differences, but that was the way of man. They believe anything that is unlike their own should be contained or worse, eradicated, for their sheer pleasure. It was appalling and made my insides turn at the thought I offered my protection to them. How could I have been so foolish?

Stopping just shy of the tree line, I took those last few moments to watch the ever-setting sun sink into the horizon only to be met with the moon's ever powerful and stunning glow. It cast rays of silvery blue light down upon all within its wake and I knew then it was my time to go. The days appear longer in this part of the world, and I would need every moment the night would spare if I were to make it to the Skogar before dawn.

Pivoting away from the men, I slipped into the darkness and removed the boots for better traction.  I knew I could not run in this armor for with each step the metal would slide together creating an unpleasant noise that could easily be heard from afar.  Once I was a few hundred paces from the others, I removed the remaining portions of the armor, apart from a pair of leather breeches, and scanned the darkness for anything unwelcome.  While the men did not appear to be near, the noise they created broke through the tree line and raced across the clearings as if it were a toxic plague attempting to devour all pleasantness in its path.  I struggled to sift through the chaotic sounds to find the underlying ones that may present danger, I was met with resistance.  I remained as I was before breaking off into a jog until I was certain there was no one nearby.

I had spent a significant part of my life in the forests of Coille, both in my youth and recently, and above anywhere else this was my home.  While the forest between there and Tuiteam had clearly changed recently, I was able to maneuver throughout with minimal difficulty.  After traveling another few hundred paces, I slowed to get a better listen.  If someone had been following me, I could not hear them now and they were clearly lost in the foliage.

Without breaking stride, I felt the heat rush over me and my body change.  My speed increased and my vision became more acute.  I was well prepared for the jaunt towards the inner sanctum and while man would have tired quickly from several miles of running, I would not.  The wind combed its slender fingers through my blackened fur, gently tickling my skin and the warmth from the afternoon sun had rapidly conceded to the coolness of the night.  The temperature change soothed my scorching flesh as I continued racing against the dawn.  Hours later, with dawn approaching, I heard something in the distance.  It was not moving as quickly as I, but it was quite nimble on foot as its steps were barely audible to me.

I thought to myself, it is not safe here.  Must keep moving.

The voice spoke back to me.  *Please keep going.  I will follow your voice and I will find you.  Just keep going.*

It was a woman, and she could hear me plainly without uttering a sound.  It was her; I was sure of it.

It is you.  Is it really you?  I asked sounding more surprised than I intended.

She was toiling over this question in her mind, unsure how I heard her.  Perhaps she had been alone longer than I knew or never taught to understand this gift.

Of course, I heard you.

*I have been searching for you for so long.*  She sounded relieved.

And I you.  I sense that you are near.

I felt that she was alarmingly near, maybe a few hundred paces or less away from me when I heard her ask me to stay where I was.  I was more than willing to abide by her wishes.  I slowed my pace to nearly a stop just steps inside a stream that opened into a pool nearby and listened for her. Her pace was quickening, and her breathing strained on top of a nearly exhausted body, she was bleeding. I could smell it growing stronger with each step she took. I stepped into the pool and lowered myself into the soothing liquid. Its cool touch relaxed my muscles and cleansed me of the sweat and filth that had clung to me from my jaunt here. I dipped fully in and let the water run through my tangled locks and cling to my tired body. I had just risen out of the pool when I heard her breathing several feet behind me. I could hear her panting and I felt my heart beginning to race. I needed to see that she was real, and I had not imagined her. I began to turn slowly when I heard her speak again.

*Please do not. I am afraid if you do, it will all be a dream and this pool shall become my grave.*

I assure you I am no dream.

I respected her wishes and did not turn towards her but soon felt the water rippling towards me. She had slipped into the water behind me and the thought of her being so close to me sent chills racing up my spine. Just when I thought I would have time to adjust to her being near to me, I felt her hands brush my back and grasp my hair in her hands, I flinched in surprise. Other than the woman in the city, I have not been lovingly touched by someone in nearly a century. I tried not to utter my unease to her, but her willingness to find and be near me surprises me. She placed her cheek upon my back and the rush the connection gave me seared through me like flames being pushed across a field from a high wind. While my heart rate was beginning to return to normal, I knew I had to see her for myself.

For months, I searched for you but found nothing I broke off.

I felt her eyes tighten against my skin, prompting me to turn towards her.  Her hair was vibrant and full of twists and curls that draped over her blushing cheeks and sun-kissed skin. When I turned her hands fell upon my chest and clung to me in a way I had never felt before.  She was afraid I was not real but not of me.  Her hands were small and soft, unlike mine, and they, too, sent a surge of heat through me.

I will not vanish unless you send me away, I thought.

Something about this broke the hold she had on the moment, and her eyes opened to me, quickly widening in surprise.

"Who are you?" she said softly as she began to pull her hands away.

I reached for her and clasped one of her hands in mine, willing her to stay, "Please do not go, I am not of whom you expected, am I?"

She shook her head and continued to pull away from me.

"Who did you expect to find while racing through Coille just before dawn?"

"Bryn, he is like me...well, like," she was stumbling over her words, and I could not tell if she was nervous or just baffled that there are others out there in the world like her.

"Us, like us?"

"But how?  I believed we were all alone in this world."

I smiled, if but briefly unsure what to say.  I relaxed my grip when I was confident, she was not going to flee from me, but she was now looking upon me carefully.

*Bryn is lost to me once more.*  Her thoughts were saddened and muffled together in a swirl of questions accompanied by what felt like a broken heart.

"This Bryn is he your-" I began to swallow the words that pained me so, but it was not without difficulty.

She turned towards me, "No, but he is the closest thing I have to family left in this world."

"Then I will help you find him," I said surprising even myself, "but we must go and quickly."

While there was a hope, I might find someone to love this broken body and spirit of mine, it probably was not her and this would all soon fade away into a distant memory.  I released her hand from mine before pulling myself out of the pool to let the water trickle down my body before ringing the excess from my long locks.  When I turned towards her, I found that she was watching me with increasing curiosity.  Her gaze may have started at my long locks and broad shoulders, but I soon found her eyes walking their way down my body.  While she was not expecting me to turn when I did, she made no attempts to hide that fact she was interested in more than just my words.

*Who is this man?*

"I am called Conall."

I crouched down and reached for her, ever hopeful she would take my hands in hers, permitting me the chance to feel the fire between us once more.  I had never felt that with anyone before and the touch, the rush it provided, was almost too much.  It provoked something primal in me, that was difficult to control, but I did not want it to stop.  It made me wonder if she felt what I did and that is what provoked her curiosity or was there something there that was deliberately left untold.  She stepped towards me, and I cupped some water in my hands before gliding them gently over her arms, watching the blood paint the surface of the pool around her.  At first, she seemed surprised but then she smiled at me, if but briefly.

"Eira, they call me Eira," her eyes darted towards mine and then away again, "and thank you.  I had nearly forgotten about them."

"It seems your body already had forgotten," I smiled showing her the scraps were all but gone once the blood had been washed away.

A faint giggle escaped her, "One of the few benefits of being what we are."

She reached for me, causing my heart to leap with anticipation, and I could not stop myself from wrapping my arms around her while pulling her from the pool.  The leather she had been wearing clung to her body, as my breeches did to mine, making it easier for the heat between us to grow and further stroking that primal urge.  I had held several others before her, but none of them made me burn for them as she did by no more than her mere presence.  I leaned my face towards hers, ever hopeful that her lips would find mine when I felt a piercing pain in my lower back.  My eyes widened in surprise and in turn causing hers to widen as well.  Her eyes fell downward towards my abdomen when I felt a second pain tear through my right thigh causing me to clench my teeth in pain, but I did not utter a sound.  Her eyes returned to me, weary and afraid.

I hastily pulled her towards me and pressed my lips to hers in a desperate attempt to hold onto that feeling before it was all too late.  Her lips were warm and soft, like her hands, and connected with mine as if they were made only to be met with my lips.  Our bodies melted together, and I soon felt her hands upon my face, caressing my skin softly.  Her kiss was a kiss of life, and I felt my darkened soul awaken in her embrace.  My heart felt heavy at the thought of sending her away, but she must not stay.  They could not have her.

You must go.  They are going to try to take me soon.

*No, I will not leave you here.*  Her thought was desperate.

Death would be a welcome end to all my suffering.  Please go now.

*I will find you again.*

I broke off the kiss and turned sharply, making sure she was shielded from the unseen assailant long enough to get away.  When I heard the brush behind me bend to her passing, I felt safe enough to look down at what pierced my flesh and found two arrows.  I quickly pulled the one through and broke the other off as I did not have time to remove it properly.

When I released what was left of them, I heard a faint whistling sound that was growing louder.  There were more coming.

I leapt towards the far side of the pool and in hopes they would follow my lead, giving her some time.  I soon found the Jagare had surrounded me, provoking the change.  The arrows continued to fly with several embedding themselves into my flesh and I felt weakened by them more so than before.  They must have been etched in poison of some sort and I would not have long to react before I would need to flee or become their prisoner once more.  I tore through the men, leaving their bodies partially devoured or thrown aside in pieces, when I heard her gasp.  The sound echoed through the forest and to me with remarkable speed.  However, nothing followed.  I turned and fled in her direction forgoing my battle with the Jagare, at least for the time being.  When I had just broken through the tree line a blaring high-pitched sound burned through my mind causing me to change back suddenly and fall crippled towards the ground.  It felt louder than anything I had ever heard and while I wanted to focus on the source, I could not bear to move.  I lay there paralyzed by the pain when I saw her long dark slender legs come into view.  It was Haxa.  I glared at her, unable to speak.

"Conall," she glanced down at me and grinned, "you do not look well at all."

She signaled to the remaining Jagare, "Bind him and cage him," her eyes quickly darted towards me and then back towards them, "should you resist, I will not be as kind next time."

The sound ceased and I sat up slowly, trying to listen for Eira, but my ears were still ringing from the sound when I faintly heard Haxa speak to the Jagare again.

"And bring her to me," she paused, "King Ferand will want to know why this one interested him so."

"She is just an elf," I croaked, "nothing more than a vessel to warm my bed at night."

I felt the lie sting as it exited my body.  Thankfully, I already looked slightly distraught, so she did not take notice.

"Is that so?" she raised an eyebrow, "Then perhaps King Ferand might wish to warm his bed with her.  She is quite stunning after all."

A growl escaped me, Haxa did not move, but the Jagare wasted no time binding my legs and arms.  To which I changed once more, shattering my bindings before lurching forward to snap at Haxa, only to find I was just out of reach when I heard that sound again.  Louder at first this time, forcing me back towards the ground where I cowered in pain.

"You heart has betrayed you, Conall," the sound stopped as she reached towards me and ran her fingers across my lips, "for that kiss was not that of lovers."

I snapped my teeth at her just before the men gagged me and threw me into a large metal cage, taking no care to remove the remaining arrows that were still lodged within my flesh.  Those broke off at several points, some above the skin and some below.  While I heal quick quickly, those may never fully heal until the remnants of the shafts have been removed, something that I would need to tend to I am sure or forever be crippled by them.  I searched my surroundings for her, but I saw nothing.  Just as I began to believe we were lost to each other once more; I heard her voice speak to me and I had hope once more.

# Unknown

Hidden high and out of sight, I watched the maiden with hair of fire slow her pace and rush towards a nearby stream.  She changed directions without warning, but moved with precision, as if guided by an unseen map.  I hastily raced through the treetops, jumping from branch to branch, when I heard her stop.  There was someone wading in the pool found at the base of the stream.  I did not recognize this man, but she moved towards him as if he were known to her.  They did not speak, and the only sound heard was that was the stream flowing nearby.  I watched them carefully for several moments when I took notice of lingering shadows across the clearing, not unlike my own.  They were not fully visible to me, but had they been and the two wading would have been alerted to their presence as well.  My attention returned to her only to find her clinging to him but still no words were exchanged.  My interest was piqued, and I continued watching them with growing curiosity.  As he turned towards her, she spoke for the first time.  Their words muffled, but the tone suggested this man was not who she had been expecting. The exchange was brief but as the man exited the pool, he reached for her giving me a clear shot of his battered face and undeniably elven ears.  From what I could see, he was unmarked, and it prompted the question, what was he doing in Coille?

She stepped towards him without fear or distrust and as I watched him lovingly tend to her, giving me the sense there was more between the two of them than we were witnessing. He stood then in one swift motion lifted her from the pool and into his arms.  I waited patiently for the two to speak again when the moment was rudely interrupted by nearby shadows casting arrows towards them, embedding two within him. What happened next was not what I expected.  He drew her near and placed his lips to hers and while it may have been sudden, it was unlike any I had seen before.

He released her, shielding her from the volley of arrows that were being cast their way, just before I heard her leap into the forest nearby.  In order to catch up to her, I could not linger long, but I had to know why he would choose to stay over fleeing towards the forest with her.  Then I saw him change into a beast and I knew then he was like her.  He stayed to protect her and, in that moment, where he stayed, I knew I must go.  I rushed towards her, quickly swinging from branch to branch until I dropped down in front of her.  She gasped and I hastily stepped towards her to place my hand over her mouth, silencing her from all nearby.  Had I waited a few more moments to detain her or fallen on top of her, I would have been grappling with a beast versus a beautiful maiden.      My sudden intrusion into her path, clearly, caught her off guard, but in the moments to follow I saw the glimmer of recognition return to her face.  She was attempting to mumble into my hand when I gestured for her silence and pointed towards the treetops.  Initially she appeared resistant to my suggestion, but as I saw the Jagare approaching from behind her there was little choice.  I withdrew my blades and in a symphony of slashes, I relieved the men of their heads.  There soon would be more to follow.  When I turned back towards her, I found she had heeded my instruction and fled up into the tallest tree.  While there was no time to hide the dead, I took a moment to relieve them of what I could and ventured up after her.

Once high and out of sight, we listened and waited for any change.  I have had encounters with the Jagare before, but this time something was different.  There was a woman with them and just like he, she was not as she appeared to be.  Cloaked in mystery, we watched her step into the forest to find the dead Jagare.  She was not pleased.  She began searching the ground for any sign of the young maiden, when she soon employed reinforcements to join her in her search.  Perhaps we had bested her this round and while I knew we could not remain here, should we choose to move now, we would surely be seen.  The woman may not have lingered here long, the Jagare appeared to search for quite some time after their initial assault, leaving us as gargoyles perched in the treetops.

We sat there with our backs hugging the tree's trunk until early midday had approached, when all had fled the forest floor. We shifted against the tree's trunk for the first time in hours, allowing our legs a moment to relax before we made the climb across the tree's branches to bring the clearing back into view. The clearing was as empty as the forest's floor, and I felt it was safe enough to lower ourselves back towards the ground. Landing at the base of the tree, we remained close together while crouched in silence. Knowing our voices could be carried through the forest if we were not careful, we could not risk speaking just yet for fear of being discovered. Once the area had been scanned and we were certain the Jagare had remained there no longer, we stood and stepped out towards the stream. I took the time to drink my fill as did she before we donned the cloaks of the dead Jagare and stepped off.

"I have so many questions," she said softly.

"As do I," I responded, "but I assure you that the answers would not comfort you."

"No, I suppose not," she muttered while dipping her toes in the cool stream, "but something is pulling at me, demanding to know."

"Then perhaps your body is misleading you," I paused, "for there is nothing about me worth knowing."

"But there is so much I would like to know," she blurted out clearly louder than she intended as she covered her mouth just as the words exited through them.

"The means of knowing what I know comes at a price, so let us leave it as I exist and therefore I am."

I turned away from her and began heading north.  If we would run, we could probably make it just after nightfall, but it may not be the wisest of courses.

"Where are you going?" she asked as she grabbed my wrist, stopping me from moving forward.

"Castle Tuiteam," I turned to press onward, but her hand would not release me.

"Why?"

I stared down at her hand upon my wrist and wondered what it would be like if I had never sought the wilds all those years ago.  Could there have been someone like her waiting for me each night to share in the joys of the changing seasons, to laugh with, warm my bed each night and birth my children.  However, these things were never meant for me, casting that hope and warmth aside was all I could do now, and I tore my arm away from her grasp just before walking away.

"For you to see how the story ends."

I kept walking and soon felt her rush up beside me.

"He's going to die, is he not?" I heard her voice break.

"Perhaps," I shrugged, "it's a wonder he has survived as long as he has."

"I cannot let him die," she whispered softly.

"You say that as if there was a choice," I felt my brow tighten at her child-like understanding.

"Is there not?" she said sounding hopeful, but hope is not my style.

"The only choice we have is permitting there to be one body or two," I said, frankly.

"Then why venture there at all if all hope is lost?"

"Call it an act of my own curiosity or perhaps to fulfill an oath previously forgotten, I care not."

"Why do you do that?" she stepped in front of me forcing me to stop suddenly or risk colliding with her.

"Do what?" I sidestepped her and kept walking.

"Never let anyone in," she paused, "What are you afraid of?"

"Nothing," I said sternly, "I fear nothing."

For the most part that was true, as I could not be who I was if I had been.  I heard her swallow hard, as if choked by my words or by her own fear growing up inside her.

"We must avoid the clearings and remain in the forest for cover," I gestured for her to follow, "this is the more difficult path, but perhaps this will permit us to remain unseen."

"And what of our arrival there, how do you intend to enter the city unseen?"

"There is an escape tunnel hidden carefully on the coastal side of the castle, it is there we shall enter."

"And your certain of this?" she sounded concerned.

"Aye, that I am," I paused, "while the entrance remains unguarded, it would be best to enter after nightfall."

"Where does it lead?"

"Into the belly of the beast," I grinned.

"Then we must hurry for the daylight is nearly spent," her pace quickened.

"Calm yourself," I held an arm out that would have knocked her off her feet had she stepped into a running pace, "for there is still time."

"Perhaps you shall remain calm, but for me, I know what lies in wait for him."

"If you choose to seek your vengeance now," I gestured forth, "then go forth and claim your prize," I added sarcastically.

She frowned, clearly displeased with the sudden use of sarcasm.

"Why not follow them and take him in the night?"

She was plotting now, does her curiosity never cease?

"For the woman, the Jagare keep in their company is not just any woman," I spoke harshly, feeling annoyed by her questions.

She fell silent and had it not been for the sound of her footsteps striking numerous twigs and leaves on the forest floor, I would have assumed she had left my company. We spent hours as we were, treading through the many twists and turns that were found throughout Coille, when we stopped several kilometers short of the castle. The sun had fallen in the sky, and I knew we would both need to rest before entering the tunnel. While Tuiteam is not filled with depraved beasts lurking about, it is filled with men, several hundred thousand of them to be more specific. All of which would be on the lookout for the man she sought by the stream and making them even more drawn to the curious beauty that was now at my side. We needed to slip in unseen.

"We will rest here for now and venture the remaining distance once night has fully set in," I told her.

She slipped out of her cloak, laying down on one of the abundant patches of moss found throughout the forest, before stretching herself out and then turning onto her side. As she lay there watching me, watching her, I knew the same thought entered our minds, had fate bound us to one another or was this merely a matter of luck? Both could have been true I suppose, however, should this go poorly for us, and I shall be beheaded, and she shall be enslaved to Tuiteam for the remainder of her unnaturally long life.

Laying my cloak near hers, I laid down beside her on my back facing what would soon be a starlit sky. She was breathing slow and steady along with a gaze that rested comfortably upon my face. I turned my head towards her and watched her once more watching me. When she did not falter or look away, I turned my body towards her and brought my face within inches of hers. I could hear her heart beating and smell sweetness upon her breath, but it was within those golden eyes that I felt something within me stir. When she did not turn away, I slid my body towards hers and placed my hand gently on her exposed hip. Her skin was warm and soft and while I expected her to pull away from me, she did not.

"If you wanted me to touch you, then you should have just asked," I whispered.

I leaned in towards her flirting with the idea of placing my lips upon hers when I watched her eyes flutter slightly at the suggestion. Quickly placing a peck upon her cheek, I returned to lay on my back, while keeping my body at her side. I heard her draw in a breath and hold it, unsure whether she wanted the kiss or wanted to scream out in anger. Part of me wanted her to erupt in anger and let out all the pain she had been holding for so long and the other part of me wanted her to tumble down the rabbit hole, losing herself in the passion she was so clearly craving. Either option would have pleased me and even though she had not moved since the kiss, she was still watching me, her eyes bright with curiosity and excitement.

"You know it would only take a moment for me to slip out of this armor," I uttered while glancing towards her briefly then returning my eyes towards the sky.

"What?!" she sounded genuinely shocked at the suggestion, "I wish nothing of the sort!"

"Then tell that to your eyes, for they have set up camp upon my flesh the moment we stopped," I placed my hands under my head and glanced towards her once more, "even now, you cannot tear them away."

"I, I can explain," she began stumbling over her words, "well, actually, I cannot."

I sat up and peeled off the upper portion of my armor and cast it aside before slipping out of my tunic, only to place it gently under her head. Her eyes were watching my every movement as if she were a hunter stalking her prey, but she would soon discover that I am the hunter in this tale, not the prey. Hovering over her slightly, I watched her place her head back down on my tunic and fiery curls fall lifeless onto the cloak beneath her, making it appear as if it were on fire, as she rolled onto her back.

"You do not have to explain it," I paused, "you find me enticing, and your ever unyielding curiosity is drawn to all that is mysterious about me." I winked at her, "Does that about cover it?"

"I never said you were attractive," she uttered sounding very unconvincingly.

"So, you do not find me attractive?" I raised an eyebrow, "Ouch, that hurt," I said with a fair amount of sarcasm.

"No, I do!" she blurted out before placing a hand loosely over her face, attempting to shield herself from further embarrassment as she was beginning to blush.

I lifted her hand away from her face, but her eyes remained closed.

"Why is it now that you choose to no longer look upon my face?" I asked.

"For I am afraid of what I am feeling," she whispered.

Not surprisingly this made me grin with delight, that is unless she was feeling overwhelming nausea at my presence, and I would rather not to think of that. Regardless, she would never know my reaction for her eyes were still clenched tightly together. I raised a hand to touch her when something stopped me. This being while curious fears nothing, but a lover's embrace makes her fracture like glass on a stone floor. Something held her back and it was not the cage wrapped tightly around her heart. I place my hand near her side, grasping a portion of the cloak within it before pulling it over her.  Her eyes opened and were once more watching me.

"There's no need," she whispered as if nearly out of breath, "I am quite warm already."

I pulled myself back and onto my side, just before closing my eyes, "Let's just say it is not for your benefit."  She exhaled heavily and I felt her shift her body towards me, inches away from mine now, before placing a hand softly on my exposed ribs, "Do not start something you have no intention of finishing," I muttered.

"I just do not want to *feel* so alone right now," she leaned in and kissed one of my cheeks and then the other.

My eyes opened to hers and she smiled at me, the way a child might, but I did not think of her as a child at all.  Sure, there was something innocent about her that I could not place, but everything other than that smile told me she was no child.  I reached over to turn her slightly before pulling her body towards mine, letting her fiery skin cast away the chill the night air had washed over me.  She rested her head in the nook that had formed between my chest and bent arm, while I pulled her hips towards mine, which I soon realized was a cruel act of torture on my part.  Having her body so dangerously close to mine made me ache in parts of my body that I had nearly forgotten were there and soon she, too, would feel my ache.  I pulled away slightly, hoping to distract myself long enough that she could fall asleep, when I felt her lift her head slightly.

"Is everything alright?"

I nodded, "Aye, of course."

She rolled her body towards mine, only further provoking my desire for her.  While I wanted to climb on top of her and claim her, I already knew that in doing so, there would be no happy ending for us.  I rolled back towards her, wrapping my arms tightly around her and opted to live with the fact that coveting her may all that was intended for us.  She soon fell peacefully quiet, and I knew she was resting.  While the idea was for us both to get some rest, I could not bring myself to leave us both defenseless in the rapidly approaching darkness.

I woke her a short time later.  By this late hour, the patrols would have finished scouting the shoreline and we should be able to arrive unseen if we stuck to the tree line.  She stretched playfully, as a pup waking from a long nap, then stood quickly to don her cloak as I donned my tunic and armor.  I watched her as she watched me hours before, for no reason other than she was beautiful in any light.  Handing her a large piece of fruit and the last of the water I had stashed away, I wished there were more that I had to offer her.  For the remaining portion of this road, would be no less challenging than that of the Ice Tower, just far less lethal.  When I was confident, she had finished, we set off at a running pace, determined to close the gap and reach the tunnel.  The forest was remarkably quiet at this hour, making each step we took more apparent to anyone or anything around us.  I turned sharply towards the coast, adding distance to our journey, but I thought it best if we permitted the crashing waves to cover the sound of our presence.  It was not long until I heard them faintly crashing in the distance and I knew it would now be safer to head north.  I watched as her pace quicken the closer, we drew, her anticipation climbing.

As the trees started to become less dense, we could see more and more of our surroundings.  Blanketed by the night's sky, they seemed duller than what would normally be found during the daylight hours.  However, when the castle came into view, her pace slowed to that of a snail, nearly tripping over her own feet, mesmerized by its grandeur as so many before her.  The castle and walls were made of the same stone it was erected from and was surrounded by fields of sleeping lavender, giving it a very peaceful feel.  Unlike most, this castle does not climb towards the clouds or through them but remained among its people.  While the kings of Tuiteam know not how to bond with their people, their chosen queens have made it their honor being seen amongst them.  The city would have benefited greatly had the Lady Beatrice lived and wed Prince Berenger, but I suppose fate had something else in store for them both.

I attempted to coax her onward when I heard her mutter something I did not quite catch.

"Forgive me," I said.

"It is so much larger than I remember," she turned towards me, "how will we ever find him?"

Follow the screams I thought to myself, but then I decided uttering something such as this towards her right now might unleash a beast, I was not willing to tackle alone.

"I have spent a great deal of time in the city," I placed my hand on the nape of her neck and squeezed gently, "I assure you that you will find one another."

She looked down and nodded, but she did not appear convinced. I wished there were more I could say that would comfort her but part of me knew we did not have time for it. Without giving it anymore thought, I began sprinting towards the castle and she quickly followed in my footsteps. While I knew elves were known for their endurance, she was remarkable, it was like she never tired. While I could not say for certain what lay in wait for us once inside the castle walls, I had a distinct feeling it was not as I might have remembered it.

We continued onward until there were only a few trees left in the tree line and we would soon be forced out into the open. Halting her movements and mine, I searched the castle wall for any sign of movement. Much to my displeasure, the guards were on point tonight and what I would have given for them to be slacking off at this very early morning hour. The last thousand feet or so to meet the castle wall could have been easily sprinted, but this may have brought unnecessary attention to two already suspicious travelers. We needed to appear as if we belonged there, and I soon felt regret that I failed to remove more the of Jagare's armor to cover her now. Her legs and bright locks, if seen, would surely draw attention, we needed her to remain covered. Stepping in front of her slightly, I pulled the cloak up and over her head, brushing her locks back into the cloak's hood before reaching the lower portions that covered her body.

I grasped them in my hands and whispered softly, "We need to move as they do.  You cannot scurry and you cannot let your body, or your face be seen."  I released the cloak from my hands and grabbed my own to show her, "Hold it tightly from the inside and move slower than you would like, that way it may be less likely to billow away from your body in the breeze."

She nodded and took her cloak in her hands and mimicked what I shown her just before I, too, pulled my hood up to cover my locks.  Taking their cloaks at the time might have seemed fruitless to an outsider but to me, everything I took was preparing for our entry into the city, for that was always the intention.  We stepped out into the moonlight valley to begin what may be our last walk in the light.  The air was crisp with a hint of sweetness and saltiness to it, more than likely from the clash of salt water and lavender in the air.  It was a welcome scent that I have frequently encountered as I venture through these parts more often than not.  It would never be my home, but I feel a strange connection here that I have not felt elsewhere in some time.

With each step, the minutes appeared to drag on as hours and I could feel the tension building around her.  I dare not turn towards her for fear of being seen but part of me begged in this moment for a gift that would siphon all emotion from her as she was being consumed by it.  This is one of the few times when an attack can be fueled by extreme emotions but once inside, those emotions would need to be banished as they could cloud one's judgment.  I sensed they were already clouding hers.  The anguish she felt was now heard with each heavily laid step and each exasperated breath she took, she needed to pull herself together.  No sooner than we reached the base of the castle's wall, and I grasped the collar of her cloak just before slamming her against the stone.  She did not utter a sound, but her eyes flared at the sudden threat.

"Pull yourself together," I whispered through my gritted teeth.

"Get your hands off me," she whispered before pressing her hands up and undermine, forcing me to release her, "I uttered nothing."

"You did not have to," I whispered, "your confusion and anguish over this man is seeping through every one of your pores."  I turned to walk away, but I knew I was not nearly finished.  I stepped back towards her and pointed my finger at her like she was a child being punished, "If you wish to die, then let it be here by my hand and if not, disconnect yourself from these emotions, so you may seek your vengeance."

Neither of us uttered a reply but as we trudged onward, I sensed a change in the wind.  If she had not yielded to my demands, then at the very least she was working harder to mask her scent and the tunnel was now within reach.  From a dense dark forest to the pale sandy coastline of Tuiteam, our journey was entering its final stages and this portion would prove to be the most difficult.  We ventured away from the wall to greet the sandy shore to begin the hunt for our hidden passage.  Following the long rocky coastline as a guide, we walked until a shadow covered nook graced us with its presence.  There were several stones and boulders that had been placed before the opening as a means of diverting attention from it, but when seen in this light, that was the last thing they were doing. Working together we freed only what we needed to get in safely without alerting any prying eyes or ears.  Once inside, we began to walk in a darkness that would not cease until we reached the hatch at the other side.

It was the knock at the door that had woke us later that morning rather than the midmorning sun and I was quickly reminded that I had not fallen asleep in my bedchamber but in the Lady Rosalyn's.  The morning's bright light shone brightly across the stone floor and warmed the space as if it were a greenhouse.  The warmth of the light accompanied by a warm midmorning breeze rushing in from the sea reminded me of nights spent on the beaches that belonged to the sound.  Even after a cool night, the sun appeared to warm the white sand beaches within minutes of its rise to the sky.  It reminded me of a much freer time.

"Lady Rosalyn," a maiden's voice spoke to her, "your father as asked me to fetch you."

I glanced down to find Rose sleeping peacefully upon my bare chest, her fingers grasping my ribs as if she were fearful I would flee while she slumbered.  I would do no such thing to her.  She had not awoken at the sound of the woman's voice, but had it not been for my keen hearing I might have missed it as well.  When the woman knocked again, I began scooping Rose and shifting to her to one side, ever fearful of what should happen if I were to be found in her bedchamber, just before sliding towards the side of the bed.  While I may have rested there, it was abundantly clear when I rose to my feet that we had not given ourselves to one another on that day, not for lack of desire I assure you.  Following my sudden movements, she was beginning to wake and she, too, was alarmed at the incessant knocking upon her door.

"My lady," the woman spoke sounding increasingly frustrated, "it is time to wake."

I heard the latch on the door lift and felt an increasing urgency to flee when I felt her hand upon my wrist, tugging me towards her.  She did not utter a sound, just merely gestured for me to follow her towards a large partition located near one of the corners of her room.  We were nearly there when I heard her speak for the first time in hours.

"One moment, if you please," she called out and I heard the latch slide back into place.

She pressed her hands into my sides, urging me to remain behind the partition, but I was not ready to let her go just yet.  I pressed my lips to hers, relentlessly encouraging her to stay.  For a moment, I felt as if my heart were going to explode in her embrace.  When she pulled away, a giggle escaped her, making my heart leap with excitement at just the sound of her happiness.  I reached for her hand and kissed it gently before pulling her towards me once more.  She giggled again and I felt like I could barely contain my desire for her in this moment.  I placed my hands upon the back of her neck and ran my fingers through her hair, kissing her already swollen lips for what may be the last time as if it were the first.

She pulled herself away once more, "We must not, or we will surely be discovered."

"Let them find us," I uttered breathlessly, "I care not."

I heard myself lie and knew that while we both knew I had not claimed her in the night, all other outsiders would never see what happened between us as such.  Not to mention her betrothed would have me beheaded for far less than the sins our lips were committing.  I brought my lips to hers once more.

"My lady!" the woman insisted.

"Forgive me," she muttered through panted breaths, "please come in."

She tore her lips away and spun around just as the door to her bedchamber opened allowing her lady's maid to enter. The woman was ranting about the hour and all the things left to do but all my eyes could see was the light radiating from Rose's hair as she stood inches before me.  I leaned in and nuzzled the back of her neck before kissing her softly, when the sound of the woman's gasp brought me back to my senses. I could not see what had shocked the woman, but when Rose tore herself away suddenly to rush towards the door, I pulled myself back behind the partition just in time to not be seen. The bedchamber door slammed closed causing a thunderous echo to reverberate throughout the space.  Unsure as to the commotion, I tried to remain hidden as my presence here would have only escalated the situation, but I listened intently.

"Please, it is not what you think," I could hear Rose's voice quiver. She was not just nervous this time, she was frightened of something, and I desperately wanted to rush to her aid.

"My lady," the woman growled through gritted teeth, "a man in your bedchamber is forbidden," I peered around the edge of the partition unsure how this could have been known to her, then I saw my tunic clenched beneath her fingers and felt my heart stop. "Please tell me you did not let this man-" her voice cut out.

I watched as Rose's face fell flat and her gaze dropped towards the tunic the woman held, "No, he did not..."

The woman scoffed as she turned away from Rose to grasp her lady's dress for the day, "My lady," the woman's tone softened a great deal, "you must castaway thoughts of this man for no good will come of it." She turned to tenderly touch Rose's shoulder and caress her cheek, "Come, let us get you cleaned up. King Ferand's men should be arriving any moment now and you want to look your best," she smiled.

With each passing hour, I knew this would not get easier for us and while there was still time to change her mind, I was not sure she would. Duty is not something easily ignored and to revoke the betrothal at such a vital time could be devastating to both her honor and King Itheal. However, the journey to Tuiteam is long, giving her time to sort out her feelings and time for me to provoke more. My thought was broken when I saw her lady's maid step towards the partition and casually toss several garments over the side.  I quickly tucked myself behind the partition and crouched down in hopes of hiding myself from her sight.  When I did not hear any further commotion, I took a few deeps breaths and peered around the other side of the partition.  Unfortunately, I peered too soon, and my sudden appearance was met with a shriek.  The woman stumbled back, shouting then mumbling incoherently.  I stood quickly, not wanting to further appear as a monster lurking in the shadows, holding my hands up.

"Madam," I spoke softly, "I bid you no ill will."

"No ill will," she gasped, "yet it is you who has touched the Lady Roselyn!" she spat, "What would King Itheal," she paused clearly taxed by my sudden appearance, "no, what would King Aldon think of your betrayal?"  The woman shielded her eyes with one hand and pointed towards the door with the other, "Begone with you or I shall summon the guards to remove you."

I closed my eyes, expecting at any moment the guards shall have heard of this disruption and would be coming for me even without her order.  Then I felt her cool hands once again on my chest, Rose had come to me even when being seen with me would have only hurt her further.  I wrapped my arms around her, pulling her tightly against me and kissing her forehead.

"Madam, I beseech you not to," Rose pleaded, "If you hold any love for me at all, you will do no such thing."

"My lady," the woman's voice sounded concerned, "you cannot be with this man, for your father will never allow it."

Rose turned her head slightly, "My father need not know of this, and I forbid you to utter a word of it outside this very room."

The woman stepped towards us and looked upon my face with pleading in her eyes, "My lord, you must see reason where she does not.  This cannot be what you wish for her."

"You know not of the love I bear for this woman or what I wish for her," I insisted, "but please heed to her request, for I wish no ill will to fall upon you."

"My lady," she attempted to reach for Rose, but my hand pushed hers away, "let Lord Bryn take his leave of us, so that I may dress you properly."

"She is right Bryn," Rose looked up towards me, "someone shall soon notice your absence had they not already."

I swallowed, uncomfortable at the idea of leaving her, "If it be your wish, then I shall take my leave."

I leaned down towards Rose, cupping her face in my hands just before kissing her lips and cheeks softly.  With each touch of her lips to mine, I felt the electricity surge throughout my body further pulling me into her, but the moment was soon broken when I heard the woman clear her throat.

"My Lord," she held my tunic out for me to grab, "it would do you a great service to don your tunic prior to your departure," she cleared her throat again, "that is, if you truly wish to maintain my lady's honor."

Had it not been for the seriousness of the situation, I might have snickered at the gesture as she had a point. I might as well bed her with witnesses should I leave her bedchamber barely dressed, for that is what everyone would see and hear echoed in the shameless steps I would take back to my own bedchamber.

"Of course," I grabbed the tunic and donned it quickly before hastily searching for the remainder of my garments.

By the time I had found my doublet and donned my boots, the woman had already ushered Rose out of view. There is so much I wished to say but now, there was not time. While I am not a pious man, in that moment, I would have prayed to any and all of the gods for her to be mine once more. Just as I began stepping towards the door, I heard the latch lift once more, startling me. I had been so distracted by thoughts of her, I was careless in not thinking of who may be lurking nearby. The sudden movement of the door caused me to backpedal onto her balcony, where there was little hope of escape should I need to.

"Madam, pardon the intrusion," King Itheal barged in bearing a sizable grin upon his face forcing me to pull myself back out of all potential view, "where is my beautiful daughter?"

The woman bowed before speaking, "Just another mere moment King Itheal," the woman said with a smile as she rose once more, "it appears the young lady overslept."

I heard footsteps followed by the King taking in a deep breath, "Rosalyn, you look breathtaking," he paused, "fit to be a queen."

"You truly have a beautiful daughter your majesty."

"Are you quite well?" he cleared his throat, "Your cheeks are flushed, and your lips swollen."

There was silence, an alarming amount of silence.

"Of course, she is your majesty, the Lady Rosalyn just had some difficulty sleeping last night and had to rush herself to be presentable this morning," the woman's voice sounded frantic.

"Hmmm, very well then," his voice sounded displeased, "Madam, please make sure that does not happen again. The Lady Rosalyn cannot appear disheveled or ill in any way for her betrothed."

"Of course, your majesty, it shall not happen again."

There was a hesitation in her voice, but I was unsure as to a potential cause. Temptation drew me in, and I peered around the edge of the stone entry to find them huddled near the end of her bed. Rose was twirling about in a long pale blue gown with long sleeves and a bodice of lace that hugged her body as I did when she was gripped tightly in my arms. She looked happy and for a moment, I was jealous of all those who could love her in the daylight. Until the tidal wave of feelings that burst through me last night, I had not realized all that I was harboring for her and now, I feel as if I cannot breathe without her in my arms. By the time my focus returned to the situation at hand, they had already returned themselves to more mindless banter and then King Itheal was saying his goodbyes.  There was something odd about his behavior, as if there was something left unsaid, but I had no means to pry.  For now, I would have to let the matter remain misunderstood as I needed to return to my chambers and quickly.  When the door closed behind him, I exhaled louder than expected and stepped out from behind the drapery found next to the balcony's opening. Attempting to fasten my doublet, I felt the air change as Rose approached me.

"Bryn," she kissed my cheek softly, "I was so afraid you were to be discovered that I hardly drew a breath."

"Well breathe now my darling, for we shall soon be together again."  I held her hands in mine and kissed her softly, confident this would not be the last.  "Please forgive me as I must go before anyone is alerted to my absence."

She nodded before whispering hastily, "Venture towards the library prior to returning to your chambers and appear frustrated.  If anyone should ask, let it be known that I had called you to the gardens but failed to wake in time to meet you there."

I nodded before kissing her hands then stepping towards the door.  Listening carefully for anyone nearby, when I was sure there was no one, I unlatched the door.  Just before stepping into the hall, I looked back at Rose in all her splendor and while my feelings for her had changed over the years, her beauty had not.

"My eyes have never beheld anything fairer than the maiden that stands before me in this moment," I glanced back at her and saw her eyes widen with surprise and delight. "Until we meet again my darling," I whispered just before stepping out into the hall and softly closing the chamber door behind me.

Making quick work of Rose's instructions, I painted on a disappointed yet frustrated facade while venturing towards the library and it was not long before others took notice. Those who did not attempt polite pleasantries, steered clear of me altogether. Perhaps I was overselling it a touch. By the time I reached the library, my thoughts had already returned to her, and I saw no point in entering. Just as I began pivoting, I heard footsteps rapidly approaching, nearly knocking me over by their sudden appearance. Much to my surprise, they belonged to King Itheal and a few members of the guard. I felt my face flush before forcing me to bow quicker and deeper than normal, giving me time to recover my composure.

"Good morning, King Itheal," I paused, "I hope you are well."

"Aye, I am," he paused, "is there something more pressing that demands your attention?"

"Pardon?" I glanced up slightly and then back towards the stone floor.

"You stepped towards the library but did not enter," he gestured for me to rise to which I did, "What drew your attention elsewhere?" he inquired.

"I realized I needed a change of dress before King Ferand's men arrived," I glanced down at my disheveled appearance as a means of emphasizing my point, "I would never wish to dishonor you in any manner."

He placed a hand on my shoulder and leaned in towards me, "No, I suppose not," he whispered, "however, I wish to speak with you regarding another matter."

I nodded as we began stepping down the hall.

"The Lady Rosalyn appears quite unwell this morning. Would you know anything of this?"

I attempted to swallow but even the air I, now, breathed felt as if spikes were being driven deep within making impossible to do so.

"Forgive me, I do not," I uttered while trying to sound convincing, "for I have not seen her since our passing through the hall last eve."

"You and the Lady Roselyn have grown quite close whilst you have been here, have you not?"

"Aye, that I believe we have," I smiled and thought if he only knew how close we had recently become, my shoulders would certainly not be donning a head much longer.

"It is important that she is well when her escort arrives."

"Your majesty?"

"You bring light into her eyes, see that it returns to them before the men from Tuiteam arrive."

"Of course, your majesty, it would be my pleasure."

Part of me wondered if I were being tested in this moment or if he really believed there was something I could do to aid in Rose's wellbeing.  I fear there has been something left unsaid, but again, I dare not pry with so many watchful eyes nearby.

"Thank you, Bryn," he gave my shoulder a squeeze before adding, "please go now, without delay and report back to me."

I nodded and felt his grip relax just before dropping off my shoulder.  Per his instructions, I removed myself from his presence and rushed towards my chambers with all haste.  Upon my arrival, I peeled off my doublet and the tunic from the night before just before tossing them into an open trunk along with several others that were hovering nearby.  As I reached to fetch a fresh tunic, I noticed the texts on my desk had shifted and were not as I left them the night before.  There was something bright within one of them lofting in the breeze that was entering from the open window.  It drew my attention towards it, and I felt compelled to investigate the matter further.  In picking up the text the bright light shown from, I now knew it was a scrap of parchment tucked within and when I opened the text, the following was there for me to read.

*The Lady Rosalyn is not who she appears to be.  She must not be permitted to reach Tuiteam.*

I did not quite understand the message nor how it was to be interpreted but there was something ominous about it.  Though the Lady Rosalyn is truly a pearl in a sea of coral, I cannot begin to comprehend how she could be anyone other than who I know her to be.  Holding the text in my hands for several moments, I replayed our time together rapidly in my mind, trying to divulge anything out of sorts. While rumors are known to swirl about all members found in royal households, I have never found the ones about King Itheal and the Lady Rosalyn to be anything but rumors. I soon found myself pacing about the chamber, contemplating who could have placed the text here and why, when I remembered I needed to return to check on Rose per the King's request.

Fetching and donning a fresh tunic and doublet, I stepped towards the door and no sooner than I reached for the handle, when someone slid another piece of parchment beneath it. Leaning in, I heard steps being taken at a quickened pace. While the wearer's shoes were heeled as most were, they hit the surface lighter than a man would have, provoking even more curiosity as to what woman would have dared threaten my darling Rose. Taking the parchment in my hands, I opened it slowly, almost fearful of the text held within.

*Library. Now.*

I hastily opened the door before rushing several steps in one direction before turning and rushing back in the other direction. I returned quickly to my bedchamber to stash the texts before rushing out towards the library. While I had no idea who or what I would encounter there, I knew I had to go there. Restraining my hair as I walked, I tried to appear as if not disheveled by the messages I had received for I had no means of knowing who was watching. When I was certain I was more presentable, I slowed my pace and turned the corner to enter the library.  It had no door shielding it from the world as King Itheal was very willing to let all who lived or visited his realm bask in the knowledge it possessed.  I frequently found myself within the comfort of its walls.  Trying to appear as aloof as possible, I strolled about in no discernable pattern when I heard someone step just behind me and stop.

"Lord Bryn," I turned to see a young page bowed before me, "a message has arrived for you."

I took the parchment from the boy's hand and opened it.

*Ascend the iron staircase.  Search for a stone out of place and enter the hidden chamber.  Remain unseen.*

"Who gave you this message?" I questioned.

"No one my Lord," he stood upright slowly, "it was placed just inside a text that was left for the custodian to find."

"What text was it inside?" I urged in a whisper.

He shook his head, "I dunno my Lord," he glanced up just in time to catch my disapproval, "for I cannot read."

I placed my hand upon his shoulder, "Forgive me, you may go now."

The boy scurried off to his duties as I scanned the room for anyone lurking nearby.  When no one came into view, I grabbed a text from a nearby shelf and opened it.  It was one thing to be found in the library, it was quite another to be found without seeking or grasping a text.  Working my way around the exterior of the room until I found the iron staircase. Peering around the nearby cases, I searched once more for any lurking eyes and ears, to which no one present paid me any notice. I took to the stairs and ascended them in a slow but steady manner, fearful a quickened pace would alert all those nearby. As I reached the top, I scooched towards the windowless walls and began scanning them with my fingers for any stone out of place.

It was difficult to locate as the walls at this height were quite dark compared to the floor below. The darkness aided in concealing me, but had it not been for my keen eyes, I might not have found it at all. My fingers managed to fall onto a coarse, pitted stone that shifted in place when I applied any pressure upon it. I slid myself downward and crouched before the stone, while the stone easily shifted, I do not believe I could have fully removed it without anyone noticing. Alternating pressure between the edges, I saw something wedged in the wooden plank beneath me. It was not part of the stone that might have possibly fallen as I shifted the stone but was clearly out of place. Running my fingers over the plank, I found the object to be smooth, not rough like that surrounding wood.

Pulling a dagger from my boot, I inserted the tip just underneath the edge of the object and applied pressure to reveal an iron spike with an odd cutout on its shaft. I twisted the spike between my fingers, carefully scanning the cutout, all the while wondering why it was placed in the plank or what the cutout could have been for. Instinctively, I placed the spike along with my dagger back inside the lining of my boot before standing.  I clung to the wall with the text in hand, reading and re-reading the instructions.  Hidden chamber?  I have been searching the castle since my arrival, ever mindful of passageways and chambers if an escape would be needed, but I never found any such chamber.

In a moment of panic, I realized I had not heeded the King's instruction and I should venture to Rose.  While I knew she had not been distraught or unwell, should the King inquire, I would not wish for anyone to present falsehood on my behalf. I took to the staircase in an unnaturally quickened pace that caused my step to ring throughout the library drawing the attention of the custodian, who was now glaring at me from afar.  Thankfully, he appeared otherwise indisposed or he might have expressed his disgust vocally.  The custodian was a wise old man with the temperament of a stream, calm and consistent most days but when disturbed he becomes out of sorts, sometimes for days.

I slide the parchment inside my doublet just before placing the text on a table near the main door and rushed towards Rose's chambers.  When I arrived, there was no response when I knocked upon the door.  I knocked again and still no reply.  Grasping the latch in my hand, I was tempted to open it, but something inside me forced me to release it from my grasp out of fear.  Closing my eyes, I thought carefully over where she might be and then I knew the garden would be the only place.  She loved it there and if she should choose to become King Ferand's bride, this may be her last day amongst its beauty.  It is there that I must go to her.

As I journeyed through the castle, I noticed the staff was quite preoccupied with the near arrival of the men from Tuiteam. The halls were buzzing with incessant chatter over remedial tasks and an overblown presentation of wealth and power. The main hall was humming with a lullaby that I could not place, but I clearly knew the melody. In passing it, I noticed the room had blossomed into a greenhouse nearly overnight draped in substantial arrangements of flowers that seemed to cascade from every angle. It was beautiful but quite overdone. King Itheal is clearly catering to King Ferand's ego as I have never witnessed such extravagance on any other occasion here or elsewhere.

Just beyond the main hall is where I saw her, standing peacefully in the sun's light. I watched her through the large glass doors, reminding myself that while as much as I may want to, I may never be able to love her the way that I would like or the way she deserves. The thought made my stomach ache and draw up in knots. I knew forcing her decision could not possibly help either of us, but I already could not stand the thought of another man touching her. I gently pushed the doors open and stepped across the threshold. The sound drew her attention and as she turned towards me, her face brightened, with the glow from the morning's light and a smile that did not appear to end. She looked very pleased to see me again so soon.

"Greetings Lady Roselyn," I tried to be as formal as possible until I was certain we were alone, "how does the morning find you?"

"Quite well Bryn, and you?" she giggled just before covering her mouth with her hand, but her blushing cheeks and wide eyes made my heart flutter with delight.

"Never better," my cheeks started to ache from the overwhelming happiness I now felt in her presence, and I never realized how little I had smiled before now, "may I walk with you?"

"Of course," she nodded, "it is lovely this time of day, is it not?"

"Not as lovely as you, Lady Roselyn."

I watched her blush again as we stepped out of the primary view of the main hall into the shade of a large pergola nearby. We were alone once more, if but for a moment and it took all my restraint not to take her in my arms and place my lips upon hers. Instead, I touched her fingers lightly with mine and I felt hers cling to mine in return. Oh, how I wish we were born of the same world and this moment were not a moment but our eternity. I leaned forward and watched her eyes close, anticipating the kiss, when I reached behind her tearing a large white flower from its home only to brush it across her cheek. She exhaled and I watched her lips quiver with what I hoped was excitement. Moving the flower onto her other cheek, gliding the petals across her smooth supple skin, when the quiver from her lips became more than I could bear. I had to kiss her now or my heart may very well explode from within my chest. Bringing my lips to hers in such a sudden and swift motion caused her to jerk slightly in surprise, but she quickly melted into my arms, reciprocating the kiss. Breaking off the kiss, I watched her eyes slowly open to mine.  While it was not what either of us wanted, it was too risky to continue as we were.  She pulled away, taking the flower from my hand, and twirling it within her fingers.  The petals of the large white flower dwarfed her hands, nearly making them disappear beneath it.  I leaned in and kissed her cheek just before brushing a few lost strands of hair back away from her eyes.

"Why is it before today I thought nothing of how your touch felt upon my skin and now, your touch is all I can think about?" she whispered.

"Perhaps it is because you are all I am thinking about as well," I whispered as I pulled her fingers further into my grasp, squeezing them gently.

"I feel as if we are in an unbearable situation," she paused to look at me, "for I fear of what will happen if we are discovered or if my heart would be strong enough to lie with another knowing what I feel for you."

Her voice began to shake, and her eyes were becoming glassy.  I knew while there would not be another for me, appearing in her bedchamber as I did, only provoked an internal struggle she may not have ever been prepared for.  It hurt me to watch her struggle and I desperately wanted to take away the pain.  However, she was the one standing at a fork in the road, not I and there is no denying what I want.

"Toil not over this today, for no good will come of it," I whispered not wanted her to linger in sadness more than is required on a day like today.

Pulling her towards me, I wrapped my arms around her to gently hug her.  Today was not about me, it was about her and about finding a secret in a chamber unknown to me.  While I did not wish to harm her further, she may be the only one who would know of such a chamber hidden amongst the walls of her home that would speak of such to me.  Not asking her would not be an option if I wished to lift the veil before our departure.

"Rose, my darling, I need to ask you something," I whispered, "while I wish to remain here with you for a long as time permits us, something demands my attention."

She looked up at me suddenly, clearly unsure where the conversation was going.

"In all your time, have you ever encountered a hidden chamber inside the castle walls?"

Her eyes shifted and I saw a flicker of recognition in them, but she did not reply.

"It is of dire importance that I find it.  Do you know where it is?" I insisted.

"Aye, that I do, but how do you know of such things?"

"For that I cannot say as I do not wish to trouble your mind or heart further."

"Bryn," she said softly, "my heart is already being forced to carry such a secret, I do not wish for there to be secrets between us as well."

I nodded knowing all too well the door that was being opened, "I fear someone is attempting to threaten your life," she gasped, "and within that room may lie the key to stopping them."

She watched me carefully and then her eyes fell towards the flower and after several more moments of silence, I heard her mumble a reply.

"In my father's study, there lies a hatch beneath his desk that leads to room which holds all that is dear to him," she paused, "I am not sure why you seek it but take nothing from there for he will know."

I nodded, "I would never betray you or your trust, my darling."

I kissed her lips softly once more and turned to flee the pergola when I felt her hand pulling mine back to her. I spun back towards her and felt her lips pressing themselves against mine, harder than before, demanding I give in to her. I did without question and felt her mouth open to mine once more, deepening our kiss. Heat rushed over my skin, and once again, I felt consumed by her and my desire for her. Everything about her drew me in and I knew that this was not the time or the place, but I could not pull myself away. Our bodies fell in sync with one another, and I knew we had to stop ourselves or a fate worse than death shall come for me.

"My darling," I started to mumble through kisses, "I dare not wish for us to be seen."

She pulled herself away to utter in between panted breaths, "Nor I, now go or I may not be able to control myself much longer," she grinned.

I winked at her before tearing myself away from her and her presence to rush back towards the main chamber where I would undoubtably encounter King Itheal, whom would be eagerly awaiting an update regarding my darling Rose.

# Commander Elgar

Wasting no time, I returned with my findings to King Edric's side. While my investigation at the Ice Tower was valuable, it yielded no results and that greatly displeased King Edric.

"You impudent fools!" he shouted as the pieces from his war table were slung across the room in a childish display of displeasure and frustration. "Not only are you telling me my wolf has escaped, but it was freed by an elf!"

"King Edric, the wolf remains on Reothadh, of that I am certain," I insisted. "The elf is of importance, I do not disagree, but we do not have the manpower to search all of Caladh for her."

"I care not if you must move mountains for her, I want her found!"

"King Edric," I pleaded, "I believe she fled upon one of the merchant vessels or perished in the sea, let the wolf be our priority."

"They will both be found, or you shall find your head on a spit just before being served to your men for supper," he growled, "is that understood Commander?"

"Aye, King Edric," I paused trying not to express my disapproval of the situation any further, "it will be done."

My men and I vacated the war room just before King Edric continued expressing his displeasure further by destroying what remained in the room as a child throwing a tantrum. The violence continued until our hearing no longer permitted us such pleasure and that is when I decided an act of subversion was in order. Kraciun and the young squire had returned with me on Lavin as I would need them for my plan to work. I summoned them to follow me as I ventured towards the prison housed deep within the walls of the castle. After leading them to a small chamber near the prison, I closed the door and let the subversion begin.

"Kraciun, you and I will take the men into the mountains in search of the wolf. Make sure your men in the tower are watching the port and reporting back all they know of the vessels delivering shipments."

He nodded and watched me as my attention turned towards the young squire.

"I need your eyes and ears. Go where you know you should not and see what was intended to be unseen."

"Commander Elgar," his voice was stiff, "what am I listening or looking for?"

"Anything out of sort," I nodded, "I care little for missed meals.  Watch for secret meetings and hushed voices, for there you will find the true purpose behind all the smoke and mirrors."

"As we are now," he whispered, "is that right, Commander?"

I nodded, "Aye, that's a good lad."

"Commander," Kraciun chimed in, "what of the elf?"

"She fled and perished within the sea's icy grasp," I paused, "we know naught of who sent her or why nor are we able to search or recover her remains.  Is that understood?"

"Commander," Kraciun looked displeased, "I will not hide behind deceit if I shall be asked."

"Aye and I shall not ask you to," I paused, "This is what I know to be true.  She did not leave aboard a ship full of serfs unseen and in her present state, she would have perished without aid.  She is surely dead."

I shifted my gaze between the two of them waiting for any sign of acknowledgement.  After a moment, they both nodded and I was ready to release them back to their duties, hoping to avoid any potential suspicion.  Patting the boy on the shoulder, I gave one final command as a cover before sending him back to the wolves who would undoubtably devour him if discovered.

"Please ensure those messages are delivered to the families of the fallen," I instructed giving any prying ears something to feed on.

The boy bowed and scurried out and up the stairwell back to the main hall. When we could no longer hear the boy, it was Kraciun's voice that broke the silence.

"Think he will make it?"

I shrugged, "Perhaps," then glanced at him and winked, "you did."

"It was not all that long ago as I can recall," he sighed.

"Aye, it was not," I stepped towards the door and began to take to the stairs leaving Kraciun in the distance behind me, "however this boy was more afraid of me than you were."

I heard a faint chuckle escape him and then nothing as I continued in my ascent. After reaching the main floor, I ventured towards the mess hall to ensure the men were well supplied along with picking up a few fixings for myself to take in tow. While other kingdoms place those of particular bloodlines in positions of power, Trocair, only gives to those who bleed for it, making us a formidable foe when challenged. In this realm, you keep what you take and no one's voice shall be silenced. I, as well as Kraciun, learned this early on giving us a clear advantage over others that were our age.

Kraciun and I were both bastard children left to be raised and then later abandoned by our mothers. In the cold darkness of this inhospitable land, you shall find your inner beast or be taken by one if left alone for too long. My curiosity was sparked in him one afternoon when I found him attempting to a pummel a man twice his size for beating a child, he could not have been more than ten or twelve years in age at the time. His empathy accompanied by the might to slay all who challenge him made him one worthy of my attention.  From that day forward I have been ever watchful of him and when given the opportunity, I have groomed him to one day lead more than the men of the tower.  Upon my arrival in the mess hall, it was not but a moment before I was noticed.

"Commander Elgar," an old woman handed me two heavy sacks and a large satchel, "the men and Lavin are well fed," she began shaking her finger at me, "you just make sure they are not the only ones who are well fed."

She raised an eyebrow and looked at me disapproving, knowing all too well that I seldom find the time to feast amongst the men and today, I should have.  For what lies within those mountains does not welcome outsiders.

"Aye, aye madam," I said as I shook my head in disbelief at how soft I was becoming in my old age.

Ten years ago, I would have flogged someone for speaking to me in such a tone and now, I cannot help in smiling while silently wishing her well.  She has been slaving away in that kitchen long before I arrived inside the castle's walls, and she will look after my men long after my body has turned to dust.  I turned to flee from her sight like a child who had just been scolded only to glance back a moment later to see her smiling at me and I smiling back at her.  I flung the sacks over my shoulder and carried on towards the south gate where I was greeted by Kraciun and several others.

"Commander," Kraciun bowed slightly, "the men have been divided into separate divisions, each with instructions on what portion of the mountains they are to canvas and what they are looking for. They stand ready and await your orders."

"Very good Kraciun," I replied and nodded.

Passing the sacks and satchel to him, I stepped towards the ladder nearby to make my ascent above the south gate for all to see. The gate was heavily lined with soldiers armed at the ready as instructed and barely moved an inch at my presence. They were trained well. Stepping into one of the few openings on the wall, I raised my hands high into the crisp air, I made three distinct half-moon slashing motions at varying degrees sending the troops off. Their steps were thunderous and echoed wildly across the barren landscape that lay ahead. It had been years since the troops were drawn and set forth in such a vast scouting party as this. It was not long before I joined the others on the backs of beasts and made way for the Glacial Pass. While there was no telling what mysteries the Ice Mountains of Reothadh would hold for us, I knew venturing there was our only option King Edric was going to give us.

As we trudged through the frozen wasteland that we call home, of course there was bantering regarding the cause and the fate of the hold, but I found my mind had drifted elsewhere. I thought of how our lives would differ should we alter the course and concede to Tuiteam's desire for power or if this journey would cause further strain on an already wounded leg. None of these thoughts were truly worthy of further evaluation, but nevertheless in what felt like an endless journey, I found my thoughts wondering back and forth through them like a needle being brought in and out of fabric as it was being stitched closed. While the wound felt better in the cold and would one day heal, my focus would not relent from the thought of a life without war, for as men we will always choose war over peace regardless of the sacrifices and accommodations that must be made for it. As much as I tried, I could not picture it regardless of the path chosen. Should we yield, Tuiteam would never stop with just us, soon their attention would be drawn towards the elves, woodland, or fire, and then what, the entire southern dominion of Caladh? I know little of King Baylon, except his temperament which was nearly as unpredictable as King Edric. Had I not known better, I would have assumed they were blood brothers in another life. As a society of miscreants, who have been abandoned by their queen and ruled by an imperious King, this could easily be plausible.

It was not until one of the men spoke to me that I was free of those incessant thoughts.

"Commander," he paused, "Commander, are you alright?"

I scoffed, "Of course I am alright you damned fool."

"You have not spoken in quite some time," he pointed to the path breaking away, "which path will you be taking?"

I glanced up at the sky just as Lavin crossed over and then back towards the paths that lay ahead, "Kraciun and I will take the lead through the heart."

Nudging my beast forward, I pushed past the other men until all I could see before me was wilderness.  The wind had died leaving the land shockingly quiet aside from the footsteps of man.  During the mind-bending haze I had found myself over the last few hours, I somehow missed our journeys towards the mountains and now they were upon us.  In the large snow-covered peaks before me, I found silence, wonder and fear all tightly woven together.  They were larger than they appear when flying above and while I knew nothing held within them would frighten me away, gazing upon them now and in this light, was as if staring into the eyes of a dragon.  May we find what we seek or be greeted by an honorable death, for surely not all would make it out alive.  I continued forward and soon heard the men fall in behind me just before Kraciun brough himself back towards my side.

"Commander," he uttered softly, "do you really believe this wolf is the key?"

"Perhaps," I shrugged, "but it is not my opinion that matters.  Would you not agree?"

He shook his head vigorously back and forth, "No, but I dare not question King Edric, for I am fond of having a head upon my shoulders."

His brutal honestly made me laugh, louder than expected and caused the beast beneath me to jerk suddenly and snort with displeasure.  I reached down to soothe its ruffled hide and felt it relax beneath my touch.

"Tell me Kraciun," I glanced at him before returning my attention to the path that lie ahead, "what you do think of all of this?"

He looked at me and I watched him raise an eyebrow as if questioning the meaning behind the inquiry, "I do not understand the purpose behind seeking these wolfs nor do I believe one beast is worth the lives of hundreds of men."

"So, you believe this is a fool's errand?"

"No Commander," he paused, "but a few packs of men might have been better suited to the task than the legion that was summoned."  He sighed, "I just know what I see does not add up to what I know."

"Hmmm," I paused, "I figured as much."

His response did not surprise me as it might have years before, but I knew he dare not deceive me.  There is no honor in deceit and while the men may be brutish, they are trustworthy for the most part, which is more than I can say for my dealings with Tuiteam.  The men began dividing into their separate groups and Kraciun and I rushed ahead to get a better look at our surroundings.  The mountains were towering, and snow covered when viewed from a distance, but once upon them, we found a gradual climb upon rock and soot that would not have been seen while upon the ground nor in the air. Looking ahead, I could see the path slowly progressing into a sheet of ice, making a safe passage nearly impossible. Signaling for the men to halt, Kraciun and I proceeded onto the icy path that lie ahead.

"Dismount here to save the beast's strength," I ordered just before dismounting, "while we cannot best the mountain, there is always a way up or through." I turned back towards the men, "Scour the area nearby for any potential route forward," I shouted.

Kraciun had already began ascending the icy slope when my attention had returned to him. He appeared to be handling the challenge with gusto and ease as if he has been here before. The thoughts crossed my mind that perhaps he had been, but it was quickly dismissed as there was no harm if he had been. Many men from Trocair have attempted the ascent as a test of strength and agility during their youth and while the mountain does not play fair, neither do they. I followed in behind him and watched as he shifted from surface to surface with minimal difficulty. As the distance between us grew, I halted my ascent and waited patiently for him to reach a plateau and report back. The minutes felt as if they had run on for hours and I could hear the men below growing restless when a noise was heard from above. It was sharp at first and then soon boomed violently against the rock and ice. I felt my ears try to bend the sound to uncover the source when I heard Kraciun call down to us.

"Incoming!" he shouted.

I watched something dark twist its way through the air and onto the surface just above me. It was a rope and with that, he had found a way.

"Release the beasts!" I commanded, "Their work here is done!"

Grasping the rope in my hands, I worked my way up and over the icy surface until Kraciun appeared just out of reach.  He was reaching over, offering me his hand of which I gladly accepted as my injured leg was feeling weaker by the moment.  Although, I would never admit to such a shortcoming as injury or old age.  With his hand, I brought myself upward onto the plateau he had found.  While the space larger than most we would find as we moved up the mountain side, it was relatively void of ice, suggesting something or someone had been here recently.  Rather than give it a more thorough inspection, I opted to anchor another rope, so more men could ascend quicker when I noticed Kraciun's anchor hammered into the mountain side.  That would have accounted for the racket I heard earlier.

As the men began funneling up the mountain side, I searched the ground and nearby trees for any suggestion that this was more than just decent luck.  However, while there were a several pines nearby, none of them appeared to have been altered by anything other than the gusts of frigid wind and ice that appeared to flow in and out of this space constantly.  There shall be no rest for us as long as we are here.  Leaving Kraciun to assist with the men as they climbed up, I stepped towards the far side to view what lies ahead.  More rock and more ice, of course, I would have expected nothing less.  Yet as I looked closer, I saw faint paths intertwined throughout the ascending mountain side, wide enough for more than just man to pass through.  I opened my search field by not only scanning the path that lies ahead, but the horizon and what lay beneath, for what goes up must come down.  With my eyes being weak and strained for the long days and nights, I could not focus as well as I would have liked and knew the sun would soon set, turning our already troublesome journey treacherous.  Soon we would have to divide further with no known certainty of ever meeting again.

"Kraciun!" I beckoned.

"Aye Commander!"

"The men will need to be divided further, and soon."

He pulled another man up and then stepped towards me, "How would you like it done?"

"Three groups: ascending, descending and one remaining here," I paused, "They are not to venture far, but more to get a lay of the land and see what paths are the most promising ahead."

"Understood," he glanced towards the climb ahead, "besides, do we really believe wolfs would willingly ascend the mountain side?"

"We can leave no stone unturned," I sighed, "I do not believe this is the path she would have taken, but that does not mean what lies above does not provide an easier path that is just not discovered yet."

"The mountain has changed Commander," he leaned in and mumbled in my ear before pulling away and whispering, "surely you must know this."

I looked upon him strangely as his behavior had changed so suddenly, I could have only assumed he was bewitched or perhaps I had been the one bewitched, for I had not seen what was right in front of me.  The route intended was not where it had been, forcing us to veer off course and up the mountain side.

"Aye," I responded barely audible, "but we cannot turn back now."

Kraciun removed himself from my side and stepped towards the men that were helping the others, "Divide the men, the Commander and I will advance onward."  He paused briefly before pointing to several imaginary points in the late afternoon sky, "Some to rise, some to fall and some shall remain…is that understood?"

The man nodded and he returned at my side, "Shall we press onward?"

"Aye, we shall for there is no time to spare, darkness approaches."

I watched him rush forward and leap towards a nearby ledge with a spirit I could not equal.  While I had no intention of letting him press onward without me, I would not do so with his level of enthusiasm.  While the men continued to funnel onto the plateau, I found myself, Kraciun and a few others making short work of the second climb.  This time, it was not nearly as steep and there was significantly more rock exposed for us to grasp.  An act of the gods perhaps or a mere matter of good fortune that was smiling upon us, I dare not question it.  However, with each strained step and each weakened grasp, I knew my strength would soon be spent.

The path that lies ahead was barely more than small shelves made of rock, forcing us to fall in one behind the other in order to keep moving forward.  It had not appeared to be man-made, more as if bits of the mountain had broken away over time and this was all that remained.  We were able to seek periods of rest when widener portions were encountered, but those were few and far between.  Mostly, we were forced to seek refuge or feast while clinging to the rock with our backs as the wind and snow scraped our exposed faces.  This was not the path I had intended for us to take and as we pressed onward, we soon found ourselves at the base of a daunting vertical climb.  Taking a few moments to assess and plan our assault upon the wall, I permitted everyone some time to replenish and relax their muscles.  While every soldier is required to spend time in the mountains, a vertical climb of an unknown distance is always draining to the mind and as this one rose into and beyond the clouds above, I knew the men would need more than just physical strength to endure.  However, before they appeared to get too comfortable, I heard Kraciun commanding them to rise.

"Rise up men," he shouted, "remove your gauntlets and fall in line."  He stepped towards the mountain side and placed his fingers carefully onto a gnarly protrusion.  "Do not tie off unless you need a temporarily release for your hand and do not tie yourself to one another," he commanded, "While it would pain me to lose anyone of you, I could not bear to lose all of you."

He was sincere in his message, but I knew this was not a request, nor would it have been had I ordered it so.  He took to the mountainside with the same gusto I witnessed hours before and without fear in his eyes.  To keep with his pace, I stepped forward while removing my gauntlets and placed my weathered hands onto the same gnarly protrusion as the one before me and began scaling the frozen beast.  Each pull towards the next protrusion on the wall further strained my already fatigued body and my muscles were beginning to burn. I began altering my pace to feel if my muscles would permit me any relief based on that, but they did not yield.  It was relentless and unforgiving.  A lesson I am certain would not be forgotten so easily.

As the sun was beginning to drop towards the horizon, our pace quickened in a last stitch effort to reach a point of safety before all would fall into darkness.  Kraciun had not faltered in speed or enthusiasm since we departed, making me long for the gusto of my youth.  Now as I watched my fingers, bloody and dark from frostbite setting in, I began to doubt my orders to venture in this direction and our purpose here.  While there was no doubting were my loyalty lies, a thought occurred to me, and a new course emerged in my mind.  One that would require a willing soul and a few more acts of subversion.  This made me grin with delight despite the chill that was settling in my bones.

The sound of rock sliding brought me back.  As I glanced around, I knew the sound had not come from above but below me.  One of the men had lost their grip or perhaps the rock had given way, releasing them to what lay below.  His cry was heard bellowing throughout the trees and off the rock nearby, he would soon meet his end.  When his voice was heard no more, there was a long silence before I noticed the men beginning to move again.  They did not appear discouraged, but had they been, there would have been no benefit to displaying it.  With his death and the feeling nearly faded from my hands, my pace quickened.  Soon night would be upon us and there would be no light to guide us.  In haste, I reached Kraciun's side and followed his gaze upwards.  Another hundred feet, give or take, then there was nothing.  As if a large dark blanket had been lain over our eyes, blocking us from seeing further up the mountain.  My mind could have been playing tricks on me, but had it not been, then there was an end in sight.  Out of my peripheral vision, I saw Kraciun rush forward, and he was ahead of me once more.

"Can you see anything?" I called out to him, but he gave no reply.

While he had risen above me, he had not ventured so far as to no longer hear my words.

"What can you see?" I called to him again.

"There is a ledge," he shouted through strained breaths, "but I cannot grasp it."  There was a pause, "The surface is iced over."

"Keep searching, I will be there soon," I shouted.

Pushing through the pain and carefully watching the placement of my hands and feet, I began closing the gap between us until he was within my reach.  There was something strange about the way his arms were hidden in front of his chest and as I crept closer to him, I noticed he was shifting from side to side in place.

"Kraciun," I spoke softly trying not to startle him, "what are you doing?"

He did not reply leaving only the howling wind to be heard.

"Kraciun, I order you to answer- "

Before I could finish, I watched him pull his legs up slightly before pushing from the rock in a leap towards an uncertain destination. There were so many thoughts and feelings swirling in my head, though none could be expressed. I hung there, clinging to rock, paralyzed as I watched his body float through the air. It was understood that time had not stopped but watching him I could not help in thinking it had slowed in some way. His movement was graceful and aerobatic in a way I had not seen before as if this were well-rehearsed and as I watched his arms extend towards a previously unseen overhang. It was not much and its surface unknown, but perhaps he saw it as something more than I.

As my chest began to ache, I soon realized I had been holding my breath in anticipation of the catch that had not arrived. I closed my eyes, willing the moment to pass, and I did not open them again until I heard boot on rock followed by a grunt that had escaped him from landing the catch so suddenly. He had made it. My body and mind appeared to have exhaled and I soon felt a sense of relief that I had not felt in hours. He made good use of his choice and I soon saw no more than his behind and the bottoms of his boots dangling from the edge. He disappeared a few moments later, but not long before I heard the familiar clanging sound ricocheting off the nearby rock and back out into the mountains.  That sound was music to my ears, and it encouraged me to propel myself on and upward.

As I drew closer, a portion of Kraciun came into view, but only for a moment and then he was gone again.  He was working hard to place a second anchor and the bits of him I could see appeared strained from the climb.  He was using the pommel of his blade to place an anchor into the floor of the ledge, directly behind the other one and the day's failure was now heavily carved into his grim expression.  Over the years I have grown to understand that attachment to those under my command are rarely met with good fortune, it would do him well to learn this as well.  I have trained and lost thousands of good men, had I felt as he feels now for each of them, the world have taken me years ago in grief.  Of course, had he known I was watching, he would not have been so careless as to appear troubled by the loss.  I will let him have this one and say nothing more of it, for we all have troubled hearts at one time or another.  I reached for the surface and when my arm quickly removed itself due to the icy surface, I called out to him.

"Kraciun, a hand please."

"Aye Commander!" he shouted back.

I heard the pommel strike twice more before rapid footsteps were approaching the edge.  Just as my eyes were drawn towards the sound, there was a cloud of dust that had dropped overhead.

"By the gods lad, are you trying to blind me?!" I shouted just as I closed my eyes, hopefully to avoid any further assault that was in store for them.

"Forgive me Commander, the wind-" he started to say.

"Just help me up," I blurted out, cutting him off.

Lowering himself towards the icy surface, he laid down upon his belly close enough to the edge that his arms were freely dangling over me.  I felt his hands wrap themselves around one of my arms, with fingers interlocked, just before pulling at it slightly.  The idea was not for him to pull me up with all his might, but to use him as another anchor and guide. Working my way up and onto his back, his grip and placement of his hands continued to change as I moved, and I soon found his intertwined fingers lowered again to provide an extra step for me.  Once I had stepped onto the ledge and no longer needed assistance, we began the task of assisting the others. One by one they rose and greeted us with relieved faces for the trials of today were now over.

# Prince Berenger

I awoke to the early morning's light breaking its way through a slight opening in my tent and I could hear the men beginning to stir.  Laying there, I permitted the sun to flood my skin with its warmth as I attempted to return to my slumber, my body and mind still exhausted.  I outstretched one of my arms searching the voided space beside me, hoping, praying, willing my fingers to find her, and let this all be a dream.  To add to my already troubled heart, there was nothing, but the sun's light found next to me.  My eyes opened again, and I sat up slowly, dropping my legs over the side of the cot where my feet were greeted by crisp blades of grass brushing against them.  I wiggled my toes through the blades, letting them briefly tickle my feet as I did when I was a child before standing to endure that long task of donning my armor.

Rarely was I to be found without some sort of armor in my position, but I often thought of a simpler life, one free from all the burdens I now felt.  I suppose that would be a fool's dream, but had I not been who I was, and my Beatrice might have survived long enough to birth the bairns I so desperately wanted to place within her belly.  It hurt to think of her but not thinking of her hurt more.  I reached over and poured a vat of water over my head and shoulders, it was cold, perhaps from remaining there from the night before, but the jolt from it snapped me back to reality.  As I began wiping off the excess, the drape towards the front of my tent peeled back and a man began to step inside.  It was difficult to discern who or why with the light shining so brightly upon his back, but I knew him to be friend not foe just from his mannerism alone.

"Good day to you Commander Berenger," the man's voice was deep and calm.

"Aye it is," I squinted attempting to meet his gaze, "how do the troops fare?"

He stepped all the way inside and the drape closed behind him, giving my eyes a much-needed break from the sun's light.  The man was one of my captains, a candid individual who I had grown to appreciate as I am frequently surrounded by individuals who are less than forthcoming.  He was short and stocky with a plump belly, one that he attributed to all the pies his wife was known to make.

"Well Commander," he nodded, "they are up and should be prepared to depart before the sun has fully risen."

Grasping at my side, which was not healing as expected, I stood with a groan, "My thanks, send the ones at the ready and I will follow with the remainder."

"Commander?" he sounded unsure.

My gaze left my body to glance up towards him, "Their early arrival will ensure the vessel is ready to depart as scheduled for I already wish this journey to be over."

"Aye, it will be done Commander," he bowed slightly and backed out of the tent.

My attention returned to the dressings that desperately needed to be changed. As I removed the bits of tattered rags, I found that the wound, while healing slowly, remained open and seeping. I reached for my pack and pulled out the arrowhead that was pulled from Vide days before and began toggling it between my fingers, searching for an answer. It was determined that it was poisoned with something, but outside of the poison we could not place where the metal or rather stone originated from. It was remarkably sharp with an ebony hazy to it, making it appear more like glass than metal or stone. Although, these details provided little insight as to the origin or purpose behind the object's creation. I returned it to its hiding place to be evaluated once more at a later date.

Donning my armor as quickly as I was able, I met some of the men by the fire as they were warming themselves and their vittles. Mostly bread filled with herbs along with cheese and salted meat. I opted for some fresh berries and cheese as my stomach was still ill at ease over the poison that may never fully free me from its grasp, a quite unwelcome feeling at any time, let alone when my strength and focus need to be at their highest. We ate leisurely and in relative silence, something that was not uncommon or worrisome and before we felt we had another moment to blink, the sun appeared to have nearly fully risen forcing us to get up and get moving.  Nearly half of the men had already departed for the vessel as instructed and the remainder were working to catch up.  I assisted where I could and then I, too, began making my way towards the vessel.

While the sound was a meager few hours' ride from our location, it was a significantly better option that venturing through the marsh.  Much to my displeasure, I venture into the marsh more often than I would care to and while it is welcoming to outsiders, it only welcomes you to become dinner.  It is said that it once was inhabited by nymphs, pixies and brownies who flitted about the valleys and river that poured in from the sound, dividing Caladh.  The great fracture that drove away a great portion of our world, also, poisoned that part of the mainland, creating the monsters that are now found within.  Some of them are known to us, but with each venture that takes us inside their world, more are discovered.

The marsh was just out of sight to the east, but as we continued our journey, I heard something moving quickly in our direction.  It was light at first, like that of someone tapping their hand upon a table, but then it grew louder like the beating of a drum.  I watched the men drop their things and stand ready, as a cloud of dust had formed and was now advancing towards us.  As I listened closely, I knew what we were hearing was hooves stamping the ground as a beast advanced.  Drawing my sword, I pressured my krigshast to advance and rushed towards the ever-growing cloud of dust.  The stamping grew louder as the two beasts synced their steps and were closing in on one another.  The beast came into sight, it was another krigshast, manned by one of my men. I slowed my pace while sheathing my sword, and the man brought his beast to a screeching halt at my sudden appearance.

"Commander Berenger!  The vessel has gone!" he shouted.

"What do you mean gone?!" I snapped.

"The men at the dock stated the vessel was released nearly a fortnight ago, they did not know we were coming," he said sternly.

"How is that possible?" I uttered just above a whisper.

He shook his head with uncertainty, and I felt myself hold back the urge to shout at him, for this was not his undoing.  I gritted my teeth, fighting the urge to press the matter with him before taking off towards the port in a gallop.  If the vessel truly were lost to us, we could not wait for its return further complicating the task at hand.  I plotted our options quickly in my mind as I rode, there would not be time to travel south, but I fear the dangers of the marsh when traveling with Ferand's betrothed.  I soon heard the men's pace quicken and the roar from their footsteps chasing after me.  The road was long but at my quickened pace, the sound swiftly came into view.  A path was cleared for me as I began making my way through the clusters of men anxiously waiting nearby.  Pulling my krigshast to a halt, I slung my legs over onto one side and slid onto the ground below.

"Where is the Port Master?!" I demanded.

A few of the men pointed towards a building lifted carefully above the sound on stilts and just as I began to take steps towards it, a man stepped out.

"Are you the Port Master?!" I called out.

"Aye, that I am," he responded, "to whom shall I ask calls upon me?"

"It is Commander Berenger, Port Master," one of the men shouted in response to which the Port Master responded by dropping to a kneel suddenly.

"Prince Berenger," he uttered swiftly, "forgive me for I did not see."

I closed the gap between us until I was no more than a few feet from him, "Rise Port Master, I wish to know why the request from your King was ignored."

"Request?" he replied sounding uncertain, "There has not been a request from the King in weeks."

"Weeks?" I heard myself repeat, "You received word from King Baylon prior to his passing?"

He did not meet my gaze, but I heard him utter, "Aye, that I did."

"Bring me the notice for I wish to read what may have been one of my father's last requests."

"Of course, Prince Berenger," he nodded quickly before scurrying back towards the building.

There were several sounds of dishevelment, as if his hunt for the request had led down a path unintended.

"Port Master!" I shouted, "Swiftly if you will!"

There were several more clangs of metal followed by the frantic muttering of a worried soul. My patience was stretching thin, and I could wait no longer. I stormed towards the building, bursting through the door to find that the Port Master had nearly destroyed all that he had in search of the request in question. There were papers and furnishings tousled throughout the space and as he crawled towards me on his knees, I knew I would get no satisfaction from this encounter.

"It has vanished Prince Berenger," his hands together with tightly woven fingers, "the request was here and now it is gone." He paused before looking up towards me, "Forgive me, someone must have taken it."

"What did the request entail?" I pressed him.

"King Baylon requested the ships be lent out to the mercenaries," he responded rather quickly.

"To what end?" I pressed him.

"Of that I cannot say for the remainder of the instructions were sealed," he looked at me perplexed at my lack of knowledge on the matter.

"Who delivered this request to you?"

He shrugged, "The hour was late, and the man was cloaked," he paused, "I could not see."

I gestured for him to stand once more, "Who retrieved the message?"

"A man, a mercenary perhaps," he shrugged once more.

"What makes you believe he could have been a mercenary?"

"He appeared just after one of their vessels arrived.  No one else would be found here at such an hour."

"Had you seen this man before?  Is there anything you can tell me about him?" I pressed him further.

He leaned in towards me and whispered, "No, but he was not dressed as a mercenary, nor did he move like one."

I stepped towards the door and closed it, for what I may need him to disclose was not for all to hear.

"How so?" I whispered.

"He moved swiftly, barely noticeable until he was in front of me," he paused appearing deep in thought, "and he was dressed like a man of position rather than a mercenary."

"Nobility?"

"Perhaps from one of the royal households," he sounded unsure.

"Could you describe what he wore?"

"No, I do not believe so," he shook his head, "however, if I saw him again I would undoubtably know it."

"Is there anything else you can tell me of this man?"

"His eyes, they were bright, brighter than any I had ever seen."

"Was he elven?" I inquired further.

He chuckled, "Never saw one of the likes of them to tell you."

I smiled forgetting how little of the world some have seen compared to myself.  I turned to leave, grasping the door's handle in my hand, "Oh and one more thing," I paused, "once this man retrieved the message, did he leave with the others?"

"Of that, I do not know," he paused, "please forgive me."

"All is forgiven, Port Master," I pulled the door open and stepped outside.

While returning to the shore I thought carefully over all that was said and all that was not. The Port Master clearly flustered by the sudden inquiry but not coached. Had he been, the responses received would have been more transparent and comprehensive, not filled with muttering and uncertainty. The thought nagged at me, why would my father lend out all our vessels to mercenaries? A cut of the profits would have been sizeable with so many at their disposal, but why? It was almost as if he was attempting to cut us off from all other kingdoms without the courtesy of justification. I felt my head begin to ache as I struggled to twist this piece about in my mind, then I thought of the man once more. A man with bright eyes? To my knowledge, man has never blessed with a light so bright it had nowhere to radiate but out our eyes, but elf kind, can hardly keep the light contained. It shines throughout their lily-white skin and radiates from them when shone to the light. They would, also, be agile enough to appear as if suddenly and then disappear nearly without a sound. Although he did not say this, I find it difficult to believe he would not have heard the man coming towards him or stepping away from him as he did not appear hard of hearing. Should this man not be elven, and I mistaken, the remark about the man's eyes would trouble me for some time. Elves have not dared to venture among us since I was a wee bairn and the appearance of them now would surely be ill-fated.  Unfortunately, this thought would need to be pinned until a later time as well as the men were growing restless.

"Send word to King Ferand, for we now must venture through the marsh," I commanded.

While the men did not utter any words or sounds of displeasure, it was clearly painted upon their faces for all to see.  The one place I never wished to venture, I now must.  Weakened and strained we shall go, but I hope the others are faring much better than I.  There was nothing more to do than grit our teeth and shoulder the burden.  As I hoisted myself back into the saddle, I forced myself towards the marsh.  Even at a distance, I felt its sickness leaping onto me, pulling me in.  Somehow, it felt different this time and that same ill-feeling in my gut had returned to me.  Something was about to change, I could feel it and while I could not walk away from an order, I knew in my gut we would not return as the men who left.

"We must deviate from the paths if we wish to keep our presence here a secret for long."  I pointed to a select few of the scouts standing nearby, "Go forth and see what you can find.  I pray there be a safer route than the one we are about to take."

Scouts sped ahead of the main pack, in hopes of pointing out any potential danger before it struck, and my confidence was high in their skill. The remainder of the men and I advanced forward in two packs, so that we may not be surrounded in the event of an ambush.  I held my arm up, demanding silence as we took our first steps inside.  It was warmer than my last excursion, much warmer.  Being closer to the sound and Tiene has placed us in sweltering heat and overgrowth of nearly all life found within.  The foliage was nearly double the size of the southern half of the marsh and the air was frighteningly suffocating.  It grasped at my throat and nasal cavity, cutting my lungs off from the air they so desperately needed.  I began pulling at my throat, straining to breathe when pulled a cloth from my pack and held it over my mouth and nose hoping to close off the toxins from entering further.  Within a few moments, I felt dramatically better, not free of the marsh's poison, but better.

"Cover all but your eyes men," I uttered through hoarse breaths.

I turned slightly hoping the visual would aid in what they may or may not have heard.  Several of the men had begun to cough and hack as they stepped inside the marsh, further alerting the marsh to our presence had it gone unnoticed previously.  Thankfully, they recovered quickly, and we pressed onward.  Scanning our surroundings, I noticed not only the foliage appeared differently, but the creatures within had changed as well.  Almost as if they had mutated from a concealed toxin.  The hares were no longer the little furry creatures that hopped around the meadows, they were nearly the size of a boar, with fangs and dark coats.  More the inner working of a nightmare than a fairytale.  Glancing around further, I noticed most of the marsh was hidden behind a dark greenish hue and an odor that reeked of death and decay.

Wet and hot, we continued forward using the sound as our guide, I felt reassured we would not so easily lose our way if we could hear the water crashing down onto the rocks at the base of the falls, just inside the marsh's border. Trudging through the sound would appear as a better option right now had it not been for the ever-changing depths of the water found there and the creatures that lurk within. The sound was home to several sirens and in their wake, being cast down the falls would be a welcome death to what they have in store for you. In all honesty, I do not believe anywhere was truly safe anymore as the waters and the lands were filled with beasts and men, both, when challenged present the potential for an unruly adversary. Then I thought of Conall, both man and beast, yet somehow found a way to survive within this region of misery.

As we trudged along the unbeaten path, I was taken back to that day. Conall was overrun by a throng of kobolds, large reptilian creatures with long skinny snouts filled with serrated teeth. In water, they appear more like serpents with their smooth, whiplike movements, but upon land they rise onto their two back legs freeing their forelimbs to wield large spears and knockdown opponents with their large, spiked tails. The sky had darkened since we first came upon them, and we watched in awe at the remarkable strength of one beast. When we were confident, the wolf had depleted most of its energy, we tore through the remaining kobolds just before he tore through us. Had he not been cast into murky pool in the marsh and turned, we may never have had the chance to reveal what he truly is. No amount of training could have prepared me for what we encountered that day nor the days that followed and while I fear little more than a broken heart, I was afraid of the events that soon would unfold when two of them are to be united under one banner.

The thought gave me chills even though I was boiling in this sauna. I found myself tugging at my armor and the fabric beneath it, longing to be free of its smothering grasp. I glanced towards the sky to aid in my estimate of how long we had been traveling, however, it was overcast and discolored preventing the sun from shining through. Whether traveling for minutes or hours, I cannot say as with each step that was taken, we felt no closer to our destination than the step before. We continued to wind our way through the varying paths ever watchful of the nearby pools and sludge that seemed to be found everywhere now, further slowly our progress. I dismounted to ease the burden on my mount and within a few moments, I heard several others slide from their krigshastar as well. Without uttering a word, I placed my hands on its reins and began pulling it forward. Night was sneaking up on us and I did not wish to remain in the thick of the marsh unequipped for the task and depleted.

It was nearly impossible to move in silence now. Each step caused us to sink further into the filth, forcing us to grunt and groan like boars in a mud hole. We needed to escape from here and quickly. The men who had not been taken by the sludge's grasp just yet began rushing towards the others, to aid them in their struggle. When out from the trees emerged, several men accompanied by large grey horses. They could not have been there long for I was certain they would not have evaded all of us. As they stepped towards us, graceful and bearing faint smiles, I noticed they were drenched from head to toe as if they had just stepped out of a bath. Aside from their sopping wet tunics and breeches, I noticed they wore no shoes or armor and their horses unbridled.

They stepped towards us slowly and without a sound, clearly unsure of our purpose here. One of them reached for me, but I did not take his hand for I fear this all be an illusion. I watched several of my men take their hands and rise out of the sludge and onto a small path of stone and moss nearby that previously had remained unseen. I still was not convinced, and I clung to my krigshast for support as I began moving once more. Their steeds aided in the extraction of several more of my men and they were soon gesturing for those men to follow them elsewhere. One of my captains outstretched his hand towards me, tempting me to take it, of which I did. I stood amongst them and watched these strangers offer their aid to us without restrictions and wondered how in all my time in the marsh I had never encountered them before now.

"Thank you for your kindness," I said softly not wanting to startle them.

They replied with only a smile and gestured for me to follow them. While I was hesitant, my men had all but given their souls to these strangers. Each man that was pulled from the sludge appeared to cling to their rescuer in a curiously familial bond, as if they were long lost friends being reunited. The further from the sludge and stench we walked the more restless our krigshastar were becoming and they were beginning to toss themselves about, pulling themselves from our grasp. I, too, felt uneasy. We were led to a large pool, relatively clear and free of debris. Several of my men rushed towards it, taking in fists full of water to drink and cleanse their bodies of the heat. The pool appeared peaceful enough and I, too, was tempted to take a drink. As I stepped towards the pool, I was pulled away by my krigshast and knocked onto my back. The impact sent a shockwave through my body and knocked the air out of my lungs. Gasping for air, I felt myself being pulled backwards along the ground. The krigshast was pulling back away from the water, and I now understood, there was something in the water.

"Away!" I attempted to shout, "You must get away from the water!"

"Commander, it is only water," I heard one of the men respond back.

Using the krigshast for balance, I brought my feet back under me and stood. Everyone was staring blankly upon me when my attention was drawn back towards the water. It was eerily calm and, in the men's, desperate need, they failed to see the trap before them.

"Get away from the water, NOW!" I commanded and my voice echoed throughout the marsh.

Despite their confusion, the men knew better than to disregard my orders and began fleeing the pool. The sudden change caused a turn in our rescuers and their once polite smiles now turned foul. All men within their reach were tossed into the pool and drug under in a furry of might and fins. Those men were not men, they too shapeshifted into something else, they were kelpies. Demonic horses from another world that seek those willing to follow them into a watery grave. When I turned the table on them, they were forced to act quickly and seize any who were within reach. My heart begged me to remain to aid the fallen, but my gut demanded I flee this land or become its next victim.

"Run!" I screamed with all my might, "All who are able flee while you can!"

I drew my sword and began violently slashing into the kelpies that remained on land. Their cries and the cries of my men tore at my insides, and I relished at the sight of the kelpie's blood painting itself across the land. Out of the corners of my eyes, I watched a few of my men remain at my side, to aid in the assault. They, too, were soon covered in a spray of darkened blood before being taken into the water to never be seen again. As I watched more of them being taken from me, I soon found myself and only one other still standing. He was a young man, fairly new to the royal guard, and probably never had the pleasure of witnessing something so vile. We stood there panting for several moments, attempting to catch our breath and reassess the situation.

"Are you alright?" I uttered.

He did not utter a sound and as I watched the blood drip down from his brow onto tear-stained cheeks and a quivering lip, I knew he was not, nor was I. Scanning the remains for anything that might have been living, only to find one of my men had somehow survived the attack and was now bleeding to death next to what would have been his watery grave. I knelt, taking his hand in mine before saying a prayer and then placing a dagger swiftly into his chest. The sudden action caused the young man to jump back with a gasp.

"Sometimes you have to hurt them to save them," I frowned knowing it was one of the worst things I have ever had to do, but I could not shy away from it. "Check for others that may still be living," I paused, "I will not leave them here to die."

"Do you not intend to take the dead?" he sounded offended.

"They belong to Boglach now," I paused, "this is all we can do for them."

We both turned to survey the land for anything living, whether man or kelpie as we soon would need to flee or be welcomed to our own watery grave, when I stepped towards a kelpie's head that had been freed from its body. I was certain it was a man when I took its head, but now it had been transformed back into a horse with smooth, dark scales like those of a fish. I was tempted to touch it as I hoped I would never again be given the chance, but once again, my gut advised me otherwise. I pulled my hand back and ran the tip of my sword across them, not sure what I was hoping to find, when I felt a sharp piercing pain in my right shoulder forcing me to drop my sword. My body tried to scream, but only air escaped me. My heart was thundering in my chest and as I attempted to turn towards the source, I felt another pain, just below the one before.  I reached to grab my sword with my left hand when I was forced forward onto my stomach, crushing my hand beneath my body.  I watched as eyes rose out of the water and knew they were coming to take me.  Pleading in my mind for the young man to see, but I knew there probably was not time.  Turning to face my enemy with my eyes wide, I greeted the bringer of my death and said a silence prayer for it to be swift.

# Conall

The journey back towards Tuiteam was not as I expected, much shorter than I could recall, and I wondered if I had been fully conscious during my return. The night's sky had choked out the sun's light, making the already formidable castle even more inhospitable. Once through the castle gates, I found we were quickly becoming surrounded by Tuiteam's populace and several clusters of the royal guard. Most were found with their mouths agape or with pointed fingers, while others were found shrieking at what I would assume was just the sheer sight of me. I appeared elven and just as the woman who tended to me fell towards the floor, frightened over the sight of my ears, others would do the same. To think of how they would react had they seen me change, for they knew nothing of true monsters.

They feared elves and, in their actions, desired not only to rid them from their realm, but to eradicate them from Caladh at any opportunity.  Unsure as to what caused their fear, I could do nothing more than close my eyes and bear the sounds of their fear and taunting.  They began throwing things upon the cage's bars violently, causing an unwelcoming sensation to spread throughout.  I would have given my soul to shift into a falcon at this moment, but I knew that was not within my power.  For protection, I agreed to stay here in hopes of waiting out an unforeseen future, but protection is far from what I received during my time here.  I hope Eira was able to find an easier path away from this land.

When my eyes opened again, we had stopped just shy of a large wooden platform where several tall pillars stood upon it with chains dangling from each of them.  These were not designed to hang someone, but for something else entirely.  My attention was drawn towards the Jagare that had once again surrounded the cage to begin poking and prodding me, tempting me to give into their demands, to which I did not yield.  The door to the cage swung open just before I was pulled outward by my legs and onto the ground, the crowd erupted with excitement.  To what end this path held, I did not know, but I knew it would end in torment.  If I turned, I could make a break for it, but with Haxa near I would more than likely not be successful in my attempt.  For after all, it was she who sabotaged my last attempt and while she was not within reach, I saw her watching from afar, cloaked in darkness, but displaying a diabolical grin that matched her menacing eyes.

Deliberately the Jagare took their time pulling me up onto the platform, permitting any onlooker willing to strike to have a chance at it. Most felt nothing more than a pat, but to the ones with rocks or staffs in hand, I could feel my bones beginning to ache.  Upon the Jagare's delivery, other members of the royal guard stepped in and began tightly locking my body within the chains scattered between the four posts.  When the final chain was latched around my neck, I was pulled upright with another roar from the crowd.  Had they only known what I was and the desire for my execution may not have been wanted so greatly.  The faces of the crowd were an array of emotion to what was happening but more of them than not, wanted to watch me suffer.  My attention was drawn back towards Haxa, who was standing calmly near one of the far walls, hands carefully placed upon the top of her staff and eyes wide.  Her long silver hair out of view, but her eyes even cloaked slightly were easy for me to find.  She was concentrating on me, but why I do not know.  Waiting for the moment when they would strike, I mentally prepared for what was to come when I saw King Ferand step onto the platform and raise his hands high into the air.  The crowd roared with delight and embraced the presence of their King, who was remarkably well dressed for the hour.

"My people," he shouted, "this elf has committed acts of treason against your king and is a traitor to his own kind!" He turned towards me to look at me briefly before continuing, "Shall we show him the same kindness he has shown us?!"

"Aye!" the crowd responded in favor of his ill-treatment although I did not nor was I what he claimed.

Stepping towards me, he stopped just within arm's reach and whispered to me, "Escape again and I shall take her head instead of yours." I pulled at the chains, frustrated and angry at the notion his eyes were now set on her, "Or perhaps I shall permit you to watch as I ravage her again and again until I am satisfied."

The chains cracked at the sudden tension I placed upon them for I could not stop myself from feeling angered over his threat. She was not mine, nor had she been, but she was the only one of my kind that I had seen for some time. I felt strangely protective of her, and it was rapidly becoming my weakness.

He grinned, "Your heart deceives you Conall," he glanced behind me briefly and then back into my eyes, "Strike him until I am satisfied."

Stepping back slightly, he folded his arms as he looked upon me disapprovingly. Only a moment or two later, I felt a clawed whip ripping through the flesh on my back. I tried to relax my body and limbs, but they were pulled too tightly to allow any give. They struck again with a thunderous crack that soon disappeared into the crowd's chants for more. Their calls seemed to blur with each crack of the whip and while I maintained my stone exterior for some time, as the whip tore fuller through my flesh, sinking its teeth into bone that lay beneath, I felt my body give a little as I began to wince from the pain. Each tear relentlessly seared in the night air and just when I felt I was nearing my breaking point, the man stopped. Although, I could not see him, I could hear him panting from the stress of striking me in such rapid succession. I removed my gaze from King Ferand briefly to glance downward as I felt my breeches were damp. There were nearly fully saturated with my blood. I began to exhale slowly when I heard him speak again.

"Have you tasted enough?" he uttered in a low tone.

I did not raise my head, but my eyes rose to meet his gaze from beneath my brow. Nothing I could say would appease his unyielding heart and he would not stop until he was given all he wanted. On this night, he would have to welcome disappointment, for I was not born to yield to him. I did not utter a sound, but a growl escaped me, and my eyes flashed before him. He pulled away slightly and then returned to me, closer than before.

"I will break you," he growled in a low voice.

His boldness gnawed at me, but underneath it all I knew he had a bruised ego.

"Best be wary of the threats you make," I growled, "for your brother will not always be near to protect you."

His teeth became tightly clenched together as the palm of his hand struck the side of my face, bloodying my lip. I ran my tongue over the split, feeling the sting of it. His weak assault made me grin, without his brother nearby nor the aid of his men, that was the best he could do to an unarmed man. A low chuckle escaped me, and I felt him grasp my hair, pulling it back tightly.

"You will yield to me," his voice demanded.

"Break me if you must, but I will not," I spat.

He retreated and began pacing before the crowd, clearly unsure of what his next action should be.  The crowd fell silent at the unexpected pause, awaiting their King's next command, then he stopped and strutted towards one of the guards.  I heard him whisper something about fetching a powder through muffled breaths but nothing more.  The guard rushed away quickly only to return a short time later with a large ceramic jar.  I watched them carefully from the corners of my eyes and then I glanced towards the wall where Haxa had been standing, she was no longer there.  Perhaps off to commit more crimes against the crown or she moved to pursue a better vantage point, I know not.  When my attention turned back towards King Ferand, he was now standing very near to me and displaying a diabolical grin.

"Since you will not yield, you will tell me all that I wish to know or suffer you shall," he whispered clearly not wanting the crowd to hear.

I scoffed at his petty threat and turned my face away. He stepped behind me and placed a hand on my shoulder before placing the other on my lower back, or at least what was left of it.  A sharp pain rushed through my back and down my one leg.  I gritted my teeth attempting to endure the pain as I felt the pain push through my abdominal wall, he had placed a hand on the arrow hole from early that day and was sliding the remnants of the arrow back and forth throughout the cavity it created.  With each pass, I could feel the shaft further splintering inside me, I closed my eyes and continued gritting my teeth.

Pulling at my hair once more, I felt my head jerk back, rattling the chains nearby, "Tell me of the maiden, who is she to you?" he insisted.

"Is your bed not warm enough with maidens of your own kind that you now seek out elf kind?" I spat, eyes open and bright with light.

He pulled away slightly before a stinging pain rushed across my skin and into every crevice found nearby. The pain took my breath away, forcing me to unclench my jaw to draw in another breath. When the pain did not cease after several moments, I jerked against the restraints struggling to free myself from their grasp. The chains cracked that the sensation and caused laughter to escape the ever-watchful crowd. They delighted in the pain and suffering of others, much to the disgust of other races. I watched their faces, laughing and mocking my pain, it was then I knew mercy nor hope could not be found among them. I pulled against the restraints again, harsher than before and unyielding, causing one of them to snap from the pressure. King Ferand drew back towards the edge of the platform, and I cast the chain towards him just before I was restrained by more of the Jagare. My skin, burning with anger, had sealed some of my wounds and stopped me from bleeding further. The pain was dulling to a more manageable level when I noticed the King had returned to my side.

"Keep your secrets for she will be found," his voice low and sharp. He gestured something to someone unseen by me and then I heard the whip crack once more, "Until I am satisfied or he collapses," he ordered. "This is what happens to traitors of the crown, so let it be known!" he shouted back towards the crowd and once again, they cheered with delight at his injustice.

Minutes drew on as hours and the pain nearly unbearable. Each time that my legs or arms would give out, he would add more powder bringing me back to consciousness and then resume. When nearly all the crowd had fled, he finally ceased, and the chains relaxed. My body lay lifeless on the cool wooden platform that had been heavily painted with my blood, these wounds may never fully heal, and I was wary of the damage my pride had cost me. She was not mine, nor had she ever been, but imagining him ravaging her was more than I was willing to endure. The price I paid for her to remain hidden, she would never know, nor should she have to bear that burden.

The King muttered something before departing for his chambers as the hour was late, but my hearing and vision were significantly diminished presently, and I was unable to understand anything further. My vision had fallen to a haze and the torches that once shone so brightly, looked little more than that of candlelight wavering in the darkness. I felt a tug at my legs and knew my body was about to be drug once more to a destination unknown and my mind no longer cared. I closed my eyes and endured the journey as my will to fight was nearly gone. My thoughts returned to her, the feeling of her lips upon mine and the freedom of the wilds, it was there I felt my mind relax.  The time of us moving about freely has passed and unless King Ferand could be stopped, it may never return.

My mind returned to the present sometime later when I felt my body collide with the sand of the cool cavern floor, and I knew I had been returned to my prison.  My eyes remained closed, but I listened to the men carefully, hoping for any sign that the King was willing to relent on his punishment at least for tonight.

"I am not certain why this elf is worth all the trouble he's caused, but the King wishes for him to remain alive," he scoffed.

"Think we should take one of his ears while he is unconscious?" the second voice shuffled his feet closer to me.  "We may never get the chance to see an elf again," his voice slightly upturned with curiosity towards the end.

"Aye, great idea mate," the first one spoke again, his voice much closer than before.

I soon could feel and smell their foul breath upon me, and their rough fingers searching for one of my ears through the bloodied strands.  I lay patiently for them to make their move and when I felt the coolness of a blade slide just behind my ear, I reach for one of them, catching them by surprise.  The first one ran in fear, while the other was quivering within my grasp.  I wanted to bash his skull against one of the many tombs the cavern held, but my depleted strength, barely permitted me to grasp him as I did.

"Touch me again and you will lose more than your ears," I growled just before releasing the man.

He scampered back towards the door, dropping something large along the way.  I could not hold focus on it, nor could I move towards it, investigating the object would have to wait.  Closing my eyes once more, I quickly fell into a deep sleep ever hopeful I would be free from these walls when I woke once more.

# Lira

We walked in relative silence, as we closed the gap between the entrance and the hatch that was waiting for us at the other end.  The tunnel was dark and musty, with very little air moving throughout giving it a stale odor that was difficult to shake.  My company did not seem to be bothered by the scent or the jaunt through the darkness, almost as if he were more comfortable here than in the light.  We treaded very lightly as any sound appeared to echo throughout the space, even without keen hearing.  It made me wonder how anyone venturing through here could have gone unnoticed or how they found their way without the light.  Nearing what I assumed would be the end of the long tunnel, I felt Drayk slow before me, gently placing his hand upon mine.  He squeezed my hand and gestured for me to remain behind while he advanced onward.  I shook my head, reluctant for us to part ways again, when he insisted I remain there.  I bit my lower lip stopping myself from uttering a sound, not willing to risk giving away our position. The hatch, was more like a door, but it was grated and made of iron, like the tunnel we found ourselves in. With minimal effort, Drayk appeared to have opened it and was pulling it back towards us. The room it opened to was almost fearfully quiet and I wondered where this tunnel was going to place us.

It appeared dark, but with faint stone walls, not metal ones as I half expected, and he soon vanished out of sight. I leaned briefly onto the threshold, but soon retreated not wishing to anger him or disclose our location to anyone that may be lurking nearby. Not sure who would have been lingering in such a place, but I was not willing to risk it. Drayk reappeared a moment later, slowly stepping towards me until my back greeted the wall. He then extended his arms, placing both of his hands firmly on the wall just on either side of my face. The sudden movement surprised me, and I inhaled sharply, unsure as to his purpose. As he brought his face in towards mine, I felt him step further towards me, bringing his hips within inches of mine. I closed my eyes willing his purpose to be known before I made a fool of myself.

He whispered to me, "This man, are you certain he is what he claims?"

"Aye, that I am," I responded, not ready to open my eyes.

"Are you certain he is worth your life?"

My eyes opened at the notion that there might be the need to trade one life for another and if so, was his worth more than mine.  I wanted to believe we both could be saved, and we would be, but with those words, I felt doubt slip under my skin.

"It will not come to that," I whispered trying to sound confident, but I heard my voice crack betraying me.

I felt him nod and pull back away from me revealing the bright eyes I had grown to search for in the dark.  Unsure of what he meant to me or what purpose he held, I felt our time together was nearly spent, although, I am not sure how.  I brushed my fingers across his cheeks and watched his eyes glow brighter, further luring me in when I felt his fingertips touch my lips.

"My heart has already betrayed me by loving a woman that was never meant to be mine," he paused, "I shall not permit it to make the same mistake twice."

I was bewildered at the revelation that was just laid before me and unexpectedly, all was becoming clear.  He sought forbidden love and was banished for it.  Depending on who she is or may have been, forgiveness would never be given by King Aldon as those markings are rarely if ever given.  They are the markings of sorrow and created by their own tears as they are forced to relive their loss or betrayal repeatedly until their heart can bleed no more.  I have never known someone to have endured the process and now looking upon him in astonishment, I noticed the pain he carried that had previously gone unnoticed.  That torment was in everything he did, from his guarded heart to the company of darkness he keeps, he would never be rid of it.

"We must go now while darkness is still upon us," he whispered forcing the subject to change.

I knew he was right, and I nodded my understanding. He drew the hood of his cloak up and stepped back into the room ahead. I mirrored his action and followed tightly behind him, unsure what may lay ahead. While it was not a room we had entered, it was a long corridor that appeared to widen as it continued onward. There were no passages that led from the corridor, and it would be difficult to move through with multiple people. I could easily see how this would be the perfect place for someone to escape. It was not long before we encountered a dead end to the passage, but upon further inspection, I noticed there was a faint light radiating through an opening in the ceiling. There was the hatch we had been looking for. Drayk reached for the hatch and pulled himself upwards towards it, giving him a much better vantage point. He hung there for only a moment and then dropped back down. Something had changed and I could see it written all over his face. I stepped towards him and once again, watched his eyes turn dark just before the hatch above us began to vibrate. I dropped down and covered myself in the event more than just a few bits of stone would fall. Shortly thereafter, I heard and felt the hatch rupture, shooting bits of rock and metal about the corridor. When I stood back up and shook the dust off, I turned towards him with a disapproving eyebrow raised. He rolled his eyes and snickered at me.

"Would you prefer to lead the way?" he uttered sarcastically before holding up his hands towards the dislodged hatch.

I scoffed before folding my arms in front of my chest, clearly not amused by his actions or commentary. While he knew little of healing magic, his ability to break in and out of places was remarkable. He wielded his innate magical gift with finesse when required, but otherwise shied away from it, treating it more as a curse than a gift. I watched him slide the hatch slightly to the side before connecting lightly with the wall and launching himself upward through the opening. He performed the feat with such grace, it was no wonder he was able to move about the tower unseen and perhaps how he was able to stumble upon Conall and I that morning by the stream. My thoughts were beginning to wander to what else he may have known or seen when I felt his hand touch my shoulder. I took his forearm in my hand and allowed him to pull me towards him. The gesture brought us dangerously close together once more and while my curiosity, no, my desire for him was at its peak, my want to find Conall was greater.

Peeling ourselves away from one another, he shifted attention towards the hatch and remaining debris, knocking the pieces down inside quickly before sliding the hatch back in place. This passage was equally as quiet as the last, but significantly lighter than the previous from a source unseen. Rushing forward we found ourselves greeted by the bodies of several fallen members of the royal guard a top of a large stone platform dimly lit by a few torches placed near the opening of what appeared to be a stone staircase located just northwest of us.  Unsure of the path to take, I grabbed Drayk's shoulder and pulled him back towards me.

"Where does the staircase lead?" I whispered.

"Towards a labyrinth of passages that slowly rise until the main floor is reached," he responded.

I exhaled heavily, frustrated, and confused over how following that course would help us when I heard him continue.

"There are a few passages that branch off from the labyrinth," he paused, "one of them contains access to the prison and the other something far worse."

Thinking carefully over our choices, I stared blankly at one of the torches on the wall, trying to focus my thoughts.

"Heading there is our only option, and our time here is running out," he grabbed my hand once more and pulled me behind him as he turned to venture up the staircase.

Though it may have been our only option, I felt reluctant to follow him and I was unsure as to the reason.  Perhaps it was just my nerves or the pile of dead guardsman that now lay at our feet, but something felt amiss about it all.  Fortunately, fate would intervene not more than twenty to thirty steps into our ascent.  We could hear the voices of men creeping towards us along with the sound of something large thudding against the stone.  The tone was soft, but audible.  As it moved closer, Drayk and I backed our way down the staircase and fled towards a dark patch near the hatch in case we needed to retreat suddenly.  He stepped in front of me and from his gauntlets drew two dark blades, razor sharp and black as shadow. Our breathing slowed to nearly a stop as we watched and waited for the men to appear. Their voices and footsteps grew louder with each passing moment, but the thudding sound remained unchanged. Their tone conveyed frustration over the mass they carried, but the mass remained unnamed.

The bickering continued until they reached the platform, where they carelessly tossed the mass onto the stone surface. It was large and blood-spattered, as I would have expected a corpse to appear after a tragic encounter with the guillotine. When it did not move, I resigned any further evaluation of it and focused on the two men who were carrying it. Not being familiar with members of the royal guard, I was unsure of their status or why they would be dragging this poor soul into the depths for disposal. They did not appear in distress, only strained from lugging such a mass down what I would assume was no less than a few flights of stairs unassisted.

"Why can we not just leave him here?" the one insisted. "Feels like we have been dragging him for days."

The second man swatted that man's shoulder, "For when Commander Berenger returns, he will surely venture down here expecting to find him," he paused, "and we ought not be caught disobeying the King's orders."

"But why this one?" he kicked the mass, "He is no different than the others."

"You hush, I wish not to be in the presence of anyone questioning King Ferand," he leaned in towards the other and whispered, "for his *cruelty* knows no bounds." He leaned down and grasped the man's arms, "Now, give me a hand before he breaks my back."

The other man bent down and began pulling the man forward by one of his legs. Their weakness was appalling, and it pained me to watch this man being drug down a dark corridor with such brazen disregard. If this man were just a man, why did they believe Commander Berenger would have any desire to see him after his passing? There was something more I did not see. I was tempted to follow them, but as they reached the opposite side of the corridor, I noticed they, too, were met with a dead end or at least what appeared to be one. They were fumbling and mumbling amongst themselves just before several loud clangs echoed back towards us. The sudden shift in sound caused me to flinch and I, once again, felt Drayk's hand find mine to soothe my weary spirit. We watched as an iron door swung opened and the men grunted as they pulled the man through it. The room beyond the door was well lit, casting a beam of light onto the platform before us. I unknowingly had stepped towards it when I felt Drayk tug me back towards him.

"We need to see what is beyond that door," I whispered.

"Nothing worth seeing will be found there," he hissed.

"Then let us rid ourselves of two potential shadows."

His eyes narrowed and shifted beyond me towards the men inside. With clear reluctance, I felt him cast my hand aside before following the wall towards the opening.  In the shadow of the door, I watched as he clung to the wall, listening, and waiting.  I followed his lead along the same wall, holding my breath for a moment until I reached his side.  The men, still mumbling, had not appeared to take notice of us allowing us another moment to survey the situation.  Though I could not see them, I could hear them remarkably well and though most of their conversation had not made sense to me, we now knew that the man was not a man, but an elf and he was alive.  Badly beaten and broken but alive.  I felt my heart begin to race at the thought that the bloody figure that was drug across the platform could have been Conall and although I wanted to disconnect myself from that thought, I could not.

There was a sudden gasp followed by the sound of someone choking.  In a panic, one of the men rushed through the door, completely unaware of the danger waiting for him on the other side.  The man was pulled into the darkness where Drayk delivered his own version of justice.  I heard little more than a pop and crack before I saw the man's body fall lifeless at our feet.  Our attention drawn back towards the room.

"Touch me again and you will lose more than your ears," a low crackling voice growled.

The other man was now scurrying his way towards the door in a half stumble, half crawl method.  Drayk did not bother to conceal himself and merely extended his arm into the doorway for the man to impale himself with his dagger.  Had he hit with more force, and he would have been decapitated.  Drayk leaned down to wipe the man's blood from his blade before shoving him aside with his foot towards the pile of dead that greeted us upon our arrival here. I stepped out from the shadows to meet Drayk's gaze, he appeared annoyed, yet pleased with the situation.

"It is a tomb," he uttered, "nothing more."

I turned to see the elf the men had been tormenting. At first, he appeared badly beaten, but as I stepped towards him, surrounded by torch light, I knew a beating was not all he had endured. My pace quickened as more of him was brought into the light and in a rush, I slid onto my knees beside him just before taking my hand and placing it gently upon the nape of his neck. His heartbeat was so faint, I had to hold my breath just to hear it. Reaching to uncover his face, I found my hands were shaking, frightened over the thought that this, mutilated mass was Conall. I brushed his hair back slowly, pleading to myself for the gods to let this be anyone else. As his hair fell back away from his high cheekbones, revealing very elven ears, I let my eyes fall towards his lips. They were swollen with a distinct notch cut into them that had scarred over some time ago. I touched them carefully with my fingertips, knowing that I had seen and felt them before.

"Eira," I heard Drayk utter softly as he stepped towards me.

"It is him," I felt my eyes welling up with emotions I did not even know I had, "we must help him."

"Eira, we cannot move him in his current state," he said softly.

"Why not? They did," I insisted.

"Dawn approaches and I have no reason to believe they would leave this man unattended for long."

Part of me knew he was right, but I could not pull myself away from the emotions that were now consuming me.

"Please do something or he will die," I pleaded, feeling my heart, and hearing my voice crack as the words fell broken upon him.

"You know I cannot do what you ask," he snapped, "I was able to close yours if but temporarily," he paused looking down upon the man that lay before us before looking back at me, "his entire body has been maimed and is beyond my aid."

"I will not leave him here to die!" I heard my voice jump causing Conall to stir slightly at the sound, "You believed I was worth saving, why not him?!"

"You could be saved," he snapped, "he may not make it through the night."

"Have you no heart at all," I reached for him, "please help me give him a chance," I pleaded.

He sighed heavily, not wishing to utter his displeasure or disapproval of the situation further as this was not his manner. He turned to step towards the pack near the door and flipped over the flap, unsure what may have been inside, I watched as he lifted it and returned to my side. As he placed it beside me, I began rifling through it, searching for anything we could use. There were bottles filled with unknown liquids, along with some vittles that I could save for when he woke, but nothing more.

"Help me roll him onto his back," I paused, "while it will be painful, it may make it easier for him to breathe."

When he did not reply I turned towards where he had just been standing and he was gone. During my search I had not realized that Drayk fled the chamber and was no longer within my sight to find. Hoping he fled to find more supplies, my attention returned towards the pack that had been left, I began opening the bottles searching for anything that he could drink or that would cleanse his wounds. However, looking upon them now, they were nearly all open and caked in a powder I had never seen before. It was dark and ashy in appearance and reeked of salt mixed with something else, something unpleasant. This maybe what is preventing him from healing as he should. It must be removed. Taking what appeared to be an ale of sorts, I reached over him while grasping his shoulder, and rolling him onto his side where I began pouring the liquid slowly into his mouth. He did not attempt to close his mouth on his own, so I aided as I could, hoping it would give his body something to cling to as I worked to clean him.

His body still terribly dark and still, I knew I could not give him all he needed, I just needed him well enough to move without him taking any further damage. The tunnel would provide the shelter and escape route as no one would think to look for us there, but getting him well enough would take time, time we did not have. I rose to my feet and began searching the room, there must be something here of use. There were a few pairs of tattered breeches which could be used to bind a few of his more serious injuries, but nothing more, when my attention was brought back towards the light.  I watched the torches carefully flicker from an unfelt breeze prompting further exploration.  The torches were sitting in small vats of oil, that not only smelled lovely, but could easily be used to seal the wounds on his back provided I could cleanse them first.  Removing one carefully from the wall, I walked back towards him when I heard the large iron door slam shut.

Running towards it, I listened carefully for any sign that the person who closed it was still nearby.  There was the brief sound of footsteps, but then they quickly faded.  I reached for the handle before tugging and pulling it frantically.  Lowering myself towards the ground, I began to focus, hoping that shifting would help ease the burden of breaking open this door when I saw them.  Several claw marks and dents scattered across the door and wall nearby, escapes had been attempted before. This place was not just a tomb, it was a prison for something other than elves and men.  This is where King Ferand has chosen to hide and torture Conall to the point of death.  This cruelty should not be allowed to continue, we must get out of here.

Stopping only to place the oil at Conall's side, I returned to my search efforts.  While this was a tomb no doubt, there must be a water source nearby as there does not appear to be a means of providing for him with any sort of frequency.  I scanned the perimeter carefully when I stumbled upon a small pool near the base of the back wall.  It was not there intentionally, but it would provide enough to cleanse and nourish his body, should he wake again.  Rather than move him towards the source, I opted to saturate a portion of the cloak I was wearing and bring the water to him.  When it was nearly sopping wet, I returned to him and knelt beside him, before pulling his head onto my lap.  There I began wringing the water from the cloak over his back, painting the sand beneath us in crimson and ash streaks.  Each pass of the water forced more of the powder out of his body, and he was beginning to respond to my touch.  His body will never be fully rid of it, but he will not be as pained by it as he is now.

While permitting the excess to dry, I found several puncture wounds in his torso and leg, reminding me of the arrows that forced us to part ways only the morning before.  Touching them softly, I noticed that they had not begun to heal either which prompted further investigation.  I found perforations stretching out from each opening leading me to believe remnants of these arrows may still inside.  I slid the tip of my finger just inside the largest one and was met with resistance.  The tip of the arrow did not feel as if it were still inside, so I felt safe to push it through.  In one quick motion, I shoved my finger inside his flesh enough for a portion of the shaft to be seen.  Conall incoherently groaned from the sensation as I removed the shaft just before running some water into the opening.  I examined the remaining openings and removed what I could just before flinging my cloak out onto the sandy surface.  Rolling him onto his back, I tipped his head back slightly to pour more of the ale into his mouth before forcing it closed again.  In small increments I did this until the bottle had been drained and his breathing appeared to be returning to normal.

He lay there peacefully resting as I look upon him when I noticed how filthy his locks had become to where their original color had nearly gone.  Brushing his hair back away from his cheeks, I wiped off what I could without disturbing him and I could once again see the color of his cheeks and pale hue of his swollen lips.  I found myself lost in wonder over him and as I brushed my fingertips across his lips repeatedly, I reminisced of the kiss they shared with mine.  It was not as I would have wished it, however every touch, every glance from him only made me yearn for him.  Even now, I felt drawn to him and though I was tempted to place my lips once more upon his, I could not bring myself to do so.

Leaning against a nearby statue, I eagerly watched the iron door while rinsing and running my fingers through his hair, which was now pleasantly soft and free from blood and debris.  As my eyes and mind grew tired from the anticipation, my attention was drawn back towards him.  His face and body were riddled with old and new scars at various staging of healing, making me wonder what path he had followed that lead him to such violent ends.  Placing my hand within the oil, I traced each wound, each scar with my fingers, attempting to carve them into my memory and understand his pain.  While I too, have suffered, nothing I have endured compares to what I am seeing and feeling now.  Each groove, each stitch, each shattered bone healed potentially stronger than before, but to be forced to see those painful memories every time you see your own reflection, must add further offence to an already battered soul. Attempting to understand his pain, only forced me to relive my own. I pulled back the leather that covered the nathair's puncture wound and noticed it was still discolored. My skin had nearly fully healed over, but beneath the surface lay a purplish hue that never seemed to disperse. Unfortunately, since I too, found myself incapacitated during my recovery, I could only hope that Drayk did all he could as I am attempting to do for Conall now. Other than Bryn, I have yet to encounter another like us in many years and I was anxious to see what he was like when he awoke, provided we both survived until the moment arrived.

In the absence of terror or company, I scanned the room once more. Some parts were darker than others due to placement of scattered torches and there was a chill to the air which comforted me since I already held a warmer temperature than most. The walls, floor and ceiling were of the same stone, leading me to believe this place was carved into the rock at one time, not built into it. However, the large stone statues and coffins strategically placed throughout the space gave it a rather eerie ambiance. Lifting his head gently, I slid myself out from under him and pulled a rolled portion of the cloak to act in my stead before standing to examine the statues further. This was not your typical hall of the dead; each statue was meticulously tended to, and some were more recent than others. There was one that drew me away from the typical cross and angelic beauties that surrounded us. A coffin, hidden from the light and with a lid slightly ajar beckoned me. With each step towards it, I felt something sinister pulling at me. I lowered myself beside it and listened, something was breathing. In a low and dry rasp, I could hear it.

"Who are you?" I whispered softly not wanting to startle them.

A sound crackled, but no words were heard. I stood and began sliding the lid as best as I could, but it only moved slightly from how it was found.

"Were you brought here to die?" I whispered.

I watched as their eyes opened and had it not been for the white of them, I would not have seen them at all. It was not a man they belonged to, but a varlet, with short dark hair to match his eyes. A foul odor was now seeping through the gap prompting my search for a cause. When I soon realized it was his own filth that he lay in causing the odor. Curiously I watched him and as his mouth attempted to move again with no sound, I rushed back towards the pool, scooping up what I could to bring to him. I let the liquid seep between my fingers and into his mouth and appeared to vanish just after touching the surface of his lips. Clearly, he had been here for some time, but was still very much alive.

"Who are you and why were you brought here?" I whispered again.

"Ur…ie…Prin…ce…Ur...ie," he uttered.

I felt my cheeks tighten from my jaw snapping shut at the revelation that a prince of Tuiteam was placed here to die. Other than being caked in his own filth, I saw nothing ill about him. I suppose the reasoning is not important, but should it become necessary, it will be his life that is given in exchange for ours.

# Bryn

I was barely a few steps outside of the garden when I was greeted by King Itheal's page.  A tall and lanky individual that when turned sideways appeared barely thicker than that of a hawk's feather and he used this to his advantage while seeking out information that was not for his ears.  He was not one of my favorite people.

"You are late Lord Bryn," he raised one of his eyebrows, "King Itheal demands a word with you promptly."

"Aye, of course," I nodded.

The page turned abruptly and began marching towards what I believed was the main chamber, but when he strode past it, my thoughts began to churn, though I dare not inquire. Fortunately, I did not have to wait long for the answer to reveal itself.  We stepped one after another into an audience chamber not far from the main hall.  The page and I bowed nearly in unison before I noticed King Itheal rushing towards me, placing his hands upon my shoulders.

"Bryn, might we have a word," he said sounding eager.

"Of course, King Itheal, how may I assist you?"

He nudged the page away and turned to walk us towards the far end of the room, "Have you received word?" his brow tightened as if to emphasize his meaning without having to utter it in the presence of others.

"Unfortunately, I have not," he was beginning to glower, "but if you would permit me to step away while you continue preparations, I feel confident that I am up to trying again."

"Tremendous, please do so at once, for I am anxious to reach an agreement with Tiene."

"Understood, I shall take my leave then," I bowed slightly before backing away and just as I reached the door to turn and exit, I heard him speak again.

"Oh, and Bryn," his tone soft, "it is my understanding that you failed to retire in your bedchamber last evening."

I felt my heart flutter before sending the sensation lower into my stomach, I turned back towards him, "Aye, that is correct your majesty."

"Shall I inquire who or what detained you at such an hour," his voice was light, but his fingers were beginning to drum against the crook of his arm with ever growing curiosity.

"The moon, your majesty," uttered with my voice pitched higher than expected, "as you know elves do not rest as you do and frequently seek solace in the company of the moon and its stars."

"Hmmm," he nodded appearing not entirely convinced by my story, "I had hoped a young maiden might have drawn your attention."

I smirked at his surprising response.  Maidens were rarely if ever mentioned in my presence, at least not since the early days of my arrival here.  Since I will outlive all the members of his court, it would not behoove me to philander with any of them.  I am confident that this has not entered their minds, or they would not have wasted breath uttering such and reminding any king of their mortality can be treacherous depending on their disposition that day.

"Perhaps the right maiden has not chosen me as of this morning and I shall have to wait another day," I smiled knowing that while this may have been a whimsical response, there was more truth to it than not.

He nodded and returned my smile before gesturing me off.  I went without any further delay.  As I vacated the room, I felt now may be the opportune time to venture into his study.  He appeared otherwise occupied and I was hoping to not need more than a few moments there at best.  In a quickened pace, I reached the study with no more than a few awkward glances, most of which seemed drawn towards my ears, not my location, which was quite typical.  When I was sure all was clear, I placed my hand upon the handle and turned it sharply.  The latch lifted with ease and the door swung open just before I entered trying to appear as if I was summoned on the off chance someone was lurking within. The room was silent, quickly I scanned the room before stepping towards the desk.

The closer I became the more I searched the floor for a hatch, but all I could see were grooves left in the marble near the legs, probably from when the desk was moved. When the desk was moved, I repeated to myself. Crouching down, I ran my fingers along the floor when I noticed a dark round loop just beneath one of the legs. I kicked my feet out before me and pushed the desk out, revealing a carefully hidden hatch. Grasping the loop in my hand, I pulled and pulled again to no avail when I remembered the spike that was concealed in my boot. I reached for it and placed it in a small opening near the center of the loop, hoping to gain leverage when the spike became lodged. My first instinct was to kick it to release the grasp the crevice had on it, but then I looked again. The piece did not become lodged in error, but it was meant to find that place. Leaning in, I tried turning it which did not work; angling it which, also, did not work. In a last stitch effort, I placed my hand upon it and pressed downward. Something inside clicked and when I grabbed the loop a second time, I felt it spin slightly in my fingers just before clicking again. It was a lock puzzle which prompted my curiosity further as to the purpose of this hidden chamber as these have not been made in over a century.

The hatch lifted, exposing a ladder that disappeared into the mouth of it. Quickly removing the spike, I lowered myself down and onto the ladder in just before closing the hatch above me and shutting out all light. My eyes adjusted rapidly, and I opted to speed up the descent by leaping from the ladder. I was greeted with another stone floor no more than ten or twelve feet from the hatch. Upon my landing dust became lofted into the air and I worked quickly to clear it from my mouth and lungs, or risk being heard should anyone enter the King's study. As the dust settled, I noticed there were candles nearby that would aid in my search if lit. I used a bit of flint found nearby to strike the stone and light one of them. The light radiated off the nearby parchment nearly blinding me with its sudden intensity. Based on what Rose had told me, I expected to find something quite different than a room chuck full of scrolls, ancient texts, and dusty wooden trunks. Uncertain where or how to begin, I started with what would appear to be the easiest, the scrolls, as I did not have much time.

While I wished to heed Rose's advice, there was no way I could search the area and let it remain untouched. I brushed off what I could before beginning to unroll and read them with precision. Only a few lines were needed to know if a text or scroll was of any importance and so far, most contained little to no value for my purposes here. I shifted through more than a dozen when I came upon one containing handwriting that I recognized. It was written in elven by the hand of King Aldon as the whimsical swirling of letters was unmistakable. He was addressing an incident and assuring King Itheal that the betrayer would be dealt with, but unfortunately the remainder of the note had been smudged or was otherwise illegible, possibly redacted later to prevent the details from being read by any others. I carelessly dropped the scrolls I had been holding in search of the remaining correspondence.  My search was short lived as the next scroll I laid my hands upon went on to add that Attor had been deemed a lorvisad and no longer considered one of his people, King Itheal may do with him as he wishes if found.

I felt myself taken back at the exposé of an elf who betrayed not only King Aldon but King Itheal as well. What could he have possibly done to deserve such a fate?  While I know this was not the purpose of seeking the hidden chamber, I could not tear my eyes away.  I sifted through a few more scrolls to no aval and then a few more before I found the remnants of what appeared to be the last notation.  It was in response to the execution of Queen Drusilla.  I must have misread that as Queen Drusilla passed from an ailment, not from being executed.  I took a breath and re-read the notation again before comparing it with the other scrolls I had found.  For crimes against King Itheal and the realm, Queen Drusilla was executed for conceiving a bairn with an elven noble, Attor. He was henceforth banished from the Kingdom of Lamprog and the fate of the child unknown. I found myself knocked back on my heels and clinging to the stone wall for support as my breath had been stolen from me.

There had to be more to the story, there just had to be. Could this have been the secret I was guided to find or was this an unfortunate reveal on my part?  I refused to let the matter rest and began riffling through the scrolls and stacks of parchment once more.  The minutes drew on and I began worrying if a safe departure would even be possible.  I talked myself into dropping the matter, for now, as I believed returning after nightfall would be possible, when I saw something once more protruding from a text just out of reach. It was high upon a shelf and carefully hidden had I been casually passing by.  I refused to let it be unseen as long as I was here.  Leaping into the air, I tapped the corner of the text with my hand and watched it cascade towards the stone floor, where several pieces of parchments shot out across the surface. With all haste, I picked them up and began reading.

Much to both kingdoms displeasure, it appears a half-elven bairn survived and there was much debate over where the bairn would reside. Too elven for the world of man and too human for the elves of Lamprog.  What became of it?  My mind was swirling and while I knew I could never unlearn what I had read, I refused to not attempt to see it through. While the fate of the child was unclear as the texts were quite vague, my instincts lead me to believe it would have survived as King Aldon would never have permitted such an execution nor stood idly by had the world of man done so.  Several parchments mentioned this situation was to be handled with the upmost secrecy and while the Kingdom of Losgadh would receive favor from King Aldon, it never disclosed what that favor would be. Then cleverly hidden in the back of the text was a scrap of parchment with the following notation written upon it:

*From this day forth the bairn birthed from this union*
*shall be known as the Lady Rosalyn of Losgadh*

*and her elven birthright never revealed.*

Once again, I found myself without breath as the news of the Lady Roselyn, my Rose, being a secret bairn birthed out of betrayal and lust was staggering.  I tugged at the neck of my doublet, trying to ease the tightness I now felt in my throat and chest.  While the information was here and for the taking, would divulging this information to anyone, including Rose, be at all useful or would this just be the means for which I was sent here?  Per King Aldon, I was to persuade the Lady Roselyn to marry another, of course at the time, I knew naught of the feelings I would develop for her, making this an even more challenging task.  However, if annulling the betrothal between kingdoms was the purpose of all of this, surely there would be a contingency proposal or was my Rose going to be the collateral damage in a war that began waging long before her birth?  The questions continued to swirl throughout my mind when I felt the need to flee before anymore life-altering revelations disclosed themselves to me.

Quickly I stuffed several of the notations and parchments inside my doublet before returning the remaining scrolls and text back to the shelves from which they came and blew out the candle.  While I knew it would not be possible to leave the room as it had been found, I tried my best to restore order to it.  With the amount of dust found creeping along nearly every surface, I was not burdened by the evidence of a few items having been shifted out of place as this place was clearly not visited with any sort of frequency.  Stepping lightly up the ladder, I listened carefully for any sign that I had been followed or that my presence here had not gone unnoticed. The room was calm and while I wished to wait longer to be sure, I did not have the time to spare.

Pressing lightly on the hatch, I felt it shift just before opening, permitting a golden stream of light to stretch across my face. I had not realized the hour and the sun had fallen in the sky. Feeling like I had just stepped out of a time warp, I oozed myself through the opening as if my body were water trying to fit through a small crack in the roof. Quietly, I pulled my legs underneath myself before lowering and locking the hatch. When no one responded to the sound of the puzzle lock shifting back in place, I felt safe enough to stand. In the early evening light, I found myself covered in dust from the chamber and if I would be discovered in such a state, more than a few items would be brought to the King's attention. Stepping towards the window, opening it just enough for the dust to cling to the afternoon air and rush back through the opening. Probably not the best of ideas since some of the dust whooshed its way back into the room and onto several nearby surfaces.

Feeling frustrated and rushed, I stepped towards the door and opened it slightly, ever hopeful of a vacant hall. Unable to see both directions, a brief judgement call needed to be made and I opted to proceed forward. Opening the door wider, I could see a maid, who had clearly just passed the chamber and another one coming to greet her. Neither of which I felt threatened by, but I was willing to wait a moment longer until they were out of earshot before I stepped out and closed the latch behind me.  Once out in the open, I continued towards my bedchamber with all haste, this time gaining significantly more perplexing looks than the time before. Placing myself in the foreground was never my intention, but with this new information and the impression that Rose may forego her betrothed for me, I may not be here long enough to worry about the people's awkward glances.  That is provided the next several hours go without a tether.

With my bedchamber insight I felt myself nearing a sprint, I slid into my bedchamber before slamming the door behind me, the sudden connection of wood and iron ricocheted throughout my bedchamber and presumably the hall as well.  I stripped out of my previous garments for something more befitting of Tuiteam's arrival as I dare not embarrass Rose or King Itheal.  In doing so caused the parchment and metal spike to dart through the air with such surprising speed they could have pierced flesh.  I scrambled to recover them as prying eyes would welcome this bit of scuttle, not just in this realm, but all Caladh.  Breaking a brick away from the window's ledge, I placed what I could in there and then the remaining parchment beneath two wooden beams in the old wooden chest where my wardrobe was being stashed for the moment.

Donning a fresh wardrobe, I was just about to rush back towards the main chamber to greet the guests when I felt a twinge inside me, pulling me back.  Attempting to shake off the feeling, I placed my hand upon the latch when I felt it again.  Eira, I remembered I had not attempted to reach her since the King's last bidding.  I would need to do so now to renounce any additional suspicion my erratic behavior early today might have caused. While I am not elven born, I do have the ability to channel certain energies. No one directly knows it is happening to them, but as a grouping of people suddenly grow tired in the middle of the afternoon or weak at the first morning's light for reasons unknown to them, you can be certain magic was involved. It is clear to me now that the energy I have been drawing from was Rose as she is at least partly elven and would provide a greater source of energy than man provided. King Aldon would have known this and that is why he wished for me to venture here as his emissary, to extend his reach. Taking a seat by the window, I closed my eyes and began to focus my thoughts on her: her face, her eyes, her hair, anything that would bring her memory forward in my mind. The closer the memory, the easier it is for me to step towards her and be heard.

In my mind I watched her laying in the grove before rushing upwards towards the skyline in hopes of a better vantage point. When she leapt towards me, her bright pumpkin hair rushed forward than back away from her face as she looked up towards me, eyes bright like the golden sun. Holding this thought in my mind, I reached for her, but was met with resistance. The resistance was different than before when I simply needed to rupture a soap bubble to find her, this time, the wall was thicker. Pushing forward with my mind, I began throwing my fists upon its surface and still it did not give. As I reached again and again, I was met with resistance and my mind was growing weak. Stretching and pushing my mind once more, I felt the surface crack ever so slightly, but it would not be for long as it was already reaching to pull itself back together. She was somewhere dark, surrounded by tawny stone walls and a sandy floor of which I had never seen.

The connection broke and I collapsed onto the floor before me, contorting and curling myself…something was wrong. My head was aching something terrible and as I reached to comfort it, I found blood streaming from my nose. The connection was not just broken, it was blocked by someone else on the other side. Whether friend or foe I do not yet know, but the something about it made the hair on my neck stand up. I pulled myself onto my knees and felt a throbbing pain take way inside my head, making my eyes and ears ache with each knock of the blood pumping through my veins. The blood from my nose began to seep once more and as the pain grew to an unbearable level, I lay my head back on the floor before closing my eyes to rest.

It was there that I awoke to the King's personal physician many hours later. There was a small pool of blood beneath my head and my vision was struggling to gain its footing to show me all who may have been present. I felt a warm breeze rushing in letting me know the hour was late, but it was not yet morning. Closing my eyes and reopening them several times forced my eyes to focus and I soon brought the men into view. There were two of them: one not much older than I and the other was old enough to be the King's father had he still been with us. The old man was muttering, and the young man rushed to follow his vague instruction. He pulled me upright, a bit swifter than expected, but with my vision nearly back to normal and my head no longer throbbing I felt well enough to stand.  As I drew my legs underneath me the young man spoke.

"Are you sure you want to be doing that?"

"Aye, I must see the King," I uttered just before feeling a dull ache return to me forcing my eyes to close.

"The King can wait Lord Bryn," he sounded insistent, "you should carry more concern for yourself at the present moment."

"Good sir," I started to say.

"Lord Bryn," he said sternly, "I will not utter the suggestion again for it is at King Itheal's request that we are here."

I nodded and then remembered that Rose's escort was to arrive today, "What of the Lady Roselyn?" I heard myself sounding a tad more eager than I had intended.  "Forgive me, did the men from Tuiteam arrive as expected?" that sounded a touch better.

"No, it is my understanding they did not," he paused, "and nor am I abreast as to the reason for the delay," his voice frank.

For someone so young, he was quite stern in manner and posture, ever eager to please his tutor, but bored with interacting with others.  Perhaps he believed he was above all the chatter that rages amongst the populace or perhaps he was annoyed from the long tedious hours that he spends toiling away over the constant sickness his position places him next too, neither reason would have surprised me, but I knew pressing him would not release him from my side any sooner. As the pain in my head began to stabilize, my thoughts turned to Eira.  Everything about this time felt all wrong.  Yes, there is always a touch of irritation when projecting oneself through a portal, but not a bloody, knock you unconscious sort of pain. Yet, barely cracking the surface rendered me helpless and I caught no more than a backwards glance.  Trying to picture the moment in my mind again, all I could see was her one side as she was turned away from me, holding something in her lap. Hidden in a cave somewhere would never have been her choice and the magic over her there was hostile.  I need to find her.

# Commander Elgar

The men were resting quietly as Kraciun remained stoking the fire that was in a constant state of unrest against the ever-blowing winds rising from the south. This patch was relatively flat compared to most of the mountain and we were fortunate that Kraciun found it when he did or surely more would have perished in the ascent. I watched him carefully from across the flames, as he rubbed his tired and achy hands, hoping to bring life back to them as they would undoubtedly be needed again tomorrow. His face was scraped in several places, but nothing that would require mending, not that he would have permitted the aid anyway. He was known to be difficult that way. Watching him now reminded me of a hunt we went out on a few years back. We had been searching for a great white bear that could easily feed some of the smaller villages scattered throughout the land and when we were finally able to corner it, Kraciun was the first to leap towards it, launching a spear into its back.  However, as the spear became lodged into its flesh, the jolt threw Kraciun into a summersault over its back and into the rocky surface behind it, breaking his hand in several places. Even then he would not admit defeat until the beast was slain and once defeated, he relied on only himself to care for his mistake.

"You can rest if you feel the need," I paused, "I will keep a watch over us."

"Thank you, Commander, but" he stopped to bite the inner side of his cheek, an old tick from childhood, "I am quite well and there will be plenty of time for me to rest later."

I nodded before shifting topics, "Had this been your decision, what course would you have taken?"

He looked up at me suddenly, "As I mentioned before, I believe a small scouting party could have accomplished the task at hand and the remaining men, left to more pragmatic affairs."

A most diplomatic response, clearly, he was unsure whether he was being tested or if his opinion was truly being considered.

"Such as?" I probed.

"Cross the sea to the northwest and seek to gain an accord with the people of Feurach and Teine."  He stopped, appearing only to gather breath as his response was rushed, "While we know Teine neighbors Losgadh, they are no friend to its people, giving us a clear advantage."

"Befriend the fire elves," I stated, sounding more like a question than a comment, "but they are known to be hostile towards outsiders."

"Aye, but I do not believe conquering the mainland is what is needed to bring peace to the land." He began gesturing with his hands, moving imaginary pieces across an invisible board, "Tuiteam intends to launch an assault upon all with an intent to conquer and rule, not seek allegiance from the kingdoms. That is where I believe that they are operating in error."

I gestured for him to go on.

"The people do not want to unite under one banner and that is why Caladh remains in a state of unrest. I believe uniting under a mutual objective would be enough to suppress Tuiteam and permit the strife on the mainland to cease."

"And what of the objective? What do you believe Caladh needs if not one ruler?"

"Commander, you, and I both know there are secrets in these lands and lands not yet discovered, why not seek them out? Allow the masses to keep their traditions and live amongst their own, but all while in the pursuit of something greater."

"You believe there is more land out there?"

"Aye, how could there not be?" he sounded surprised, "The great divide fractured our world and while we know of numerous islands outside of the mainland, who is to say there are not more of them or another mainland yet to be found."

His voiced upturned with excitement, and I knew he had given this topic some thought, even though it had never been requested of him.

"And you believe this lost world can be found?" I prodded further.

"Aye, we have just been too busy squabbling over nonsense," he lips pressed tightly together, "have you not ever wondered why dragons have been seen but not found?"

I sat there pondering his question and his course of action. There was strength and merit to it. For all my years, I had not ever asked myself that question nor would have attempted to fathom such a notion. I was trained to conquer and that is the path I have trained the men to follow, but while King Edric and I are too old to change our ways, this man may be the one to pave the way for all.

"Then let us do just that," my voice firm and matter of fact.

"Commander, I…I," he began stumbling over his words, "We have orders to follow, and I do not wish to deceive my king."

"A commendable attitude and one I respect. We shall conclude that of which has been started, but upon our return I suggest you heed to your true calling."

"Commander, I do not believe I was born for the path you are suggesting, nor would I be very good at it."

"Kraciun," I paused waiting for him to meet my gaze, "have the courage of your convictions and the people will follow you…I will follow you."

"But you and King Edric are friends, what has changed?"

"Who is to say that anything has changed between us? King Edric has been a fine ruler, but as his mind and body slip further into the abyss, I long to see a successor worthy of the challenge."

"Commander, I have no desire to rule as you know," he paused, "I just do not wish to watch my brothers continually fall with nothing to gain."

"Then take what is within your right to take and perhaps it will be you that changes the fate of men," I insisted.

He watched me carefully with his eyes narrowed and brow tightened, thinking carefully over his next move. Accept my proposal and his life would immediately change, refuse and he would always wonder what might have been. The choice I believed would be simple, but neither option came without risk. We sat there in silence for several moments, me watching him, him watching me, when he spoke again.

"For that, I must execute King Edric," he sounded uneasy over the matter.

"Aye, you know the throne must be seized for power to be given, but once given you will fall into the line of Trocair and that can never be taken from you."

"Is this what you have been preparing me for?"

"No, what you just told me, I could not have taught you. You began preparing yourself for this many years ago, I just did not see it until this day. So, unless you concede to the mountain, this kingdom may possibly one day be yours."

He nodded but did not appear comforted by this notion as so many before him. I was just a varlet when Edric seized the crown, and he carried no less burdens that Kraciun now does. Both well trained and capable men, but while there was no denying that Edric wanted the crown, Kraciun appears hesitant for reasons unknown to me.

"And what of the Queen?" he mumbled softly.

"She abandoned her King long ago," I responded.

"But what if she should return?"

"But nothing, the instant King Edric perishes, she is no longer our Queen. A man's right to the crown cannot be refuted if it was taken in proper order."

"Proper order? I do not understand."

"The crown cannot be taken by ambush, you may openly challenge the King or take him in silence, but it must be witnessed to ensure no foul play was at hand."

"How do you know all of this?"

"There was a time when I, too, thought of a different path. Only as I watched many attempt the challenge and fail, it was then when I embraced my talent for strategy and strived to be the right hand of the King instead of the King himself."

He nodded. While I felt like the discussion was far from over, the seed had been planted and soon would take hold. Not a moment later, I watched him stand and step towards the ledge with his arms folded, clearly deep in thought.

"Not thinking of jumping, are you?" I spoke with a fair amount of sarcasm in my voice.

A chuckle escaped him, "Never, for I am not a coward nor a fool."

That made me smile. Although he would not see it, nor would I want him to as I would not want to appear soft in any way. I knew what he was doing in a sense, plotting the next day's course as a means of distracting him from the thoughts and questions that were now undoubtedly swirling within his mind.

Seeking the Wolf

He never rested or at least not that I have seen, not since he was a young lad, and now, I fear he would rest even less so if he believed all the world would soon be watching.  It is a heavy burden to seek and bear the crown and one that should never be taken lightly, but I believed he was ready and watching him now, I knew that he would agree.

We woke early the next morning, with snow covered faces, to a bright and golden sun.  Kraciun had already began preparing some vittles for the men and I think it was the smell of the meat searing over the flames that woke me, more so than the sun's warm light.  I sat up slowly, feeling my body ache with each twist and turn, just before stretching my limbs and gazing out across the mountain peaks.  The wind had ceased, if but briefly, permitting all to gaze over the crystal-like snow-covered peaks that were now glistening as the sun's light creeped over them slowly.  From this height, we could see outward for miles, presenting a picturesque and deceiving view of the hostile landscape.  It was then, that I could see a faint trail carefully woven between the peaks, that shall be the course we will take.  For what was good enough for beast, shall be good enough for man.

Reaching for a flagon of ale, I slugged it back quickly letting its cool touch coat my dry throat and empty belly, further reminding me of how long it had been since our last meal.  I did not need to wait long, for one of the men brought something small and wrapped over to me.  I nodded my thanks and pulled back the cloth, there was some smalls bits of what more than likely used to belong to a bird of sorts and a chunk of bread to help fill the belly. Vitals while traveling high into the mountains tend to be smaller as we travel light, and the larger predators isolate themselves to the caves and lower trails. My hope is that the vantage point will permit us to see what was previously unseen as the dense forests on the ground limit all we are able to see. Alas, had the wolf been spotted; we would already have been on the move.

The men were oddly quiet this morning but appearing in much better spirits than the past eve. Permitting them a few more moments to devour their vittles would be the extent of my generosity today. There was a lot of ground to cover and while the seed had been planted for a potential new king to rise above King Edric, we still had orders to follow. When I was sure the men had finished, they packed quickly, and we set off on the long road ahead. By foot, it would be at least two or three days until we reached the other side, but I had hoped the men on the lower trails would have found an easier route.

Along the way, the grey clouds moved in slowly to block out the sun and made time appear to standstill. We no longer knew the hour or had it to guide our way, further increasing the skill needed to advance and I no longer heard Lavin's cry. Although, with the dense cloud coverage and low ceiling, it would be nearly impossible for even his eyes to witness anything of use. Despite the gods working against us, we pressed onward. We reached the ridge and followed it until we were faced with Paseigh-Shruthach, it was the coldest portion north of the Ice Tower and known to be coveted by the island's most treacherous predators. While we came to seek the wolf, that would not stop others from taking notice and the mountain's howl grew louder with each step we took towards it.

The pass was a vast crevice that had been left behind when our world was divided.  In nearly perfect division the mountain of ice had been broken in two equally monstrous masses of ice which held between them the path we must now take.  Riddled throughout the pass were caves and nooks, large enough to house both man and beast, leaving all sorts of danger lurking as darkness approaches.  As we continued advancing, the howl that was once growing louder than a mother's call, had now faded into near silence, leaving the dark passageway nearly void of all sound. Each step echoed throughout the crevice and further announced our presence. I signaled for two of the men to lead the way and scout for what may lie in wait, they moved forward without question. We had not ventured more than twenty steps when the sound of something cracking followed by a hastened sound of something sharp striking the ice, rushed towards us. We halted our pace, clinging to the icy floor, unprepared for what may be waiting in the passage ahead.  When the scouts had not returned to us nor did the racket continue, we slowly began moving forward once more.

There was no sign of the men sent forth, but one of their axes was soon found imbedded into the wall of the icy passage. Upon searching the area, we found no footsteps or signs of a struggle, only the axe was all that had remained of them.  The crevice that once appeared so large and open was appeared to close in above us and narrow ahead of us, growing darker, prompting us to ignite a few torches to light our way.  Just as the flints began to spark, we could hear something shifting from above. It sounded like fingernails drawn across metal forcing us to cover our ears from the high pitch that was rapidly invading them. A few of the men were fortunate enough to ignite their torches revealing what appeared to be a sheet of ice moving towards us from the peak of the crevice. The light appeared to anger it and bits of it began breaking off and falling towards the ground near us. The noise had now progressed to such a pitch that only beasts would have been bothered by it and as I took my hands down from my ears, I gazed upward to find the sheet of ice was not ice at all. We were being surrounded by grotesques.

Grotesques are large, carnivorous, gargoyle-like creatures that are known to hide in caves and caverns due to their hatred for light. While they once were viewed as guardians of the ancient world, the fracture mutated them into something else like so many other creatures of their time. They were white, like alabaster stone, but appeared more crystal-like when at rest which is why we would not have paid them any notice before now. Most possess large, jagged wings that assisted in their movement across vertical surfaces as not all caves are open enough for them to fly about, but not all do. Their bodies thin and generally, no larger than a man's even when well fed, but their wings make them appear significantly larger adding to their menacing presence. Their feet and hands appeared more claw-like than human and there were only three fingers and toes found on each, of which I had not previously known there to be. Their faces perhaps were the most terrifying as they always appeared to be grinning with delight when found, never appearing off guard, or threatened by weary travelers or other monsters.

More men had taken notice of them and soon lit their torches in rapid succession, hoping to force the grotesques to flee from our sight, when our attention was drawn towards one of the scouts they were now holding tightly. To my surprise, he was alive, but I could not be sure for how much longer as multiple points of his body were now encased within their equally jagged tails. Watching their faces watching ours, patiently waiting for our emotions to run over, but they did not know of the men whose company they now kept, and we would not be shaken so easily. I held a torch in one hand and slowly drew an axe from my belt. They did not appear amused nor threatened by this and I waited for any sign of what was to come. The man they held, would never be permitted to be free again, but what of the remaining men?

Kraciun did not shift from his position, but I began slowly stepping backwards towards the entrance to the pass. The men following my lead forced the grotesques to undoubtably take notice and they did not appear pleased. Their grip on the man grew tighter and I watched Kraciun drop his torch to draw the two axes his belt held. He had no intention of going quietly. Now scanning the walls, I found there to be nearly double my original estimation. We could not outrun them, but if we were able to reach the opening, then there was a chance the light may detour their course. I quickened my backstep and with each step, they thundered like a drum playing the melody that would be the man's untimely undoing. Out of anticipation, a few of the men broke out in a sprint and others soon followed provoking the already eager grotesques.

The man's voice silent just before he was torn into pieces and the grotesque's launched themselves away from the icy walls in a wave of high-pitched squeals that was designed to make the prey cower in fear. We did not cower. As the men and I soon became surrounded, I lashed my axe through the air towards the beasts with a powerful battle cry that drew the attention of the grotesques allowing the men a chance to strike first. The match had been set and with my cry, the others followed, creating a vortex of sound that rushed towards the beasts, weakening their defenses. They recoiled in surprise from the sudden sound and our blades sunk deep within them. Their cries now flooded the space and soon all that was heard was the sound of metal striking ice and the dying sounds of a once so hopeful pack of grotesques. We had won this round.

# Conall

To my displeasure, I found my eyes had opened facing a familiar tawny stone wall, but what I had not predicted is that I would not be alone.  My head had been lifted and placed upon something other than the sandy floor beneath me, as I reached to run my hand across it, I felt the smoothness of leather pulled tightly over a woman's lap as the legs I felt were much smaller and softer than a man's would have been.  While weary and riddled with pain, I longed to know to whom was left to my company.  Was it by order of King Ferand that this poor soul be tortured as well, or had she been brought to mend me?  I did not know, but as I ran my hand across her thigh once more, I heard her exhale as she was beginning to wake as well.  She shifted her legs slightly and began running her fingers through my long locks as a means of pacifying her anxious heart.  I recognized this woman's touch and even though I was weak, there was something about her scent that I recognized as well.

Attempting to turn slightly and bring her into view caused pain to flood my senses and force my eyes to close tightly, willing it to release me from its grasp.

"Conall, try not to move," the woman said softly, "you are days from being a fraction of your former self."

I recognized her voice as well, but how could this be?  I mustered what I could, pulling myself up and unto my side, held barely upright by two very strained and shaking arms.  My body struggling just to breathe.

"Eira," I muttered through dry, panted breaths, "But how? Why have you come?"

She appeared slightly startled, but recovered quickly, "I came here for you…I could not let you die."

I felt my heart skip a beat at the thought she put herself in danger for me as I did for her, but then my heart sank at the notion of her being imprisoned here alongside me, "Perhaps you should have for this is no palace but a prison," I mumbled, "you must go and quickly."

"I will not leave here without you," she leaned forward bringing our faces close together and placing her hands upon mine.

"You must," I insisted as I attempted to pull myself further upright, "they cannot know you are here."

"Why?" she placed her hands upon my shoulders carefully applying pressure as a means of insisting I remain as I am.

"For you are the one they are now seeking, and I am uncertain of what their intentions are for you."

"Do not worry, we have a way out," she paused and glanced towards the door, "however, the way seems to be shut if but temporarily."

I brought my legs underneath me slowly as the pain in my back remained relentless and placed my face in my hands. "Then it is already too late," I whispered.

"No, it is not," she insisted, "A friend, accompanied me into the castle with the intention of getting you out of here."

My attention was quickly drawn back to her, "Does this friend know of what we are?"

"Aye, that he does.  He is elf-kind, so he understood the risks of coming here."

"And he did so willingly?"

"Aye, he is the same elf that helped me escape the Ice Tower of Reothadh just days ago."

"And what did this elf request in return?"

She did not utter a reply, either unsure of whether she should tell me what he requested or fearing why a request was not made.

I brought myself closer to her and took her hand in mine, "What did this elf request in return for his aid?" I insisted.

She shook her head, "I did not ask," she muttered softly.

I sighed and returned her hand to her, "But yet he knew just how to enter the castle without being seen and this same elf was able to extract you from the tower alone?"

She nodded.

I looked upon her in shear confusion as everything she was stating did not add up and while I wanted to question her further, my strength was quickly fading.

"Here," she handed me a small bottle, "drink this. There is not much, but it will help."

"Where did you get this?" I asked quickly before taking a moment to smell the contents.

"It was left behind by the men who brought you here, presumably by mistake as they fled from your presence rather quickly."

"You were here when they brought me?"

"Only just before," she paused, "and those men were killed moments later."

I drank the liquid quickly, "How long has it been?"

"I am not sure, for the light never enters or fades from the cavern," she reached forward to touch my arm, "not long I would presume as the young prince hidden in the stone coffin is still alive."

"He still lives?" I heard the surprise in my voice.

"Aye, barely but he is."

I nodded, faintly remembering the events from days before and not wishing to speak of them further.  Looking down I noticed my breeches had been washed of the blood that once so heavily coated them and the arrow shafts, once embedded, now missing.

"I removed them while you were recovering and did what I could to cleanse the remaining," her eyes scanning me for any sign of approval, "your breeches of course remain unchanged as I did not feel it was my place to undress you…without your permission.”

I felt my brow tighten, unaccustomed to the kindness of others, “Thank you for your candor and your discretion. Others would not have been as kind.”

“I am merely repaying the kindness you once shown to me.”

“You should have stayed away,” I growled, “I gave myself to them, so that you might get away.”

“I never asked you to do that!” she shouted back at me sounding hurt.

“You did not have to,” I spat in return, “for everything you felt, I felt. You were afraid and given another moment, they would have taken you as well. I pushed you away to save you!”

I heard my voice crack, pained further by her lack of ability to see the future that now lay before her. I was angry with her, and I wanted to push her away…I needed to push her away, force her to leave this place so outraged she may never wish to come back. For out there, our kind could possibly continue, but only if she lives. Yet, my heart felt something else for her now and it would not let me push her away so easily. With each plead I pushed towards her two more came back at me begging me to take her in my arms and kiss her once more. It was an urge I had not felt before and while the physical state I was in was temporarily suppressing this urge, it shall not remain so indefinitely.

She placed her hands just above my collarbone, one on each side and whispered, "And how is it that you knew what I was feeling?"

Once again, I was greeted by the warmth our connection provided and it further provoked not only my curiosity but my desire for her.

"For we are not like man," I uttered frankly as my eyes widened slightly, "they need to see your reaction to gauge how you are feeling. I…we…physically feel what each other is feeling, providing us with more *intimate* knowledge rather than leaving it up to one's interpretation of the situation."

Her eyes said she understood, but the feeling I was getting now was uncertainty and trepidation.

"Surely you must know this?" I uttered hoping that the confusion she was feeling was in error.

She shook her head, "My mother died when I was quite young and there was no one to teach me these things."

"But the one you were seeking," I stopped myself, "surely, he must have known or sensed something while in your presence."

She shook her head again, "I think we just believed we understood each other in a way others did not, nothing more." She paused, "Besides, Bryn is younger than I and…"

"You are young as well, no doubt," I interjected.

She looked appalled at my perception and pulled herself away from me quickly, folding her arms across her chest, "You presume to know too much."

"If I speak falsely, then forgive me, but everything I can see, and sense tells me you are no more than two, possibly three centuries in age, just after the great divide."

"Aye," she said sounding surprised, "but how, how could you know that?"

She was undoubtably curious, I will give her that, but I am astonished at what little was passed down to her by the ones before her. Either that or she was being purposely unaware for reasons unknown, but nothing about her behavior suggested that to me.

"I am just a touch older than you and while you appear to have spent most of your life in relative isolation, I have been in the trenches, continually seeking out others of our kind."

"A touch?"

"I was birthed just over a century before the great divide."

"Oh, just a touch," she smiled briefly before lowering her arms, and a glimmer of hope was sparkling in her eyes, "were you able to find any others?"

Out of shear exhaustion, I lowered myself onto the cloak near her, attempting to minimize my discomfort further when I saw her turn herself towards me to meet my gaze. With the light from the torches now reflecting from her bright locks, I was reminded how truly vibrant they were, and I wanted to feel them within my grasp once more. I reached for her with one of my arms and was forced to pull it back suddenly as I felt one of the wounds on my back break open, causing a burning sensation to run throughout. I grimaced and she quickly reached to cover it with a portion of her hand.  The warmth she provided, soothed the open wound and I once again felt the heat grow between us.

"Forgive me," I inhaled deeply, "I usually heal much faster than this."

"It must have something to do with the powder," she said softly, "I have never seen anything quite like it."

"Nor I," I whispered, "but it burns like acid in an open wound and slows the healing process."

"Perhaps it saved you from turning before eyes that were not meant to see, but I was not able to get it all out with what I could find here."

"I appreciate what you did for me," I paused taking a moment to gaze into her equally bright eyes, "no, what you are doing for me," I uttered nearly breathless, "for I know you do not have to, nor were you asked to."

She smiled at me and reached to brush her hand across my cheek.  What was it about this woman that enthralled me so?  While I have seen others like her, I have never had someone rush to my aid as she did and I can feel something within her, clawing its way to the surface.  There was something she was not saying, but everything about her was screaming it.

"Eira," I said softly not wanting to break her thoughts.

"Huh," she uttered softly, still appearing lost in them.

"Why did you come back for me?"

"I already told you," she whispered, "I promised I would find you again and I intended to keep that promise."

"But why?  You know naught of me, nor do you owe me your loyalty."

She shifted her legs and hips to one side before lowering herself next to me, "Something inside me that I have never felt before refused to let you go."

Her eyes remained bright, and I could see the light returning to mine in the reflection her eyes provided.  I was healing and while a part of me wanted to take her in my arms once more, my body just could not bear the anguish of it.  I placed my hand upon one of her thighs and watched her eyes dart towards my touch with growing anticipation.  The feeling I was getting was stronger this time, anticipation mixed with confusion and desire.  An odd mix of emotions which forced me to pull my hand back slightly, in hopes of calming those emotions.  Her eyes found their way back to mine as she leaned in towards me, I watched her eyes close just before placing her lips upon my cheek.  Everything about her drew me in and even though I knew she should not stay; I felt compelled to indulge in my desire of her while it remained.

I reached for her, placing one of my hands against the back of her neck with my fingers slowly intertwining themselves into the locks of hair that they had found there.  Her eyes remained closed but as I held her head within my hand, I willed them to open again to give me the satisfaction of meeting their gaze.  For her eyes glowed bright like starflies found at night in the fields of Feurach.  I longed to take her there and lay with her in the fields, leaving behind the urgency and fear that our current predicament holds us in.  Her eyes opened slowly just before one of her hands found its way onto my chest, tracing the curves of my muscles and scars as if she were carving a sculpture of me in her mind. I could not resist her any longer. In the moment just before my lips found hers once more, her eyes grew wide and then wider once more. Her gaze fled from me and rushed towards the door; she heard something. I watched her watching the door and used her body as a guide of what was to come. We did not shift, but both of us were now intently listening to what may be moving on the other side of the door, someone was coming.

I tightened my grip slightly on her neck, drawing her attention back towards me, "Eira, you must hide for they cannot know you are here," I watched her carefully, waiting for a sign she was willing to do as I asked, but there was nothing. "Eira, you must do this, and should they take me again, I need you to not follow, just leave this vile place…for you need not know the wicked things King Ferand will do to you if found."

Her eyes grew dark, as if the light in them was going out, but she nodded. Whether or not she intended to follow my instruction, I did not know, but as she tore herself away from my sight, I rushed to pull myself upright. We could now hear the locks on the door shifting open and soon we would be greeted by the faces of those who came to look upon the beast. I listened carefully, but other than the movement of the locks within the door, I heard no voices nor footsteps. Quickly straining to stand and prop myself against one of the statues nearby, I felt the air change slightly as the door slowly opened. However, the one that stepped across the threshold was not what I expected.  The male figure heavily cloaked in black with a hood pulled up and draped over his brow, shadowing his face, said nothing, only walked towards me.  As he moved towards me, I noticed he was tall, much like myself, and moved with little noise or disturbance to the ground he walked upon.  He moved more like a dancer than man and without seeing his face I knew this man could not have been human.  I raised a hand emphasizing his need to halt where he stood, but he did not yield to me as so many before him did.

"Have you come to gaze upon the beast," I paused, watching his behavior remain unchanged at the sound of my voice echoing through the cavern towards him, "or was there something you wished to discuss?"

He stopped several feet from me and just looked upon me as if I were a royal jewel on display for his viewing pleasure.

"Who are you?  Why have you come?" I insisted trying not to appear winded by the strain all of this was putting upon my body.

He exhaled before beginning to speak softly, "I assure you, who I am is not important.  Who I am to her is what you should be asking yourself?"

I felt my chest tighten as I held my breath, waiting for more to be revealed to me.  He reached to push back his hood revealing bright green eyes and the lily-white flesh that surrounded them, his gaze intense and brooding.  I wanted to call to her, but I knew I should not, nor would I want him to sense anything I felt for her.  I looked him over carefully as I watched him do the same to me.  We appeared remarkably similar, but I was certain he was not one of us and I was suspicious of his purpose here.

"You were the elf that aided in her escape from the Ice Tower, are you not?"

"Ahhh," he grinned, "so you have had a few moments to get acquainted I see."  He glanced around the cavern, "Where is she now?"

"I am here," her voice soft, "I was afraid you had been discovered."

She rushed towards him throwing her arms around his neck and his arms around her, hugging each other tightly.  His eyes did not close but remained watching me as I watched them.  My heart feeling betrayed by their embrace.  I could not help but turn away from the sight of it as a new sort of pain washed over me.  That was when we heard it, the sound of two hands clapping together amongst an evil laugh that resonated its way into the chamber, sending chills through me.

"I must admit," a man uttered, "you had my brother and I fooled into believing you knew naught of this woman," he paused and stopped clapping, "and yet, she came to your aid so easily."

"Ferand," I growled just before stepping towards her only to be met with the elf's darkened gaze.

My eyes began darting between the three of them and the threshold, desperately searching for a means to escape while the chance lingered.

"Drayk," she whispered, barely audible to even myself, "we must go now."

She touched his hand with hers and I watched his expression budge ever so slightly and only for a moment before it returned to the stern face he strolled in here with.  Something within him was stirring and I intended to find out what as he was not what he seemed.  He was hiding something.

I quickly reached for her and pulled her away from him. She swirled into my arms, and I tucked her behind me, trying to shield her from whatever was intended next.

*He will not hurt me.*

He is not what he seems.

I turned my head towards her slightly, when I felt her hands wrap themselves around my arms.

"Remarkable are they not?" Drayk spoke, "So protective of one another."

*I do not understand what is happening.*

Her words were steady, but her thoughts were beginning to run together.

You must go, now, while the door remains open.  I insisted.

Ferand stepped forward and placed a hand on Drayk's shoulder and grinned with delight, "I must say I had my doubts," he paused leaning slightly to bring her back into view, "but now that I see her, I am not sure how you were able to resistant *claiming* her."

I clenched my teeth tightly together, willing myself to let his comment pass.

Go. Now. I urged.

She lowered her arms and changed quickly before bursting around me, knocking Ferand towards the ground but missing Drayk for he sidestepped just in time. Returning to seek her vengeance on them, I dropped down to change when I heard a howl escape her. Drayk's hands were pressed firmly against her side, holding something in place. I changed quickly to rush to her aid, when a familiar blaring sound pierced my ears, causing us both of us to cower on the sandy floor, writhing in pain. While I knew she was still there, I could no longer hear or feel her, but my eyes would not leave her. We changed back quickly and when she did, her eyes focused on Drayk, who was now straddling her body, holding a small, pointed object before her eyes. The sound slowly began to dissipate, but I was not strong enough to stand. I lay there, watching them, unsure of her future, when I heard him speak to her once more.

"Their venom may no longer be as potent, but taking these has proved most beneficial," he grinned.

"Why are you doing this?" she uttered through the pain.

"For you, my darling girl, are the real treasure," he said, frankly.

I watched her melt before him, placing all the pieces together in her mind. It finally made sense and the pain she was now feeling would soon be felt by us both.

"I was the target the whole time," she uttered it as a statement, but I could tell she needed to hear him say it.

"Everything you saw, I wanted you to see," he leaned down and kissed her forehead softly, "and none of this was by chance."

He stood quickly leaving her body ashamed and bleeding on the sandy floor.

"What would King Aldon think of your betrayal?" she spat, "Drayk, you owe him your allegiance."

"Oh," he grinned again, "not much I would presume for I was reborn the lorvisad known as Drayk many moons ago by his *own* hand.  For within me burns a dragon's fire and my vengeance shall be taken upon all King Aldon holds dear.... including you my darling girl."

He turned to walk towards the door, where Haxa was faintly seen hovering just across the threshold, looking just as I remembered her, when I heard Eira speak once more.

"Through all the smoke and mirrors," she stopped clearly out of breath, "may I at least know your given name?"

A sound of amusement escaped him, "Since we have grown so close," he glanced over his shoulder towards her, "I will permit you this one courtesy," he paused, "Attor was my name."

As Haxa and Attor faded from our sight, I watched Ferand crouch down beside Eira.  Unsure of what his intentions were, but the thought of him touching her made my blood boil with rage.  I watched him place a hand on her waist before dragging his fingers up and onto the side of one of her breasts. She lay there helpless and in pain, with tears now streaming down her face as the future that was previously unclear to her was now coming into view.  He turned to look upon me with malice and lust in his heart, which only further enraged me.

"I told you I would break you and in due time, I will break her as well."